Advance Praise for

The New Land

"In *The New Land,* David O. Stewart goes deep into the lives of a band of immigrants who landed in Maine before there *was* a Maine. This is the rare historical novel that has it all: a family love story, a panoramic war story, victories and losses in the daily struggle for survival, and, from the shadows, the quiet but unmistakable thrum of the tragedy of the European invasion of North America."

—Patricia O'Toole, author of acclaimed biographies of American figures, including *The Five of Hearts: An Intimate Portrait of Henry Adams and His Friends*

"A dazzling and wrenching novel of history that marks the beginning of an American epic. A story of immigration, the inheritance of violence, and the love of a father for his son, told in language that stings with salt and sawdust and gunpowder. A novel of our revolutionary past that speaks truth to our fraught and furious times. David Stewart is a master of history and the human heart that beats within it."

—Kent Wascom, author of *The New Inheritors*

"Sweeping in scope, keenly researched, and deeply felt, *The New Land* will capture your imagination and your heart. David O. Stewart has delivered an absolutely engrossing read."

—Brad Parks, international bestselling author of *Unthinkable*

"This compelling novel brings Stewart's finely-wrought characters into danger and heartbreak in the wilds of colonial America. The brutality of survival in colonization and war is rendered in sensitive detail, making for a vivid family saga."

—Carrie Callaghan, author of *A Light of Her Own* and *Salt the Snow*

"Writing in the tradition of Kenneth Roberts, David O. Stewart has produced a well-researched, rousing saga of colonial and Revolutionary War New England. The story transports the reader to the mid-18th century German settlement of Broad Bay, on the rough and raw Maine frontier, and to the turmoils and adventures of an immigrant family who sacrifices, prospers, goes to war, and helps to build the United States."

—Thomas Crocker, author of *Braddock's March: How the Man Sent to Seize a Continent Changed American History*

"David O. Stewart's historical novels always hook readers, and his new novel *The New Land* will have fans eager for the rest of the coming trilogy. Stewart shines as one of our leading authors of historical fiction."

—James Grady, author of *Six Days of the Condor* and *Mad Dogs*

"In *The New Land,* a grand saga begins. David O. Stewart tells the classic tale of European settlers arriving on the New England coast, where they encounter hardship, winter, war, and a world indifferent to their sufferings and strivings. But he tells it from a fresh new perspective, through the eyes of German immigrants, like the skilled storyteller he is. You will live in this world. You will come to know these people. You will root for them. You will want more of the Overstreet family. And you'll get it in Part II and beyond. But you must begin *here* to let David Stewart sweep you into the past. You'll be happy you did."

—William Martin, *New York Times* bestselling author of *Cape Cod* and *Bound for Gold*

"Sweeping across a panorama of pre-Revolutionary War New England, *The New Land* presents memorable and engaging characters who show us—sometimes uncomfortably—what life was like as our nation was being formed. David Stewart's deep experience in chronicling those fraught and fascinating times pays off many times over with a multigenerational family saga, a love story, and an action adventure of real people trying to carve out a legacy in a new and unforgiving land. David's fans, both longtime and newcomers, will eagerly await the next installments of the Overstreet saga."

—Mark Olshaker, novelist, documentary filmmaker, and coauthor of *Mindhunter* and *The Killer Across the Table*

"A compelling origin story of an American family and the new nation where they carve out a home. David O. Stewart's prose makes you feel the sea spray, hear the saw's rasp, and smell the musket smoke."

—Tom Young, author of *Silver Wings, Iron Cross*

"David O. Stewart reminds us that the people who invented America weren't Americans when they came here, they were improvisers and gamblers laying odds that this rough wilderness would be better than the servitude they fled.... If you love historical adventures, *The New Land* delivers history with the punch of a thriller."

—Eric Dezenhall, author of *False Light* and *The Devil Himself*

"An engrossing saga of hope, determination, and bravery. Johann and Christiane risk everything to cross the Atlantic to Broad Bay, where they are devastated by the false promises of charlatans, the harsh land, and the ever-present threat of native attacks. Only through faith, grit, and the power of love do they secure a future and build their family's legacy. David O. Stewart's action-filled prose creates an unforgettable story."

—M.K. Tod, author of *Paris in Ruins*

"David O. Stewart is a rare talent—a superb historian who is also a gifted storyteller. *The New Land* marks the arrival of an inventive, thrillingly vivid American saga."

—Daniel Stashower, author of *The Hour of Peril: The Secret Plot to Murder Lincoln Before the Civil War*

"No one knows U.S. history—its nuance, intrigue, and back stories—better than David O. Stewart. In *The New Land*, he takes us back to the frontier of a new nation, and to hopes and struggles that resonate with us today."

—Tim Wendel, author of *Escape from Castro's Cuba* and *Red Rain*

Also by David O. Stewart

Historical Novels

The Burning Land, Book 2 of the Overstreet Saga (forthcoming, May 2022)

The Resolute Land, Book 3 of the Overstreet Saga (forthcoming, November 2022)

The Lincoln Deception (2013)

The Paris Deception (2015)

The Babe Ruth Deception (2016)

Histories

George Washington: The Political Rise of America's Founding Father (2021)

Madison's Gift: Five Partnerships that Built America (2016)

American Emperor: Aaron Burr's Challenge to Jefferson's America (2011)

Impeached: The Trial of President Andrew Johnson and the Fight for Lincoln's Legacy (2009)

The Summer of 1787: The Men Who Invented America (2007)

The NEW LAND

DAVID O. STEWART

To Linda —
With best wishes,
David O. Stewart

PERMUTED PRESS

A PERMUTED PRESS BOOK
ISBN: 978-1-63758-080-6
ISBN (eBook): 978-1-63758-081-3

The New Land

Cover art by Elaine Tabol

PERMUTED
PRESS

Permuted Press, LLC
New York • Nashville
permutedpress.com

Published in the United States of America
1 2 3 4 5 6 7 8 9 10

To Flora, August, Lucy, Scarlett, and Rex,
whose story this is, too

A dream is not a very safe thing to be near...It's like a loaded pistol with a hair trigger: if it stays alive long enough, somebody is going to be hurt. But if it's a good dream, it's worth it.

William Faulkner, *The Unvanquished*

TABLE OF CONTENTS

†

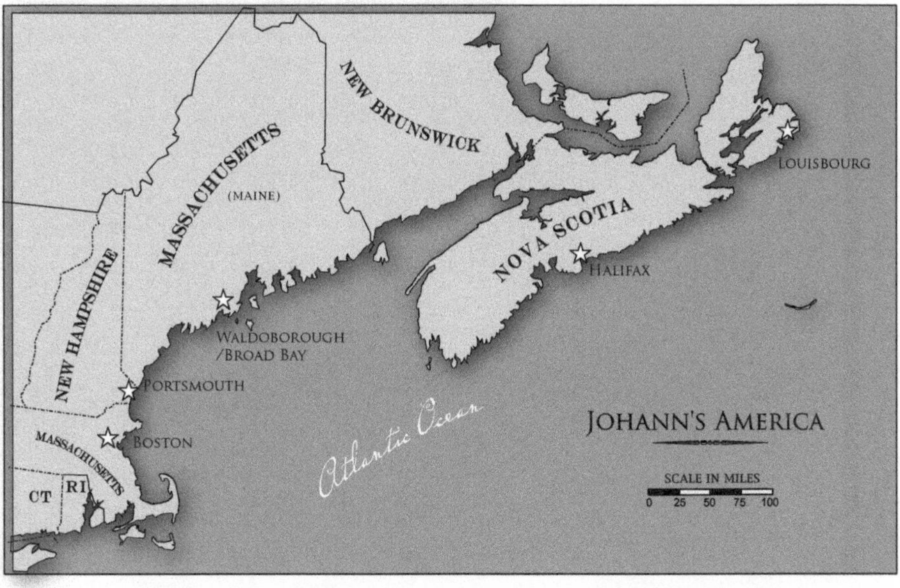

Cartographer Paul Rossmann Illustration Design

PART I

1752

†

CHAPTER ONE

†

"You there, John—it's time."

The mate's voice was gruff, roughened by a lifetime of shouting over windroar and wavecrash, but not angry. Johann Oberstrasse nodded without turning. The English always called him John, never recognizing German names. "Yes," he said to the far horizon, where the slate-grey sky met the blue-grey water. "It is time." The mate moved away.

Even as the deck of the *Mary Anne* heaved with the march of foam-crested waves, the immensity of ocean and sky had a calming quality. Johann shifted his weight but didn't leave the ship's rail, pinned by the keening and moaning that rose from the deck below. A wind gust or a snapping sail might cloak those sounds for a few moments, but the undertone of despair always seeped back into his ears.

The sounds had started when they were only a few days out of port. Fevers and illness swept through the seventy-odd families seeking new lives in America. Deaths introduced an edge of madness, arias of grief breaking out to punctuate the steady recitative of anxiety and fear. After more than a week, with pestilence rendered more lethal by the sea's cold and damp, the passengers knew the rituals of burial at sea.

When it came to delivering bodies to their eternal resting places, Johann had more experience than most. Professional soldiers do, if they stay alive. The body must be prepared, often simply rolled in a blanket or a coat. Everyone nearby must pause in respect, head bowed. Even an enemy, when his breath has gone out and his dreams have stopped, commands that respect. There must be words. They can be short and simple, but they must be said. When the silence falls, it must be allowed to linger, but not too long, especially if there are many dead to bury. Then the body is lowered into the earth and covered.

At first, the burials on the *Mary Anne* jarred the passengers. A measured pace marks the lowering of a body into the ground. It takes time to cover it. At sea, bodies plunge overboard, making lively splashes. The separation from the world of the living is sudden, total. No stone marks the lost life. Johann's imagination pictured the bodies drifting down past the monsters of the sea, perhaps dissolving before reaching anything that might be called a resting place, bits of the person washed by waves into every corner of the globe. Aboard the ship, only a vacancy remains.

He straightened and pushed back from the rail. His hair and face were wet. He couldn't be sure if it was spray from the sea or moisture from the sky. His soldier's greatcoat didn't keep out the cold. This was the fifth burial since they left port. It would be the worst. He must shut off his imagination. He must be strong. He had no choice.

A sailor with a sour look stepped around Christiane, who was curled in front of a storage chest on the windswept deck. Despite the cold, the sailor was barefoot, the better to scramble up and down the rigging. Christiane clutched baby Walther, shielding him with her cape. She kept a hand on the bundle next to her, wrapped in a frayed blanket sewn shut on three sides. Her eyes didn't meet Johann's. Her face was set, as terrible as he had ever seen it. It showed nothing and everything.

The mate returned with a Bible. He said something in English, but the wind tore away the words before Johann could hear. Johann had learned that language while serving with the British in the

Dettingen campaign, when the English king rented the Landgraf's army for his war. That's when Johann learned that the English would never know his name, would always call him John. They had no feel for German, no need to know it. On the *Mary Anne,* he conveyed messages from the German passengers to the crew and back again, so he knew more of the people in both groups, and more about them, than he cared to know. In the army, the more that people knew about you, or thought they knew, the more trouble they could cause.

Nungesser the schoolteacher stepped forward. Not a preacher but a literate man and a godly one, he acted like a preacher on the *Mary Anne.* There was no other, and the grim days required someone who knew the Bible and could be patient with grieving souls. Nungesser even knew a little English.

Leaning over to speak directly in Johann's ear, he said, "I will read something short, in German." Johann had said words over comrades and over men he fought against. Never for a child. Never for his child.

Johann crouched next to Christiane. When she looked up, the feeling rushed back. Not until Johann left the army did he come to know Peter, then nearly three. He was such a little fellow, at first shy of Johann but soon trailing behind whenever he could. The fever had been too much for him, so God took him. Johann could see no use that God could have for such a small one. Christiane's eyes filled. She had so many tears. He placed his hand against her cheek. She looked down and nodded.

Tall, blonde Fritz Bauer stood on the other side of the blanket that held Peter. They would hold that bundle between them. The Bauers had lost their youngest in the weeks in the Netherlands, waiting for the ship, nothing to do but worry while spending their little money. Fritz and his wife Ursula buried their little girl in a soggy, unfamiliar land they would never see again. At least she was in the ground, her place marked. Johann didn't look at the others gathered around the railing. Some had stayed below, too ill to come or too busy nursing the sick. The sailors hung back.

Nungesser stood at the rail. He turned to the people. He had the slouch of a tall man. After clearing his throat, he asked the forgiveness of the Almighty for their sins. He asked Jesus to care for the blameless dead like Peter and to bring them greater peace than they knew on earth. He asked the Lord to bring peace to His people on the *Mary Anne*. He led the Lord's Prayer. Then Nungesser opened his Bible and read a passage from Exodus, one the passengers had repeated since the burials began.

> Behold, the Egyptians marched after them; and they were sore afraid: and the children of Israel cried out unto the Lord.
>
> And they said unto Moses, hast thou taken us away to die in the wilderness? wherefore hast thou dealt thus with us, to carry us forth out of Egypt?
>
> Is not this the word that we did tell thee in Egypt, saying, Let us alone, that we may serve the Egyptians? For it had been better for us to serve the Egyptians, than that we should die in the wilderness.
>
> And Moses said unto the people, Fear ye not, stand still, and see the salvation of the Lord, which He will show to you today.

Nungesser muttered, "Amen." A few echoed him. Unsteadily, he began to sing "A Mighty Fortress is Our God." Some joined, their words trailing raggedly behind the simple tune. Johann looked at Christiane, her head on Ursula Bauer's shoulder, tears again tracking down her cheek. Her arms were folded over Walther, his head under the cape. The fever had first struck him, the younger one, but he recovered swiftly. They had thought Peter would get better too.

When the singing ended, Johann and Fritz lifted Peter. The bundle weighed so little, even with ballast rocks knotted into the shroud. Johann nodded. They stepped on a platform that the sailors placed next to the rail for burials. Johann nodded again. They tipped the blanket. The small body, bundled in the coarsest linen, slid out. Johann barely heard it enter the sea. He kept his eyes on the water, away from Christiane's eyes.

Then he closed his eyes and said farewell. Through his last year in the army, during drills and on sentry duty and through all the dreary business of soldiering, Johann had talked to Peter in his mind, telling him things that Johann had learned and that a boy should know, that a father should teach him. When he got home, Johann called Peter his little soldier, but Christiane said not to do that. She said she was not making soldiers for the Landgraf to rent out to fight other people's wars. Johann had minded when she said that, because a soldier, even a rented soldier, could be a man of honor and duty, but he had said nothing. Her father had land so her brothers never had to be soldiers. The Oberstrasses of Kettenheim had no land, so Johann, orphaned early and shuttled from uncle to cousin to aunt, became a soldier for the Landgraf.

She only said that once. Christiane was no nag. But it lingered and grew in Johann's head. He had always thought his *dienst*—his faithfulness to duty, even to the Landgraf—was the best part of him, but what she said made him less certain. He made up his mind to no longer be a soldier, not one who is hired out to kill for another man's profit. Going to America, leaving behind all they knew and all that Johann had been, boiled down to those words. No more soldiers for the Landgraf.

A cross-wave slammed him against the rail, lifting him up on his toes. He looked down at the white and green water. A hand gripped his arm, holding him. Fritz was staring at him, concern on his long horseface. "Yes," Johann said. "Yes. It is not my time." Johann realized that Fritz was holding the blanket in his other hand; Johann had let it go. Johann straightened and blinked. They stepped off the platform as two sailors reached to move it away.

Johann sat on the deck with Christiane and Walther, their backs against the chest that held extra ropes. The spot, out of the traffic of busy sailors, offered some shelter from the wind. He opened his coat so she could lean inside its warmth.

"Walther was very good," he said.

He felt her head nod. She had been quiet over the last few hours. When they saw life leaving Peter, she had shrieked, screams from another world, then sobs that became goose-like honks, mucus streaming from her nose. Walther joined her wailing. Johann couldn't comfort a baby who heard such sounds from his own mother. There was no comfort. Johann didn't know how long the screaming and sobs lasted. He had been lost in them. It was madness, madness that terrified him. He had longed to leave the dark hold where their sleeping space was, to get out in the air, but Christiane wouldn't move, not away from Peter, so he had stayed.

"I'm cold," Christiane said.

"We can go below."

"No. The air there. Walther needs clean air, even if it's cold."

"The weather on the sea is no better than back home."

They fell quiet, lulled by the ship's plunging and the windsong in the rigging. Johann lost track of time until Walther began to stir, his soft noises knifing through the ship's background din. Grey light slanted from the west, from beyond the ship's bow. "We must eat," he said. "All of us."

"I'm not hungry," she said, her voice husky, near a whisper.

"You must eat, so that Walther may eat."

He helped her up. They were nearing the end of their own supplies. Soon they would have to eat ship's rations. They would be charged for every scrap, probably for much they never received. Without Peter, their food might go farther. The thought brought Johann shame. Peter was such a little fellow.

Johann led them down the steps of the hatch, descending into the fetid warmth of too many bodies crammed too close together. The stink hit like a slap. His gorge rose. He fought the instinct to hold his breath. He tried to take air through his mouth as he wove around people and piles of belongings that loomed in the dark, ducking his head under the ship's crossbeams. Hammocks hung from the ceiling, some occupied, some not. Here, for once, his lack of height was an advantage.

He steered Christiane to the rear corner that they had made theirs, clinging to a shred of privacy but no more. Christiane sat with her back to the cabin, Indian-style, and let Walther wobble on his stumpy legs. A shiver passed through her as she re-draped her cape, then reached into the sack for their remaining food.

Except there was no food. She peered in to be sure, then told Johann. He repeated the investigation of the sack, finding only a cloth, four spoons, and a cup for drinking. He took a moment and breathed once, hard. Christiane closed her eyes. He sank to his knees and ran his hands twice through each of the three sacks that held the things they had taken from their chest, which was stowed away. He found only his second shirt, Christiane's second apron and dress, a few rags for Walther. Nothing to eat. He searched through the blankets that were folded and piled, refolding each. Then he did it all again. Blood pounded at his temples. The food—cheese and biscuits and salt fish—was gone. His brain felt slow. It happened during the service, Peter's funeral. Who could do such a thing?

Without thinking, he patted his shirt for the pouch that hung from a leather cord around his neck. Their money. Still there. He sat back on his hams and passed a hand over his face. Rage flooded through him. The Lord would be hard on such a thief. The Lord would impose His justice. That was what He did for the Israelites so long ago.

But waiting for someone else's justice, even the Lord's, wasn't Johann's way. If He couldn't be bothered to save Peter, He would be little use for this. Johann thought of his bayonet. That weapon, plus his greatcoat and his soldier's boots, were what he had to show for fifteen years in the army. In the high troops, a despicable crime like this would bring 500 stripes with a stout stick. Some sergeants would make the thief run the gauntlet a dozen times. Johann didn't like the brutality of the gauntlet, but theft is a serious crime, one that undermines fellow feeling. Johann reached into the smallest of the sacks. His fingers found the bayonet's rough metal socket. He unwrapped the weapon and slipped it into his coat pocket. He looked down the length of the great cabin, dimly lit by an occasional candle and small pools of bright where hatches opened to the deck.

Families sagged in listless groups, some in hammocks, some on the deck. A few children ran here and there, mostly for the pleasure of moving. Even for the healthy, the voyage was dreary days and nights wedged into the cabin with two hundred others. Johann's suspicions for the theft fastened on two passengers. He had never liked their looks. They pushed in front of others and complained. He knew he should keep an open mind about who the thief was. Thieves, good ones, don't look like thieves. Maybe, he wondered, it was a crewmember? They were a rough-looking group, living a dangerous life with few comforts. Most seemed to view the passengers with a mix of contempt and resentment.

His rage was subsiding. He had no way to find the thief. If anyone saw the theft, they should have told him by now. This wasn't the army, and Johann wasn't a sergeant here. He had no power to inspect the possessions of others, looking for the missing food. Food all looks alike, anyway. How could he tell a bit of cheese was their bit of cheese? He would have to leave it to the Lord's justice. Still, Johann would keep his eyes open, see what turned up.

He rewrapped the bayonet and put it back in the sack, then took a cup to the water barrel. He drank and brought more back for Christiane. Walther was climbing on his mother's folded legs, then burrowed into her bosom. "You keep me warm, don't you?" she said to the baby, then drank.

The food was definitely gone, Johann said. They would have to eat ship's rations. Hardtack plus a little salt pork. She nodded and said, "We knew this would come."

"You must eat," he said. "You and Walther. You must become fat and strong."

They moved to lean their backs against the ship's wall. He spread a blanket over her. With Walther at her breast, she fell asleep.

Until this voyage, Christiane would never have sat so boldly against him where others might see, a baby in her blouse. He had admired her sense of propriety, but that was an early casualty of the crowding on shipboard, where passengers ate and slept, dressed and performed personal acts, all under the gaze of others. In a few days, the close quarters had dissolved the habits of a lifetime.

Some of Christiane's auburn hair had escaped from her cap and lay against her cheek. Her skin was pale in the half-light. Her smile could startle him with its brilliance, but her mouth fell into a hard set when she rested. Her face turned stony, that of a stranger. From the talk of other men, he knew he was lucky in his wife. Christiane didn't gossip. She didn't carp. And she comforted him in the way that a man needs a woman to do. He shook his head to stop his tears. She and Walther had no need for a weeping man.

One of Christiane's hands shielded Walther's head. Her hands had reddened and toughened. They were still only when she slept. She had stopped knitting when Walther first fell ill, then while Peter suffered. Johann would have to check that the knitting needles—good ones from pig bones—were still there.

Snatches of song came down through the deck. Above, at the ship's stern, the evening prayer group was meeting. He could hear Nungesser's uncertain tenor above the others. When Christiane claimed this spot in the cabin, they hadn't known it would let them hear the singing. Christiane liked it. She clutched his shirt with one hand.

"Want to go up to listen?" he asked.

"No, not tonight."

"I'll help you into the hammock."

"Let's stay here; Walther can sleep here."

It was awkward. One of the ship's planks pressed hard against his ribs, but he stayed where he was. His breathing slowed, but he didn't sleep. When he closed his eyes, he saw Peter fall to the water, so he opened them again.

CHAPTER TWO

†

Johann snored softly. Moaning came from halfway across the cabin, where the Drechslers nursed two children with fever. Christiane heard more pained sounds from another direction, she didn't know from which family. She felt weak, jittery, balanced on some unstable edge, her mind roaming through dark and sad places.

It was barely one day since Peter died—or was it two? Time lost its shape in this gloomy space. However long it had been, now she could think of Peter's name, have him in her thoughts, without reeling from the scorching flame of losing him. There was still a stab, an urge to cry out, but it didn't consume her. It left room for her.

Her mother had warned about the sea and its terrors, its storms and its shipwrecks, its pirates and its diseases. Peter might have died even if they had never left their village, though he had always seemed strong. It was Walther who struggled more in his first months. Yet Walther shrugged off the fever that stole Peter away. Perhaps that meant that Walther was meant for some special purpose. She would like that.

She knew her mother prayed for them, even without knowing about the boys' fevers. Christiane had never found much solace in church rituals; that was something she and Johann shared. She wished that prayer would help her now, or help Johann, that they might find peace for Peter wherever he was. Did he still float in the water? Had he reached the ocean bottom? Had some sea brute made a meal of him?

A sob tore through her, and she clutched the baby. Johann started. Through tears she shushed them both. She knew her thoughts were bad but what could she do? No Bible readings or pastor's sermon ever kept away her bad thoughts.

She was with child again, she was certain, though she had said nothing about it. Before Peter sickened, she hadn't wanted Johann to worry about her. He worried enough. She valued that. A man without worries is a fool who brings only sorrow. Yet she tried to protect Johann from some worries, ones he could do nothing about. And there was no reason to tell him this, after Peter. When this new baby's time came, they would either be safe in America or they would be with Peter below the waves.

She dropped her head close enough to feel Walther's breath on her face. Her mind slipped away again. She thought of having babies and then burying them. Or casting them into the sea. She saw herself doing it again and again. Peter had been part of her but then no longer, and now he was gone. She couldn't see him now, not ever again. She wiped her face with a corner of the blanket. An empty feeling opened inside. She placed her hand over her stomach. It was too early to feel the baby. She was too thin. How many times could she give herself away to a baby, then watch what had been part of her, what she still felt to be part of her, die? How soon would there be nothing left of her?

Her mother had been rough with her brothers, angry when they did something reckless or foolish, when they treated so thoughtlessly the life that had cost her dearly to give them. "Don't expect me to weep at the grave of such a fool," her mother would say, as though a mother could choose how much grief she would feel when her child was gone.

It had been Christiane's idea to go to America. Johann thought it was his. When she accepted him as her husband, she had admired his bearing, the respect he commanded as a common man who rose to be sergeant, a man with *dienst*. Her father had questioned the match. Johann had no land, and Christiane wasn't bad to look at, she knew that. But she was the fourth daughter, and the dowry money had run out. Johann required no dowry. She overheard her mother say that Johann was respectable and probably wouldn't beat her, that was enough. That would be better, Christiane had thought, than two of her sisters had done.

Christiane grew to care for Johann but to hate the army, not only because it took him away. Even when he was home, he was still in the army. Christiane couldn't tell if the soldier's life ground harder on him each year, or if she learned to see better the toll it exacted each time he left for a campaign of more hardship and more danger. Always quiet, he grew quieter. Christiane couldn't bear for him to continue, to keep killing or be killed for his precious *dienst*. And she knew he couldn't be satisfied living in Hesse, working on her family's land or hired by another landowner. A man like Johann couldn't be that way. Christiane couldn't ask it.

When Peter came, she realized it was up to her. If she did nothing, she would watch her sons march off in the Landgraf's uniform, like their father. They had no land. She went to find the man in the market, the one who talked about America, always in a loud voice.

He was short and fat, with eyes that never rested on what he saw. She didn't like his looks, like a man who shortweighted grain, so she wasn't sure she could believe what he said. They called men like him, men who recruited for America, the soul-sellers.

The soul-seller said that in Massachusetts, in the Maine district of Massachusetts, the soil was rich, the land empty, the seasons gentle. He had a pamphlet, just a sheet of paper folded down the middle, describing a settlement in Maine owned by a man named Waldo. General Waldo. It was a strange name. The paper, he told her, said that General Waldo had land for settlers who were willing to work hard to grow fat and rich.

She thought he must be lying about some of it, maybe all of it, but she had to do something. She brought the pamphlet home and left it on the table. She said nothing to Johann about it. He picked it up and read it, but said nothing. He placed it on the windowsill. After he left in the morning, she put it back on the table. He read it again that night. On the third night, she asked what it said. He told her that it offered land that settlers could work for, and only half-fare to get to America where the English were, a land called New England. People in their parish had gone to America before but always to Philadelphia. Johann was intrigued by New England. He had fought beside the English during the war and learned some of their language, or enough of it. They weren't so bad. Their officers were better than some German officers, and they were good fighters. They did what they said. Why, he wondered, does this man trade land for our work and only charge half-fare? Is the land bad? Is it full of these Indians and bears? It's too good to be true, this New England.

She didn't answer. There must be something wrong, she knew, with the land or the offer or the ship on which new settlers were to sail. But it was the only way for Johann to get land. They had to go. He said he would talk to Fritz Bauer about it; Fritz knew about land. Then maybe Johann would go to the market and speak with the man who looked like he shortweighted grain. She nodded. She had been in her final month with Walther, heavy and sluggish, so Johann expected no more from her.

The prayer group's hymn came down to her in snatches, then the deck boards creaked as the group broke up. She felt Johann start awake in the dark. He gripped her shoulder and said her name. She leaned into him. Her tears came but not the sobs. She shivered. Johann stroked her cheek, then reached to cover her with his coat. Awkwardly, he placed it over her and Walther. She hoped it would be warmer where they were going. It was still only September.

CHAPTER THREE

"Yes, potatoes, that's what we'll want to be growing." Fritz Bauer's tone, usually mild, brooked no disagreement on this point. Standing at the rail, he leaned down to be sure Johann heard him. The two men, both early risers, met most mornings before their wives and children climbed from the semi-consciousness that passed for sleep in the stinking cabin. The sea swells came from behind the ship, pushing it westward toward America, regular enough that even non-sailors could roll with them. A clan of porpoises danced and tumbled alongside the ship.

Johann had heard Fritz before on the subject of potatoes. Many times. His friend was a hired man in their village. The Bauers had never owned land. But Fritz had studied and thought about crops and soil and rain and sun until he knew more about them than Christiane's brothers ever did. Johann had bristled when Christiane's brothers mocked his ignorance of the land, but they had been right. For a soldier like Johann, a farm was a place you stripped of livestock and crops as you marched through. New recruits wasted time sniffing around for a likely milkmaid or two.

Veterans concentrated on what could be eaten. Soldiering was no way to learn about growing seasons, insects, tending crops. Because his family's survival in the new world would depend on his ability to raise food, Johann listened to Fritz and tried to remember what he said. Remembering was easier because Fritz often repeated himself.

"In the army," Johann said, "I thought I would never want to eat another biscuit. When we marched with the English and the Scots, it was biscuits, biscuits, and more biscuits. Potatoes sound good."

Fritz smiled. His fair hair blended naturally with the freckles across his forehead and the bridge of his nose. "What would you give today for a warm roasted potato?"

"Ach," Johann said, his mouth watering, "I shouldn't think of such a thing. But they will grow where we're going?"

"I think so, yes. The potato wants to be cool, not like in Virginia, which is supposed to be so hot. Where General Waldo's land is, north of Boston, I think should be a good home for potatoes."

"And the soil?"

Fritz shook his head. "The soil I don't know. They say it's the finest soil, of course, but they also say that gold coins fall from the trees."

They stood in silence. The sea was calmer today, the wind less biting.

"And Christiane?" Fritz said.

"She is sad. It's hard for her. Peter…" His eyes smarted.

"Ursula will be with her."

"Yes." Johann rubbed his forehead with his fingertips. A look of exasperation crossed his face. "None of us has enough to do. We look at the sea. We feel how sick we feel. We think about how much we have lost and imagine how other things may go wrong. It makes us weak."

He caught a whiff of coffee from the sailors' galley. For a moment, the acrid aroma overrode the stench from the cabin. The ship's watch would change soon. Johann had picked up the ship's rhythms. Five watches of four hours each, then two dog watches of two hours around sunset. Bells announcing each half-hour. The sailors, never idle, repaired sails and the ropes that held them in place, scraped and scrubbed surfaces, spread tar and grease and oil, paint and varnish. They climbed the masts to unsettling heights, let sails out and gathered them up as the captain read the restless wind. Discipline lay at the center of the sailor's life, as it did for a soldier. To face danger, each must know what he must do and what others will do.

Johann remembered what had bothered him when he first woke up. He leaned close to Fritz and spoke softly.

"We have a thief," he said. He picked a louse from his collarbone and crushed it with a thumbnail. It left a smear of red on his thumb. He wiped it on the rail.

Fritz kept looking at the sea. He didn't speak.

"I'm sure," Johann said. "There is no other explanation for what is missing. During Peter's service, he stole food from us."

"Listen," Fritz said. From below the deck came a piercing wail. "Someone is dying. Maybe old Kuchel." The man, a smith in his home village, had to be over forty.

"He has suffered."

Fritz turned to him. "What of this stealing? We are two hundred people, living like animals, with no washing, not enough food, nothing to do, plus fevers. And dying. Dying that tears at our hearts because we left home with hope. And so there is stealing. What do you expect?"

"We cannot have thieves. This cannot be like a jungle. We're going to America to make a new world for us, not a new world for thieves."

Fritz sighed. "What's been stolen?"

"Our food. Fish, cheese."

"I'm sorry. We'll share with you, Ursula and I, but this isn't the army and you're not the sergeant major here." Johann flinched inside. He had never been sergeant major. He didn't serve long enough to rise to such a high rank. But Fritz and others in his home village had decided he had been a sergeant major, and Johann never corrected them. He would have liked to be a sergeant major. Fritz kept on. "Would you steal to feed your wife? To feed your child?"

"I would not." Johann's jaw set.

A glance at his friend's face persuaded Fritz to change his ground. "How would you find the thief? The food has been eaten, for sure. So, there is no evidence. Will you look inside our stomachs? Better that Ursula and I will share."

"I thank you. For Christiane, while she feeds the baby, I accept. But the food was wrapped in a cloth that Christiane brought with us, and the cloth is gone too. It is blue and has a shell pattern. It was from her mother."

"How will you look for it—sneak around in the night and go through everyone's things? What will you do if you find it? Will we have a trial? Johann, this is madness."

Johann turned a level gaze to his friend. "We must show that we are men. That we cannot be taken advantage of like this. And that we refuse to live like pigs, snatching food from each other."

Johann didn't wait for a response. He walked over to the burly Dutchman, the bosun who directed the crew. Johann thought of him as the ship's sergeant. To make himself understood in English, which the Dutchman did not know well, Johann spoke loudly and slowly, gesturing more than usual. The Dutchman nodded. Johann returned the nod, then went below to see Christiane and Walther.

That evening, about half the families came up on deck for dinner. The rest stayed below, nursing others or sickened by the moderate seas of that day.

Each family had its routine for who carried the cloth square and who spread it on the deck, anchoring the corners against the wind. If they still had their own food, the wife handed it around. If they were on ship's rations, the husband stood in line before the ship's cook—a small, greasy man, a stranger to soap—for a shred of salt pork and biscuits. A clerk noted each ration as it was handed over.

Christiane and Walther settled next to the Bauers, who shared their fish. After Johann brought back the family's rations, he overheard a man on the square next to them. He was complaining that the cabin was unhealthful. Johann leaned toward the man, supporting himself with a hand on the deck.

"I agree," Johann said. "We must clean it or more will die like our boy did."

After extending to Johann his sympathy, the man asked how they could clean. "So many are sick and weary. Do we have enough to do the work?"

"If anything gets wet," the wife objected, "it'll never dry out."

"It won't be easy," Johann said, "but if we work together, we can manage it." He explained what he had arranged with the bosun.

After breakfast the next day, one person from each family should come on deck to join the cleaning party. It could be a man, a woman, or a child, so long as each could work. At the same time, other family members should bring their things—blankets and clothes and anything else—up to the deck to air out. If the items could bear washing, they could be washed, or at least rinsed in sea water. From the sailors, the work crew would get brushes, scrubbing stones, and buckets, then they would return to the cabin to scrub the flooring and sleeping surfaces. During the cleaning, the hatches and side ports for the cabin would be open to the air.

If a family didn't wish to participate, they could mark their space so the work crew would leave it alone.

"There are people too sick to move," the woman said. "If you're washing the floor, those people, their things, will get wet."

"Yes," the man broke in, "and shouldn't the crew do that sort of thing?"

Johann shrugged. "The crew will not do this, so either we clean ourselves or we live in filth."

When the man agreed to the plan, Johann moved on to the next family gathered around its cloth square, then the next. There were more objections. It was too cold. Too damp. But Johann pointed out that the days were growing shorter, and it would only get colder. Better to do it now. Most agreed. They were, as Johann had hoped, weary of the squalor and glad for something to do.

The sea was strong the next day. Water surged over the forward deck when *Mary Anne* plunged into a wave, then slid over the aft deck as the prow climbed the next crest. Then a fierce rain pockmarked the water's surface. The masts, carrying few sails in the heavy weather, creaked and groaned as they leaned forward and back, then side to side. Some passengers hung on ropes and rails, green and yellow puke streaming from their mouths. Others stayed below, wedged into corners or against posts, heads over buckets, lurching with the jolt and sway of the ship. The *Mary Anne* was far from a new ship. The sailors called it a tub. Johann told himself it had survived many storms and would endure this one.

Johann, who didn't get seasick, called off the cleaning but remained on the deck as the rain relented. He fidgeted through the afternoon, staring at the lightening sky. He should be glad for this, he told himself. A stronger wind should mean a faster crossing. Christiane stayed below with Walther.

The next day was calm, so they started cleaning early. Johann distributed buckets with water and some with vinegar, plus brushes and sandstone rocks and sand for scrubbing. Perhaps thirty people started, most with a vengeance. There was a pleasure in scouring the grimy boards, watching the grease and filth run down the cracks and out through the scuppers at the ship's edges. The bosun came down to ask if the passengers had what they needed. On other ships, he said quietly, the crew would do such cleaning twice a week, but they were too few on the *Mary Anne*.

Hard words came from families that had refused Johann's invitation. One woman kicked over a water bucket. She shouted at Johann, "Can't my husband even die in peace?"

"Of course," he said, "but his peace will be greater if there are fewer mice and less bad smells."

Johann did his share of scrubbing. He hauled blankets and clothes up the hatch for washing, refilled buckets, cheered on the others. Despite his years of soldiering, he was still lithe and quick. On the main deck, Ursula used a stave to pummel clothes and blankets in a barrel of sea water and lye. Christiane, holding Walther, picked lice from the wet scalp of the Bauers' five-year-old, Sigrid.

"Good hunting?" he called with a smile.

She waved him over. "You're next. I've watched you scratch!"

Heartened by the passengers' work, Johann returned to the cabin and moved toward the rear on the left side. It was where the Reuters from Darmstadt slept. They were city people, so Johann didn't trust them. Not that everyone in Kettenheim village was filled with virtue, but the city men in Johann's regiment were always more likely to skirt the rules. Also, Heinrich Reuter claimed to be a cooper, but his hands said that was a lie, that he labored with a pen and his brain. The hands of Frau Reuter, a large and loud woman, might build barrels. She was directing their two children, a boy and a girl, both sturdy and florid like their mother.

"Can I help with something?" Johann asked.

Frau Reuter looked up from her knees, where she scraped with holystone. "It is you who arranged this?" she said.

"I spoke with the bosun about it, yes."

"You must see that everything is washed twice." She wagged a forefinger at him. "The first time, we simply stir up the vomit and shit and the smell gets worse. Then new water, and we wash again. The second time, it begins to get clean."

Johann smiled. "I'll tell everyone you said so."

She gave his arm a sisterly swat. "Tell them you said so. They listen to you. We must do this every week, perhaps more. We were like pigs in a sty. May the Lord bless you for this."

Johann lingered for a minute near her, shifting to try to gain a better view of the Reuters' belongings. He could see a blue cloth hanging off one of the hammocks. The light was too dim to show if it was Christiane's.

"Ludva," Frau Reuter called to her son, a boy of eight or so. Tucking hair behind her ear, she pointed the boy to the hammock Johann was looking at. "Take those things up. I'll wash them." She stood with a groan and smiled again. At a loss for a way to investigate his suspicions, feeling shame for suspecting a woman who seemed so open, Johann nodded and moved on.

At dinner that evening, with clothes and blankets drying on the top deck, most passengers ate with good appetite. Johann's shirt was damp from washing but no longer stiff with sweat and grime. He and Christiane ate only hardtack and water. She still picked the maggots out of the hardtack and threw them aside. Johann swallowed his down without a thought.

"They will make you strong," he said with a smile, "and they don't taste any worse than the hardtack. Just swallow."

She shook her head and wrinkled her nose, eyes trained on the crumbs of the disassembled biscuit on the cloth before her. She put some in Walther's mouth as he sat on the square cloth. He strained to climb up on his mother and walk, then to crawl away. His pleasure in having arms and legs brought smiles to his parents. Walther looked up into the ship's rigging and squealed. Johann reached out both hands to squeeze his son's middle, which produced a cheerful noise.

"Did you look at the Darmstadt people as they were washing?" Johann asked. "They have a blue cloth like your mother's."

Christiane swept the biscuit crumbs into the palm of a hand and stuffed them in her mouth. She chewed hard, swallowed some water from her cup, then chewed more. "Johann," she said around the mouthful, "am I to dig through everyone's clothes for you? Frau Reuter seems a decent woman."

"I can't say the same about Herr Reuter."

"You have no reason to say that other than you don't care for how he looks, which is something he cannot control."

Johann held his tongue. He took the measure of a man quickly, judging his character on how he looked and moved and spoke. People showed their character if you paid attention. He trusted his judgments, but usually kept them to himself.

Christiane drank more water. With a finger, she dislodged hardtack from her back teeth. She reached under her apron and pulled out the pamphlet from the soul-seller in the market at Kettenheim, the one about General Waldo's land. It was soft from frequent handling, some of the words now faint. She handed it to Johann to read in the failing light. Christiane knew it by heart, but she listened.

Johann skipped the introduction, which described General Waldo and America, and also the rough map of the area to be settled. The sketch showed a river that entered a bay that led to the ocean. Christiane had memorized the map too.

Using a voice meant only for her and for Walther, Johann started with the description of the settlement and the terms for the settlers. In the town, each family could place a house on a quarter of a morgen, the amount of land that a man can plow in a morning. The head of the household would own that house and lot. For farmland, each family could buy another fifty morgens outside of the town at two shillings per acre, with three years to pay. He stopped after that passage. Christiane looked over. It was so much, as much as Christiane's father and three brothers owned among them. What would that much land look like in one piece? So long as that part was true, it didn't matter what else was. Johann read it again, then continued.

General Waldo would build a temporary shelter for the settlers to occupy when they arrived. He would build a church. He would provide beef and pork and wheat and Indian corn and salt, enough for the settlers to establish themselves. Each family would receive a cow and a calf and a pregnant sow, plus three axes, four hoes, a spade, and a handsaw. It was signed by General Waldo, Hereditary Lord of Broad Bay.

"Fifty morgens," Johann said. "On the river."

"It doesn't say it's on the river."

"Ours will be on the river. I will see to that." His eyes glistened. "We'll live there on our own. No Landgraf to take our sons, or to take our money in taxes. We will make our own way with our own hands, with the hands of our sons and daughters."

She hugged Walther tighter and closed her eyes. Johann's hand was on her arm, and she felt his warmth as he leaned into her. "If I had known we would lose him," he said, "I wouldn't have come. Not even for fifty morgens."

CHAPTER FOUR

†

"What do you mean?" Anger clotted Johann's voice. "Explain, please." He leaned over the wooden table to look into the eyes of the man behind it, who was pointing to an entry in a tally book. The sunlight was golden.

"The boy was on board for more than half of the crossing, so you must pay the fare for him."

"My son, my son died long before the halfway point of the journey, yes? That is the dividing point. Look there," he pointed at the book on the desk, "look in the ship's record. We were no more than eight or nine days from port when he died. We had the funeral. It will be in the records. We have been crossing, what, four or five weeks since then. We could not have been halfway across. That is not possible."

Johann tapped the book with his finger. Fritz stood next to him, nodding, though Fritz knew almost no English. Their wives, each holding a child, were behind them.

When the *Mary Anne* had neared Portsmouth harbor that morning, Johann and Christiane had crowded against the ship's rail with the others. The world looked new. It smelled new, the loamy aroma of land mingling with the astringent sea air, birds calling down as they flew overhead. Christiane found the mix intoxicating.

The voyage had seemed endless, a procession of grey days and black nights, of sickness and misery. Some days Christiane had not allowed herself to think what America would be like. Other days she dreamt of it with all her heart. Now she wanted nothing more than to rub black earth on her skin, to trace her fingertips over green leaves and dig her nails into the bark of trees, to sit quietly where the world didn't heave and dip and heave again, where her eyes no longer scanned the horizon for deliverance. She wore a clean apron she had saved.

Portsmouth didn't look like much. Raw wooden buildings straggled along the shore. Farther back, the buildings were more like shacks. A stiff ocean breeze might knock them down. Above the small port loomed the forest edge, the vastness of America, where bears and wild Indians held sway, where civilization ended.

The man and his table commanded the end of the gangplank. No one could leave the *Mary Anne* without the approval of this man with his grey complexion and shiny, matted hair. A guard loomed on either side of him, pistols and knives jammed into their belts. The man's voice was nasal, his face pinched. His accent wasn't the same as the British, but his clothes were fine, his waistcoat a black and gold silk brocade. He eyed Johann coldly as he opened a second book, the ship's record.

"All right, then. It says here that *Mary Anne* had passed the halfway point for the journey by September 14. Your son—Peter, correct? —he's recorded as dying on September 16. So you are liable for the fare for the child. That was explained to you before you got on the ship. You must pay the fare for everyone who makes at least half the voyage."

"How can that be possible?" Johann said. "We left port on September 7. Now it is the end of October. You mean that we reached the halfway point after nine days, and it took us five more weeks to travel the rest of the way?"

"The sea," the man shrugged. "Winds and tides. It's the life of the sailor. Your fare comes to thirty-five pounds; thirty for the Bauers. If you don't have the money, you must go over there." He nodded at a forlorn group huddled at the side of his table.

They were the ones who couldn't pay, not even the half-fares that General Waldo had specified for his settlers. They were marooned in the New World, unable to pay to arrive and unable to pay to return to Germany. They couldn't remove a single possession from the ship until somehow, someone paid their half-fares. Their fates would be determined by the half-dozen well-dressed men who lounged on the shore behind the pier.

From the bosun, Johann had learned of this system. Redemptioners, the sailors called them, these forlorn ones. When all were gathered, the well-dressed men would step forward. They might pay the half-fare for a German who looked like a good worker, one with a vigorous step and bright eyes. In return, the redemptioner would sign an indenture, agreeing to labor for the well-dressed man until the half-fare was repaid. Some indentures lasted three years. Some lasted five. The work could be as light as household labor or as heavy as clearing forests.

And what if, Johann had asked, you looked too sick or too weak to labor, so that no well-dressed man would pay your half-fare? The answer was that the captain kept you on the ship until you grew stronger or died.

"Why, this is outrageous," Johann said to the man behind the table, his voice rising. Walther squawked and pointed at a sea gull as it landed a few yards away. Christiane bounced the baby and shushed him. Johann burned with humiliation, standing before his wife and his son and people who knew him. "You're cheating us."

The man fixed him with a sharp look and deepened his voice. He leaned forward on his elbows. "No, Herr Oberstrasse, it is you who propose to cheat us. We promised to bring you here to the New World. Here you are. Your life in America stretches before you. The terms of your passage were explained. Can you prove that you weren't halfway across when your child died? Where is your evidence?"

"It only makes sense. What you say makes no sense. It takes nine days to go more than half the way, and then it takes six weeks to travel the rest? Do you take us for fools?"

The man sat back and shrugged. "You and your family must step over there." He waved toward the forlorn, then called out, "Next."

The guards stepped forward. They were large and smelled of animal fat. Johann felt Fritz's hand on his arm. Walther began to cry, squirming in his mother's arms. Johann looked back at Christiane. Still white-hot inside, he reached under his shirt for his leather pouch and counted out the coins on the table. Fritz paid too.

"Please," Johann said after the man swept the coins into a large pile on the table, "show me in the book where you are recording our payment?"

"Next!" The man looked over Johann's shoulder, and a guard herded them to the side of the pier, away from the redemptioners. The guard pointed to a small ship tied up at a separate pier. "The sailors'll put the chests out on the pier over there. Carry yours onto the sloop after that."

They walked unsteadily, unused to land. Something calmed Walther—dry land, or maybe it was America. Johann breathed easier to see their chest carried onshore. It held everything they still owned: hand tools, bedding, clothes, the prayer book and Bible that Christiane's mother had pressed on them.

A gust blew Johann's coat open. He suppressed a shudder. His anger slid into a fear of the omens around this landing. In his first minutes in America, he had been cheated like some ignorant peasant back in Hesse. Now they would have less money for settling the land. General Waldo had made promises, but what were promises worth? What did Johann know of this country? He could see how wild it was, how wild and immoral its people were.

When Christiane took his arm, he placed his hand on hers. At least, Johann thought, they would never set foot on the *Mary Anne* again. They would never descend again into that foul cabin, breathe air that had been breathed dozens of times, lose all dignity living on top of each other.

"Stop here," she said. They let the Bauers walk ahead. She kissed their baby and fixed Johann with a smile that was far too lovely for his mood. "We are in America, Johann. You have brought us here for our new life. Let's always remember this moment."

She nudged him to look around. Under his feet, the land still felt odd, tilted yet solid in a way he hadn't felt for so long. The sunshine glowed on the land. The sky sparkled with blue. Sigrid Bauer started running up the slope to the town, shrieking with joy, her mother trailing behind. "The leaves, Johann," Christiane said. "What colors they are." The trees shimmered with oranges and golds and reds, reflecting in the water from the opposite side of the harbor. She touched his cheek with the fingers of one hand. "Thank you, Johann."

"Yes," he said. He clenched his teeth against a surge of feeling. He had meant to do so much more for her and for Walther. And for Peter. He should have. And yet still she gave him this smile. "So. We are people of America now."

His head was stuffed with all the things they must do. Get land. Clear it and plant it. Build a home and raise crops and cows and chickens. Christiane must learn English, and Walther must learn to make his way in this world. They will have children, many children. All of them people of America. They will stand on their own. He felt a rush of energy and hope, an eagerness for this testing to come. He looked over at Christiane, hungry for another smile. She gave it to him.

* * * * * *

The sloop was too small for the hundred remaining settlers. Johann and Fritz had planted their chests next to the starboard rail, their families following to sit on them. Sigrid jumped up and down when the sloop cast off in mid-afternoon. The next ground they walked on would be Broad Bay, their new home.

Christiane thought of the hardships already passed, of those buried at sea, of those who fell into indentures that morning. They had left familiar places and traditions, had gambled on a journey they could not expect to return from. She pushed those thoughts out of her mind. For Johann and Walther and her, the time was at hand. Anticipation pulsed through everyone jammed onto the sloop's deck.

"Say," Johann said to a crewmember who was shouldering through the press. "Where is General Waldo? Will he meet us in Broad Bay?"

The man grinned. "General Waldo? Meet the likes of you?" After he had gone a few more steps, the crewman called back, "If you see him, point him out to me, will you?"

Johann felt his ears warm. He was glad the other settlers didn't know enough English to understand the sailor's words, though they couldn't miss the mocking tone. "So?" Fritz asked. "Will the general be there?"

"Maybe not," Johann said.

About an hour from Portsmouth, the wind died. Through the night, the sloop barely moved. The passengers fell silent. As the hours crept by, their discomfort grew. Those with physical needs pushed to the rail and relieved themselves in a range of contorted postures. As one man struggled through the crowd, another called out, "Take a piss for me, would you?" There was laughter. Another said, "Shall we swim there, lads?" The laughter was less.

In the morning light, the crew brought out a keg of fresh water, but it soon ran out. There was no food. Christiane swayed on her feet. Johann made her sit on the deck, her back against their chest. A few hours later, a breeze nudged the ship to life. The ropes and wooden joints creaked. A few hours later, the words ran through the ship. Broad Bay was near.

Clouds almost filled the sky when the sloop shifted toward an opening between two shores. Christiane stood, then rose on her toes. Johann turned Walther's face to the land and pointed, saying in English, "This is your new home." The smudges along the shore, Christiane thought, must be cabins. Four crewmen strained to drop the heavy anchor in what had to be Broad Bay. They shivered to a stop. Christiane barely noticed the cold wind coming off the water.

After lowering a dinghy from the stern, the crew ferried settlers to shore. Another dinghy came out from the land to speed the process. The Oberstrasses were among the last to reach the short pier. The settlers gathered in a clearing near the water. They gazed around in wonder. Some wept. Some embraced. Some fell to their knees.

From her knees, Christiane set Walther on the ground, her hands hovering on either side of him. He crouched and slapped the ground. Johann joined them. He took off his hat. In a voice only she could hear, he said, "Thank you, Lord, for bringing us here safely. We will care for this land as You would wish. And may You care for our Peter."

Nungesser walked in front of the settlers and removed his hat. He held his Bible in his other hand. He smiled and spread his arms.

"There is a passage in the Book that we may hear now as never before. It is in Exodus, where Moses speaks when the Israelites reach the Promised Land." He turned to a page:

> And the Lord said, "Before all thy people I will do marvels, such as have not been done in all the earth, nor in any nation: and all the people among which thou art shall see the work of the Lord; for it is a terrible thing that I will do with thee."

Many "amens" rose up. To Christiane, they sounded heartfelt.

CHAPTER FIVE

†

Walther had rotated in his sleep, placing his feet in his father's chest and his head against his mother's arm. Johann covered him with the blanket and stood quietly in the dark, his boots in one hand and his coat in the other. Their first morning in America, yet still they slept with the others.

The shelter building was no more fit for humans than *Mary Anne* had been. It had once been a garrison. It had clay floors, no windows, and holes in the roof to release woodsmoke. Johann and his family slept in a room with the Bauers and another family, each with its chest of belongings. The room opened to a passage that led to a central opening. The suggestion of light was enough for Johann to sneak past sleeping forms. He stopped at the fire that smoldered outside the entrance. He pulled on his boots, hopping when his foot snagged halfway into the second one, then shrugged into his coat. The diffidence of the pale half-moon matched the chill of the morning. A few settlers had slept outside, but close to the fire. They didn't stir. America's disappointments, Johann suspected, were only beginning.

Broad Bay settlement had no road, nothing wide enough for a wagon to pass along. There was only the clearing, the pier on the river. Off to the right a dozen cabins, mostly occupied by English settlers, crouched along the river. Johann took the narrow track, slightly muddy and wide enough for only one, that led from one cabin to the next.

Next to each cabin a small boat or canoe rested on the shore. The river, called the Medomak in General Waldo's brochure, was plainly the main thoroughfare, with boats the best way to get around. The brochure had not said there was no road. Johann would have to learn about boats.

A few cabins had cows tied next to them. Some cabins huddled next to the charred remains of earlier shelters. The settlement had been burned by Indians five years before, Johann had learned the night before. The brochure hadn't mentioned that either.

To explore farther, Johann had to enter the forest. Fingering the bayonet in the belt of his coat, Johann set off. Some chickens ignored him as he passed.

Upriver, the path disappeared into woods. Rocks and tree roots reached up for his feet while branches poked at his face. He paused every few hundred feet to listen. When he first stopped, the silence seemed complete but for his own breathing. If he stood long enough and steadied himself, sounds emerged. Light watery tones from the river. Owl hoots. Birds waking up, their calls unfamiliar. A breeze brushed leaves against each other.

He slowed at a meadow that stretched up from the riverfront. He paused and stared at the land. This was what he had come for. It was right on the river, and it wouldn't take months to clear off the trees that otherwise darkened every vista. He would want Fritz to look at the soil. Johann was no judge of soil. Was the land too steep for good farming? Also for Fritz.

This meadow was probably taken. General Waldo surely had snapped up the best for himself. But Johann might find something as good, maybe farther from the settlement.

He started again, the sky brightening on his right. He entered another patch of bush and scrub trees that cut off his view. A scream tore through the air. He froze. He gripped the bayonet and tried to slow the hammering pulse in his ears.

It wasn't a human scream, he decided. A wild animal, not one he knew. Outside Kettenheim, the forest held boar who grunted and snuffled. He once saw a chained bear who could be goaded into a roar of annoyance and rage. This scream was different, higher-pitched, more ragged. He decided to turn back. He moved quietly at first, wary of disturbing a wild creature, then began to relax and pick up speed. When he reached the first cabin and the beginning of the path, he released his grip on the bayonet. Now, with more light, he could see where the path veered into the woods, then vanished.

He slowed to examine the cabins. They were rough affairs. Their doors faced the river and had no windows on their inland sides. Hewn wood piled high next to each. The forest offered wood in abundance. Smoke rose from several cabins, which had chimney arrangements of varying designs. At one cabin entrance, a dark shape hunched before a fire that was just beginning to catch. The figure fed small sticks into the flickering pile. Johann made enough noise to warn of his approach. A cow tied to a small tree eyed him but said nothing.

"You're either a giant bear," a deep voice called out, "or one of those ignorant Germans that swam ashore yesterday."

Johann stopped. "Just an ignorant German."

The man stood and turned. He was tall and ruddy. "Not that ignorant," he said, plainly embarrassed. "I thought you—"

Johann held out his hand. "Johann Oberstrasse. The very ignorant Johann Oberstrasse."

"Truly, sir, I meant no offense. It's just, most of you people don't know English." He took Johann's hand and pulled him toward the fire, then reached for more branches.

"I know English from the army," Johann said. "I fought for your king at Dettingen."

The man smiled. "Not for Robert McDonnell's king you didn't. That's where you got them soldier's boots, did you?"

The lilt in his words told Johann that the man was a Scot. They were violent soldiers, he knew, as ready to fight their friends as their enemies. The two men watched the fire. Saws and woodworking tools were laid out under a lean-to. A rack of animal pelts stood away from the cabin. Young voices came from inside. The McDonnell family. "How long have you been here, at Broad Bay?" Johann asked.

"But a few months. Came up from Boston. General Waldo's so desperate for settlers that he'll take Germans and Scots." He pointed at the remains of a cabin. "The settlement got a poor reputation when the savages from St. Francis burned it. They scalped a bunch and hauled off another bunch. Some survived, but most lost their taste for the neighborhood."

Johann had heard about scalping. Some settlers spoke of little else. Though he had made war his profession, scalping seemed barbaric. McDonnell was at the pile of wood and logs. He lifted logs and pushed others aside, searching for the right one.

"I wonder," Johann said, "if I might ask about the land."

"Only if you can work and talk at the same time. Grab the end there." Johann sprang to the log and helped pull it from the pile. McDonnell dropped one end on a tree stump and reached for a measure that he laid against the log, then marked with a knife the spot where he would cut. When he picked up his saw, he nodded to Johann. "Steady it, eh?"

As McDonnell's blade bit into the wood, releasing the sweet sawdust smell, Johann said, "We came for the land, but they say we can't mark off our lands until spring. We are here. We came for the land. But they say we must wait."

McDonnell sawed steadily, pulling the teeth through young wood with a powerful pressure. Then the blade jammed. "See here. Reach under and brace the log so it don't close up on me." Johann did as he was told. McDonnell picked up his rhythm. "You'll have no trouble from us who are already here," McDonnell said. "We have our land, all we can manage. Your business is with Waldo and his man."

"Yes, but the talk yesterday was that no land will be assigned now. Not until spring. And they had no money for us. There was supposed to be money for each family." After the extortion at Portsmouth Harbor, after paying for ship's rations for much of the journey, Johann had fewer coins left than he had expected to have.

McDonnell's saw broke through the log. "Roll that one over there," he said. McDonnell pointed to the side of the fire, then turned back to the wood pile to find another. "There's little enough use for money here," he said over his shoulder. "Nowhere to spend it. Here, it's labor that matters. You can trade your hands and your back. Now, for instance, I need to build another room here. We've got four little ones, and that's a lot of squirming and squealing in the one room. You help me with that, and I'll show you how we do things, give you a hand with your work."

When Johann didn't say anything, McDonnell looked up. "I'll pay you, man, and I'll show you how to live here, which is worth a hell of a lot more than anything I pay you."

Johann stepped over to help with the next log that McDonnell had selected. "I'll bring my friend Fritz, he's a farmer, smart about such things. With him, we'll finish your work even faster. He's to teach me about farming, and you will teach me about America."

They rested the new log on the stump. McDonnell measured, then marked the place for cutting. "If you're really a soldier"—the man waved at Johann's midsection, where the bayonet handle showed—"that could come in handy."

Johann reached down to steady the log, then remembered to support it from underneath. "I have no gun. Only the bayonet. I came to America for peace. To beat my sword into plowshares. To become a farmer."

Making his first stroke carefully, pulling the saw through the mark he'd made, McDonnell grunted. "The savages'll decide how much peace you'll be having, but you might want to think over being a farmer. The growing season's short. The soil's not as good as it looks. Nice crops of stones. The treasure"—the man pointed to the forest with his free hand—"is out there."

"What is in the forest but wild animals and Indians? They are treasures?"

McDonnell smiled as he pumped the saw. "The forest, man. All that wood. Now we just use it for firewood, ship it down to Boston to heat the houses of rich men who sit on their fat arses all day. But it's the treasure of this land, and not for burning. Wood for building houses and ships; tall trees for masts; fine wood for furniture."

Johann nodded, thinking. But he had more urgent questions. "What's he like," he said, "this General Waldo? Have you met him?"

"Wouldn't know him from Adam," McDonnell said. He placed his saw down and stepped away to add some larger branches to the fire. "I bought this place—and the farm connected to it—from a man whose family had been here when the Indians came through. Sold out cheap, he did."

"What do you hear of him, the general?"

McDonnell grinned. "They say he's a slippery character. How else does a man grow that rich? Is he already cheating you?"

"Is he a general in the army?"

"Aye, not that it's a proper army, of course. Things around here, you see," McDonnell grinned again, "the rules aren't always the same as on the other side of the sea."

"And his agent, Herr Leichter, what's he like?"

"Is he the one with the fine waistcoat?"

"I haven't seen him yet, but he sounds like the only man in Broad Bay to have authority."

"Well, I haven't dealt with him either. I reckon he can't be any straighter than the man he's working for."

Johann didn't care for the sound of any of that, but the sun was almost fully risen and he should get back. He stood and reached out his hand again. "Robert McDonnell, I thank you."

"Don't thank me till I've done something for you."

"You have made me a little less ignorant. This is good." Johann started to leave, then stopped. "Did you hear that scream, perhaps half an hour ago?"

McDonnell shook his head as he walked over toward the tool shed, speaking over his shoulder. "No, not a scream. Was it like a woman or a man?"

"No, like an animal."

"Might be a bobcat. They get into arguments. Or maybe an Indian who wanted to sound like a bobcat. Or a Frenchman who wanted to sound like an Indian wanting to sound like a bobcat." He turned to his tools, then looked back. "Say, Herr Oberstrasse, you might keep this in mind. Winter comes on fast. And it stays for a hell of a long time."

Back on the path, Johann thought about what McDonnell had said, especially that last part. One of the sailors had talked about the winter in Maine, but they had winter in Kettenheim. It got cold and snow fell. This couldn't be very different. Johann resolved not to mention McDonnell's warning to Christiane.

When he reached the clearing, Christiane was helping another woman lift a large kettle with stout sticks. They guided it to a hook over the now-blazing fire. The way Christiane straightened and placed her hand at the small of her back reminded him of how she moved when she was pregnant. Was she with child again? It would have to be from before the voyage, that much he knew.

He didn't speak until there were no people around them. "Has Herr Leichter come ashore yet?" Johann asked.

Instead of answering, Christiane held Walther against her shoulder, pointing his face toward his father. Johann grinned and nodded to the baby. "Yes, yes, good morning, young master, and to the mistress as well. You slept well?"

Walther answered in his own tongue, neither English nor German.

They sat on a log to the side of the firepit. "I think your son prefers the land to the sea," she said.

"That may not be for the best. It seems the people here spend much time on the water." He waved at the cabins. "Everyone has a boat. They must use them for fishing and for moving things." He extended a finger to Walther, who began to gnaw on it with his four teeth. Peter, Christiane said, had more trouble when his teeth were coming in, but Johann didn't remember that. He had been with the army in those days.

"Even with these boats," she said, "they always sleep on the land?"

"Probably, yes. So what of the young master's mother? Does she prefer the land?"

"Absolutely, yes. Also breathing air that doesn't stink and also not hanging over the sea to use the privy."

"Ah, the tastes of a fine lady. America may be a difficult home for such a one." He smiled.

"And no," she said, "Herr Leichter has not come ashore. He probably prefers to eat his porridge first, something we might do as well." She nodded toward the fire, plainly looking forward to a meal without hardtack. She lifted Walther to her shoulder.

"How much flour is there?"

She tilted her head and ran her eyes over him, then back at Walther, who was making insistent noises and reaching for her blouse. "Not much. Not for all of us. A few days, maybe." She began to move Walther off her shoulder.

"Yes, yes." Johann straightened and nodded to Fritz Bauer, who was emerging from the shelter. Two women were stirring the kettle. Johann found the smell of hot porridge seductive. "I'll get the bowls and spoons." He stood.

"I have them here." She pointed to the ground next to her feet.

He sat again and began twisting a twig. "They say we are all to farm together, to prepare, plow, and plant one large plot that everyone will build on in the spring. You know what that means?" Busy with Walther, she didn't answer. "That means, of course, that some will not do their share."

"There's no time for growing anything before the snow," she said. "They say the winter is hard. Very hard."

When she sat next to him, he reached over and placed his hand on her midsection. She put her hand on top of his, then looked up with shiny eyes. She nodded.

"Were you going to say?" he asked.

She smiled. "I wanted to be sure."

"God is blessing us in this new land. He will be the first of the American Oberstrasses."

"Perhaps *she* will be the first."

"Yes, yes, of course. In the spring?"

"Yes, the baby will bring the warm weather."

"There's so much I must do," he said.

He kissed her forehead and pulled her to him, not caring who might see. "Christiane, I walked out to see the land. This meadow I found. It was green and gold. The soil is dark. The trees, they're like giants. It's hard to imagine them falling at the hands of mere men."

"I could see from the riverside."

"It's beautiful here."

"And we will have fifty morgens of it," she said.

"We will have our fifty morgens." Another woman was stirring the porridge, so Christiane stayed with him. "I just met an Englishman," he said, "a Scotsman. I can work for him, learn from him how to live here."

"He's a good man?"

"Yes, his yard was neat. He measured his wood. The corners of his cabin were squared."

He stood and stared at the sloop standing offshore. "The food for us, the tools, they must all be out on the ship. There's nowhere here on land that they could be. I've looked." Christiane reached down to stroke Walther's cheek. Johann kicked at the ground. "But I don't know where they could be on the ship either," he said. "That ship, it's not so large."

He looked back at the shelter. It was made out of a few timbers, with brush interwoven for walls and roof. Turf was laid on top. It looked flimsy, not likely to survive a harsh winter. It already had stood for at least a year or two, he told himself. It would have to do.

Where in Christ's name was Leichter? He feared the man was a scoundrel. And that the general was too.

CHAPTER SIX

With Walther burrowed into a basket on her arm, Christiane picked her way along the rocky shore. Her heart felt lighter than it had since they left Kettenheim. Up ahead, Ursula and Sigrid Bauer carried a heavy pot between them and sang a song about a cat who sneaks into a house to drink cream. Other women were farther in front. Christiane hummed her own tune to Walther. The sky was grey and cold without threatening rain.

Her mood surprised her, for the news hadn't been good. After a week of evasions, the settlers knew the truth for certain: General Waldo's promises meant nothing. The Broad Bay settlers would have to make their own way. The sloop had held enough food for them for two weeks, if managed carefully. A few bags of coarse flour, some salt beef, plus corn and squash and beans.

"It is better," Johann had said. "We must know this country, not wait on that rich turd to put food in our mouths." Christiane wouldn't have minded having some food put in their mouths, but now she thought Johann might be right. They would make their own way.

Johann had worked for Robert McDonnell the day before, earning a pail of buttermilk. At night, she and Johann drank the rich liquid slowly, sharing it out to Walther. As it filled their bellies, they began to feel giddy and brave. Johann said the best thing about working for McDonnell wasn't the milk, but what he was learning. Johann had watched the McDonnells eat clams and lobsters. Robert said they could be found near the shore, there for the taking at the right time and in the right place. She and Ursula and Sigrid were going to the place Robert said, at what should be low tide. They were hoping for bounty.

"Look," Sigrid shouted, her voice between a squeal and shriek. She dropped her handle of the pot and ran out onto a rocky beach, then down to the damp sand lapped by waves. Out in the bay, the waves rose to frothy white tips.

Here the river widened to become the bay. Christiane hurried to Ursula and lifted the other pot handle. At the water's edge, where Sigrid shouted and pointed, the water boiled with dark-shelled creatures who darted forward, then paused, then darted in another direction, sometimes climbing over each other, apparently oblivious to the arrival of hungry humans. They looked like giant bugs. Farther on, three women stood shin-deep in the water, pouncing to grab lobsters and dump them in baskets as quickly as they could, flinching from the evil-looking claws.

Sigrid began to cry. A dark object fell from her hand with a splash, then scurried away. "It bit me!" the girl called out.

While Ursula comforted her, Christiane placed Walther on spongy ground just above the high-water mark, where he could do little but pick up stones and eat sand, a dish he wasn't likely to enjoy. Pulling off her shoes and cape, Christiane tucked her skirt up into her waistband and pushed up her sleeves. Taking a breath, she waded into the icy water. She instantly lost the feeling in her feet.

Trying to respect the powerful pincers that each creature waved menacingly, Christiane found a stone that seemed to fit her hand. She tried to sneak up on the creatures, but they scooted off each time she lunged. Off-balance, she sometimes fell into the water, banging her knees on rocks. She looked back at Walther, who was crawling toward her, his small voice somehow cutting through the sound of waves and wind.

Ursula snatched a creature up by its tail. Twisting around, it swiped at her with a claw. Ursula dropped it with a startled cry.

"Sigrid," Christiane called to the girl, who was sniffling and sucking on a finger. "Come help me." The girl took careful steps into the water. "See those two?" She pointed at lobsters between them. "Chase them, toward me." The girl nodded. She splashed at the lobsters, shouting but not getting too near. One veered away from Christiane but the other did not. On one knee, she brought her stone down hard. It splashed and cracked against the creature's shell. She handed the lobster to Sigrid, who took it with her good hand and ran to drop it in the pot, whooping all the way.

To sharpen their tactics, they studied the creatures' ways. Christiane and Ursula, rocks at the ready, stationed themselves about twenty feet apart, with Sigrid between. The girl chased creatures toward one woman, then toward the other. Then they shifted down the shore, or farther into the water, or up toward the land. Many lobsters scurried safely away on zigzag paths, claws swaying in triumph. But some fell to the smashing rocks. Christiane began to anticipate their patterns, how far they would run before changing direction. Sigrid learned to approach slowly, then spring and splash. Each time a stone smashed down on another shell, a shout of triumph rang down the beach. Walther joined their shouts from the shore.

Soon enough, two dozen creatures lay in the pot, covered with water to keep them fresh, a few still feebly waving feelers.

Grinning, the huntresses sat on the shore, rubbing the feeling back into their feet and gazing at the bay while seagulls circled overhead. Two especially bold gulls stood nearby, stealing sidewise glances at the pot.

"What part do you eat?" Sigrid asked.

"Inside the shells," Christiane said, pointing. "There's meat there. Sweet meat."

The girl wrinkled her nose. "Really? And it tastes good?"

Ursula pulled the girl to her, bringing happy laughter. "It'll be delicious—our first feast in America!"

"How do you cook them?"

"We boil them up in this big pot, and we must do it soon."

"Now, young mistress," Christiane said, "it's time to hunt for the clams."

Sigrid flounced back into her mother's arms. "I'm tired."

"Can you watch Walther? Keep those horrid creatures from biting him?"

When Sigrid nodded, Christiane handed the baby over. He had worked his arms free from the blanket and was sucking on a fist. Christiane headed back into the frigid bay.

The water soon numbed her feet again, so she teetered precariously over the rocky bottom. Johann had brought clam shells from the McDonnells so she would know what to look for, but nothing under the water looked right. Several times, she reached for what turned out to be stones. She steeled herself to wade in deeper.

The water was at mid-thigh before she saw what must be a clam. To get it, she had to plunge her arm into the water up to her shoulder. A close look revealed that this was indeed the clam. "See?" She held it up for Ursula, still in shallow water. "Like this." Looking back down, she saw another. Then another. They surrounded her.

Her teeth were chattering by the time her basket was full. When she reached the shore, her whole body was trembling.

Ursula ran up with Walther and Christiane's cape. "You're shaking like a wet dog!" she scolded, wrapping her up and shielding her from the breeze. "We should have brought another blanket." They knelt on the shore, and Christiane and the baby huddled in her arms. Christiane's vibrations slowed, then stopped. "Sigrid," Ursula called, "bring the shoes."

* * * * * *

Propped against the wall of their room in the dark, her cape over her shoulders, Christiane sank into the unfamiliar feeling of a full stomach.

Frau Reuter had shown her how to cook the strange creatures, then how to manage their protective shells. Johann was standoffish, still convinced of the Reuters' thievery on the *Mary Anne,* but the woman seemed perfectly nice. The clams proved chewy with a strong salty flavor. Inside their shells, the lobsters were soft and tender, as sweet as Johann had said. They drank the cooking water as broth. Even Walther had gorged on his share, emitting happy squawks while he gobbled down mashed-up lobster meat. When he sighed in his sleep, the sound touched Christiane's heart. What could he dream? Of the tossing of the sea, which he had known for nearly half his life? Of creatures with shells and strong claws who skitter across the bottom of the bay?

Johann snored next to her on their bower of branches and leaves. It wasn't soft, but it kept them off the chill ground. Today, he had hauled timbers to a clearing that was set aside for the new settlers' cabins. Fritz had come to the shelter at sundown, shaking his head. "Your husband," he said to Christiane, "he's a crazy man. No sun, no moon, not even stars, yet he works. He's like a bat."

An hour later Johann arrived, frustrated that he was too exhausted to keep working. He was desperate to build a cabin before winter, one based on advice from McDonnell. The cabin would only be for this first winter—he'd build something better for the next one—but he wanted to be out of this shelter, to have a place that was theirs alone. They hadn't come to America to live with all these people.

Christiane was proud that she and Ursula and Sigrid had brought back dinner. They would keep gathering these creatures when they could, at least until the water froze. They also could catch fish and salt them for the winter. The English settlers lived on fresh meat that the men shot in the forests: deer and something they called moose, a great huge animal but not dangerous. Johann would have to learn to hunt, which meant he needed a gun. In Hesse it was forbidden to hunt, though some did so anyway. Either the Landgraf or his nobles owned the forests and also the animals in them. In America, you could hunt wherever you liked.

She lifted her knitting from her lap. As a girl, she learned to knit in the dark. When bad thoughts had come in the night, she couldn't get out of the bed she shared with her three sisters. So she kept her needles and yarn within reach and knitted without looking. Her fingers told her what she needed to know. How much slack there was on the yarn, how wide each row was coming out, when to change pattern, and when a stitch slipped that had to be pulled out, which after a while was almost never. Her fingers worked without hurrying. Her hands knew what to do. They freed her mind to go where it pleased.

She had planned to knit many things on shipboard, but she hadn't. First there had been seasickness. Then Peter fell ill, and she had no time to be sick. And then he died and she lost heart. She shouldn't have, but she did.

She had been making a hat for Peter, but it would become a mitten for Johann. She would have to make hats for her and for Walther, warm ones, but Johann's hands came first. For his working. He went through mittens so fast, faster than anyone she had ever seen.

Five years before, her father had arched his eyebrows when Johann came to say he wished to see Christiane after church services. Standing behind Johann, who was neither tall nor wide, Christiane waited for the answer, squeezing and twisting her fingers, too nervous to look. Her father gave his consent.

After Johann left that day, her father asked why she wanted him, this ordinary-looking man with no land. Christiane's brothers were all big men, and her father was proud of that. And they had land, too, which all of the family was proud of. Christiane didn't answer. Most people couldn't see Johann's strength, but she could. She had from the very first, from before Kettenheim's folk started to speak of him, with a trace of awe, as the sergeant major, even though he was only a plain sergeant. The village granted him the higher rank because of how he carried himself, how he spoke, how determined he seemed, and the wars he survived. Kettenheim had never produced a sergeant major, not that anyone could remember, not out of all of its sons who went into the army. Johann said he didn't feel bad about never correcting the mistake. If he had soldiered long enough, he told her, he might have risen to sergeant major. He liked having people make an error in his favor, for once.

Later, after they were married, her father said he understood why Johann was sergeant major. When Johann helped with the harvest, he took fewer breaks than her large brothers and he reaped more grain. She brought water to the fields and watched him work, his face locked in a neutral expression but his body filled with intensity, almost a rage. Her father taunted his sons with Johann's example. Such big men they were, he would say, but still outworked by this slender fellow, barely half their size. Weren't they ashamed? Her brothers had been glad to see Johann return to the army. She smiled at the memory.

She put her knitting aside and stood too quickly, her balance off. She automatically placed her hand over her belly. The baby was growing, giving her hope. It would give Johann hope too. She wished for a girl, one to work with her. She envied Ursula having Sigrid.

When she stepped out of the shelter, the canopy of stars made her feel small. They were the same stars as in Kettenheim, she told herself. They had come with her to this new, unfinished place. Pulling her cape tight across her belly, she hugged herself for warmth. Johann was right about the beauty here, but she also felt the danger. The forest was all around. The men said it was filled with Indians and Frenchmen, both capable of terrible things.

She began to shiver. She should have worn her shoes. She turned back to the shelter.

CHAPTER SEVEN

†

"Egad, man, what do you think you're doing?" McDonnell pointed at Fritz Bauer with his mallet. The lanky German was trying to hoist a long timber by himself. Johann dropped his saw and hurried over. Together they carried the timber to what would become the north wall of the McDonnells' new room.

"You lads are willing enough," McDonnell said as he turned back to his measurements, "but you need a bit of care. Don't want to end up hurt."

As Johann had suspected from their first encounter, McDonnell was a meticulous carpenter. He worked from a drawing he kept inside his cap, though he had spent so much time planning the new room that he rarely looked at the drawing. He was working on the door that would connect it to the current room. With pride, he had said it would be the first inside door in Broad Bay. Johann and Fritz were preparing the logs for the outside walls, a task that required more muscle than skill.

"Will you look at that." McDonnell lifted the door from the ground and set it against the cabin's outer wall. He stepped back to gauge its four wide slats, joined by three stout crosspieces. "That oak was a damned big bugger to bring down but, Lord, the wood is a treat."

Johann ran his fingertips over the slats. "These boards," he said, "they're as smooth as boards from a mill."

"Smoother, Brother John. Smoother."

"How do you do that?"

McDonnell grinned. "The hand of a master, young sir." He pointed his mallet. "Watch and learn. I'll be starting a mill of my own soon, up on the stream that runs through the willows. Just a one-man operation. The water flow won't be enough sometimes, but you'll want to bring your lumber there for cutting."

He squinted at the sun, which was dropping toward the horizon. "Let's finish laying out that north wall, then pack it up."

When the logs were set out in order, the thicker ones positioned to serve as the base, McDonnell called into the cabin for the children. Two straw-haired tykes tumbled out and began climbing over the logs. A third waddled out deliberately, holding her mother's skirt with one hand. The fourth rode in Maggie McDonnell's arms.

"Boasting again, weren't you?" she said to her husband. "I could hear you, even with all the hullabaloo from these ones."

He laughed and waved at the door. "Just have a peep and tell me I'm wrong."

As he and Fritz made to leave, Johann lingered a moment over McDonnell's saws. Johann didn't yet know the uses of every tool. He understood the plane and the gauges, and the drill with its bits, and the braces. There were scrapers, too, and several sizes of saw. That last one was what he needed.

"Go ahead, man," McDonnell called out, "take what you need." McDonnell detached one of the children from his leg and lifted him to his shoulder. "And be careful with this business of working in the dark. Even Scots know better than that."

"We'll be a bit later tomorrow, as I said," Johann said as he reached down for the second-largest saw; the big one would be too much for him. He reached down for the measure, as well.

"Right, right, your meeting with Waldo's man. I saw the sloop. Mind your tongue now. You don't want to make him an enemy for life."

"You're a fine one to talk," Maggie McDonnell said. "When was the last time—"

Robert held up his hand. "It's excellent advice nonetheless. Now let these hard-working men be on their way."

Johann was looking forward to confronting Leichter, Waldo's agent. So many promises had been broken. But with at least an hour before dinner, he stopped at the clearing that held the logs for his own cabin. He built a fire to provide some light, listening to a riot of birds chattering through the day's end as they swayed crazily through the trees, then soared into the sky, looking for just the right perch. He smiled at the jabbering of dozens of squawking birds. Humans weren't the only creatures who preferred speaking to listening.

The pale firelight quivered with every breeze, so he dragged the logs close to mark the places for his cuts. He liked working with wood. McDonnell was a fine teacher. He laid out his work precisely. He respected the grain of the wood and its knots, selecting pieces to minimize waste. He checked and rechecked his measurements and cared for his tools. Johann tried to copy those habits, the practices of a craftsman.

He propped the log on a stump, then drew the saw through his mark. He pressed through the downstroke, trying to exert the steady pressure that McDonnell used. The sawdust smelled sweet.

When he had got through the log, he looked at the six still on the pile. The cabin, he had reckoned, would require at least fifty. He had to level the ground, erect the walls, fill the chinks and gaps with mud and clay and dry grass. Then a frame for the roof, which could be thatch woven with reeds and branches, but should be at least two layers thick. He hadn't yet decided what to do for a chimney. The cabin wouldn't have finely worked surfaces inside, not like McDonnell's. The door would be crude, the single room drafty and cold. But they might be the only new settlers to have their own cabin for the winter. He wanted to give that to Christiane, to greet their new child in their own home.

He straightened and took a breath. He could feel the advancing winter. So much to do. He had to ignore the fatigue. He decided to drag the big log, one of the pines, to his working area near the fire. Then he would return to the shelter.

He heaved the log's end up to waist level and steadied himself with a breath. When he stepped backward, the other end of the log stuck on a rock or a root. He gave an extra yank and lurched back when the log broke free. His heel caught on something. The saw? His balance fled. As he fell back on his seat, he tried to push the log off to the side, but it was heavy. His right foot took its weight with a thud, then turned sideways. Agony ripped up through the ankle and leg. He gasped and squeezed his eyes shut. His breath turned into panting. Pain shrieked in his brain. He spun sideways to reduce the strain on his foot.

When he opened his eyes, he wasn't sure if he had passed out or not. He tried to control his breathing. The sputtering fire made little dent against the dark. He tried to ease his foot free by twisting onto his right side, supporting himself with a hand. No luck.

He couldn't feel the foot. Hauling his other leg up, he placed its toes against the log. He strained to roll it off his foot. It moved up an inch, then another, but it had to climb over the wide part of his foot. His left leg began to twitch. He gathered himself and roared with the effort.

"Johann!"

"Here, Fritz! Up here!" The footsteps were close. "On the ground." Johann waved his free hand.

"My God. What have you done?" Fritz crouched next to him.

"I fell. The log's on my foot." Johann nodded at the timber. "I can't get it off."

Fritz took in the scene, then stepped to the log end that rested on Johann's foot. Squatting, he raised the log and pitched it to the side. Johann still couldn't feel his foot.

He hung on his friend's shoulder as they struggled to the shelter in a three-legged stutter. He felt a pang of shame when Christiane ran to him. Others, busy with dinner and chores, looked away as Fritz helped him onto a log that faced the common fire. Fritz told her what happened. There wasn't any blood around his foot. That seemed good. Perhaps his good soldier's boot had protected him.

"We have to take off the boot," Christiane said, kneeling next to Johann.

Johann shook his head. "Don't. It's swelling. And it will swell more without the boot, and then I'll never get it back on." He closed his eyes to ride out a wave of pain. "I must meet with Herr Leichter tomorrow. That comes first."

"You must stop this madness of working in the dark," Christiane said. "You must slow down. You'll kill yourself and then what good will you be to Walther and me?"

He had appetite only for broth from the boiled fish that Christiane had prepared. Soon he felt feverish. He slid to the ground with his back against the log. The pain surged, then relented, then came back. He stayed outside at the fire, sometimes staring into it, sometimes clenching his eyes to pass through another spasm from his foot.

His head was in Christiane's lap, her hand on him. "Where's Walther?" he asked.

"Sleeping. With Ursula." She had been eager to tell him how Walther had taken many steps that afternoon, leaning forward in his funny, desperate lurch, each foot hitting the ground just in time to keep from landing face first. She would tell him tomorrow. Walther would show him.

Johann sucked in his breath and tensed. His foot was on fire again. Sweat popped on his face. Then Christiane was standing over his leg. Fritz was next to her. "What are you doing?" Johann asked.

"The boot," she said. "It has to come off."

He didn't argue. Christiane gingerly lifted his knee. Fritz tried to work the boot down, tilting it to clear Johann's heel. Nothing. "Pull hard," Johann said. "It can't hurt more than it does."

Fritz knelt, gripping the bootheel with both hands. He yanked and strained. Both men grunted. Johann gasped. His head fell back against the log. Fritz tried again, more violently. And again. And again. Johann came awake with Christiane's hand stroking his face.

"It won't come off," she said. She leaned back and picked up a knife. "We must cut it off."

"No," Johann protested. "What will I do in the winter without a boot?"

"What will you do without a foot?"

"If I have no boot, I will soon have no foot."

Christiane handed the knife to Fritz and gripped Johann's leg.

* * * * * *

Leichter leapt nimbly from the workboat onto the pier. His bright green jacket and satiny brown waistcoat set him apart in the frontier setting. A man of middle years, his face bore the expression of a person who smelled an especially vile odor. At Broad Bay, such odors came from rotting fish innards and imperfect human sanitation. The day was changeable, cloudbanks chasing each other across the sky, sunlight alternating with gloom.

Leaving the pier, Leichter seemed to glide over the uneven ground. Johann wobbled on his good foot, leaning on Christiane on one side and a stout stick on the other, envious of the man's mobility. Rough linen wrapped the injured foot, swollen to nearly twice normal size, ugly colors emerging beneath the skin. It could bear no weight.

They stood at the back of the small crowd of new settlers who hoped to speak with General Waldo's agent. Walther twisted in Christiane's arms. Johann, feeling weak, could see that despite Leichter's fine clothes and careful carriage, he was not a man of the drawing room. He had the look of someone who knew hard work. A man to be reckoned with, one who would not overlook slights.

The settlers grew silent as Leichter approached. The men removed their hats. The agent stopped and cast his eye over them. No English settlers had come to the pier.

"Good morning," he said in a strong voice. "I bring welcome from General Waldo, the Hereditary Lord of Broad Bay, who is pleased that you have completed your journey to this new world." Though his accent was German, he spoke in English, which meant that most couldn't understand his words. They shifted uneasily.

"As you know," he continued, untroubled by the settlers' confused looks, "I am the general's agent. Talking to me is like talking to General Waldo. The general has two rules that you must respect in Broad Bay. The first is that you cause no trouble with the Indians. Your predecessors did that and you can see what it got them." He gestured at the burned cabins. "The general follows a policy of peace with the savages. If you violate that policy, you will be sent away from this community." He paused to make eye contact with individual settlers.

Nungesser, the schoolteacher and unofficial pastor, cleared his throat and raised his hand tentatively. "Please, your honor," he said, "if you might speak in German…"

"Broad Bay is a British colony," Leichter said, "and all its business is transacted in English. If these people wish to conduct business with me or with General Waldo, they had better learn English." The agent clasped his hands behind his back and bounced up on his toes. "And General Waldo's second rule is that you must work. We have nothing but hard work here at Broad Bay. But we also have great opportunity. If you cannot do this work as a settler, then you must return to Portsmouth and work there until you pay off that part of your fare and the cost of your homestead, both of which the general has already paid for you."

Leichter scanned the blank faces. A small smile played on his lips. "All right then," he resumed, "who here speaks English?" He turned to Nungesser. "You, sir?"

"Yes, sir, I speak some English." Johann tried to raise his hand, eager to launch into his questions and concerns. The movement caused him to lean on his bad foot. A stab of pain bent him over. He could barely stay upright.

"Fine," Leichter said to Nungesser. "You explain these two rules to them. I must see the Indians. When I return, you and I will meet. I will respond to questions that you gather from the others. I will speak only through you." Leichter wheeled and strode back onto the pier, then climbed into the boat. The oarsmen pushed off and started up the river.

Christiane helped Johann sit where they had been standing. His foot throbbed.

That evening, the settlers met around the common fire. Nungesser stood at the center. The men were nearest the fire, the women in the next ring out. Johann stood behind that second circle, leaning on Fritz and on his stout stick. When Walther wouldn't settle down, Christiane had to walk him around the clearing. She let him walk on tiptoe, hanging onto her fingers. Whenever she steered him near the meeting, he began to squall. Christiane thought he had another tooth coming in.

Nungesser began with a short prayer, then said, "Herr Leichter returned this evening, so I will see him in the morning. What do you want me to say to him?"

A wall of complaints crashed in on him. The general had broken his promises about food, about tools, about land. They had no weapons to fight off Indians. They would starve. There was no church or minister to care for their souls. Some would pay with their lives for those broken promises. Over and over came the complaint that they had no land yet. When would he assign the land? They had come all this way for the land.

The pain fractured Johann's focus. Early on, he started to speak. The men turned to him. His thoughts blurred. The words didn't come. He shook his head and looked down. The meeting moved on.

After an hour, the complaining slackened. Nungesser, nodding and listening, had said little. Now he spoke: "I have heard, and what you say is right. Promises, important ones, have not been kept. But also, shouldn't we be careful with our complaints? We can't afford to offend Herr Leichter or General Waldo. We need to preserve good relations with them. We will depend on them to keep us safe and to support us. We have nowhere else to turn." A resigned murmur passed around the fire. Heads shook, but the passion had drained from the men.

Johann couldn't stand it. Anger cleared his head. "*General Waldo,*" he called out, "depends on *us*. He has not kept his promises and now he wishes for us to settle the land, to sweat our lives out so he may grow richer, to take whatever risks there are to take while he is safe in his bed."

"We're all disappointed," Nungesser said, "but we must remember that he can replace us. He replaced the first group of settlers. That's why we're here." Nungesser didn't have to point to the charred cabins. "But we cannot replace him. There is no one else who will assist us, who even knows we're here."

"By asking nicely," Johann said, "we will get nothing. That is the way of the world. We must be strong. That is the only way."

"So," a voice called out, "we must be strong by working in the darkness, is that right?" The laughter that followed caused Johann more pain than his foot had. He squeezed Fritz's shoulder as he strained to see who had spoken, who mocked him before everyone. "Steady," Fritz said softly. "Steady, Johann." A deep weariness seized Johann. It took all of his strength to stay upright. He kept his eyes fixed on Nungesser.

"So it's settled," Nungesser said. "I will ask about the land, and the provisions, and the tools. And I will preserve warm feelings between the general and we settlers." He looked from side to side. Johann had no strength to argue. It was useless, he knew. These men weren't cowards. Nor were they fools. They had always bowed before the strong and the rich. They were accustomed to it. They didn't expect that to be different in America.

The Obserstrasses spent the night before the common fire, watching it dwindle. Johann sank into a feverish state of half-wakefulness, but resisted moving. Christiane also got little rest. At least Walther, worn out by a day of irritation, slept deeply next to her. When Johann fell still, he felt the emptiness of the continent around them, the darkness of the woods. What would they do if his foot didn't heal? Where could they live? How would they eat?

An owl hooted, a penetrating, hollow sound from the stories of childhood, tales of bears and wolves and black forests filled with danger. Back home, such animals lived in the forest away from the village. In America, they would be outside their door.

CHAPTER EIGHT

†

The embers of the common fire spat and hissed as a morning drizzle leaked from low clouds. Christiane woke with a start. Walther wasn't there. She hurried into the shelter, hoping that Ursula had him.

Johann was left on his own. The foot was no longer an inferno of pain, only a dull ache. When the drizzle accelerated, he rolled onto all fours, grunted his way up to kneeling, then propped his good foot under him. Jamming the staff into the ground for balance, he rose unsteadily. Once erect, he tried a little weight on the bad foot. It complained, but he could move it. Perhaps it wasn't broken. Pulling the staff close to his right side, he limped into the shelter to find his family.

Christiane, cradling Walther, whispered that Johann should stay quiet and rest. He settled against the wall, half-upright, then dropped into a doze. When he awoke, he wrapped up in a blanket and worked his way back outside. The drizzle had relented. At first, his presence, seated on log at the common fire, stifled the women's conversation while they did their chores and watched the children.

As the day wore on, with Johann doing nothing but shifting his seat from time to time, he became invisible. The women's talk resumed.

Christiane left Walther with him while she hauled out their blankets and clothes and spread them on bushes for airing. Johann wondered at her confidence that the rain wouldn't resume, but said nothing. Then she went to the river to rinse out Walther's swaddling clothes. Johann slid from the log onto the ground to play a hide-the-pebble game with the baby. Everyone in the clearing watched as Nungesser was rowed to the sloop to meet with Leichter. Their hopes traveled with him.

A weak sun had passed its highest point before Nungesser dropped awkwardly into the small boat for the ride back to shore. Christiane was feeding the baby inside. Johann levered himself back up on the log. When Nungesser approached the common fire, his stride was purposeful but clumsy. He was no athlete. His black suit, black cape, and black hat accentuated his customary sobriety, though flushed cheeks and a look of self-satisfaction suggested that sobriety might be an illusion.

Nungesser waved for people to join him before the fire. "Come, friends," he called. His moon face smiled unpersuasively.

Johann stayed on the log. He could see Nungesser only when someone shifted to give him a sight line, but he felt too weak to stand. Also, he didn't care to call attention to himself, not after the derision of the night before. When Christiane approached with Walther in her arms, Johann pointed for her to step to the front. She stood next to Fritz and Ursula.

"I bring the best wishes of Herr Leichter on behalf of General Waldo," Nungesser began. "He made a point, again, of emphasizing how much General Waldo values the importance of *his* settlers—he said that the general always refers to us as *his* settlers—to the future of Broad Bay."

"Enough, Nungesser," a voice called out. "The land. What of the land?"

The schoolmaster cleared his throat. "Herr Leichter assures us that the land will be allocated in the spring, on the terms promised. Each family will get the 50 morgens, but next year we also will labor on a common plot that will be created over there." He pointed to a level stretch of land north of the settlement.

"What of raising our own crops on our own land?"

Nungesser turned deliberately to the questioner. He waited a beat. "We may do that on our own time, after laboring on the common plot." An ill-tempered ripple passed through the crowd.

"And payment for the lands?"

"I'm pleased to report that the general will still wait three years for payment."

Another voice broke in: "When does the three years start? Does it start after we're through laboring on the common plot? We can't raise our own crops while we're raising his." A murmur of agreement rose.

Nungesser looked puzzled. "The starting point—that was not discussed." After an awkward silence, he spoke again. "Some provisions will be delivered by the dinghy this afternoon."

"Is it everything that he promised?" This came from a woman. Johann thought the voice was Frau Reuter's. He still didn't trust her husband, but had almost decided that she was all right.

"Herr Leichter said there have been shortages in Boston, so prices have been high. So we will have to supplement the provisions ourselves."

"What of the tools?" Fritz asked.

"Happily, there are many tools," Nungesser said, "and they will be available for sale this afternoon." Johann smiled grimly. He had meant to be the one to negotiate with Leichter. He knew more English than Nungesser did and would have been adamant. Now that the news from Leichter was so disappointing—even infuriating—he was just as glad that Nungesser had to deliver it. Would the news be different if Johann had negotiated? From what he had seen of Leichter and what he knew of Waldo, he thought probably not.

"Wait, now," Fritz called from his seat, "General Waldo is supposed to provide the tools, not sell them to us. That's what the paper said." Other voices agreed.

"Do you have the paper?" Nungesser wheeled on Fritz.

When Fritz didn't answer, Christiane spoke up. "We do. We have it. That's what it says. I can get it."

Nungesser shrugged. His oval face took on a resigned look. "I asked about paying for the tools, and Herr Leichter said that if any settler needed credit to purchase tools, it would be available. There would be no need to repay for three years, as with the land."

"So when does *that* three years start?" a voice called out.

Nungesser ignored the question. He looked back at the sloop. "You can see that they're bringing the provisions now, so you men can help store them. The tools will come next."

* * * * * *

"That man is a fool," Fritz said through clenched teeth as he crouched next to Johann. "We're at General Waldo's mercy so long as Nungesser speaks for us."

Johann shrugged. "He may be a fool, but we're at General Waldo's mercy no matter who speaks for us. I doubt I could have done better. What else are we to expect from the Hereditary Lord of Broad Bay? We are his peasants."

"So what do we do?"

"Until we have our land, we act like his peasants. What else is there to do?" Fritz stalked away. Johann hadn't seen him so angry. He wondered if his own calm came from his injury. And last night's humiliation. Nothing like shame to focus the mind.

Christiane joined him on the log. "You will have to do this now," he said, "getting the tools. They'll set up down at the pier. There will be men with guns to make us quiet. I don't think I can get down there. Even if I got there, I would only collapse."

She nodded. "So, shall we trade as we talked about?"

"Yes. We have the hoes and shovels from your father, and the buckets. We can raise food with them."

"But it's the wood, you keep saying that."

"Yes, I listen to Robert McDonnell and I believe him. It's the wood. I must learn to harvest it and use it." He waved at his foot. "Also, I must be more careful."

"So, which tools?"

"Not fancy ones for making cabinets and chests, not all the chisels and such that McDonnell has. Get saws, two if you can. A good ax. A good plane. I don't think we can pay for more."

"Nungesser said there will be credit."

"We spit on General Waldo's credit. It's a fool's comfort." He looked down at the riverbank. Men were unloading a few barrels of flour and salt pork. "What we really need is a rifle." He looked over at Christiane. "For hunting."

"But you've never hunted."

He smiled and shook his head. "Only men on a battlefield, with a musket. It's not the same. In the woods, you must be sly and quiet and smart. On the battlefield you must be lucky. Let's see about the money."

Christiane knew that Johann didn't need to count the money. He could recite to the penny how much they had. But she waited. When Walther began to crawl toward the fire, she ran after him. When she returned, Johann had emptied his leather pouch into his palm. She sat close to him to shield the coins from prying eyes. He counted them out, dropping each into her cupped hands. It came to four pounds, fifteen shillings. Johann cursed and sighed.

"A gun?" she said.

"Not unless the general is giving them away. They may not even have one." He held the pouch while she slid the coins back in, keeping one eye on Walther. Every day, the baby moved faster. "Look for McDonnell. If he's there, ask him to help you."

"Not Fritz?"

"McDonnell knows this place. Look for him."

"You trust him? After only these few days?"

Johann nodded. "We must trust someone. And Christiane, trade with them. Like you do in the market." She smiled. "If they won't speak German, use fingers for the numbers. Numbers are the same in every language."

She put the leather pouch around her neck and wrapped Walther in a blanket, then joined the other settlers waiting near the shore. Two boats were returning from the sloop, loaded with tools. The settlers drifted into a line that roughly respected how long each family group had been waiting. They talked little among themselves.

As Johann had predicted, two men with pistols in their belts stood behind the man with the tools, who announced his name as Armstrong. Because he spoke no German, and the settlers spoke no English, the trading was slow. Both sides used gestures and spoke loudly and slowly, as though volume and pace would render an unknown language comprehensible. Christiane couldn't understand why Leichter didn't trade himself. He could have done it in German in half the time.

Walther amused nearby settlers by grunting through a bowel movement, which Christiane pretended wasn't happening. Then he grew restless, twisting in her arms and crying in dismay. She tried songs and bouncing. After nearly an hour, Ursula came by with Sigrid and asked if Walther would like to go with them. Christiane agreed with pleasure, warning that Walther needed a cleaning. She immediately missed his warmth in her arms. She kept her eye on a large saw, a smaller saw, and an ax. They were unsold when she came face-to-face with Armstrong.

Armstrong eyed her with a grin and called back to the gunmen. "Look here, gents, I'm to do business with the apple dumplin' shop, I am." He lifted his three-cornered hat in an ironic salute. Appreciative sounds came from his audience. Christiane returned a half-curtsy but didn't smile. She walked over to the items she wanted and touched each in turn.

"All right darlin', if it's business you're after. You"—Armstrong pointed at her—"want these?" He lifted up the two saws she had touched, but then hefted the wrong ax. The one he lifted was too small, more like a hatchet. She said so in German and walked over and touched the one she wanted.

"More with the hubble-bubble," Armstrong said, swapping the axes. He set it down next to the saws. Christiane looked the question at him with an open hand.

Armstrong gestured at the pouch she clutched in her hand. "Let's see how much you have, then we can see what you can buy."

When he reached for the pouch, she turned away and shook her head, saying, "Nein, nein." This was not how to trade.

"Now listen, missus, until you learn the King's English, we're going to have to do business a certain way. Now hand it over." He gestured behind her. "There's folks waiting. Let's get a move on."

She told him in German that she wouldn't be treated that way. She held up one finger for how many pounds she would pay. "*Eine* pound," she said. Then all ten fingers to show how many shillings. She pushed both hands forward and said, "Shillings."

"Missus, that's insulting, to me and to General Waldo." He waved her away. "You go on and come back when you can parley like a civilized person."

"Armstrong!" The deep voice came from higher on the riverbank. Christiane turned and saw Robert McDonnell coming near. The line moved so he could pass.

"Look out, boys," Armstrong said over his shoulder to his guards, "here comes our very own Scottish laird. Guess he's got to the apple dumplin' shop before me." The smirks returned.

McDonnell nodded to Christiane, then turned to Armstrong. "Frau Oberstrasse will give you two pounds for the lot of them. Cash money."

Armstrong stroked his chin theatrically. "Sounds like a partial payment to me. We could arrange credit for the balance."

"Ready money, Armstrong, that's what we're talking about."

The trader turned to Christiane. "Is that what we're talking about, missus?"

She looked to McDonnell uncertainly. He leaned closer to Armstrong and spoke in a low voice. "You can see, Armstrong, she can't understand a word, just another dumb cabbage-eater. But you don't want to be taking advantage of a lady, do you?"

"Well, it wouldn't keep me awake at night, now would it?" More appreciative sniggering. McDonnell kept his expression severe. Armstrong sighed deeply. "I suppose I could take four pounds for the three of them. Nowhere near their worth, but—"

"Two pounds, eight."

"Aw, don't be doing this now. You'll get my stomach all in an uproar."

"Two pounds, eight."

"I'll let them go for three pounds, but I don't want to see either of you back here today." He looked at Christiane and lifted three fingers. She looked at McDonnell, who nodded. "*Drei* pounds sterling," he said. She turned away from Armstrong to count out the money. She handed it to Armstrong. McDonnell picked up the tools.

"*Warten sie*," she said. "*Eine gewehr*?" Both men looked confused. Christiane raised her arms as though she was pointing a rifle and said, "Boom." Armstrong smiled. McDonnell turned to Christiane so they could have a private exchange.

"How much is left?" He pointed at her pouch. She poured the remaining coins into his hand. He shook his head and returned them to the pouch. "Not half enough."

When they reached the common fire, Christiane thanked McDonnell, who carried the tools. "I'll just leave these with John," he said, then pantomimed his meaning. She repeated her thanks and went for Walther.

Johann sat up and smiled at the sight of the tools.

"You found her?" Johann said.

"Aye, it was fair easy. She was the only pretty woman buying tools." He set the tools next to Johann. "I need you back at work, John. The two lads I had today were so worthless I sent them away at noontime."

"Tomorrow. This is much better now. It's only pain."

"When you're able. When you're able." He sat on the log next to Johann. "Those tools are solid enough. When Waldo actually does something, he tends to do it fairly. And your missus did fine." He poked Johann in the shoulder. "Tried to buy you a gun, she did."

"A rifle?"

McDonnell gave him a puzzled look. "Haven't seen one of those around here. No, a musket."

"Not enough money?"

"Not nearly. Want these inside?"

"Leave them here. I'll look them over." He lifted the smaller saw and inspected it.

"Mind you keep that sharp. Find yourself a whetstone."

"Yes, yes. Soldiers know how to keep blades sharp."

CHAPTER NINE

The next morning, Johann woke clear-headed. He had more movement in the foot, no fever. His appetite was back.

He rose and grabbed his coat and boots—the good boot and the one slashed down to the ankle bone. Using the staff, he limped to a log at the common fire. His breath forming mist, he pulled on his greatcoat and buttoned it. Then he pulled on the good boot. He unwrapped the bad foot. It looked an ugly range of colors, but the swelling was down. He rewrapped it with only half of the linen, then tried to work the slashed boot on.

Getting down to the riverfront was awkward going. He had to drag his bad foot to keep the slashed boot in place, but he grew more pleased with each shuffling step. He could work. Then he would work on their cabin the following day, Sunday. People might talk about him working on the Sabbath, but there was no choice.

The dawn's half-light softened the far border between the river and the forest. With no wind blowing, the river was calm, a mirror of the heavens, even of his thoughts. He needed to think. He couldn't think in the shelter, surrounded by so many arms and legs, so many mingled dreams, so many smells and groans. He needed to speak to God. Clinging to the staff, he sank to his knees.

Johann closed his eyes and fumbled for the thoughts that had troubled him since his accident. He had sinned again, his old sin, the one that always hung over him like a sharpened ax. The sin of pride, the first sin of Satan. It had started with Peter. He had been so angry over that. He still was. He hugged himself with both arms and stopped a sob. He couldn't forgive God for taking Peter, not for that, but how could he judge God? He knew it was monstrous to judge God—for him, a sinner, to do it. But he couldn't stop. Peter had been blameless, a small child. What purpose could God have in taking him? God couldn't mean to punish Christiane. She did nothing to incur His wrath. She never would.

It had to be him, the prideful soldier who stole men's lives for money. He was the object of God's wrath, the one whose sins were repaid by the blameless boy. He shook his head and squeezed his eyes.

Johann made himself look across the water. He had to face his sin. His pride hadn't ended when he left the army. When he arrived in this land, he meant to tame it in a single week. By making a show of working so hard and accomplishing so much, he meant to win favor—with Christiane, with the Germans and the English, with McDonnell, with Armstrong and Leichter and General Waldo.

Johann had aimed to lead the settlement, to seize the place close to the general's agent that Nungesser now held, but instead he had made himself a laughingstock. He had aimed to claim his land within days of arriving here, but no land claim would be recognized until spring, if ever. He had aimed to build the first cabin of a new settler, but he had to sit nursing his foot while other men worked. And winter was coming, a winter—so the English said—like none he had known. He had to provide for his family. He had to make a place for the American Oberstrasses.

He sat back on his heels. God had exposed his sin, shown how ridiculous he was. Perhaps God could forgive his sin, but Broad Bay would not. He must let go of this pride. It poisoned everything. It wasn't his place to understand why Peter died. He must accept it. He could not think it was right, but he couldn't be angry with God. He must put his energy to understanding this vast and wild place. He could not change America to fit Johann Oberstrasse. He must change to suit it. This was what God wanted of him, and what he owed to God and to Christiane and to Walther and to the baby who was coming. He thought again of Peter and let the tear form at the corner of his eye. He gazed down the river to the bay. This might be a cold place, but it had water and woods and land. The land that they came for.

He made his way back to the fire and returned to their corner of the shelter. Only Christiane was still there, Walther asleep in her lap, under a blanket. She was knitting, somehow, with one wrist supporting the baby's head. She smiled at the way Johann dragged himself across the ground. She held up what he knew would be a mitten. "Almost done."

"Good," he said. "I'll need it. Back to work today."

"Your foot?" she asked.

Lowering himself, he shrugged. "Better. I was lucky. But the boot is a problem."

"We can bind it with linen. When the swelling is gone, I'll sew it shut."

* * * * * *

The mid-November sun warmed Christiane's face as Johann told her that they could live in the cabin soon, perhaps after five more days of work. He could keep working on it after they moved in.

"We must wash everything," she said. "We won't have another chance until spring." It already had snowed twice, though not much snow. "Won't it be fine to start in the cabin with clean things?"

"Yes," Johann agreed. "The only things that will stink will be us." He squinted at the sky. "Will there be time to dry everything?"

"If we go quickly. We can go to the river, upstream so we don't do it in front of everyone here." She turned to him. "And you can help carry, before you work on the cabin."

Johann wished the cabin were made better. The notches at the corners were uneven and the walls not exactly vertical. But McDonnell thought it would hold up, even under heavy snows, so long as Johann swept the roof as soon as the snow fell. The hearth was bare ground surrounded by rocks, with a hole in the roof above to draw out the smoke. Johann was working on a rope connection to raise and lower a cover on the smokehole, depending on the weather. He had started working in the evening again, but only work that involved no lifting or cutting. The night before he had filled cracks between the logs. When the wind blew, those cracks felt like gaping holes. He wedged sticks and even rocks into the gaps, then sealed them with mud with grass mixed in. He daubed the cracks from both the inside and outside. After it dried, the mud sometimes cracked, so Johann had to seal it again. When Johann complained to McDonnell about the problem, his new friend laughed and said he'd be resealing the walls until the cabin fell down.

Johann was embarrassed to compare his cabin to McDonnell's. The Scot had brought fine planks with him from Boston and was using them for the inside walls. He had rigged up the small mill on a nearby stream and was planning a larger one on the Medomak, but not until the next year.

For all the cabin's faults, Johann thought it might do. It was on a small rise, which would keep water from running in. The clay floor would be damp and cold but he could do no better now. There were no trees close by, so they would get what sunlight there was. It was big enough for the three of them—even for four of them—as much space as they now shared with two other families in the shelter. He was building a sleeping surface to keep them off the ground. Johann knew this cabin would never satisfy him, but their next one, the one on the land they received in the spring, would show what he learned from building this one. That one would be better.

Walking along the river, Christiane felt almost gay. They would soon leave the shelter and start a new life. She smiled at Walther, nestled atop a pile of blankets and linen. Christiane had recruited Ursula to join the washing, so she and Sigrid carried similar bundles. Johann and Fritz trailed them, each carrying his family's clothes.

When the women pronounced themselves satisfied with a riverside spot, Johann and Fritz dumped the clothes. Before he left, Johann gave Christiane his bayonet. "What will I do with that?" she said.

"You'll know if you need to," he said. She left it on the ground next to a large tree.

The women set to the washing with energy. They pounded the blankets and linens and clothes against large rocks, dislodging the crusted filth of the voyage and their first weeks in America. The soap from General Waldo was harsh in the cold water but there was a satisfaction that came as the blankets became more flexible, as the dirt tinted the river water and swirled away. They decided to wash everything twice. They draped soggy items over the sunniest bushes to dry.

Christiane had parked Walther next to a small pile of rocks which he was banging against each other, mimicking the women, pointing at them with his stones and squawking. She stopped him when he tried to taste the rocks. Sigrid explored the plants along the shore and chased sparrows that flew close to her, bold and unafraid.

Near noon, at the end of her second round of washing, Christiane began to finger the stiffness of her dress. It was so dirty. The sun was still strong. The winter would be long. She pulled it off and went to work on it, wearing only her shift. When she finished with it, she called to Ursula, "Will you watch the baby for a minute?" Ursula waved.

In a quick movement, she shed her shift. The swelling of her belly made her smile. That was why her balance wasn't always right, why she sometimes felt warm when others were pulling on extra clothes.

Kneeling naked on the shore, Christiane scrubbed the shift with soap and pounded it, then waded in to rinse it. After repeating each step, she spread it to dry. She had thought she would wrap herself in whatever blanket had dried the most, but instead picked up a bar of soap and plunged into the frigid river with a shout. She got as far as waist level. Her breath came in gasps and giggles as she speedily washed. She ducked her head in backward and worked the soap into her hair. She felt in her scalp for the lice that tormented her. She found one, then another, swiftly digging them out and crushing them with a thumbnail. She would check Walther, as well. His hair was coming in, the same light brown as Johann's.

Another splash and a shout came from behind her. Ursula was in the river, too, laughing and washing. Her skin and hair were pale and delicate in the sunlight. She would make a perfect duchess or princess.

"Can I come in?" Sigrid shouted from the shore, running to them.

"Yes," Ursula said, "but quickly, quickly. It's so cold."

Christiane saw Walther crab-walking toward the water, drawn by the excitement. She ran to the shore, lifted off his dress and swept him up, then grabbed the little girl's hand. The three of them ducked into the water with shouts of "Brrrrr, brrrr." Even Walther tried to make that noise. Ursula greeted Sigrid with a bar of soap and began to wash her. When Christiane ducked Walther in the water, he screamed, then began to cry. They all laughed, and Christiane spun him around to distract him.

That was when she saw them, two of them, standing next to a scrubby tree. She froze. They had dark skins, much darker than the bathers, but she couldn't make out their faces. Their hair was long. Their clothes looked to be of leather. One cradled a musket. The other held his musket by the barrel, resting the stock on the ground.

Christiane hugged Walther with both arms and began backing towards Ursula, keeping her eyes on them. The baby, sensing her mood change, quieted. "Ursula," she said over her shoulder, but was drowned out by splashing and happy shouts. She gripped her friend's arm. "Indians"—she pointed with her chin.

Ursula looked over, then began to drag Sigrid from the water. "Mama, no! I don't want to stop," the little girl objected. Her mother said nothing. Christiane followed, watching the Indians, who hadn't moved. Was that good? She stumbled over a rock but didn't fall. Were there others? Were they hunting? Why would they hunt so close to the settlement? Were they at war? Where was Johann's bayonet?

Heart racing, she crossed the narrow shore to pull a blanket from a bush and wrap it around herself and Walther. She shivered from the damp wool, then found the bayonet. Ursula had already wrapped herself and Sigrid in wet linen.

When Christiane turned to look, they were gone. "Where are they?" she said.

"I don't know," Ursula said.

They walked to the edge of the water. "They vanished," Christiane said. "I never heard them. Not when they came or when they left."

"What do we do? Everything's wet. And heavy."

Christiane didn't answer. She stared into the woods without seeing. The forest had secrets, but she knew none of them. She tried to think as she fingered the bayonet. "We've been foolish." She crouched down on her heels. Walther was crying again. She stroked his head and held him closer. "They could have taken us, or done… anything."

"Yes."

"But they didn't."

"No."

"We should go back."

"They could get us on the path."

"At least we would be closer to the others."

"The men were going to come to help carry."

"Do you want them to carry our bones?"

They folded the soggy clothes and blankets, stacking them into three piles, two large ones for the women and a small one for Sigrid. They wore as many of the damp things as possible, which made the piles a little smaller and made the women feel more secure. But only a little. They strained to lift the sopping loads and staggered off. They stopped several times to shift their grips, lean against tree trunks, and catch their breath. When they neared the settlement, they set their loads down and spread things to dry in the slanting sun. They dawdled in the light themselves, hoping to dry what they wore. They had nothing else to put on.

Walther dozed on Christiane's shoulder. Ursula combed out her daughter's hair with her fingers, then released her. When Sigrid chased a blowing leaf, the two women exchanged a look of relief. "We've been lucky." Christiane said. "Will you tell Fritz?"

"Of course." Ursula tilted her head. "Sigrid will blab it no matter what I say. Will you tell Johann?"

"Of course." Christiane then raised one eyebrow and gave her friend a sidewise look. "Perhaps not everything."

"Not about bathing?" They shared a smile.

"Didn't that stop before we saw the Indians?"

"Long before," Ursula said. They both smiled. "Husbands." They laughed.

"Mama," Sigrid came running back from a curve in the path that afforded a view of the settlement. "Those Indians, they're over there!"

When they reached the shelter, they saw the two Indians near the pier, bold as brass. They couldn't be sure it was the same two, though that seemed likely. Animal skins lay on the ground between them and Armstrong, the trader. The other settlers were trying not to gawk at the visitors, but without much success.

Christiane studied the savages. Their tunics were of animal hides, as were their capes and leggings and moccasins. Beadwork decorated the capes. Christiane wondered if they had left the women alone because they had come to trade, not for war. One Indian had a soft pelt, perhaps beaver, tied to his belt and hanging between his legs. They wore necklaces made of shells and rings through their noses. Their hair hung loose from leather bands around their heads. Christiane's eyes kept going back to the nose rings. That must have hurt. Perhaps that was the point, to show strength in the face of pain.

"A fine thing," a woman said nearby, "the way that trader kisses up to them. He should send them off to trade with the Frenchies."

"You won't be so high and mighty," another woman said, "when we're all starving over the winter and they bring fish or squash to trade."

The first woman wheeled on the other. "Don't you go telling me they're our friends. They wiped out this settlement once, and now they strut through here like they own it."

That night a full moon lit the way for Johann and Christiane to walk to their new cabin. He carried a bucket of water. Christiane, carrying Walther, told the shortened version of their encounter with the Indians at the pond. "I was afraid," she said. "Should I have been? Are they our enemies?"

Johann clucked his tongue. "Yes and no. You heard Leichter when we first got here. General Waldo's policy is that we must be friendly. But we know that they resent us, and they have killed many settlers. I think you shouldn't wash clothes so far away." They were at the cabin. He began to build a fire to light his work for the evening.

Christiane inspected the cabin's walls. Johann had filled many of the cracks. She tried to imagine what it would be like to live inside for the next cold months, with no windows, only the light from the cracks, or the fire, or the smokehole.

"Was this land," she said to him, "this land we're standing on, was this Indian land?"

"It all was. There were no white men."

"And their tribe is the Penobscots?"

"The ones today? Yes." He was beginning to mix mud in the bucket, spreading grass into it. "They live to the east, but they've dwindled. Diseases. They look strong, but they fall to disease like we do. More than we do."

"So are they our enemies?"

Johann shrugged as he began to daub the mud into a crack. "Sometimes, yes."

CHAPTER TEN

†

The sharp cold made the air feel brittle. The late February snow crunched under Johann's boots as he moved across the ridge. Sound carried farther in the cold. The wintry sunlight angled through bare trees. His breathing echoed in his ears as he shifted the canvas sack on his shoulder and plunged through the heavy going.

In December and through Christmas, Johann had hoped the warnings about winter at Broad Bay were exaggerated. Winter came to Hesse, every year. It snowed and grew cold for weeks on end. How much worse could Broad Bay be? The Indians had survived these winters for as long as time could remember. Johann refused to be frightened by a season that the savages endured.

January and February modified his thinking. Unless Christiane left their water next to the smoldering fire, it froze overnight. Their two woodpiles dwindled at an alarming rate when the snow piled up. When he could dig them out of the cabin, he spent hours chopping and hauling firewood. On some days, though, he couldn't get out of the cabin, pinned inside by harsh winds and swirling snow that attacked his eyes and nose and seared his lungs. When the fire cast enough light on those days, he read to Christiane from their Bible, mostly the stories from the Old Testament that he liked best, while somehow she made her fingers knit more caps and mittens they could trade for food.

The cold crept through every crack in the walls, making new cracks by shattering the mud he had smeared on so generously. It was perpetual war. He chipped dirt from the cold floor with a hatchet, warmed it by the fire, poured in water to make new mud to reseal the walls.

They slept together, all three huddled under every blanket and cape they owned, fingers curled into fists inside their mittens. Snot had run from Walther's nose for four weeks without a break. Johann couldn't understand why the baby didn't run out of it. Walther whimpered constantly, though he seemed feverish only once, and then only for two days.

On good days, like this one, the sky cleared and the wind blew somewhere else. Johann could push the snow from their door and stamp down a path to the rest of the world. Then he could cut and haul more wood. At least he was moving his legs and arms enough to warm himself, even sweating into the shirt he hadn't taken off since Christmas. He always cut more firewood than they needed, then traded some at the clearing for the salt fish that was keeping them alive and the wool that Christiane knitted. He stockpiled wood to sell into the Boston market whenever the river ice melted and trade resumed. He shared the fish with Fritz and Ursula in the shelter, who suffered from the bloody flux. He emptied their bucket of watery shit, silently congratulating himself for getting his family out of that swamp of contagion.

At least once a week, twice if he could, he walked out to the line of deadfall traps he had built with Robert McDonnell's advice. The traps were so simple that even Johann mastered them. He drove four posts into the ground, two by two, with enough space between them for a small log. Then he braced one end of the log on a trigger stake which raised that end about eight inches high; he stabilized the raised end with a second, horizontal stake. The final touch was the bait, usually salt fish, held down by the trigger stake and stretching back into a pen built of rocks and branches. The hungry muskrat or beaver or possum, tugging on the bait, would wrench out the trigger stake, crashing the log down on his head.

The traps weren't foolproof. Snow could bury them. Sometimes the animal got away with the bait. Johann's scent, steeped in the wood smoke that filled the cabin, doubtless kept some animals away. But winter was hard on them too. They were hungry. He usually found kills in at least two traps, sometimes more. The meat from the small animals brought welcome variety. He was saving the pelts to sell in the spring, though muskrat and possum were not much in demand. Beaver, though rare, brought a good price.

Trapping was building Johann's connection to this new country. It made him live in the land, tramp through it, know it. He watched for the animals' signs, eager to understand how they lived, how they moved through the forest. He was learning the tracks they made. Deer tracks had two halves, each oval, though he had no weapon to bring down a deer. He could bring one home, he complained to Christiane one night, only if the animal ran up and surrendered. Rabbit tracks came in clusters of four. Muskrat tracks also came in groups of four but with space between the prints. Footprints of raccoons, who ventured out rarely, showed five separate toes. Toes in fox tracks were more rounded.

He read the tracks to decide where to place his traps. The best locations were in lowlands, near water, close to the homes of beaver and muskrat, lands that tended to be separated by hills and ridges like this one. If a site produced nothing for two weeks, Johann searched for a better spot. The more he trapped, the farther from the settlement he ranged.

He also was trying to learn to pass through the woods without sounding like an entire regiment. If he ever got a rifle and could hunt for larger game, moving quietly would be important. Recently, he came upon two Indians with rifles, crouched behind a large oak tree. He froze, not knowing their intentions, but followed their gazes to the top of a crest, perhaps a hundred yards away, where a deer stood, a rack of antlers giving him a lordly air. Luckily, the deer stood upwind and Johann's heavy steps hadn't spooked him. The Indians slid away in pursuit, advancing on their toes. They didn't swing their arms or their guns. When they disappeared over the crest, Johann tried to mimic their stealthy walk. He found it exhausting.

Today he had already visited five of his six traps, making a lopsided loop through the woods. When he thought of the two muskrats in his bag, his mouth started to water. The last trap was down from this ridge, far to the northeast of the cabin. He picked the spot because he could make out the shape of a beaver lodge at a nearby pond. Christiane had learned how to cook beaver, and one of those pelts was worth some extra walking.

Johann glanced at the sun. It probably had two more hours, long enough to check the trap and get home. The baby would come soon. Johann would have to fetch women from the shelter when the baby was ready. Christiane shouldn't be by herself then.

He reached a point where the ridge looked down on the trap. Fury swept through him. An Indian, wearing a cape of skins and a fur hat, crouched at the spot, stealing whatever animal had been snared. Johann bent over, scanning the ground before him. The Indian looked around, then lifted the trap's log off the carcass. His furtive movements were a confession. It was theft, something that Johann couldn't tolerate, not in a hungry winter with a baby and a pregnant wife. Trappers had a code. No white man would poach from another man's trap. The system would break down if anyone could take a kill from any trap. McDonnell had been clear about that. General Waldo's policy of friendship toward Indians couldn't include letting them steal.

Johann pulled the bayonet from his sack, then looped the sack back over his shoulder. He couldn't leave that behind. Losing the two animals already gathered would be too high a price to pay. He took off the mitten on his right hand and stuffed it in his waistband. He couldn't have his hand slip on the bayonet.

Johann passed behind fir trees, staying in shade when he could. To use the bayonet, he had to get close. He wanted the sun over his shoulder, shining in the Indian's eyes. This man must be from close by, a Penobscot. They couldn't let the Penobscots steal whenever they wished. Where would it stop?

Closing to fifty yards distance, Johann saw that the man had rested a musket against a deadfall log. Unless the gun was loaded, which Johann thought unlikely, it wouldn't be much use in a close fight. Johann kept advancing.

At about thirty yards, he saw the man look up, alert. He had the kill in one hand; it was a beaver, stout-looking. That strengthened Johann's resolve. He wouldn't give up a beaver. The Indian had heard or smelt or sensed something. He had the beaver tied to a leather thong that he draped around his neck with other necklaces and two other animals. He gripped the gun and rose, then scanned the woods.

Johann broke from cover, sprinting as fast as slick snow allowed. When the Indian raised his musket, Johann gave a war shout from deep in his belly, hoping to rattle the man's aim. When he looked ready to fire, Johann dove to the ground. A shot boomed. Thanking his luck as the sound bounced around the hills, Johann scrambled up. The Indian was climbing the opposite slope, moving north, away from Broad Bay. Johann slung his sack back over his shoulder and set off.

The Indian churned through the snow in moccasins. Behind him, Johann's boots sank too far into the snow to work up much speed. He dropped his pace to one he could sustain. His surprise ruined, he would have to run the Indian down.

The Penobscot, checking over his shoulder, saw Johann's pace slacken. The Indian tried to burst ahead, but he slipped to his hands and knees, rolling onto a shoulder to keep the gun out of the snow. He was up again, moving at a steadier rate. Sprinting wouldn't work for either of them.

Johann's thighs burned as the effort stretched out. He could match the Indian's pace—the musket and the heavy beaver slowed the other man—but he couldn't gain. He was grateful the Indian wasn't on snowshoes. He must have intended to stay on frozen streams where moccasins would work better.

Grim and silent, Johann pursued in the fading light. The Indian led him over ridges and across frozen marshes. The gap between them shrank a little. They were leaving Broad Bay behind. Johann didn't know this country. The sack of carcasses weighed on him. He kept on.

When the Indian disappeared over the top of a slope, Johann fought the urge to speed up. He thought of the tortoise and the hare. He must be the tortoise, a lethal one. He set his jaw and pumped his legs. He squeezed the bayonet handle. He focused his mind. He would bring down this offender of the proper order, this threat to Johann's family, this offense to God. The rightness of his mission washed out the fatigue and pain that waited on each wind-swept ice patch, in each thigh-high snow drift. He must be pitiless, implacable.

The two men staggered up hills and picked their way down steep grades. They strained to avoid the misstep that could be fatal. The Indian hugged a ridgeline for most of a mile. Johann still couldn't close. He knew they wouldn't meet another white man out here. He hoped they didn't come upon Indians.

His quarry darted downhill. Gravity allowed him to widen his lead. Johann, following, used gravity to step up his cadence. He had closed a third of the distance by the time they reached a swale at the foot of the slope. Frozen hard by months of winter, the boggy stretch posed little obstacle until the Penobscot reached a narrow stream. His foot smashed through a layer of ice and into frigid water, then sank deep. Thrown off balance, he pawed at the ice with his other foot but found no purchase to pull out of the stream. He tried to vault out of the water but failed and fell back. The water drenched his musket. Johann held his pace, drawing to fifteen yards, then ten. With a grunt, the Indian hauled himself to the stream's far side.

The two men faced off across the narrow water, which now splashed through the gap the Indian had smashed in the ice. The Penobscot gripped the gun by its barrel and faked a swing at Johann, who slipped to one knee. Johann saw the tomahawk in the Indian's girdle. When Johann hesitated, the Indian resumed his flight.

Johann worked up the stream to a narrower spot. Gathering himself, he leapt across, landing on his hands and knees, but not in water. Being dry might be an edge. He began to close again as they worked up another slope, now heading due north.

Johann had to plan the fight. The other man was large, larger than Johann. He looked strong. He already had led a chase for several miles. He had the musket as a club and the tomahawk for close work. Because it would take two hands to swing the gun with any force, he couldn't wield both weapons at once. He probably also carried a knife.

Johann had only his bayonet. Longer than most knives, its handle fit Johann's hand. Its wicked triangular shape made an ugly wound. It was meant for stabbing, not for slashing. When he got close enough, Johann might need a heavy branch to fend off the swinging musket.

He could hear the Indian's breathing. The stink of animal fat came back to him. The gap shrank to ten yards as they labored up another slope. At the crest, the Indian lost his footing. He began to slide, then turned, braced to defend himself. Johann leapt forward. He meant to land on top of the Indian, making the man's gun useless, but he landed short. Grabbing desperately, he yanked the Indian's hair, provoking a roar as the man fell back into Johann. Their fall jarred the musket loose.

The Indian spun, leaving a hank of greasy hair in Johann's hand. He reared back to swing his tomahawk, then grunted as his footing failed. The weapon flashed an inch in front of Johann's face. The swing carried the Indian to Johann's side. Johann fought to rise, feet pawing the ground. Unable to stand, he rolled downhill to duck a backhand swing of the tomahawk which took the man off-balance to Johann's other side.

On his knees, Johann let the sack slide off his shoulder and shed his remaining mitten. He launched himself at the Indian's middle. This lunge came up short too. As he fell forward, Johann clutched at the man's belt with his free hand, then stabbed up with the bayonet. The thrust glanced off the Indian's belt. Switching his grip on the bayonet, Johann stabbed down hard into a thigh. The Indian roared again and swung the tomahawk straight down, reaching over Johann's back and hammering the right side of his ribs. A fireball of pain loosened Johann's grip. He fell away from the Indian.

Bright blood shone on the snow. Johann hoped it was the Indian's. He shifted the bayonet to his left hand. He had to strike quickly, while he still could, protecting his injured right side. The leg wound would limit the other man. The carcasses around his neck would too.

Johann stood carefully, staying low. He circled to his right over uneven ground. The Penobscot rotated in place, favoring his gashed leg. He waved his tomahawk and kept his dark eyes fixed on the bayonet.

Johann feinted to his right. The Indian shifted to meet the thrust. Johann found solid footing and feinted back to his left. When the Indian spun back, his foot slid. Pushing off hard, Johann drove his shoulder into the Indian's chest and stabbed up with the bayonet. The blade sliced through a leather vest and linen shirt. Johann felt it plunge into flesh and put his weight behind it. Hot blood slid over his hand. He pushed again on the bayonet and twisted it sideways, deep into the man's guts. The Penobscot grunted and fell back, unable to resist. He grunted again when his back hit the ground, the tomahawk flailing weakly against Johann's back.

The bayonet lodged in bone. Johann let the weapon go and reached both hands to the Indian's throat. He drove his thumbs into the Indian's windpipe. His hands slick with blood, he leaned in with all his rage. He felt the Indian's resistance stop, and then his life. Johann squeezed for another minute, then another, until he was sure. He couldn't afford to be wrong.

Johann rose to his knees. He fought for breath. His heart thundered. He wanted to gasp deeply, to fill his lungs with cold air, but his ribs shrieked if he tried anything more than a shallow panting. He reached around to his back. The pain was fierce. Touching around the wounded area, he found no tear in his coat. The blade hadn't penetrated. It must have been dulled by wood-chopping or neglect. If it had been sharp, Johann might already have bled to death.

Still panting, he stared at the Indian's face. It was tan and lined. The man was probably five years older than Johann. Why had he run? It was the wrong move. He was larger. He had better weapons. He should have stood his ground. Flight only wore out the older man, making the fight more even. He had underestimated Johann, thinking the white man would give up the chase. Johann was used to being underestimated. It was an advantage.

As his breathing slowed, another thought crowded in: General Waldo's policy that the settlers cause no problem with the Indians. This man, whose belt included ten rows of valuable wampum, who carried a musket and had reached a substantial age, might be a respected figure in his tribe. The Penobscots, who seemed always on the edge of war, might not shrug off his killing. That was why General Waldo's policy was one of peace. Could a single killing trigger a war? Why not? It could in Europe.

He decided to conceal the body and tell no one about it. They were far from Johann's trap line, far from the settlement. The man's stab wounds and throttling could have been inflicted by anyone, white or Indian. Johann would drag the man to a low place and conceal the spot with snow, branches, even rocks. By the time someone found the body, it might not even be recognizable. Johann reached down and closed the man's sightless eyes, his skin already cold to the touch. Johann's fever to kill was gone.

He took the animals from around the man's neck. One was the fat beaver from Johann's trap. It would bring a good price. The other two were muskrats, likely stolen from someone else. Johann had traded the man's life for them. To recover his bayonet, he put a foot on the man's chest and pulled down and out. He took the other man's knife and found the tomahawk in the snow. The knife had no special markings. He could keep it. But not the tomahawk, which he stuffed into the man's wampum belt. He fingered the belt. It had value, but it felt wrong to strip him of his clothes, leave him naked to the winter and the animals. Johann had killed to stop a crime, not to rob the man. Johann instinctively looked at the man's feet, shod in moccasins with intricate beadwork. Every week or two, Christiane had to re-stitch Johann's slashed boot. After battle, boots of the dead were an accepted item of plunder. But the moccasins looked flimsy. The traction Johann gained from digging in his bootheels may have saved his life. If he wore these moccasins, people might want to know how he got them. He had no way to pay for such a fine pair.

And what of the musket? Johann looked it over. It was drenched from the stream and from lying in the snow, but was in fair condition. The spring and hammer and trigger worked smoothly enough. The barrel was straight and cleaner than some he had seen. Johann longed for a gun for hunting. He might bring home a deer or even a moose that would feed them for days. He could defend his family with the musket. But how could he explain acquiring a gun in the dead of winter? That he found it in the snow? His neighbors would talk. If he was to conceal this killing, he would have to conceal the musket. He resolved to find a separate, safe place for it so he could retrieve it when he had thought up an explanation for how he got it.

It took time to find a low spot where a fallen tree and underbrush would conceal the body. Johann scooped out the snow, stopping every few minutes to wait out the pain in his back. The man was too heavy to carry, so Johann dragged him, then covered the body. Finally, he walked backward from the spot, using a long branch to spread snow over his own footsteps and the track and blood where he dragged the corpse. He placed the gun in a hollow tree trunk some distance away, using a cloth to wrap the mechanical parts.

With clouds gathering and the light thinning, Johann ate snow for the water. He stuffed the carcasses into his sack, then used the branch to smooth over the site of the fight. He wedged the Indian's knife in his belt and began the long trudge home. He wasn't sure of the way or the distance. During the chase, he had focused on the man ahead of him, not noticing landmarks. He retraced their tracks until the skylight faded to a moonless sky. A light snow began to fall. He would have to reset the trap where he interrupted the theft, but there was no time for that. He fought to ignore the pain. His wound seemed to be swelling.

His mind cycled back to the Indian's mistakes. The savages were supposed to be mighty warriors, yet this one had blundered when confronted by a smaller man with only a short, bladed weapon. Were a few trapped animals so essential to the man's family that it was worth a fight to the death? Maybe the man had been half-mad with hunger, his judgment distorted. Was there something about Johann that unsettled him? Did the Indian fear that other settlers were close by? Or was he simply a man of faint heart, not a fearsome warrior at all? Surely the savages, despite their bloody reputation, had men like that. All races did.

With a start, Johann realized he had lost the trail. Had he gone beyond where the chase started, or simply veered off? He climbed a ridge for a wider look. Nothing was familiar. Pines rose like open umbrellas, long bare shafts with conical greenery at the top. He searched for the North Star, but snow clouds obscured it. The man had fled northeast, so Johann had to travel in the opposite direction.

After dropping his sack, he blew on his hands through his mittens and stamped his feet. He stretched an arm to test his back. A lightning bolt of pain stopped him. Waiting for the spasm to relent, he closed his eyes, then concentrated on searching the horizon. He sniffed the air for wood smoke. He hunched against a wind gust. Weary from the chase, the fight, and his wound, he knew he couldn't stay out for the night. He had heard about trappers who curled up behind a windbreak, wrapped themselves in a blanket, and waited for sunrise. But he had no blanket and feared freezing to death. And Christiane might give birth at any moment. He had to choose a path, the right one, and get home.

He thought he saw a break in the trees. It seemed to stretch for some distance. That could be the river. He squinted, shielding his eyes from the snow as it fell, muffling the sounds of the forest. The more he squinted, the more Johann thought he had no choice. With a moan, he shouldered his sack and started off. The night would only grow colder. The snowfall might accelerate.

Johann's progress slowed, but he kept on, still puzzling over the Indian's tactics, searching for an explanation that satisfied him. In this weather, he didn't fear animals. Bears would be in their winter dens. Wildcats wouldn't attack a man unless he was obviously injured. A wolfpack might be trouble, he supposed, but he could do nothing about that risk now. He was using a solid branch about four feet long as a staff. That would be his defense against wolves.

As the snowfall eased, a half-moon cast a low glow that backlit the clouds in front of him. He thought he saw a white plume to his left. The scent of smoke spurred him on. The smoke thickened, becoming much too thick for that time of night, when settlers let their cabin fires dwindle. He thought he heard a woman's shout.

He drove himself faster.

CHAPTER ELEVEN

"Christiane," Johann said from the entrance.

She was terrifying in the firelight, leaning back against the cabin wall nearest the fire, her knees drawn up to her swollen belly. Her face shone bright red. Her unseeing eyes were glassy. A candle flickered on the floor next to her.

"Close the door," Ursula said sharply, though the door consisted of three blankets pegged into logs above the entrance. "Don't bring those animals here. We need wood."

Christiane's face dissolved into a grimace, and she began to moan.

"Get the wood!" Ursula shouted at him. She took Christiane's hand and spoke soft words that Johann couldn't make out. An older woman who helped at Broad Bay births, Frau Schultheis, was dipping hot water from a three-legged pot over the fire.

"Walther?" he asked.

"At the shelter, with Herr Bauer," the Schultheis woman said. She must have brought the pot, since he and Christiane didn't have one.

He went for wood. He stashed the carcasses under a canvas sheet, then piled snow on it. Hauling the wood loosed the pain of his back. Christiane was crying when he returned. "More," Frau Schultheis said.

After his second trip, he fed the fire. "Stay there," the older woman said, nodding toward a far corner. "Better you don't watch." She and Ursula were on either side of Christiane, helping her stand. Christiane's eyes passed over Johann without a trace of recognition. "We'll walk, dear," Frau Schultheis said. "It helps the baby find his way."

Christiane nodded. She shuffled a few steps. Watching, Johann felt fatigue overtake him. He started at the sound of Christiane's groan when she turned. He passed a hand over his eyes and drank some water from a cup.

"When did she start?" he asked.

"Midday," Ursula said.

"She's not taken this long before."

Frau Schultheis turned a stern face to him. "Hush, you."

"But she's in pain."

"Of course, she's in pain. She's having a baby. This is woman's lot. We have nothing for her, not even tobacco, but she's a tough little cat. She's done this before."

But Johann hadn't. He had missed the births of their sons, away on campaign both times.

Christiane gave a cry and sagged heavily on the other women. "It hurts," she said.

"Yes, dear," Frau Schultheis said, "let's get you in the chair."

"Please," Christiane breathed. The women grunted with her weight. Johann got to his feet and took Ursula's side. He supported Christiane as they lowered her to the birthing chair he had banged together from lumber McDonnell gave him. It was better than lying on the floor. Frau Schultheis pushed him aside. He fed the fire and fanned the smoke up to the ceiling, then returned to his corner.

The midwife reached up Christiane's skirt. She massaged both sides of Christiane's belly. "Here," she called over her shoulder to Johann. "Pile the leaves under her."

He was close when Christiane screamed, the sound tearing into his bones. Her eyes were clenched tight. "That's it," the midwife said softly. "That's it, dear. The baby's coming." She dropped down between Christiane's knees, spreading them, placing her hands under her thighs and repositioning her.

Johann stepped back uncertainly. He dropped into his corner. His back and ribs were on fire. The dead face of the Indian hung before him, the life he had just taken, the stench of the Indian's grease and guts and blood still on him, the bayonet in his waistband, the Indian's knife on the other side. The connection was clear. This agony of Christiane's was God's punishment for his bloody killing, for the violence in Johann's heart. God kept punishing the innocent to teach the wicked. He recoiled from the unfairness of it. He closed his eyes and begged God not to do this thing. Punish me. Punish me. Another shout came from Christiane, one that lasted.

"Good, dear," the midwife said. Ursula wiped Christiane's face. Christiane clutched her hand. Johann sat in the cesspool of his sin, forced to watch God wreak vengeance on his wife and his baby.

"It's coming," the midwife said. "I see the head. You're close, dear. You're doing well."

Christiane began to cry again. "No more," she said. "No more. Please. Make it stop." Ursula leaned close and whispered to her. Christiane sucked in her breath and issued a sound close to a roar.

"He's out!" the midwife called. "He's out!" She held the baby's head in her hands and pushed the cord from its neck. Its hair was matted and smeared with fluid. "Take another breath, dear, then you'll have your baby."

Christiane sobbed and thrashed her head from side to side. Then she roared again, and the baby came in a rush and squirt, its legs curled up. With precise movements, the midwife clipped the baby's cord and wrapped the baby in a blanket. "She's a girl, dear," Frau Schultheis pronounced. Ursula took the baby and wiped it dry. She rewrapped it and handed it down to Christiane.

"Just a bit more, dear," the midwife said. "Don't mind me." Using the cord, which dangled like a tail from Christiane, she pulled out a clotted mass and wrapped it in the leaves Johann had spread. "Here," she said, turning to him. "Take this to the woods and bury it. You must bury it deep so she won't have so much pain."

Johann accepted the bundle but was flummoxed by the direction. The earth was frozen solid half a foot down or more. He would have to hack at it with an ax. "Go," she said. "Do you want this poor thing to be racked with pain? As deep as you can."

Johann pulled his mittens on. They were all he had taken off since reaching the cabin. Holding the bundle in one hand, he lifted the ax and left.

The job took nearly an hour, digging through the snow, then battering the ground. He feared he would shatter the ax handle, but the earth finally yielded. Twice he heard small cries from the cabin, almost like a cat mewing. His daughter. His eyes welled up. He was grateful to hear no more cries from Christiane. Perhaps God understood that Johann had been enforcing His law on the trapline. Or perhaps God would turn His vengeance only on Johann, where it belonged. Johann felt purged, filled with light. By the time he had filled the hole and covered it with snow, a grey dawn lit the sky behind the cabin. Most of the clouds had fled in the night.

He brought more wood. Christiane lolled back in the birthing chair, her shoulders against the cabin wall. "Right, then," Frau Schultheis said. "Carry them back to the bed."

When he knelt, Christiane gave him a sleepy smile, the baby at her breast. He slid an arm under her legs, the other behind her back. He felt the barest weight when he lifted them. He turned to the sleeping area, far from a proper bed. In the warm weather, he vowed, he would build a fine bed for Christiane and another for the children.

When he placed Christiane down, she gave a small moan.

"What?" he said.

"It's sore. Down there." The women swept in with blankets and helped Christiane shift. "Right, then," the midwife said, straightening up with a sigh. "I'll be off."

Johann pulled off his hat and reached his hand out. "Frau," he said, "may I say thank you, for you are a blessing from God."

The woman smiled, which gave her apple cheeks a less severe look. "She's a fine girl, and you have a fine baby. No more traipsing out in the woods when you should be here looking after them."

"No, ma'am," he said. "May I send home a couple of muskrats with you, to show our gratitude? I can skin them for you."

The woman shrugged. "That would be fine, but you needn't skin them. There's nothing wrong with Herr Schultheis doing a little work for his supper."

Johann left with her and dug out the muskrats.

When he returned, Ursula stepped from the fire and took one

of his hands. “You look tired, Johann. You were so late. We didn’t know what to think. Christiane was afraid.”

“It was stupid. I got lost. I’m not yet a man of the forest.”

“You must rest,” she said, “with your new baby.” He sat near Christiane. “Christiane,” she said, “wants to name the baby after her mother.”

“I know,” Johann said. “Hanna. Hanna Oberstrasse.” He closed his eyes.

Ursula settled in the corner where Johann had been. She was asleep in a moment.

CHAPTER TWELVE

Johann woke up to his daughter's soft noises as she strained for Christiane's milk. Ursula bent over the pot that hung over the fire, the smell of porridge blending with the smoke.

"She's beautiful," Christiane said. He rolled on his side to stare at Hanna. Her eyes were shut as her mouth worked. He twisted to ease the pain in his back. The movement didn't help. "Touch her skin."

He trailed a forefinger over the baby's cheek. "Like her mother."

"Pah," Christiane said, "not since I was her age." She smiled at the baby.

"She's the first Oberstrasse of America," Johann said.

"We're all from America now," she said. She gestured up to Ursula, who stood with a bowl of porridge. "Now, you eat. You must be starving."

"Have you eaten?" he asked. She nodded. He took the bowl and shoveled in the hot mush. It warmed him from the inside. Sitting back and closing his eyes, he gave thanks to have made it back here to his small family. He was a prideful fool, risking all of this over a beaver and two muskrats. He leaned over and kissed Christiane's forehead.

The day was nearly half gone, but he had much to do, starting with clearing six inches of new snow from the cabin's entrance and roof. Bright blue sky peeked through patchy clouds. He emptied their pot and chopped wood, cutting extra so he could bring some to Fritz as thanks for Ursula's help. He gutted and skinned the remaining carcasses. He was still learning how to preserve the pelts for trade, but made a fair job of it, taking special care with the beaver. He stored the pelts in a cache he had dug and kept covered with stones. The meat would make a dinner stew for them and the Bauers. He brought in clean snow to melt for water. Through it all, he ignored waves of pain from his back, which loosened a bit as he worked.

Near dinnertime, he carried the extra wood to the shelter. He found Walther in the care of the stout Frau Reuter, playing a game with her young daughter that involved sticks and clapping. He felt a pang of guilt for still disliking Herr Reuter.

"A little girl?" she said. He grinned. "She'll be a blessing for you all."

He pressed the extra firewood on her. He would chop more for Fritz and Ursula. Then he gathered Walther up. "We go to meet your sister, all right?" he said.

"Mama," the boy said, and Frau Reuter laughed. "He's been saying *that* all afternoon."

"Yes," Johann said, "we go see Mama too. Do you know," he asked the woman, "where Fritz Bauer is?" She shook her head and shrugged. He thanked her again.

They found Fritz and Sigrid stamping their feet before the common fire, holding mittened hands out to the warmth. Several settlers congratulated Johann. The midwife had spread the news. He smiled and ducked his head to each.

Fritz explained that he and Sigrid had fished with spears through holes in the river ice. Herr Leichter had been teaching settlers how to fish that way, using a wooden decoy fish on a string. One person dragged the decoy through the water. If a real fish came near the surface, the other struck with a barbed spear.

"It was freezing," said Sigrid, "and we couldn't make any noise at all."

"Yes," Fritz said, "she is an excellent fisherwoman." He offered to bring to dinner the two fish they'd speared, but Johann insisted the stew would be plenty.

* * * * * *

Next morning was grey again. While splitting wood, Johann favored the side that took the tomahawk blow. It would heal. He'd told Christiane that he hurt his back when he slipped on the trail and fell on a log. It could have happened that way. His mind still churned over the killing. Why didn't he just scare the man off? That would have cost him the beaver—the Indian made sure to take that with him—which Johann would have minded. Plus, the man had shot at him. Johann was justified to retaliate against that attack. And why wouldn't the Indian come back to steal from Johann again? It was just luck that Johann had come upon him. He may have been stealing for weeks without Johann knowing. As long as the thief reset the trap and smoothed over his tracks, there would be no way to know.

When Johann reached this point in his thinking, though, his heart seized up. General Waldo's directions were clear: no quarrels with the savages. But it was more than just flouting the general's policy. Johann had meant to kill that man, had run him down, and then he killed him. Did he still have the taste for killing from serving the Landgraf? Would this land bring out the violence and anger in him, the parts he tried to conceal from Christiane, from everyone?

He stopped chopping and looked up at the unyielding sky. Those clouds, he decided, wouldn't bring snow. He needed to reset the trap where he'd found the Indian. He could check the other traps on the way. He began to pile the wood to carry inside.

"Brother Oberstrasse!"

Johann turned. Nungesser, about twenty paces down the path, peered back in his owlish way. Next to him stood Leichter, the general's agent, wearing a beaver hat and a jet-black coat with brass buttons. A settler hung behind them. Johann knew the man slightly. Wagner, he thought. Josef was his given name. A young man, one with some money but not so much energy. And a handsome wife.

Johann dropped the wood and walked down to them, pulling off his mittens. He extended his hand to each. His stomach was shaky. They must know about the Indian. There could be no other reason for such a delegation.

Leichter took the lead. "I hear," he said, "that you have had a happy occasion. Allow me to offer my congratulations, and General Waldo's."

"Thank you."

"And the little girl's name?"

"Hanna, after my wife's mother." Johann gestured back to the cabin. "I would invite you in, but my wife is still—"

"Of course, of course," Nungesser said. "She needs rest, and so does little Hanna."

"General Waldo will be pleased to hear this news," Leichter said. "He wishes Broad Bay to be your home, and the home of all your generations."

"As do we," Johann said. He couldn't get a good read on this Leichter. He dressed like a dandy and sometimes spoke like a man of learning, but his bearing and movements were those of a man of action. Of a man like Johann.

"We've come about something else," Nungesser began, "something from two days past." Johann's stomach dropped.

"Yes," Leichter said, "we understand that you were out in the forest long into the night, that's what Frau Schultheis said."

Johann repeated the lie that he'd gotten lost tending his trapline. He tried not to appear nervous. "It was a dark night, and snowing," he added.

Leichter made a sympathetic noise. "Ah, but then we come to Herr Wagner's tale." He tilted his head toward the mute member of the delegation. "He was in the forest that day, as well." Leichter turned. Switching to German, he told the younger man to speak. The man nodded uncomfortably and cleared his throat.

"I was out with my musket—it's one I bought from Armstrong. I've been hunting with it. A week ago, I shot a deer," he said eagerly. "We shared the meat with some others." Not with my family, thought Johann, but he waited silently. Trouble was coming. He would have to accept any consequences. He wouldn't apologize. They would see that as weakness. "I was on the ridge, over to the east and north of here." Wagner pointed that way. "Wasn't finding any game. Well, I'm not very good yet, as a hunter. I make too many noises."

Leichter shifted his weight, conveying the impatience of all three listeners. Wagner cleared his throat again. "I heard a shot on the far side of the ridge and went to see. That's when I saw you taking out after that Indian. You were on one side of a trap, and the savage, he was on the other side, running away."

When the narrative trailed off, Nungesser prodded the young man. "And you saw."

"Yes. Yes. I saw you keep chasing that Indian. You followed him right up and over the ridge until you disappeared over the other side. He had a gun but you didn't, so I figured he'd taken the shot at you, maybe when you found him at your trap."

"Why," Leichter asked, "didn't you follow Herr Oberstrasse to help him in his pursuit?"

Wagner shrugged. "I watched for a few moments, figuring out what was happening, then realized I should help, having a musket and all. So I started after him. But," he turned to Johann, "you started about 200 paces away, something like that, and then you were 300 paces ahead, and then more. It was difficult to go fast in that snow. You both moved so fast. I was slower. I knew I'd never get there in time to help. And the musket's no good at such distances. Listen, I've got to tell you," Wagner nodded with a type of respect, "you looked like the vengeance of the Lord, the way you went after him. I wouldn't want to be on the wrong side of you, not for anything."

"So, Herr Oberstrasse," Leichter said, "what have you to say about this?"

Johann took a breath. "Herr Wagner speaks the truth. I found this Indian, a Penobscot I think, stealing a beaver from my trap. I surprised him and went after him."

"And?" Leichter asked, "did you catch him?"

"Yes."

"And?"

"I got my beaver back."

"And the Indian?"

"He won't be stealing from traps again."

Leichter looked off into the woods. "I see," he said. "And what did you do with the body?"

"I concealed it. I know General Waldo wants us to get along with the Penobscots, so I hoped no one would find it. I didn't want to cause a problem for anyone. For all of us."

Leichter gave a slight smile, flicking his eyes back at Johann then looking again into the woods. “It was rather late to think of that, wasn’t it?”

“Perhaps. I don’t think the Indians will be good neighbors if we let them steal. They need to know that they can’t. He would have stolen again.”

“Ah, you’ve studied the Penobscot?”

Johann tried to keep the anger from his voice. “I have studied men.”

“Yes, well. So have I,” Leichter turned to face Johann. “And so has General Waldo. You did right, Herr Oberstrasse. We want to show the savages we are peaceful, but we cannot be peaceful when we are…provoked. You were provoked. We do not tolerate stealing and harassment by our people, or by the savages.” Johann was gratified by the words, but still felt on edge. There was something ominous about Leichter’s manner. “Tell me, since you didn’t have a gun, what did you kill him with?”

“I have a bayonet, from my time in the army.”

“Herr Oberstrasse,” Nungesser broke in, “was a sergeant major for the Landgraf, where he learned to deliver cold, hard steel.”

Leichter raised his eyebrows. “A sergeant major, and yet so young?”

Johann decided to correct only one of the errors. “Not so young,” he said.

Leichter clapped him on the arm. “If you keep charging Indians with only a bayonet, you may never become old.”

Johann shrugged. “A soldier’s habits die hard.”

“They need not die at all, not at Broad Bay. You are, I think, a man who should have a rifle. Would you like that? We have a couple from good German gunsmiths in Pennsylvania. They offer advantages over a bayonet.”

Johann nodded. “We used muskets in the army, but a rifle would be better.”

“I can issue you one, with powder and shot, but you must agree to come to the aid of your neighbors when needed.”

“Of course. I would do so anyway.” None of the men looked at Wagner, but they all had the same thought about the younger man.

“Of course you would. Come to the landing in an hour. We’ll fix you up.”

They left after another round of handshakes. Wagner mumbled another apology. Watching them leave, Johann felt a tingle of excitement as he pulled his mittens on. He would have a rifle, and he could go back for the Indian's musket. Maybe he should give the musket to Fritz. With the rifle, Johann could hunt for deer, maybe even the very large moose. He would be in debt for the rifle, but for once the prospect of debt didn't bother him. Was this new world changing him? He wondered. It might be a wonder if it didn't.

He knew he would have to tell Christiane about the Indian, about the rifle, and that he was going to be a soldier again, at least some of the time. Everyone on the frontier was a soldier, he thought. This time, he'd be fighting for himself and his family, not for the Landgraf or for a foreign prince. That would be better.

CHAPTER THIRTEEN

"Here, it's just up here," Johann said, steering toward the shore. He and Fritz slid from the small boat into the shallow water, then pulled the boat up on land. Johann pointed to a large boulder. "Starting there, and reaching back into the woods. Fifty morgens is maybe fifty rods or so, depending on how wide the riverfront. Right here would be good for a dock."

Johann reached into the boat for his rifle and Fritz's musket. He kept the rifle nearby when he was working, and carried it when he left the settlement. As much as Johann hated debt, Leichter had set no due date for payment for the rifle, and they needed it. It took longer to load than a musket, but its accuracy was far superior. He had fired it only enough to learn its ways. Powder and shot were dear, and not available on credit. He had taught Fritz about the musket, but his friend brought it only when Johann reminded him.

The melting of the river ice meant Armstrong would soon be taking cargo to Boston, where the kitchens and fireplaces of the wealthy needed Broad Bay's firewood. Because the Medomak provided the only way to haul wood, Johann and Fritz swapped some of their wood for the use of Leichter's boat to travel up where the forest was untouched.

This trip, though, wasn't for business. With Maifest two days away, Leichter loaned them the boat for free. Today's load was for the bonfire in front of the shelter. After the long winter, the settlers were more eager to celebrate spring than they ever were back home.

Lifting his hat to scratch his head, Fritz pivoted to view the site. "It looks fine," he said. "Enough slope that most of it should stay above flooding, but not so much that you can't farm it. Still," he squinted into the woods, "it has many trees. Much to clear."

Johann shrugged. "Yes, but if I'm to become a carpenter, I'll have a good supply of wood. There are oaks and maples, over there." The men moved toward the tree line. "The soil," Johann said. "How is it?"

Fritz reached down and sifted dirt through his fingers. He plunged a knife into the earth. The soil had a yellow cast. He licked a forefinger and used it to carry a few grains of dirt to his tongue, then spat them out. He walked a few paces away and did the same thing. Then again farther from the river.

"Well?" Johann said.

Fritz shook his head and put his hat on. "It's no better than any around here. Too much clay. Many crops won't like it. And, like everywhere, many rocks. Potatoes will grow. Cabbages too. The local squash and pumpkins. Maybe the corn of the Indians. And pasture for animals."

"Good land for a carpenter?" Johann smiled.

"Good land is wasted on a carpenter."

"Fritz, you don't like the land, but yet you still plan to farm?"

"I'm a farmer. I'll make things grow, even here." The men started back to the boat. "How will you get this parcel? Leichter says they will be assigned, and none are to be this far upriver."

"Yes, I know. I'll have to find a way." He stopped and looked around again, already feeling like the proprietor of this lovely spot. "Why don't you take a parcel up here? Right over there." He pointed to adjacent land. "We could start North Broad Bay."

"If you can arrange it," Fritz said, "the Bauers will be pleased to join you here."

Johann wagged a finger at him. "You'll be glad you did. We'll need a boat, too, and a sled for the winters."

"And a horse to pull the sled?"

Johann smiled. "Was I putting the sled before the horse?"

Back on the river, Johann paid little attention to the pale green of the newly-leafed trees. He reviewed the tasks he faced. With the days growing longer, he could get more done, and on Sundays he was helping McDonnell build a boat. For each Sunday of labor, he received a quart of buttermilk and a quart of corn meal, plus he learned how to build a boat. Christiane complained that Johann neglected his soul by working on the Sabbath. He told her that God will understand that he cannot rest.

* * * * * *

For weeks, the rumor had flown through Broad Bay that General Waldo was coming to visit, but he never arrived. Johann could hardly hang around waiting for the man.

Johann and Fritz had just left to cut wood for Maifest when Christiane heard men's voices outside. Wrapping the baby and pulling Walther away from the sticks he was building into a pile, she stepped through the blankets at the cabin's entrance. Herr Leichter and two others were listening respectfully to an older man who spoke in English.

"—damned poor job of it, Leichter. What sort of cabin is that?" The man's voice carried easily. His face was bright red, and his blue eyes shone like marbles. His long hair was tied back in a knot. Neither his clothes nor his tricorn hat was finer than Leichter's, but his quality was plain in his knee-high boots and walking stick. "For the love of Christ, just look at it. It's topsy-turvy, leaning every which way. By God, we need to build solid stuff, stuff that will last for years. Not like this."

"General," Leichter said in a voice that wasn't entirely respectful. "This settler arrived last fall and had only days to put this up so his family wouldn't be in the shelter over the winter. He will build something far stronger this summer, after the land is allocated."

"Why isn't he doing that now? There's been time since winter?"

"He cuts firewood to trade to Boston. I expect he will then buy supplies and tools and start on a new cabin."

"You *expect*, do you? We need to run this settlement on more than your expectations." Leichter's lips tightened. Christiane couldn't follow the English, but she didn't need words to feel the tension between the blustering general and his agent.

"General," Leichter said, "we should start out if we're to reach the parley in time."

"And what are the chances that the damned savages will be there on time?"

"It's a mark of respect to be on time. And an insult to be late."

"Yes, yes, yes. Off we go in those bloody canoes." Waldo waggled his stick down the path to the settlement. At that moment, his eyes met Christiane's. She made a small curtsy. He saluted her with his stick and said, "Missus." After a few strides, he called out to Leichter, "Well, at least they're a fertile bunch of scoundrels."

Near the end of the day, as Johann and Fritz rowed a load of wood toward the settlement's pier, they saw General Waldo's sloop at anchor in the bay. It flew a banner with an eagle pattern that Johann recognized from the brochure. The banner of the Hereditary Lord of Broad Bay. Men clustered near the pier, staring at a post that had been set in the ground with a paper nailed to it. Johann's stomach clenched. It must be the land allocation.

When they reached shore, Johann resisted the urge to rush to the notice on the post. He must not seem overeager. He and Fritz carried their load to the lean-to that sheltered firewood to be traded with Armstrong, careful to mark which was theirs. Then, in the fading light, they approached the post.

On the paper, Johann could make out a drawing of Broad Bay, along with the path of the Medomak. The pier and the shelter were marked also. Johann had to wait for the men in front of him to leave before he could see the lines that marked out different land parcels. They looked to be roughly the same size. He couldn't be sure that they were all as large as fifty morgens, but they might be. Initials appeared on each parcel. He looked for his. He ground his teeth when he found them. That land, he knew, was hilly. And it had no riverfront.

"Do you see yours?" Fritz asked.

"I do."

"You see," Fritz pointed, "they allocate no land above here. Nothing near what we were looking at. The settlement won't reach that far."

That didn't mean, Johann thought, that it couldn't reach that far. "Where is yours?" he asked. Fritz pointed to a parcel to the south, where the land tended to be more level. It had a narrow river front. "I don't know it," Johann said.

"Nor I. I'll be there at sunrise."

Johann smiled and gripped Fritz on the arm. "You must go and tell Ursula. I'll get my things from the boat."

Johann lingered before the map, though the dark was coming on quickly. The last upriver parcel looked to be a mile below the land Johann wanted. So he wouldn't be taking it from someone else. And he wasn't afraid of being that far from the other settlers. He turned to look out at Waldo's coaster. He might row to it, ask to speak with the general and plead for the land. Leichter, he knew, thought tolerably well of Johann. He might even support such a plea. But interrupting a man at his dinner—especially a powerful man like the general—was probably a poor idea.

Johann retrieved his rifle and was halfway to the common fire when he heard voices behind him. Two war canoes were sliding onto the shore. Leichter stepped out of one, splashing in the shallow water. A well-dressed man with fine boots climbed from the other, uttering a series of oaths and groans. That must be the general. Johann walked to the shore and doffed his hat.

"General, sir, good evening," he said.

"Yes, yes, good evening," Waldo said. He didn't look at Johann. He turned to Leichter. "Where the devil's the launch from the ship? Are we supposed to mill around all night waiting for them to realize we're here?"

"General, sir," Johann said. "I can row you out in Mr. Leichter's boat."

"That would be most satisfactory," Waldo said. "Leichter, you might well have thought of that yourself. We're lucky to find Herr…"

"Oberstrasse, sir. Johann Oberstrasse." He beckoned the two men. "Please, this way." Johann pushed the boat into the water, and all three men stepped into it.

"It seems, Herr Oberstrasse, that life in Broad Bay involves a good deal of time with wet feet."

"I suppose," Johann agreed, beginning to row but not too fast. "Sir, I hoped to speak with you about the land allocation, on the map." Even in the dim light, annoyance was plain on the general's face. "I don't wish to complain or even to claim any parcel allocated to someone else, but there is a parcel that was assigned to no one that I could make very productive for the settlement and for you."

"Really, Leichter," Waldo said without looking at Johann, "perhaps we should have just swum out to the ship."

"Actually, General," Leichter said, "Herr Oberstrasse is a valuable settler. He's the man the chief referred to during the parley, who killed the Indian who was stealing."

"Indeed." Waldo took another look at Johann. Meeting his look, Johann rowed with a firmer stroke. "So, you are the sergeant major who runs down Indians with a bayonet?"

"Yes, General." Johann was uncertain. Was it good that the incident came up during the parley with the Indians? "I hope I haven't caused a problem."

Waldo loosed a laugh like a bark. "Quite to the contrary. You've managed to get the attention of those savages, shown that some of our people have some actual backbone. The savages, it seems, call you 'Snow Runner.'" Leichter nodded in agreement. "I must tell my recruiters in Germany to find more sergeant majors."

"Your Excellency," Johann said, "the spot I mentioned is upriver from the parcels that have been allocated. It's almost a mile beyond the last one. As I said, I think I could make it much more productive than the parcel my family was assigned."

Waldo cocked his head. "You'd be exposed to attack by the savages."

"Ach, that will only be for a short time," Johann said. "This land will fill up swiftly. Such rich land. There will soon be settlers all around that parcel. Another man here, Fritz Bauer, is willing to bring his family to join us on an adjacent parcel."

This time Waldo's laugh carried something close to warmth. "Leichter," he cried, "we have a man after my own heart. He understands that Broad Bay will bloom with ever more men and women." He said to Johann, "Sergeant Major, you shall have the land you request, though only fifty morgens of it, and subject to approval by Herr Leichter, of course. You will be Broad Bay's first line of defense against the savages."

"That's why I have the rifle." Johann nodded to the rifle on the floor of the boat.

"Leichter," the general said, "you will manage this."

"I'm sure Herr Oberstrasse and I will come to an agreement. We'll draw up the deeds in the morning."

"Very well," Waldo said. "Say, Oberstrasse is such a mouthful. If my German doesn't fail me, that translates to Overstreet."

"I'm not certain, Excellency," Johann said. "I think perhaps it would be 'high street' in English."

"Highstreet. I don't like that. Too commercial. So long as you're going to be Broad Bay's strong right arm, why not take the land in the name of Overstreet? That has a solid English ring to it."

* * * * * *

In the morning, Johann and Fritz met Leichter at the landing. They rode upriver in Leichter's boat and walked off the boundaries for both parcels, marking them with piles of stones. Leichter wrote up the deeds when they returned to the pier. "Shall it be John Overstreet, then?" he asked Johann. "If you're becoming an Englishman, you might as well go all the way."

Johann shrugged his agreement and signed the new name.

After hurrying to the cabin, he presented the deed to Christiane, who traced his new signature with her finger. "So," she said, "we are all Overstreet now?"

"Yes, I suppose so."

"Walther Overstreet," she said. "Hanna Overstreet. They're good names." She thought for a moment. "You have no regret—John—to lose your name?"

He smiled. "You call me Johann."

"And I am Frau Overstreet?"

"Mrs. Overstreet, I think."

She grinned at him.

He put the deed in his leather pouch with their coins and stashed it below the sleeping surface in the cabin. Flushed with excitement, he insisted that Christiane and the children come to see their new land. He carried Walther through the path along the river, then through the woods when the path played out. Christiane followed with Hanna.

At the site, he held his hand out like a performer in a show, then swept into a bow. "Mrs. Overstreet," he said, "welcome to our land. The land of the Overstreets."

Christiane took a few steps and scanned the area while he described the boundaries, then pointed out where Fritz and Ursula would be. Turning in place, she said, "It's beautiful."

Johann set Walther down and strode along the shore to show the far boundary, then into the woods, then back. He lifted Walther, whose happy noises matched his father's mood. "Look, Walther," he said, his eyes greedily taking in the land and trees. "I think it's more than fifty morgens. More like sixty, don't you think? Just have a look."

Christiane walked to a stand of firs. Vines trailed under the trees, showing pink and white blossoms. She leaned down to smell them, drawing Walther's curiosity. When he came over, she snapped one off and held it up to his nose, showing him how to sniff it.

"They call these mayflowers," she called to Johann, who hadn't moved, transfixed to be standing on his own land. "Let's call this Mayflower Hof."

"Why not Mayflower Farm?" Johann said.

She stood and shook her head. "No, Mayflower Hof. To remind us of our old home."

Johann came over and embraced Christiane. "Never in Hesse could we own land like this."

Walther began to cry and reached for his mother. She brushed a dark fly from his arm. It left a red spot on his skin while he continued to cry. Johann rubbed the spot. "Walther Overstreet," he said, "say hello to your new neighbors, the flies. The Indians keep them off by smearing their skin with bear fat. Would you like that?" He swept up the little boy, who began to giggle. "Yes, yes, Walther says! Bear fat for everyone!"

"No, Johann," Christiane said, wrinkling her nose, "not if you wish to come inside Mayflower Hof."

PART II

1755

CHAPTER ONE

Stepping out of his cabin with his new wooden bucket, Fritz Bauer was thinking about Armstrong, the trader from Boston. That villain, to Fritz's knowledge, had never given anyone at Broad Bay a fair price. Robert McDonnell talked about inviting another trader to come to the settlement, but it hadn't happened and probably wouldn't. Armstrong must have a deal with General Waldo, maybe with Leichter.

Three skinny chickens and a skinnier rooster fluttered out of Fritz's path, flapping and squawking. Ursula aimed to breed them up to a flock of respectable size, but the quarrelsome rooster—also acquired from Armstrong—didn't seem up to the task. After bidding the birds good morning, Fritz paused to gaze at his farmstead.

He never tired of this view, especially in these cool mornings of early summer, when all was promise. New shoots of squash and cabbage showed through the raw dirt in five orderly rows. Potatoes flourished here, just as he predicted. Some might be ready in a month. Fat bumblebees hovered over a mayflower vine. Sigrid, only eight, tended the plants every morning, taking pride in their progress. They were flourishing. She had Fritz's knack for growing things.

He smiled to see Johann already out in the next field, working an iron bar under the edge of a large stone he had started on two days before. Johann called it the kaiser rock, swearing that he would remove it or die trying.

Even though Johann preferred carpentry, his pride drove him to claw every rock out of his field, stacking them on the half-built stone fence between their farms. Fritz had contributed stones from his field, perhaps half as many as Johann had. For Johann, every stone on his land was a personal insult. Fritz waved when his friend took a rest. "I'll come over after I milk the cow," Fritz called. "We'll go at it together."

Johann waved back, then returned to his unequal task. Johann's rifle leaned against a smaller rock. He was always reminding Fritz to take his musket with him, even on his own land. There was war now with the French and their Indian allies. If Fritz loaded the musket with buckshot, Johann urged, he wouldn't even need to aim it. Fritz didn't argue with Johann, but he didn't much see the point. He wasn't going to stop an Indian raiding party with a single shot.

Fritz was glad he had moved his family next to the Oberstrasses—the Overstreets, he corrected himself. Broad Bay was growing, even though disease took some every year. Fifty more families had landed since Fritz and the others staggered ashore. Johann was a generous neighbor, always willing to pitch in and help. Not a man of high spirits and jokes, to be sure, but capable and true. And their women took pleasure in each other's company. Women grew lonely in Broad Bay, on the edge of this new land, especially when the men were away hunting or trading. Ursula and Christiane were like sisters, sharing chores and children—three for Christiane now, and the Bauers' two girls. Fritz still hoped for a son. There was time for that.

Fritz heard the faint ring of a cowbell. The breeze ruffled the leaves on the trees. Fritz's milk cow stood in the pasture, beyond Sigrid's vegetable patch. She must have jostled her bell. Speaking in a soothing voice, Fritz approached the cow and stroked her soft muzzle. Armstrong, to be fair, had not cheated him on the cow. She was healthy and a good producer. He dropped to one knee and positioned the bucket.

The pasture could support more animals than the cow, but they couldn't afford swine yet, or sheep, and certainly not a horse. He wasn't so sure about ever getting sheep. They graze so heavily that they can spoil the land. A dozen tree stumps taunted him from the south side of the pasture, as did four piles of wood stacked there. More work. He would have to rent Reiser's ox to pull the stumps, also to haul the wood to the river. From there, he could use Johann's boat to bring the wood to the villain Armstrong. The trader would claim much of Fritz's profit, but there was nothing to do about it.

As he rose with the bucket of fresh milk, Fritz heard the bell again. It came from the woods. It was probably one of the pigs belonging to the family on the other side of these woods, toward Broad Bay. Heilman's swine were always getting into other people's property, tearing up fields and raising havoc. With six children including two sets of twins, the Heilmans struggled to keep track of anything, especially their livestock.

Fritz set down the bucket and covered it with a cloth. He smiled to see Johann stretched out almost parallel to the ground, straining every muscle against the kaiser rock. They'd try to move it together, or maybe Fritz could persuade his friend to leave the kaiser on his throne. Not likely, Fritz knew.

The bell rang again, more faintly. The animal must be moving into the woods. Johann stepped slowly into the trees. He didn't want to spook the animal and drive her farther away. He called out gently and heard the bell again. Yes, she was over to his left, toward the Heilman farm.

* * * * * *

Johann, panting, let go of the iron bar, leaving it wedged at a sharp angle. He looked over to the next farm. This would be an excellent moment for Fritz to come help with this damned rock. Johann was prepared to admit it. He couldn't budge it by himself.

He couldn't see Fritz. Ursula was walking stiffly toward their cow. Johann knew that walk. It wasn't going to be good for Fritz, who must have wandered off, no doubt looking at a flower or a bird with colored feathers. Dear Fritz, with the heart of a poet. Whenever one of Fritz's spells of dreaminess and curiosity exasperated Ursula, he would croon to her, "Oh, *liebe* Ursula," to a tune of his own devising. He always coaxed a smile from her. Johann envied that gift, which had won his friend such a fine wife. Johann had never been so good at winning smiles from girls.

Since Fritz wasn't going to arrive any time soon, Johann walked around the stone, looking for an angle he hadn't tried. The blasted thing was squarely in the middle of the second garden he had planned for Mayflower Hof, which needed to be ready in about two weeks. Which meant he had to solve this problem now.

After two circuits around the rock, he decided to split some wood. Fritz might not arrive for hours. After dinner, Johann could work at his carpentry shed. He loved the summer days, how the light stretched on and on. He could get so much done while Walther and Hanna and Richard, the baby, played, and Christiane knitted.

"Johann." Ursula's voice came to him. "Have you seen Fritz? He left the milk." She lifted the bucket in illustration.

Johann shook his head. "I'm waiting for him to help me. Didn't seem to be planning anything else, but you know Fritz."

Ursula looked back to the woods. "It's been too long, even for him."

"Maybe he saw something to hunt?"

She shielded her eyes. "His gun's over there." She pointed at the cabin.

Johann reached for his rifle and called to Christiane. When she came to the door, towheaded Richard in her arms, he said he was off to find Fritz. A quick flash of concern passed over her face, then she smiled at Ursula. "Bring the girls over, and your sewing," she called. "The children are wild today. They need friends." Johann pointed to Fritz's musket and said to Ursula, "Keep that with you, all right?"

Ursula looked flustered. "I've never fired it."

"Christiane knows how. Stay near the cabins."

In the woods, Johann found a faint path where the pine needles looked to be scuffed every few feet. He crouched and held his palm over the ground to focus his eyes in the shade. He couldn't make out footprints. Someone might have walked here, toward the Heilman farm. It could have been recent. That was logical. Maybe Fritz had business with Heilman. Johann moved forward quietly, staying low. A tingle of danger tensed his shoulders, something more than the alertness he always felt in the forest. Ursula was right. Something was wrong.

After a hundred paces, about halfway to Heilman's, Johann tensed. Blood pounded in his eardrums. The forest floor painted the scene. Many feet had dug into it here. Feet had slid and pushed and stomped in a struggle. A scrap of buckskin hung on a low branch of a half-grown tree. It wasn't Fritz's. He was wearing linen. The Penobscots wore buckskin. Johann's eyes shifted to a dark spot on the forest floor. He touched it with a finger. Sticky. He smelled it. Blood. He drove the idea of scalping from his mind.

He followed the signs. Broken branches and scuffed ground shouted the story. Something was dragged to the river by men who made no effort to conceal their path.

Trying to be quiet, Johann hurried to the shore. Breaking out of the trees, he saw no trace of this terrible party of men. His boat sat upstream, to the right. Voices in German carried from the Heilman farm. Penobscots sometimes knew French, occasionally some English. Never German. The sun to his left was up almost to the crest of the trees, mocking him in its ordinariness. Just another morning.

Johann cursed himself as he hurried to Heilman's. He knew Fritz wouldn't be there, but he had to be sure. He had seen Fritz, what, less than an hour before? Fritz had called to him, then walked away a bit. Johann should have reminded him to bring his gun, reminded him to be on his guard. Fritz needed reminding. If Fritz had a reason to go into the forest, why hadn't he come back for his musket first? Why hadn't he asked Johann to go with him? How could this happen with Johann right there?

Johann shook his head and clenched his teeth. He'd never had any trouble with whether he was his brother's keeper. He knew he was, certainly with Fritz. And the savages took him right from under Johann's nose. Fritz was in an Indian canoe now, either a corpse about to sink into the river or a captive on his way to Canada. Terror would spread through Broad Bay.

When Johann reached the Heilman farm, three children and two adults were in frantic pursuit of a hog that had escaped from a dilapidated pen. "Johann," Karl Heilman shouted, "head him off! Drive him back to us!"

Johann waved his arms at the snub-nosed brute, herding him toward his owners. Two younger children, laughing and shouting, put their arms around the pig and held him, then grabbed the rope around his neck. The animal looked strong enough to escape their grasp easily, but he seemed to have had enough freedom. The children tugged him back toward the pen and his next meal.

It took only a moment to learn that Fritz hadn't been there, nor had anyone seen Indians. Karl Heilman, short and thickly built, turned to his oldest son, a ten-year-old wearing breeches that had fit him two years ago and his father's shirt, which billowed in the breeze. "Run to the settlement," the father said. "Tell Herr Leichter that Indians have captured Herr Bauer. Tell him we need men to search. Herr Overstreet and I will start."

The boy, his eyes wide, turned to Johann, who nodded.

"Go," the father said. "Then hurry back and stay with your mother." Heilman looked at Johann. "We're not likely to find him, you know." Johann just looked at him. "Right, then. I'll get my musket."

"Meet me at my boat."

Trotting back toward Mayflower Hof, Johann fought the empty feeling and the rage. He was already missing his friend. How was Johann going to say to Ursula the things he would have to say? Johann had known that Fritz was no fighter, yet he persuaded Fritz to move his family to this more vulnerable place. A worse thought was gnawing at him. Could this be the Penobscots' retribution for Johann's killing of the man he caught stealing from his trap? Or God's retribution? That was long ago. Years ago. But the Indians don't forget. Nor does God.

CHAPTER TWO

When Johann pushed the boat into the current, the children were quiet. The bow sliced into the water with a soft sound. The somber end-of-day light matched the grief hanging over them, cancelling the joy the children usually felt over a boat trip. Ursula's sorrow was enough to sadden them all.

For two days, while the men looked upriver for Fritz, Ursula and her girls had stayed with Christiane. Ursula had prayed and bitten her lip. Her eyes leaked tears only a few times. She held grimly to the hope that the searchers would find Fritz, or he would walk out of the woods unhurt, maybe confused, explaining that he had gotten lost. She would be angry at first, she knew that, but soon they would laugh about it.

On the second night, Johann returned alone. Christiane and Ursula were on the bed with the baby, their backs against the planked cabin wall. The four older children grouped around the table Johann had built only that winter. Seven pairs of eyes looked at him. He didn't have to speak. He took off his hat and dropped his head.

Ursula broke then. Her wordless cries filled the night. The children wailed along with her. Christiane, baby Richard in her arms, hugged her friend. Johann knelt to gather the others. He made low noises, pulling them into his arms. Sigrid broke free and ran out into the night.

Johann hurried to the door, pulling the smaller ones with him. Sigrid had stopped, sobbing, a few paces away. He called her name. When he called her a second time, she rushed past him and flung herself on Ursula. The other children followed. Johann sat on the bench at the table and closed his eyes. It was knowing but not knowing. Fritz wouldn't come back, they knew that now, but they had no idea what had happened to him.

The searchers had little chance of overtaking the raiding party. The Penobscots had a head start, their canoes were swift, and the rivershore and woods provided endless concealment. Johann and Heilman had worked up the east side, looking for evidence of a boat having been pulled from the water. When Leichter and three others caught up in canoes, they scoured the western shore. At the portage around the falls, the signs of human traffic were too many and too jumbled to tell them anything. Above the falls, they put in and kept on looking into the night. Every hour that passed took Fritz farther away. If he was alive. Johann had argued to keep going upriver on the second day, but the others insisted on turning back. Their families were exposed to raiding parties too.

Neighbors, mostly on foot, came by Mayflower Hof through the next day. They brought food and small things. They offered to pray. Ursula wouldn't see them, so Johann intercepted them outside the cabin. He received the gifts and listened to their words. He thanked them for their prayers. They told him that Leichter had called a meeting that evening before sunset. He knew he had to go. They all would go.

More than two hundred men, women, and children clustered in the clearing before General Waldo's fenced compound, which stood where the shelter had been in their first winter. Not since the early days had Johann seen so many together. Anxious faces turned to the Overstreets and the Bauers.

Only the two oldest children walked on their own. Each of the younger ones, made shy by the sadness and the large gathering, nestled in a parent's arm, face against a parent's neck. The crowd opened so they could pass to the front. Some offered words, reached out to touch an arm, to make eye contact, nod.

Leichter, followed by a red-jacketed British army captain, stepped through the gate in the wooden palisade that circled the compound. It was a rude structure, though by far the largest in Broad Bay, and commanded the river landing. Because the general spent little time in the settlement, Leichter was its most frequent resident. Sometimes Armstrong the trader stayed there. Leichter was dressed for work—leather breeches, leather vest, loose shirt. His face was grim. The captain's uniform was smudged and sweat-stained. The two men stood until the crowd fell silent.

"You all know why we're here," Leichter started, speaking German for once. "First, I would ask Herr Nungesser to lead us in a prayer for the safety of Friedrich Bauer."

Nungesser's voice came from the right side of the crowd as heads inclined to the ground. "We pray for the return of our brother Fritz, that you take him into your special care," he said. He opened his bible to a marked page and peered at it in the failing light. "We call on the words of Genesis, that the Lord may watch between me and thee, brother Fritz, when we are absent one from another. We beseech thee, Lord, to look over our brother, and that You bring comfort to his family, as the psalm says, because when we cry out to the Lord in our affliction, He responds tenderly. While our troubles may not go away, His loving response to our prayers can help us face them with renewed strength. Amen."

"Herr Nungesser," Leichter said after a short pause, "if you would step up here. Please translate what I say for everyone." The agent switched to English. "The first thing I wish to say is that we will continue to seek Fritz Bauer. There will always be hope. We know of captives who have been recovered months and years later." His voice carried conviction, but few in the crowd had any hope. "This is Captain August Shaw, who commands at Fort St. Georges. For the last year we have been on the border of the war between Britain and France, but now we are part of that war."

The soldier took a step forward. With his uniform and his soldier's posture, he looked like a race different from the weary settlers in tired work clothes. Holding his hat in one hand, he paused for Nungesser's translation after each sentence or two. Shaw related that in the last month, Indian raiding parties had struck coastal settlements, attacking lone settlers. "They won't meet us in open battle," he said, "so they look for people who are isolated, who they can capture or kill. Sometimes the settlers get away. Sometimes they become captives in New France. Sometimes they're killed."

While Nungesser translated, Johann thought how Fritz wasn't really alone when he was taken. He and Ursula had been nearby, though useless. The captain resumed. "Their cowardly tactics include preying on farmers in their fields and luring people into the woods, so no one should go alone into the forest." More translation. "The more exposed you are, the farther you are from other settlers, the greater your risk." Johann could sense Christiane stiffening. Hanna wiggled in his arms. He was holding her too tightly.

Johann raised his hand. The soldier looked at him. "Captain, sir, if there's an attack, it takes many hours to get to Broad Bay from Fort St. Georges. Will soldiers be stationed here?" The fort was less than a dozen miles away by foot, but the woods were so thick that most travelled by boat, a route that led around two peninsulas and through several islands.

"I've nine soldiers to protect this entire section of the coast." When his statement was translated, a murmur passed through the crowd. "I've been told that no more soldiers will be available. So, no, there will be no soldiers at Broad Bay. You, like other settlements in this colony, will have to defend yourselves."

A man asked in German whether there was reason to expect more attacks at Broad Bay. After Nungesser translated the question, the captain said, "We have to be vigilant along this entire frontier. The French have inflamed the Indians, and they have armed them. Many Indians don't want to see settlements like Broad Bay succeed. They want to have the forest take over your homes, to push us back across the ocean and return to the days when only they lived here, when they hunted and fished without white men. But we'll not leave. So the war will not end soon."

"What about the French ships?" a man asked in English. Johann recognized the voice of Robert McDonnell. "They can attack our trade up and down the coast. How can we feed ourselves if we can't trade?"

"The Royal Navy is patrolling these waters, but it's a very large area. We're recommending that merchant vessels arm themselves." He spoke firmly and swept his eyes over the settlers, using the pauses for translation to emphasize his points.

"This is King George's land, which he has seen fit to share with you. He will do his best to protect you. But it is a wild land, filled with wild things, which you knew when you chose to come here. If you wish to hold the land, you must fight for it. I have counseled with Mr. Leichter on the best way for you to do that, which he will discuss with you."

"Say, Captain," McDonnell called out, a smile playing on his lips. "By the by, this war of ours. How's King George doing? Is he winning?"

The captain straightened, his face unmoving. He put his hat on, spun on his heel, and walked back into the compound.

Leichter, in German, asked the settlers to come closer. The men stepped forward while women and children hung back. He presented the plan quickly. Broad Bay must change how it lives. If the settlers stayed on their farmsteads, the Indians would pick off more of them. They must build four defensive stockades, spread through the settlement, and take up residence inside them. General Waldo's compound would be one stockade. Each stockade must be large enough for sixteen families. Captain Shaw and Leichter had identified good locations for the other three stockades, locations on high ground or in the center of open clearings, giving them good sight lines against attacks. One stockade would command the river and the settlement's water supply. As he described the locations, some of the settlers nodded. Leichter stopped and asked for questions.

"How thick must the walls be for these stockades?"

"A single log's width is fine," Leichter said, "enough to stop a musket ball. The Penobscots don't have cannons, and we can't build anything that would withstand the guns from a French ship. But each stockade will need a high observation deck, so we'll always have someone on lookout."

"Who owns the land for these locations?"

"General Waldo owns this site and the one next to the sawmill. He will donate those to the settlement until this crisis is over. The other two are on allocated lands, so we'll ask the owners to donate the lands for a limited time. We may be able to have the settlement pay some form of rental."

"How will we live? How will we farm if we're huddled into stockades?"

"We can leave the stockade under armed escort. So that means that you men will have to form a guard. We need volunteers for that. The guards will take different farmers to their lands on different days, on a rotating basis."

"We'll never have enough time to do all that needs to be done!" came a voice. A second said, "This isn't practical. We'll be prisoners. We can't live like that."

Leichter fixed his eye on the second speaker, a tall, broad-shouldered man. "Perhaps you should ask Fritz Bauer whether he would be willing to live like that." He took a breath. "It is your choice. I cannot force you. You can choose to change nothing about the way you live and wait for the Indians to come. Maybe you'll be lucky. Or you can follow this plan. It's the best we have. We live in a time of war." When he stopped, the settlers talked to each other in low voices. Leichter waited for them.

Johann spoke. "I don't like this plan, Herr Leichter, but I think it's the best we can do. And it's only temporary. The war can't last forever."

"Must we decide tonight?" came the question.

Johann turned to the voice. "What will be different tomorrow?"

After a silence, Leichter clapped his hands. "All right, then. I will take names tonight of those who volunteer for the guard. All men must help with building the stockades. We'll form regular work crews."

As the settlers began to disperse, Johann turned to Christiane. "I must do this," he said.

She nodded and held an arm out for Hanna. The little girl resisted, burrowing her head into her father's shoulder.

"I'll be at the boat in a few minutes, sweetheart," he said to her.

The volunteers gathered before Leichter. He said he needed twenty-four men, but there were only nineteen. "Others will join," Robert McDonnell said from the second row.

Leichter leaned toward McDonnell. "You, you and Bennett, how will you understand the Germans?"

McDonnell shrugged. "How much German do we need to know when we're under attack?"

Karl Heilman, Johann's neighbor, asked if Leichter would be the captain of the guard.

"No," the agent said. "I won't be here all of the time, and the captain must be. You should choose your captain. Someone whose word you'll follow without questioning."

McDonnell pointed at Johann. "The sergeant major," he said. "Agreed?"

The others nodded. McDonnell said to Leichter, "I didn't need to know German for that."

The men were eager to get their families back to their cabins, so Johann spoke quickly. He set up an informal system for the guards to carry messages from one to another, at least until the stockades were built. Leichter took the volunteers' names, then copied the list for Johann. "Will McDonnell be a problem for you?" he asked.

Johann shook his head. "No, he knows more German than he lets on. In fact, I'm inclined to make him my lieutenant."

"Is that wise? Will he follow orders? He made no friend in Captain Shaw."

"Captain Shaw and his nine soldiers won't save us. Robert might."

CHAPTER THREE

†

Christiane loathed this fourth winter in Broad Bay. Johann, like most of their neighbors, lost himself in the drive to put the settlement on a war footing. Lumber had to be cut and hauled for stockades. Stakes had to be driven, living quarters built, and farms converted to provide the greatest amount of food with the least amount of tending.

Johann helped with everything, especially building the living quarters. His woodworking skills still lagged behind McDonnell's, but he had learned much. Using thick timbers and narrower planks from McDonnell's mill, he had built their home at Mayflower Hof with mortise and tenon joints, a tongue-and-groove construction that eliminated nails or pegs. Each of Johann's joints was tighter and firmer than the one he made before. He had the patience for the work. He meant to do it well.

Using his careful joints, he had doubled the length of the cabin's walls beyond what was usual in Broad Bay. He cut windows in two walls, covering them with thick boards on grooved tracks that slid open and closed. To heat such a large space, he installed fireplaces at both ends, with clever piping that drew the smoke from the cabin but screened out all but the most furious wind gusts. As Johann had hoped, other settlers admired his work, then hired him to improve their cabins. He had begun on floor planking for Mayflower Hof when Fritz disappeared, which changed everything.

Johann's focus now was the guard. He set a rotating schedule so two guard members, loaded muskets in hand, walked the length of the settlement twice each day. They were to watch for signs of Indian activity, though such signs could be hard to detect. The guards encouraged settlers to be vigilant and asked about suspicious sights or sounds. A single gunshot, Johann decided, would be the alarm. When someone complained that there would be false alarms if someone fired a gun by accident or shot at game, Johann was unmoved. Better too many alarms than too few.

By mid-July, settlers began moving into the stockade converted from General Waldo's compound, which was named for the Prince of Wales. To set an example, and because Mayflower Hof was so exposed, the five Overstreets were among the first to take up residence. They crammed into a single room a fraction the size of their new cabin, with none of its clever adaptations. As more settlers piled in, Christiane's unhappiness grew. By winter—another freezing, wind-whipped season—they were enduring the misery they had known on *Mary Anne*: confined for months, rebreathing other people's air, eating only salt fish, knowing only shreds of privacy.

They shared common walls, which meant they shared personal habits and noxious smells, bugs and mice, loud arguments and soft endearments. When they stepped outside their room, they entered spaces occupied by fifteen other families. No disease could be avoided. Whenever Christiane managed to impose cleanliness and order on a corner of their world, in came filthy feet, bone-biting cold, or the whimpering of an ailing child. She feared for Walther and Hanna and Richard, fears that made her short-tempered, like her neighbors.

For two half-days each week, each family could return to its farm in the company of two guards. The visits were too brief to maintain the cabins and fields, or to stop the forest from reclaiming land that had been so difficult to clear. Johann and Christiane worked on the Bauer farm too. Ursula came with them, but listlessness often overtook her, deadening her eyes and slowing her mind. Christiane tried to be patient with her friend, who had lost so much, but could not always contain her frazzled annoyance. At night, Christiane prayed for a larger heart, a spirit that would love and nurse Ursula and her girls through this terrible time.

In mid-November, in the dark hours before another frosty dawn, the earth shook with a low growl, as though it would crack open. Women in the Prince of Wales stockade rolled from their beds to their knees, praying aloud. Children cried and hugged each other. Men scrambled into the courtyard, looking anxiously to the heavens, then at the earth, then at the heavens again. The earth stilled after ten seconds or so, but the shaking had seemed endless. Near the end of that churning, a log fell from the observation platform with a crash, knocking the front gate askew.

As the women and children ventured out uncertainly, they asked if this was the wrath of God upon their land? Or some massive weapon of the French? Attendance jumped at Nungesser's prayer meetings. It was months before they learned that the earthquake had struck all of New England.

In the bleak winter days after Christmas, the compound simmered in surly watchfulness. Christiane asked Johann one morning how long the war would last. It had already been almost two years. How long could nations fight? Johann drew his lips tight. He didn't know, he said, but the last war between Britain and France took eight years. Walther will be half a man by then, Christiane said in a rising voice, and will have known only this as his home. Johann had no answer.

Later that morning, Frau Reuter, the one with the thieving husband, set Christiane off. That shrewd woman had quieted Johann's suspicions by praising him and by the energy she brought to her work. Johann had a fondness, Christiane knew, for the strivers of the world, the ones who took on hard jobs and laid on the elbow grease. Frau Reuter seemed to be one of those, but Christiane knew what that cow really was underneath her false smiles: a close, grasping woman who manipulated people to her own ends.

Richard was nursing as Christiane tried to knit with unfeeling fingers. Poor little Hanna was curled against her, her thumb in her mouth, her breath crackling with thick phlegm, her skin waxy. The girl had been feverish, off and on, for at least two weeks.

Christiane had been up with her several nights, wiping her brow, humming, praying.

The slap she heard was loud. It could have been anyone. But Christiane knew the cry that came next, the hiccupping and snorting that only Walther produced.

She flew into the compound, carrying both little ones. That cow was bending over Walther, her cheeks red, shouting at him, her finger an inch from his startled face.

"What's this!" Christiane called, trying to keep the blanket around Richard. She almost lost her balance on the courtyard's packed snow.

Walther turned wide eyes on his mother, but Christiane went for the woman. "What are you doing?"

Frau Reuter brandished a pewter spoon with a hand. "Your boy had this spoon of ours, one of our set that came from my mother, that she got on her wedding day. Why, he's nothing but a thief, and we can't have thieves here in Broad Bay. I won't live with thieves."

Stepping between Walther and that cow, Christiane felt the anger rise. "Well," she said, "then you should move out from your entire family, which is nothing but a den of thieves, filthy stinking ones at that." Other children and women, transfixed, gathered round.

The Reuter woman put fists on her hips and leaned back. "Ah, so this is what I hear from the wife of the great sergeant major, the man who stands by while his neighbor is snatched by savages. Maybe he was just hoping to get some time with his neighbor's pretty wife, eh? You're all such good friends! While you hold the baby, of course, there's nothing I can do about your vile accusations."

Having noticed Ursula nearby, Christiane handed Richard over and set Hanna on her feet. "I accuse you. You and your kind are the thieves," she shouted.

The other woman glared at Christiane. She spat. "You peasants are beneath me. I don't truck with such scum."

"Yes?" Christiane screamed. She flung herself, tearing off the woman's bonnet and reaching for her face. Her fingers became entangled in Frau Reuter's hair so she couldn't pull back for a slap or punch, so she pushed and pushed the heavier woman, driving her back into the onlookers, finally tipping her over. Frau Reuter fell heavily. Christiane jumped on top. Her arms were free. She pummeled the woman, shrieking and crying, rage pouring out while the woman shielded herself with her forearms. Shouts came from around the compound, piping children's voices at the far edge of frenzy. Christiane ignored them all.

Strong hands gripped Christiane's shoulders and pulled her up. When she struggled, the hands lifted her off her feet, denying her purchase for a solid blow. Her bellows and shrieks continued as Frau Reuter scrambled to her feet. The other woman came after her now, but the strong hands spun Christiane around. Frau Reuter bounced off Robert McDonnell and slipped to her knees.

"Now, now," his deep voice said, flat and calm. "Are you done?" Christiane's feet reached the snowy ground. His hands still held her shoulders. Her anger drained, replaced with shame. She covered her eyes and started to shiver with the cold, her naked hands aching. Walther grabbed her leg and began crying. She felt Ursula's arm around her.

McDonnell looked down at Frau Reuter. "She's done. How about you?" The woman struggled to her feet and turned away.

"Listen, folks," he said to the others, some stunned, some smirking. "I know most of you can't understand the king's English, and I don't know what the hell this was about. But we've got plenty of Indians and Frenchmen to fight without going after each other. Everyone go on about your business."

Back in their room, Christiane sank onto a bench. She pulled Walther into her arms until he finished his wailing. He had been playing with the spoon, he said, just playing with it. He didn't mean to take it. She hugged him. When he grew quiet, she spoke. He shouldn't just borrow something like that, she said. He must ask the owner. He always must ask. He nodded. "Will you punish me now?" he asked.

She shook her head. "You're a small boy," she said. "You must learn this. But if it happens again, then you'll be punished." She patted his leg. "Now, get wood for the fire."

With Walther's help, she rebuilt their fire, then took Walther back into her lap. Together they stared into the flames. Ursula came to the door, a fussy Richard in her arms and other children trailing behind. "He wants his mother," Ursula said. Christiane waved them in.

Later in the day, watching the children run in the snow of the courtyard, Ursula and Christiane had a moment together. "Nothing she said is true," Ursula said. "About Johann, I mean."

"She's a wicked woman. Johann thought so from the start, back on the ship. But I must make peace with her. We could be in this cursed place for years. With her." They squeezed each other's mittened hand. "But not today."

"No," Ursula agreed. "Not today."

Christiane still had to face Johann. He returned late, like always, from working on the Governor Shirley stockade, the last one to be built. She didn't know what to expect from him. He was careful of his position in the settlement, worried to set a proper example.

When he arrived, he knelt to rinse his hands and face with water from melted snow. She handed him a cloth. In a small voice, she said, "I have something to tell you."

He gave her a serious look. "I worked this afternoon with Robert McDonnell."

She blinked. "He told you." She grabbed the hands he was drying on the cloth. "I'm so ashamed, Johann." She began to weep. "We quarrel like children. We act like children. We say terrible things. It's like being on the ship, but worse because we're not ever going to get out of here. It's going to go on and on. It's purgatory. Johann, I swear, I don't know how much of this I can take. I'm losing my mind."

He dropped the towel and pulled her to him. He was smiling. After a moment, she pulled back and looked angrily at him. "I make a fool of myself and my family, disgrace myself forever in Broad Bay, and you sit there like some happy child who's just been given a second pudding. Do you care nothing for what people think of me, what they think of you to be married to such a lunatic?"

Johann tilted his head back and laughed out loud. She threw the cloth at him and stood. He grabbed her hand and pulled her to him.

"Christiane, Christiane, my love," he said. "Now everyone in Broad Bay knows what I've always known. That my wife, the mother of my children, is a lioness. That we are a family of lions. They won't forget."

He leaned back and gave a loud roar that ended in another happy laugh. "Walther," he called to the boy, who sat on the bench, staring with wide eyes. "Come here and roar with me and your mama!"

The boy ran into his father's arms, and the three of them roared. A small voice came from the bed. "Mama."

"Oh, Hanna, lambie." Christiane fell into the bed and dug the little girl from the blanket. "What a mother you have," she said, cradling her.

"A lioness of a mother," Johann said.

They laughed again. When Richard started to cry, they decided he was roaring too.

CHAPTER FOUR

Through the spring and summer, the grim reports trickled in. A farmer was found scalped and dazed near Brunswick. He died. Another in Pemaquid fought free from captors. A raiding party burned three farms in North Yarmouth. The royal governor in Boston offered a bounty for every Indian scalp, inciting whites to match the Indians in preying on the weak and defenseless.

On a cloudy day in June, two settlers noticed that loose cows were trampling a common field of cabbages on the river's west side. Bringing muskets, they crossed the river to gather up the cows. A war party killed and scalped one and carried off the other.

The drumbeat of grim news drove some settlers to Boston, which was too big for the Indians to attack. The departures—about thirty families so far—left more room inside the stockades, but also shrank the number left to guard them.

When Frau Schultheis and her family left, Ursula stirred from her despondency. She announced she would help with births in the settlement. As midwife, Ursula began to make a place for herself. Her assistant was nine-year-old Sigrid, grown solemn and diligent since her father's disappearance. Ursula refused to consider leaving Broad Bay. This was their home, she insisted, and where Fritz would come if he escaped. Some Indian captives had emerged years later. She and Fritz came for the land. She wouldn't give it up. Johann and Christiane lent her the money to pay General Waldo. They also helped her and her girls with food.

Within two or three weeks of each bulletin about fresh Indian depredations, the settlers' fears would begin to dissipate. They grumbled again about stockade life, about venturing out only under armed guard. One time or another, most sneaked off on their own to work on their farms, to see to a chore, to pick some berries that should be ripe, to fetch clean water, or simply to breathe in an open place, looking at the river, no one else around. The world outside the stockades taunted them. It was so wide and exciting, filled with adventure and riches waiting to be gathered, yet so deadly.

Armstrong, during a trading visit, reported that settlers down the coast had started using dogs to guard them. When the Penobscots go to war, he explained, they smear their bodies with bear grease, which dogs can smell from hundreds of yards away. The dogs alerted settlers to danger better than any human senses could.

By a lucky coincidence, Armstrong brought two dozen scruffy dogs with him, along with bear grease for training them. In a vivid demonstration, he had someone wave a cloth stained with bear grease from a distance of nearly a quarter mile. In a matter of seconds, each dog erupted in a frenzy of excitement. The reaction was the same if the animal was a hound or a terrier or had mixed ancestry.

Johann bought one with a russet brindle coat and vague forebears. He named her Freya, after the goddess of war. Christiane and the children spoiled Freya with their own food through the summer, indulgences that didn't soften Freya's disposition when she joined Johann on patrol. Unfortunately, her barking could be indiscriminate. Squirrels, rabbits, and windblown leaves set off the same raucous warnings. But she also reacted to bear grease.

"I don't mind a nervous dog," Johann told McDonnell one day in late autumn, when they were walking three farmers in the direction of the Pemaquid peninsula. Two of the farmers had each brought a son along. All of them carried hoes and buckets. "Freya is nervous for me." The dog crossed the path to roust some dark birds from a bush. Johann noted the red chevrons on the blackbirds' wings. They were the sergeants in the winged army.

As captain and lieutenant of the guards, Johann and Robert huddled each week to adjust schedules and talk over developments, but they rarely patrolled together.

"If you want someone to be nervous for you," McDonnell said, "pick anyone in Broad Bay. The whole place is jumpy as hell."

"Better too jumpy than too relaxed."

"Sure," the Scot said, "but too many false alerts make people indifferent, too relaxed. You know that."

Johann knew that. Alarm shots thundered across Broad Bay at least twice a week, sometimes more. They drove settlers into the stockades and brought guards on the run, guns in hand, powder and cartridge bags over their shoulders. So far, only one alarm had produced an actual Indian ambush, but that didn't mean the savages weren't there. The Indians' ability to melt into the forest still impressed Johann. What the false alerts did mean was that the settlers responded more slowly each time. Some might even ignore an alarm. When there was real danger, that could be fatal.

"What did Armstrong tell you?" Johann asked. "Anything new?" The trader had landed the day before. He and McDonnell sometimes drank whiskey into the night, having grown friendly since discovering that they both refused to enter the stockade named for the Duke of Cumberland, the scourge of Scotland during the Jacobin rising ten years before.

"Nothing good," McDonnell said. "There's rumors of war parties coming down from the St. Francis. The Indians've got their crops in, so they're ready to raid."

Johann grunted at the mention of the St. Francis bands. "They're fierce," he said, "and they know war."

"That they do," the other man agreed, "and the French have armed them. If we have to fight, we'll run out of powder and ball before they do. Also," McDonnell said with emphasis, "they travel in numbers. In the last war, Armstrong says, they're the ones who took on whole settlements, like this one, instead of picking off one or two at a time like our locals do. That attack on the Kennebec last fall—that was the St. Francis tribes, and it was damned bloody."

"They come a long way to make war."

"A couple hundred miles. That's why they like to bring some trophies back, like women and kids."

"So, what do we do?" Freya started barking at the forest to their left. The men crouched, and Johann held out a hand to halt the others, who also crouched. After about ten seconds, the dog fell silent and started sniffing around her, then alerted again to the same spot in the woods.

"See anything?" Johann whispered.

McDonnell shook his head. Freya started sniffing off in another direction, no longer interested in the woods. McDonnell shrugged. "Maybe a deer." The group started walking again.

After about twenty paces, Johann said, "We don't have enough guards to increase the patrols, and the folks in the stockades want to get out more."

"I know," McDonnell said. "We need to lose a scalp or two to get everyone's attention again."

"If they attack a whole settlement, they come just before dawn, right?"

"Yup."

"How about having at least two men take that last shift before dawn up on the watchtowers? Maybe one of them'll stay awake."

"Maybe make 'em take dogs up there."

"They'd have to carry them up the ladders."

"Small dogs."

Both men smiled. "All right," Johann said. "We'll get the men together on Sunday after prayer meeting and talk it over."

They neared the three farms on the peninsula. Each farmer moved to his own land. One pushed his son toward potatoes that should have been dug a week before. By hand gestures, Johann and Robert divided the visual fields each would monitor.

Johann looked at the sun to mark the beginning of the two hours they could stay. The days were shortening and the leaves beginning to turn. Another winter in the stockades lay before them, but this day was a gem. The sun heated his face and hands as the early chill lost its bite. Fluffy clouds hurried across the sky, their shadows racing over the land. Christiane had suggested they eat dinner that night just outside the stockade, looking out at the river. Johann was looking forward to it.

The yellows and greens and oranges of the leaf trees danced in the breeze next to sober, dark firs. In addition to their guns, each guard carried a knife and a tomahawk. They couldn't fend off a sustained attack, but the Indians usually wanted easy pickings, not battles.

Then again, attackers might come by canoe before dawn, conceal their canoes and hide in the narrow strip of trees between the path and the bay. They prized boys as captives, young enough to be raised in the tribe. There were stories of abducted whites who refused to return home after years with the Indians. Johann always wondered about that.

Indian life might not be any worse than life in the stockades. Once, while hunting, he had watched a small Penobscot camp. Three or four families lived there, doing the sorts of things that Johann and Christiane did with their family—preparing food and clothes while children played, scolding when necessary, speaking to each other, sometimes smiling. The Indians didn't believe in the Word of God. They had their own ideas about how the world was made and the spirits that fill it. The part of their world he never understood, even less than he understood scalping, was that no one owned land.

"Robert," he said.

"Yes."

"Why don't the Indians own land?"

"By God, they own land. They think they own this whole bleeding continent. That's why they're so dead set on driving us back into the sea."

"But that's the whole tribe that owns the land, right?"

"Sure."

"Why don't individual Indians, the families, own land? They don't have that, right?"

"You're quite the philosopher today," McDonnell took a moment. "I guess it's how they live, hunting and fishing. That needs too much land for any one man to own."

"Not back home in Hesse it isn't. Our nobles own the hunting land."

"You're right." McDonnell was quiet for another spell.

"But," Johann started again, "they plant and raise crops, like we do. Yet none of the Indians owns the land they farm, right?"

"Don't believe they do." McDonnell chuckled. "Are you thinking on trying to buy some from them?"

"They might offer a better deal than General Waldo." They both smiled. "You know, it just seems like the thing we're most different about. We've both got religions. We've both got boats and weapons and war and shelters and families and farming and hunting and fishing."

"We've got lumbering," McDonnell said.

"They use the trees too. They cook over wood fires, and their wigwams have wooden frames. Their canoes are made from bark. All I can figure out that's really different between us is the land."

"You may be right, John, but I doubt that changes much. Even if we only wanted to hunt and fish the land without sharing it out to each other, we still would be moving the Penobscots off of it. The Indians fight each other over land, over which tribe gets to hunt where. To them, we're just another tribe."

"Maybe so. But their friends are the French, who sell land like we do."

"The French," McDonnell spoke with a deeper voice, "don't settle the land the way we British do."

"Or we Germans."

"Or you Germans. The French just set up trading posts and make money by cheating the savages. We come to stay, to build homes, to be part of America."

"That's it, you see. We come for the land."

"All right, then. We come for the land. So, tell me, is all this deep thinking somehow connected to what Maggie says, that you folks are having another child?"

Johann smiled and nodded over his shoulder at his friend. He felt his ears redden.

"It's little wonder the Indians are angry," McDonnell said. "I swear that the Overstreets are going to overrun the entire continent all by themselves."

"We'll still be two behind the McDonnells."

McDonnell grinned. "It's a punishing thing," he said, "this business of enjoying your wife and what it leads to. Maggie says that'll be three in four years for you. You need to start leaving that woman alone."

"My Bible tells me to go forth and multiply."

"God was talking to the Hebrews, not to the Germans."

"Or to the Scots."

Each man continued to watch his share of the woods. Johann checked the sky. Another hour.

CHAPTER FIVE

The birth of Franklin Overstreet came at the end of a frigid March. The people of Broad Bay had marveled over a warm January. The river didn't freeze until nearly the end of the month. Even February wasn't so bad. No one risked pulling a full sled across the Medomak until the gales of March blew away every hope of an early spring.

As befit the squally month, Franklin's arrival was stormy. Christiane's labor lasted much of a day in the smoky stockade room while a blizzard howled outside. Ursula, assisted by Sigrid, did what she could, but Christiane's torment dragged into the night. The storm trapped Johann in Ursula's room with the children—his three and Ursula's small one, Herta. A neighbor came with a pot of warm porridge. Johann told Bible stories he had heard as a child. Walther loved the one about Daniel in the lion's den. Then Johann had to tell more stories. He tried to remember others he had heard Christiane and Ursula tell, but Walther kept correcting him when he got them wrong. In Christiane's final hour, just before dawn, her shouts competed with the winds that screamed through the stockade.

The ordeal drained Christiane more than the earlier births had. She was too weak to leave the compound for several weeks, seeming to grow paler and thinner. It didn't help that Franklin arrived angry with the world, his temper worsening as spring tiptoed into Broad Bay. He was quiet only when he ate, which he did voraciously, and when he slept, which he did rarely. If Johann tried to hold his new son, Franklin's little body went rigid with rage. His face turned scarlet. Only Christiane could comfort him, so she spent every day with this tiny tyrant, shuffling across their room with Franklin in her arms until she collapsed on the bed, which was Franklin's signal to begin screaming. The other children, even Johann, learned to sleep through Franklin's fury, but Christiane wasn't allowed. She sometimes wept as she tended to him. His cries, erupting through the night, drove Ursula and her daughters to move to an empty room farther from the Overstreets. Neighbors assured Christiane that the baby would grow out of it. A few whispered that he was possessed by demons.

Watching Christiane grow more haggard, her energy ebb, Johann felt helpless, snared by his obligations. During the days, he had shifts with the guards, both on the watchtower and escorting settlers. As captain, he fielded problems all day and many nights.

He had agreed to McDonnell's proposal that the guards earn money for the whole settlement by hauling firewood for shipment to Boston. The farmers could never bring in decent crops under these conditions, McDonnell had argued, so they had to draw on Broad Bay's one source of wealth. Some guards complained that they wouldn't be able to take care of their farms. "We're in a war," Johann said. "This is what war is like. Small people like us, we suffer. We do the best we can. We take the fish, we take the shellfish, we take the wood. And we pray for victory and peace."

When a few were unmoved by Johann's words, McDonnell stepped in, speaking slowly in the hope they could follow his English. "You can't take proper care of your farms, am I right?" He made a hoeing motion, then wagged his finger. "So"—he wielded an imaginary ax—"why not do something that you can make a little money at?" He rubbed his fingertips together in the universal gesture for funds. The men nodded.

Johann organized logging parties and shipping schedules. They took the trees from land the settlers hoped to farm when the war ended, then shipped the wood out on coasting sloops that had to evade the French.

In the evenings, while his family tried to sleep through Franklin's fits, Johann worked on his carpentry. He brought his tools into the room Ursula had vacated. He made it his workshop, daring anyone to challenge him, the captain of the guard. Working by firelight, he built furniture for their room. A bed for the children. A second table. Stools to sit on.

As he worked, Johann ached for his real wife to return, not this spectral figure enslaved to the baby. When he brought her mayflowers in the spring, she barely noticed. The idea seized him that childbirth was war for women. So much was the same—the pain, the fear of the unknown, the risk of death. And it had to be endured over and over. He couldn't stop resenting Franklin and his constant demands, even thinking of the helpless baby as their enemy, an evil force dropped into their lives. The thoughts shamed him, made him promise God that he would be a better person, but then the thoughts stole back into his mind.

On an evening in June, Johann was working late when Franklin started up again. Johann tried to stop his ears to the din, but then heard a soft, almost mewing sound. Christiane. He put down his tools and walked into their darkened room. She sat slump-shouldered on the edge of their bed, a hand on Franklin, who was on his back, screaming. Johann could tell that Walther and Hanna were awake, their eyes following him. Only Richard slept.

He reached down and lifted the baby to his shoulder and placed his hand along Christiane's cheek. "Rest," he said. She nodded, then twisted onto her side, facing away.

Grabbing a cloth to wrap around the baby, Johann carried him into the courtyard, then opened the gate.

"Captain," a voice came from the watchtower. "That's not permitted."

Johann said nothing. He closed the gate behind him. Everyone would thank him for taking Franklin away.

Johann walked to the river, his arm under Franklin's bottom, a hand on his back. He bounced the baby gently and sang to him. He walked up and down the shore, back and forth. Franklin didn't relent. His spine was like iron. He threw his head back, his mouth open in the light of a thousand stars and a sliver moon. His cries grew more frantic, more urgent. Johann could feel the baby's fury infect him. The hideous noise was blotting out his human feelings, the kindness and warmth that are every baby's right.

Johann felt jittery, his muscles strung taut, a terrible weariness and anger in his soul. It had been building for days, weeks, now months. He had to fight the reasoning that formed in his mind, reasoning that seemed so seductive, so obvious. The baby is miserable. The baby is making everyone else miserable. The noise never ends, it crawls under your skin and into your brain and never lets you alone, noise that no human should have to endure. Everything else has been tried. So only one course is left. There's only one way to stop the noise.

He shook his head. This was madness.

Franklin carried on for another minute, then broke off. He choked for a second. Johann looked down and saw him fight for breath. Franklin widened his eyes and belched. He took a breath, closed his eyes, and screamed again.

Johann sat on the ground with his back against a tree. He faced the river, holding his son before him, leaning the small body back against his drawn-up knees. Franklin's screams suddenly sounded sad. The boy was inconsolable. Somehow he knew the horrors of this world he had been dropped into, the bloody death and disease, the viciousness and fear and loneliness. Johann felt himself open up inside. A tear came from his eye. He smiled at Franklin and brushed his knuckles against the baby's cheek. Ah, poor baby, he thought. Poor, poor baby. Tell me about it, he whispered. It will be less terrible if you share it.

Franklin broke off in mid-cry to take a double-breath, one with a hiccup in the middle of it. He opened his eyes and looked at Johann, then shifted his head. Johann nodded to him. "Hello, Master Franklin," he said. He felt this tiny being enter his heart. Franklin peered into the dimness to one side. His spine of iron relaxed. He yawned. Soon he was asleep.

Sitting by the river with the exhausted baby, Johann had a waking dream. Christiane was next to him under the tree, her head on his shoulder, her hand holding his arm. He hadn't felt her touch in so long. When the dream ended, Franklin was looking at him, turning his head side-to-side in a grey dawn. The baby began to grunt and push his hand into his mouth, chewing on it. He was hungry. Johann smiled. "For that," he said, "we need mama."

Christiane said nothing when he sat on the bed. She sat up and held her hands out. Franklin greedily locked his mouth on her breast. She closed her eyes and rested her head against the wall. When Walther approached, Johann put a finger to his lips, then helped him dress. The boy was six now, not big for his age. No Overstreet would be. Walther's blue-grey eyes were calm. They conveyed a self-possession unusual for a child. Like his mother. Perhaps, Johann hoped, like his father too. He wondered if Peter would have had that. The other two slept when he and Walther began to slip out of the room.

"Johann," Christiane said softly. He looked back. "You'll come back to walk with him?"

"Of course," he said.

Franklin didn't change completely, not right away, but the screaming part of his days became shorter, then shorter still.

CHAPTER SIX

†

When Richard grew ill in the winter of 1758, seven Broad Bay settlers had already died from the smallpox. More had sickened and then recovered. One of those was Walther, who proved as resilient as he had been during the ocean crossing. This time, Walther was tired and feverish for a day, then developed a rash. But he never descended into full-throated smallpox. Christiane hoped that Richard, who trailed faithfully after his brother on most days, would be like Walther that way.

They moved the children's bed into Johann's workroom next door. Johann slept there with the healthy ones while Christiane cared first for Walther, then for Richard. She couldn't be sure if she'd ever had the smallpox. There had been two outbreaks in Kettenheim when she was a girl.

Richard's rash evolved into angry red sores, then welts formed on his arms and back and stomach and face. They sometimes oozed a clear, vile-smelling pus. He tried to be a brave boy, but he was hot and his head hurt. The mouth sores made him cry. It hurt to swallow, so he didn't want to eat. Christiane made the porridge thinner and thinner so he could get something down past the sores.

Every day, Richard looked forward to the times when Walther and Hanna stood at the door to his room and called out to him. They said they missed him, how he would be well soon and come play with them. Richard's mouth and throat hurt so badly that he couldn't make them hear his answers, but he never looked away from them. Johann, holding little Franklin, stood behind while they waved to their brother. Late at night, while the three small ones slept, Johann slipped into Richard's room. Christiane wouldn't let him near the bed—they weren't sure if Johann had had smallpox either—but he stayed until she shooed him out to sleep.

Richard's sores started to scab over, which Christiane hoped was a good sign. When the blisters near his eyes seemed to heal, she worried less that he would go blind. She tried to keep him cool, wiping around his sores with a wet cloth. She prayed. She told God that no one would mind scars or pockmarks on such a fine boy. Richard didn't need to be pretty, if he could only be spared.

At the end of the second week, he vomited thin, green bile. He vomited again and then again that day, though there was nothing in his stomach to bring up but his own flesh and blood. She was losing him. She stopped praying. She lay with him in her arms, sometimes humming, sometimes whispering what a wonderful boy he was. She never let him see tears. When Johann and Walther and Hanna came to the door the next day, Richard couldn't open his eyes to see them.

She didn't weep on the day he stopped breathing. She had been building the fire, cursing the winter, with her back turned. When she turned to him, he was gone. She knelt next to him, then placed his head on a folded cloth. From the door, she called to Johann. She handed him two buckets for clean water. He gripped her arms hard, but she shook her head, then let it droop against his shoulder.

"I've set aside the boards," he said. "It won't take long." She nodded. "I can help you wash him."

"No," she said. "You mustn't get sick too. You take care of us."

"Do you want Nungesser?"

"No."

She washed Richard slowly. His ribs stuck obscenely from his torso, his icy skin stretched taut between the scabs. She gathered the cloths and blankets she had used with him and changed to her other dress. When she tied the apron over it, she had to adjust the top. It was loose. She hadn't been able to eat either. They would burn her dress, Richard's clothes, everything he touched. She sat on the bed's edge and gazed at him, feeling her heart grow hard. She couldn't do this again.

Next morning, Johann and McDonnell built a bonfire at Mayflower Hof to soften the earth. They dug the grave, then returned to town. More than fifty neighbors joined the procession back to Mayflower Hof with the coffin, snaking along the still-frozen river. Most of the guards came. They carried muskets. Johann was surprised by how many people. There had been many burials since the smallpox struck.

The grave was behind the cabin on the north side. It was the highest ground, looking out at the two firs Johann had left standing near the river. He stood behind the coffin, holding Franklin in one arm and his Bible in the other. McDonnell had brought three stools. Christiane sat between Walther and Hanna, her arm around each. It was too early for flowers, so each child held a small branch from a holly tree, the waxy green leaves bright against the snow. Christiane held one too. Johann had one for himself and one for Franklin.

For Richard, Johann read the passage he used to read for his soldiers when they had been killed, from the book of John, about his father's house having many rooms. Johann thought of Peter, too, when he read the last words, "And if I go and prepare a place for you, I will come back and take you to be with me that you also may be where I am." Richard and Peter never met, yet they were brothers. They might meet.

Christiane met Johann's eyes when he looked up. Then she looked out at the river. She longed for a fire. It had been so long since she'd been warm. Richard must have felt that way.

Johann nodded to the group. The mourners shuffled by. Christiane didn't stand. She murmured thanks for their words. When they were gone, all except for McDonnell and Ursula and her girls, they knelt again at the coffin. Johann and McDonnell set Richard in his grave. Each of them dropped a holly branch with him. Then the men spaded the earth in.

* * * * * *

"John, I'll tell you one thing about Alec here," McDonnell lit his pipe with a burning twig while he waved toward his slender son, who was tall for his thirteen years. "He's clumsy enough for three people, but if you give him a solid base, he'll hit a squirrel in the eye at a hundred paces."

Fair-haired, with porcelain skin that showed blood running blue beneath it, the boy blushed with pleasure under his father's words. McDonnell was addressing Johann's objection to meeting at McDonnell's cabin for their weekly review of guards business. Evening visits to cabins were strictly forbidden, but McDonnell liked to argue his way around rules. "Alec's better than most of our so-called guards, so we're fully meeting the requirements that at least two guards be present with the owner."

"You twist the rules to suit yourself." Johann hunched close to the fire, its light bouncing off the snow that McDonnell had cleared from the fire pit. With stiff fingers, Johann began to light his own pipe. He usually didn't allow himself tobacco. He minded the expense of it, and also the whole idea of a substance that existed solely to burn up. But this was McDonnell's tobacco. That was different.

"Aye," McDonnell agreed, "and thanks be to God that I do. What a torture to live by other people's rules." He drew on his pipe and looked toward the river, where only a few ice chunks flowed by. "Feels like more snow, don't it?" Johann nodded. It was only mid-March. The snow would fly for a while longer. "Armstrong may be here soon. Will you have the furniture to trade?"

"Two tables and six chairs."

"The chest of drawers?"

"They're not right yet."

"Ah, John, John. I love your honesty, but it's a barrier to making a living. I'll bet they're fine."

"They're not right," Johann repeated. "You're not worried that the French will get Armstrong's sloop?"

"Of course I am. But it's either take the risk or eat the tables and chairs for dinner. We need to trade. Armstrong's always made it through. I wouldn't put it past him to have a side deal with the French." He turned to his son. "That's not the sort of thing to be said to anyone who's not sitting at this fire right now." Alec nodded. McDonnell asked Johann, "You're still all right with me making the deal for both of us?"

"Yes. He likes to do business with you. He doesn't care for me."

"Why would he care for you, you being such a murdersome son of a bitch? He knows that old McDonnell, why he's all right for a Jacobite. A bit of a lout maybe, but right enough with a few drinks in him. That Overstreet fella now, so quiet, and with the stare of a killer. I'd be afraid of you myself if I didn't know what a sentimental fool you really are, mooning over that skinny wife of yours."

Johann smiled to be companionable, though he never liked talking with other people about Christiane. But McDonnell was his only real friend in Broad Bay, at least since Fritz. "If I'm such a killer," Johann said, "then why would he cheat me?"

"You and your German logic. It'll be the death of us. You don't follow at all. He would never cheat you. But he would give *me* a better deal." McDonnell looked over his shoulder at his son, who was attending to every word. "Alec, why don't you go check the woods on the other side." The hectoring tone was out of his voice. When the boy was gone, McDonnell started again. "John. You see, Maggie's been talking to me. She's worried about your Christiane. She says the girl won't eat. Maggie brings her food, good stuff that she should be saving for her lout of a husband, but she says Christiane don't eat it. Is she all right?"

"Yes, Robert, she is." Johann stopped. "No, no she's not. She's sad about Richard, about how we are living." He had been thinking that day that his little boy had barely three years on this earth, most of it in that filthy stockade. That wasn't what they'd come to America for. He ran a hand through his hair. "We're both sad, but as you say, I'm just a murdersome soul, so I go back to work while she stays sad." He had tried the other night, had put his hand on her hip as they lay together, in the way they both knew. She had whispered, "No," then rolled away. He shook his head as though the movement would clear out an unwelcome thought. "I thought she was bringing up her food once, after dinner, spitting it out. She said she didn't, that she was just spitting, but I don't know."

"She's not eating dirt, is she? A woman did that back home. She ended up crazy as a loon."

"Christiane's not crazy."

"No, that's not what I mean. What I mean is, Maggie and me, we're worried."

"I know." Johann took a breath and looked up at the sky. "I'm worried too. It's good for Maggie to keep coming by. I know Christiane's glad to see her."

McDonnell puffed on his pipe. "I've wondered how they talk to each other. Maggie doesn't know a word of German."

Johann smiled. "Christiane knows more English than she lets on. I've taught her some. When I speak it with the children, she listens."

Alec came back around the cabin. "Sit here and warm yourself, boy," McDonnell said. He turned to Johann. "You know this great gawky thing has been mooncalfing around about a young girl?"

"Pa, that's not true."

"Nothing wrong with that, boy. McDonnell men like the girls, and vice-a vers-a, as they say. Mooncalfing is the first step. But," McDonnell grinned, "I need to tell Mr. Overstreet which one."

"Pa!"

"He's like the father for that poor girl, so I need to speak of this. Your ma told me to, so you know that leaves me no choice." He faced Johann. "It's that other long drink of water, the daughter of your friend."

"Sigrid?"

"That's it! Sigrid. Right, Alec?"

The firelight revealed the boy's shame, embarrassment, and pride. He said nothing.

"But Sigrid," Johann said, "she has only, what, eleven years?"

"She as tall as her ma, and as pretty as her ma, and any day now she's going to fill out like her ma. I warned him that she probably doesn't speak a word of English, but he's at an age when that doesn't matter much, and I'm not sure it should at any age. However you slice it, John, you"—he pointed his finger—"are going to be lying awake at night trying to figure out how to keep the young bucks away from that one."

Johann put the uncomfortable thought aside. He would need to speak with Ursula about this. Women understood these things better. He sat forward with his hand on his knees, signaling a change in tone. "Robert, do we have any business about the guards?"

McDonnell sat forward, mirroring him. "There's tomorrow night, Nungesser's big meeting. He's going to tell us we're all damned. Most of the guards'll be going to hear how the Four Horsemen of the Apocalypse are rampaging through Broad Bay."

Johann shook his head. "What were they? Pestilence, famine, war, death? They're here. The people are without hope or spirit. They're listening to him."

"Aye, it's hard times. As hard as I've seen. With the boats running to Boston again, I wouldn't be surprised if we lost more families. It takes desperate times to make people start listening to a numbskull like Nungesser. I've never known anyone less likely to know divine will."

"Something has to change, Robert. It's more than three years we've been in the stockades, afraid of the Indians, afraid of the French, hearing all the terrible stories and not making our way." Johann stood and paced before the fire. "We can't go home because we spent our last shilling coming here, and we have nothing back home anyway. After more than six years here, we still have almost nothing. Land that's turning back into forest."

McDonnell stared into the fire. After a minute, he said, "That's about the size of it, at least until King Louis and King George decide the rest of us can live in peace."

"I came here so kings wouldn't control my life, so I wouldn't answer to them and their stupid quarrels. So I wouldn't have to die for them. And yet every night I lie down in that damned pesthole with my poor family, having achieved nothing for another day, just waiting for the pox or some fever to take us away."

"Well, Armstrong says they're gathering a grand fleet and expedition against Louisbourg. If we can take Louisbourg, that'll clear the French off the water and push the Indians back up to Quee-bec. Then we can get out of the stockades."

"Didn't the settlers take Louisbourg in the last war, only to have King George hand it back to Louis?"

"That they did, won it fair and square, and that the king did, too, give it right back he did. Don't expect me to defend that cursed man. He killed my kinsmen."

"If there's no way out of the stockades but to fight for Louisbourg, by God I'll do it. Let's get on with it."

The two men and the boy watched the fire die down. McDonnell stood and started throwing snow on the fire. "For tomorrow night, the Marlborough stockade and the Cumberland will need men on the watchtower. You can cover one with old Schroeder. I recruited him for it. He's made no secret of the fact that he despises Nungesser."

"All right."

"I'll cover the other with Alec."

"Robert, wait a minute. The boy's only thirteen."

"Alec's taller than half the guards, shoots better than most of them, and can see farther than all of them, including you and me. He'll do fine. Actually, I think we should get him into the regular schedule."

"I'll think about it."

"See, Alec. I told you Mr. Overstreet would listen to reason." As Johann stood, a grin came over McDonnell's face. He leaned over and said softly, "And wait till that little girl hears that Alec's one of the guards." He winked.

CHAPTER SEVEN

While two seamen pulled the boat's oars in rhythm, Leichter cocked an eyebrow at Johann. "D'you care for the general's boat?"

Johann rubbed his arms against the chill. He gave a small smile and shrugged, squinting into the rising sun, its silver reflection spreading across the bay. General Waldo's sloop had arrived the evening before. This morning, Leichter arrived at the Prince of Wales stockade with an invitation for Captain Overstreet to breakfast on shipboard. Johann was glad to have a clean shirt for the day. He had scraped his cheeks red for the meeting.

He knew what the meeting was about. For two weeks, Broad Bay had talked of little else than the expedition to Louisbourg. Not even the melting of the river ice was more important. King George was rousing Britain's military might to protect his settlers in the new world.

After Johann scrambled up the sloop's ladder, two men in matching hunting shirts and coats pulled him up over the rail. Each had a pistol in his waistband and picked up a musket once Johann was aboard. Leichter climbed up unassisted, then gestured for Johann to enter the captain's cabin. He didn't follow.

"Ah, Captain Overstreet," Waldo said, looking up from a writing desk. "Welcome." He beckoned a sailor with a teakettle to enter. "Tea, Captain? We have cream and sugar."

Johann sat at the indicated place. The table was set for two. The meal began with porridge that didn't compare to Christiane's, but moved on to roast chicken and a poached fish that were unlike anything Johann had eaten. He wished Christiane might have such food. That would keep her appetite keen.

Waldo, dark eyes hooded under his heavy brow, ate steadily, without passion, evidently feeling no need for conversation. He watched Johann eat, then offered an extra biscuit as Johann's pace slowed. Johann took it. Steam rose from it when he broke it open. Waldo pushed a small dish of honey across the table. Johann spooned it over the biscuit. He was glad to be bribed with this fine meal. He already wanted to do what Waldo would ask him to do. Christiane had agreed.

When Johann finished the biscuit, Waldo nodded for more tea, then waved the sailor from the cabin. Johann admired the china teacup for a moment, then admired the cabinet work that lined the cabin. Made in Boston, he thought. He would like to be able to build such compartments. They followed the curves of the ship's walls and sealed neatly with latches. With an effort, he looked back at Waldo.

"Captain Overstreet, I need your help."

"General."

"You have heard of the expedition to Louisbourg, I trust." Johann nodded. "You know that a bunch of us Yankees took that godforsaken fortress thirteen years ago, no thanks to His Royal Majesty's admirable army?" Johann nodded. "And then the half-wits in the foreign office decided to give it back to the frogs when they signed the peace, so now we must capture it again, except this time the frogs know how we did it last time. And this time they'll have a fleet there to stop us." Johann nodded again, while Waldo drank off his tea.

"You can speak, can't you?"

"I can."

"Ah. Good to have that settled." Waldo pursed his lips in a disdainful look. "Well, the bastards are taking over the expedition this time round. They're ginning up a great spanking army, one large enough to scare the frogs all the way back to Paris. We Yankees are riding along to lend a hand here and there, but the bastards in the red coats will be in charge. Theirs to be the glory. With any luck, theirs to be the bloodshed."

Johann nodded but couldn't entirely suppress his amazement. "Ah, I surprise you, Captain? It's deuced unpleasant to be a loyal subject of the king and to be treated like some rustic idiot with no more idea how to take Louisbourg than how to take a shit."

Johann smiled.

"Ah, Captain, you are familiar with the British Army?"

"I fought alongside them. I was at Dettingen."

"So you witnessed our king's most glorious victory, eh?"

"It is called a victory, General, but no battle is glorious. Dettingen wasn't."

"Spoken like a man who fights other people's battles, yet never gets the credit for winning them, eh, Captain?"

"Louisbourg will be very much my battle. My family and I have been unable to live on our land for more than three years. Our son died of the pox. My wife is, well, she is like all of us, weary of how we must live, like prisoners in this new land. To end this war, I will fight."

"Well said. As you're the only trained soldier in this settlement, and already the captain of the guards, I will appoint you captain of the Broad Bay company of irregulars."

"We must discuss this," Johann said, "this Broad Bay company. Many of our neighbors have gone to Boston. The pox has taken others. We have few guards. If we send many soldiers to Louisbourg, the Indians will see. They'll attack our families."

Waldo pursed his lips again and pushed his chair back from the table. He turned in his seat so he could cross a leg over his knee. "How many men do you think Broad Bay sent to take Louisbourg last time?"

"I don't know."

"Two hundred and fifty." The number startled Johann. Today, the entire settlement might number that many if you included the women and children. "Of course, we can't do anything like that now."

"We have thirty guards now, who all can shoot. Most are fit. A few are too old for a battle."

"We'll need most of them."

"General, you can't expect men to go off to war if they fear their wives and children will be killed while they're away. They won't stay at war."

"You're saying the men of Broad Bay will desert their duties? The bastards won't like to hear that. They'll hang 'em."

"I'm saying the men of any place will defend their families first."

"I've instructed Leichter that he will stay here in Broad Bay until your ranger company returns. He will take charge of defense and the guards." Johann nodded. Leichter was a capable man. "So, Captain, how many can we bring to Louisbourg?"

Johann thought for a moment. "Fifteen."

"Twenty."

"Perhaps twenty. Perhaps eighteen. But we'll have to train more guards to replace those who go."

"Do it quickly. The expedition will gather in Halifax next month. We'll have the best equipment His Brittannic Majesty can provide. The soldiers will be kitted with the coats and hunting shirts that those fellows on deck are wearing."

"There are other matters." Impatience crossed Waldo's face, then he nodded. "I'll need to appoint my own sergeant."

"Who would that be?"

"Robert McDonnell. He acts now as my second for the guards."

"McDonnell. Isn't he a Jacobite?" Waldo maintained a bland expression as he posed the question.

"We Germans don't know those distinctions. He knows how to be a soldier."

"Well, our king has recruited Highland regiments for the expedition, and there's doubtless many a refugee from Culloden in them. What else?"

"What will the pay be?"

"Ah. Excellent question. Seven pounds sterling per month, per soldier."

"In silver?"

"Yes, in silver."

"And if the final month is not a complete month, we will be paid a proportionate share of the seven pounds for that month?"

"Captain Overstreet," a smile played over Waldo's face, "I form the suspicion that you have been trading with Mr. Armstrong. These are Yankee questions, not German ones."

"To be German is not to be a fool."

"I take your point. The pay for the last month will be proportionate, as you say."

"And for any who die in the expedition, their families will be paid a full share for their service."

"Unless," Waldo raised an eyebrow, "we have to hang them for desertion or insubordination." Johann nodded and prepared to stand. Waldo took advantage of the pause to lean forward. "You haven't asked about your pay as captain."

"It must be more than seven."

"Ten."

"That is fair." Johann looked over Waldo's shoulder for a few beats and furrowed his brow. "Who will command the expedition?"

"A fellow by the name of Jeffrey Amherst."

Johann shook his head. "I don't know him."

"Well, you would never have seen him on a battlefield. Apparently he's never had a fighting command. A staff officer, don't you know." Waldo sighed. "Most of his fighting will be done by this strapping new brigadier, James Wolfe."

Johann tilted his head a few degrees. "A red-haired man?"

"Never laid eyes on him. Be on warning. The word is that he hates all Americans. Thinks we're stupid and cowardly. I'd give him a wide berth."

"And you, Excellency? You'll be at Louisbourg?"

"I'm supposed to be advising General Amherst and the high command, fat lot of good that's likely to do. I've been writing memoranda until my wrist hurts. I'm sure they use them to light fires with." As they stood, Waldo spoke again. "Captain, I've spoken very candidly this morning." Johann nodded. "There's a lot about this expedition that makes my blood boil, but all of us who care about Broad Bay know that we have to win this fight. If we can take Louisbourg—take it *again*—our trade will open up, the French will be set back on their heels, and we can push them back to Quebec, then to France. Louisbourg's the key. With any luck, we'll get you men home before the snow falls again."

"Yes, General." Johann stood at attention and saluted. Waldo did the same, then smiled. "Do us proud, Captain. I'll be watching, and so will the bastards."

* * * * * *

Christiane had Franklin on one hip as they approached the landing. She took Johann's elbow with her free hand. Fog had hung over the bay for most of the morning, but a breeze was blowing it off. The wind promised fair sailing to Boston, where the Broad Bay rangers would join others destined for Louisbourg.

Johann carried Hanna, her eyes red from crying tears that Christiane was holding back. Walther carried his father's pack with his second shirt, mittens, and second pair of stockings. Freya patrolled in front, pausing to greet a large retriever. Johann looked fine in his ranger shirt and coat. His three-cornered hat featured a captain's blue cockade. Other families stood awkwardly at the landing. Anxiety muted their voices. Few could say what was in their hearts.

Christiane understood why Johann must go. He was the only soldier in Broad Bay. The others would follow him. If the expedition succeeded, then life in Broad Bay might become normal. And, of course, his *dienst* demanded it.

She thought of the coming months as God testing them again. He never seemed to tire of it. Before they left for America, her pastor back home had said that God would never lay a burden on her that she couldn't bear. She knew now that wasn't true.

Leichter greeted them at the water's edge. "Captain," he said with a smile, "shall we load the first group?"

Johann looked around. "Perhaps in five minutes. Let them know so they can say their good-byes." Still holding Hanna, he crouched before Walther.

"You must always help your mother and take care of her. I couldn't go without knowing you'll be here to do that. Can I rely on you, Son?"

The little boy nodded. He pulled up his arm in a salute, but Johann quickly took hold of that hand. "Only soldiers salute, Walther. You will not understand this now, but it is my wish that you never become a soldier. Let me be the last Overstreet to do that." They shook hands.

Christiane couldn't help smiling as he stood. "You're also the first Overstreet to be a soldier."

Johann gave his relaxed smile, the one where his eyes softened. "Be well, Christiane." She nodded, her throat suddenly closed up. Franklin rubbed his head against her shoulder. Johann embraced her quickly, squashing Franklin and Hanna slightly. He lowered his head to look into Christiane's eyes. "I will come back. I always have. You must be here for me. All of you." Her tears began to spill.

"Don't do anything brave, Johann," she whispered. "Promise me."

He kissed Franklin and Hanna, then set the little girl down next to her mother. He hugged her and Walther together. Lifting his pack, he nodded to Leichter.

CHAPTER EIGHT

The Broad Bay rangers, in double file, moved quickly through the damp woods. It was their third week in the small British town of Halifax, Nova Scotia, which meant they were three hundred miles from Louisbourg in a place where the sun never shone. The rangers carried their muskets against their bodies, right hand gripping the stock, left hand under the barrel. Only Sergeant McDonnell, the best marksman, carried a rifle. When a shot rang out, the double line split, half the men diving to the left and the rest to the right. They scrambled to what cover they could find and reached for their cartridge boxes. More shots echoed over the hills. The rangers readied their guns while lying on their backs, rising at least part way to load powder and ball, a tricky business when under attack. But they couldn't carry loaded muskets through wet country. That would mean soggy cartridges and damp powder.

McDonnell, who trailed the column, slid forward on the sloppy ground and tapped the leg of the man in front of him. Wilhelm Koch, who was too old for any army, rose to his hands and knees and began to move diagonally away from their line of march.

McDonnell followed. After forty yards, the two men began to circle their attackers. They knew that Johann and Alf Meisner were following a mirror path on the other side. The other men began to fire. Then came the bosun's shrill whistle.

A British colonel rode down the slope on a dapple grey. "Form up!" a Highlander sergeant bellowed to his troops. The attackers, three dozen tartaned men, emerged from the woods and jogged into two lines. They stood at rigid attention. The Broad Bay rangers, their dark coats mud-spattered from their dive for cover, moved less briskly into their double line. The Highlanders, even without their impressive headgear, were taller and broader than the rangers, except for McDonnell.

"All right, then," the colonel said as he halted his horse. "Take a good look at yourselves." The men in both groups looked around with some puzzlement. "You men of the 34th." The colonel faced the Highlanders. "You look clean and bright. Still have your hats on. And our provincials are quite filthy, ain't they?" Several Scots smiled. "Unfortunately, war ain't a tea party, gentlemen. If this had been a fight, those fine plaids would be covered with blood. Your blood."

The colonel turned to face Johann. "Captain, what was wrong with the ambush?"

"Their men were well-concealed, sir."

"I know that. I asked what was *wrong* with it. You and your sergeant noticed that right off, didn't you, Sergeant?"

"Yes, sir," McDonnell said. "They came at us only from the front. Indians would put a few before us, like they did, but they'd keep most behind and drive us back into that trap."

"Captain," the colonel turned back to the Highlanders, addressing their leader. "What was wrong with the counter-ambush techniques?" The colonel walked his mount down the line of Highlanders, then called over his shoulder. "Ranger Captain. What was wrong with your techniques?"

"We were slow getting out on the wings."

"You were not," the colonel said. "You moved quickly. Try again."

"There weren't enough of us to turn the ambush against them." Johann nodded at the Highlanders. "After a while, they might've overrun us."

"Then why did you attack?"

"They might run. We know the woods and they don't. And you don't want to get run down from behind. Not ever."

"Also, Captain, you got dirty, didn't you, all that crawling around for cover?"

"Yes, sir."

"Dirty but alive. The enemy," the colonel spoke to the Highlanders, "knows everything that this man just taught you." He turned to the Highlander sergeant. "Return to camp."

Johann allowed his rangers to drink from their canteens and brush themselves off. "Dirty but alive, eh?" McDonnell called out to them. The rangers grinned. A couple of them laughed. The Highlanders marched off in parade formation, four abreast through the woods.

"I'll bet that's how Braddock and his boys marched too," McDonnell said to Johann.

"We're on the same side, Robert."

"What's got you in such a turmoil?"

"I don't like being set against our fellow soldiers."

"You heard the man," McDonnell said. "We're teaching them."

"And they're hating us for it. We don't want to be in a tight spot some day and have those Highlanders say to themselves, 'Ach, those ranger lads, let's see 'em teach their way out of that."

McDonnell looked surprised. "Since when can you talk like a Scot?"

"Di'n' ya know? 'Tis me third language, I reckon."

The rangers had to wait on the shingle beach for a boat to take them back to the transport ship that served as home. Halifax was too small to accommodate the thousands massing for the attack on Louisbourg. Dozens of ships, including three huge ships of the line that bristled with sixty-four guns each, rode the swells in the harbor. Johann compared the bustling scene with the quiet of Broad Bay, where the whole settlement buzzed over the arrival of Armstrong's small coaster or Waldo's sloop. His thoughts rarely strayed far from the Prince of Wales stockade and the Mayflower Hof and Christiane. It had been a bad time to leave.

"Well, well, well, look what we've got here." The rough voice was followed by a few grunts and chuckles. Johann looked up. It was the 34th Highlanders arriving at the beach. "Say, Jock," the voice continued. It came from their sergeant, a man of middle height but built like a barrel. Curls of russet-colored hair strained to escape from his crested headgear. "Do you reckon those turd-sucking provincials are through wallowing in the mud for one day? Maybe we should help them have another go at it?"

Johann, his mind lingering on his regrets, rose too slowly. McDonnell strode past him, pointing his finger at the other Scots. "Don't make me laugh. You fellas couldn't find your arses with both hands, which is exactly what the colonel was trying to explain. Or are you all too pig-stupid to understand?"

"Lads, you hear that?" the other sergeant said. "Just as we thought. These fairy boys are after our arses, with both hands. I say we ram our boots up some provincial arse."

At the same moment, McDonnell and the other sergeant went for each other. McDonnell used his height to drive the other man to the ground, but the Highlander pulled him down, then rolled him over. Men from both units formed a ring as the fighters regained their feet and began to circle, edging one way, then feinting the other. Both were quick. Johann looked for the Highlander captain, but couldn't see him.

"Sergeant McDonnell," he called out sharply. His voice barely penetrated the clamor. He stepped into the ring between the sergeants, holding his hands out. "Sergeant, I order you to step back!" McDonnell shifted his eyes to Johann. In that moment, the Highlander dove around Johann and drove his shoulder into McDonnell. Legs churning, he pushed the ranger back into the shouting crowd until both lost their footing. Johann jumped after them. The shouting stopped abruptly as Johann was grabbing the Highlander's arm.

"Who's in charge here?" The sharp voice came from a man on horseback. The Scots snapped to attention. Johann turned to face a white horse topped by a tall, florid man with ferrety features. The red hair told Johann who he was.

"General Wolfe, sir," he said, saluting. "Captain Overstreet of the Broad Bay rangers."

"Justify yourself, sir." The general, though a young man, had mastered an expression of disdain that encompassed everything before him.

"No justification, sir. A failure of discipline."

The sergeants were on their feet, each at attention. Wolfe offered them some of his disdain, then turned to Johann. "Captain, you're no Yankee. How did these irregulars"—the word plainly disturbed the general—"end up with a German officer?"

"We're settlers on General Waldo's land, sir. In Massachusetts."

"Yes, well, that doesn't signify for this lack of discipline, does it?" Johann said nothing. The Highlander captain came running onto the scene. After saluting, he said, "General, sir."

"Where in the blue blazes have you been, Captain…?"

"Grant, sir. There was confusion about our sleeping quarters, sir."

Wolfe turned his disdain on the Highlander. "I dislike excuses, Captain. They aren't manly." Wolfe sat erect on his horse. "Refer these two"—he nodded at the sergeants—"to my headquarters tent in the morning for convening of a court-martial."

* * * * * *

Next morning, Captain Grant and his sergeant were outside Wolfe's tent when Johann and McDonnell arrived. All four wore spotless uniforms, the Americans in cream-colored hunting shirts and black coats, the Scots in brilliant scarlet and kilts. None looked like he had slept well. Grant and Johann took off their hats and nodded to the guards at the tent's entrance. A guard ducked inside the tent flap, then pulled it aside for them to enter.

Wolfe sprawled in a camp chair, a long leg stretched out on a table covered with papers and a half-furled map. The captains came to attention and saluted. The general kept his eyes on his work, forcing the captains to hold their salutes. The plan was for Grant to commence the appeal.

"At your ease, gentlemen," Wolfe said, looking up. Intelligence brightened his eye but couldn't improve his features. A chin dimple made his weak jaw recede farther. His narrow brows didn't inspire respect. He stood up, stork-like on slender legs. He was a head taller than Johann, half a head taller than Grant. "So, this is when you tell me that these brutes are essential to your companies, that they are good men who had a bad moment, and that I should allow mercy to light my way to grace so we may link arms and go thrash the French." He looked at each man. "Oh, and it won't happen again. Am I correct?"

"Correct, sir," Grant said.

"That was better, Captain Grant. But what are we to do about discipline? What kind of soldiers can we expect these men to be, least of all these rabble from the provinces who afflict us, if we close our eyes to brawling sergeants?"

"We don't argue against discipline, sir," Grant said. "Both men should be reduced in rank to corporal and should receive other punishment the general deems fit."

"Not broken to private soldiers? If they're corporals, you can elevate them again when I'm not looking. Isn't that true, Captain Overstreet?" Wolfe looked at Johann.

"It is, sir," Johann said.

"What have I omitted from your petition for these sergeants?"

"Nothing, sir."

Wolfe returned to his chair and leaned back, tenting his fingers in front of him. "Call them in."

Johann stepped to the tent flap and summoned both men.

The slouching general allowed the sergeants to stand at salute for a full minute. "By the grace of your captains," he finally said, "I will not have your balls sliced off and fed to you one at a time." He stood, though he couldn't use his height to intimidate McDonnell, who was eye-level with the general. "I consider you both an embarrassment to this army. If you wish to make me happy, please commit an additional transgression so I may proceed with the agonizing punishments I am postponing." He nodded at them. When they didn't leave, he shook his head in annoyance. "Go."

The captains turned to face Wolfe, who addressed Johann. "Why are you familiar, Captain?"

"Sir?"

"Your face, your bearing. Why are they familiar?"

"I was at Dettingen, sir, with the Landgraf's regiments. When you lost your horse."

"Of course! That bloody useless nag. What a nightmare that day was, the goddamned orders going every which way. You—" he pointed at Johann and snapped his fingers—"you're the bloody wizard with the bayonet."

"It was a hard fight, sir."

"Do your men know how to use the bayonet too?"

"I've taught them what I can."

"Keep on doing it. It could matter a great deal. Colonel Bosworth says your men do well in the woods, with ambush and counter-ambush."

"We have to know the woods, sir. They're all around us."

"Light infantry, eh? That's the answer. The goddamned tactics come straight from Xenophon, though I can't get anyone in this army to understand it. Small groups, mobile, adapt to the land, strike hard and fast." He looked up at the two captains and made a face. "Xenophon?"

"Don't know him, sir," Grant said.

"The tactics sound right, sir," Johann said.

"Hard to get in trouble agreeing with the general, eh, Captain?"

"The tactics still sound right, sir."

"They say it's fighting like the savages."

"It isn't, sir."

"How is it different?"

"The Indians won't stand and fight even, sir. They don't like that."

"Yes, I see. And we call them primitive." Wolfe pulled on an ear. "Do you know why I just did what I did, letting those fools off?"

"Because they're good men, sir," Johann said.

Disdain came back to Wolfe's feature s. "Hardly," he drawled. "It's all this drilling, Captain. The men must be drilled, of course. The landing will be a damned tricky business, and then the fighting's going to be tough, in the shadows. But the drilling's hard on real fighters. Sometimes they need a fight."

"Yes, sir."

"Next time they do it, they'll hang."

"Yes, sir."

Wolfe's smile returned. "And you and that thug of a sergeant really are settled on Waldo's land?"

"Yes, sir."

"God help you. Waldo's more of a scoundrel than Louis of France is."

CHAPTER NINE

Johann decided to leave General Wolfe's party early. He had been flattered to be among the captains invited, but when he entered the Great Pontac coffeehouse, eyes adjusting slowly to the bright light of three roaring fires and uncountable candles, several British officers had looked right past him. The experience repeated itself. He was, it turned out, invisible to British captains.

He spotted some ranger captains and moved in their direction. They, like him, seemed torn between eagerness for a friendly face and a wish not to admit their social inferiority by bunching together. At the punch bowl, he passed a word with General Waldo, who seemed equally ill at ease. The rum punch warmed Johann. He smiled as he nodded to the tune the musicians played—three fiddles, four flutes, and a drum, but they made a cheery noise. It had been five years, at least, since he'd been in a place of leisure like this. Whenever the war ended and he established his carpentry business, he would take Christiane to taverns like this in Portsmouth or Boston.

When General Waldo left, Johann took it as a signal. Sidling toward General Wolfe to bid him good evening, he passed Captain Grant of the Highlanders. They exchanged shallow nods.

Stepping into the cool evening, Johann felt at peace with the world, an odd feeling at the beginning of a campaign. Yet he felt the fellowship of the fighting men gathered in this town. It was in the air. It wasn't, perhaps, enough of a reason to justify the gore and agony of a battlefield, but it was a real thing.

Putting his hat on against the raw night, he found Wilhelm Koch standing before him, saluting. Koch, a short and intelligent man, rarely saluted. Johann's good feelings evaporated.

"I've come with bad news, sir. I'm sorry to do so—"

"Out with it," Johann said.

"It's Robert, sir."

"Sergeant McDonnell."

"Yes, Sergeant McDonnell. He's been arrested, sir."

Johann took Koch by the arm and led him down the street to where they couldn't be overheard.

Johann's heart sank as Koch related the tale. McDonnell, dissatisfied with the meal offered for the rangers on their last night before taking ship for Louisbourg, had decided that he and Koch should go fishing. As they set off in a borrowed boat, with nothing but fishing string and hooks in their hands, they were stopped by a provost marshal's patrol.

"But they let *you* go?" Johann asked.

"They did. The officer in charge announced that it was the sergeant who must answer for the crime. They were calling it theft of the boat, but then the sergeant was charged with desertion at the court-martial."

"There's already been a court-martial?"

Koch drew his mouth into a grim line. His large features and deeply-lined face looked desperate in the thin lantern light. "They tried him quick as lightning. I gave my evidence, told them we were just going to fish. We were going to return the boat in an hour, maybe less. He's to be shot in the morning. The officer in charge, he was a colonel name of Cameron, he said the fishing story was a ruse to conceal our intent to desert."

Johann was quiet for a few moments. "What will you do?" Koch asked.

"Beg, I suppose. Goddamn his eyes. All he had to do was not get arrested."

"I feel terrible about it, sir. I told him it was a bad idea, but you know how he gets, so excited like. The men are going to be frantic."

"Wilhelm, go back to the men and for God's sake, tell them my strict order is that they must do nothing. They can't help Sergeant McDonnell now."

After Koch left, Johann paced in the fog, willing the voices in the coffeehouse to move on to farewells. General Waldo was probably back on his ship for the evening, but that didn't matter. Waldo was just another Yankee, no matter how rich or how many times he called himself the Hereditary Lord of Broad Bay. He had no power in this army. Only Wolfe could help. Rain began to fall, first a few drops, then more steadily. Johann pressed himself against the coffeehouse wall, trying to squeeze under the roof's overhang. He was wet to the skin before enough officers had left that Johann resolved to try his luck.

"Dear God," Wolfe cried out when Johann came through the door and shook out his hat and coat. "What a sorry sight I behold!" Johann did his best to salute.

A disgruntled serving woman was lugging the punch bowl to the back of the coffeehouse. Three other officers slouched in chairs and sprawled across tables. Two gazed without focus into the middle distance. The third slept noisily. Wolfe was bright-eyed and cheerful, but not sloppy. He regarded Johann with amusement. "Captain, I insist on officers—even ranger officers—knowing enough to come in out of the rain, except during campaign. And we are *not* yet on campaign."

Johann held his waterlogged hat with both hands and took a step into the room. The serving woman glared at him as she returned to gather up mugs. He was dripping on her floor. "I am sorry to appear like this, but I have an urgent matter."

Wolfe looked sharply at him. "Captain, surely you know that disturbing the general during his party is a poor idea."

"Your Excellency, I waited until I thought the party over." He gestured with his hat, triggering a fresh round of drips. "It is a question of life and death, in only a few hours." Wolfe's response was to grunt softly and take a chair, stretch out his long legs and cross them at the ankles. Johann told him about McDonnell.

When he was done, Wolfe said, "Colonel Cameron's a good man."

"Sergeant McDonnell is a good man too. This is a mistake. He just was going fishing, which was stupid beyond my reckoning, I admit it, but he shouldn't be hanged for it."

"This is the sergeant who was brawling the other day?"

Johann nodded.

"Hardly the flower of our army, eh, Captain? How many chances is this one miscreant to get? This army is going on campaign, Captain." Johann nodded. "It's going to be hard, bloody, and bloody unpleasant. This is precisely when the men become nervy, when desertion becomes a real risk. We must be severe."

"He had nothing with him. No weapon, no blankets, no canteen, no food. Just fishing string and hook. No ranger, no American, would desert like that."

"In my experience, Captain, criminals are rarely intelligent. A lack of foresight and planning is a hallmark of the criminal act." Wolfe stood. "You know I can't overrule my own officer. Why would you think of asking me? No sergeant could be worth that."

Johann took one more step toward Wolfe and held out his hat. "Yes, sir. The sergeant is my friend. We've served in the guards in Broad Bay for three years. For us Germans in the settlement, he was important to us, *is* important to us. I take full responsibility for him. I will accept any discipline you think right for my failure to control him. But you must understand. We are not British soldiers. Sergeant McDonnell is my friend. He's a friend of my family."

"Well, that's a damned stupid thing. Subordinates aren't your friends. War isn't a personal matter."

Johann took a breath. "General, we're not soldiers, not like the others. We're neighbors. We care for each other's children. We fight for our homes, not your king."

Wolfe stood abruptly. His eyes were cold. "You could be cashiered for that, Captain, and worse. Don't say such a thing to me or anyone in this army again." He nodded once. "Good night."

* * * * * *

The slow drumbeat filled the harbor in the morning. Like every morning in this part of the world, it was cool, moist, and breezy. The Broad Bay rangers came ashore in boats.

Assembling them on the shingle beach, Johann said this would be the worst day of their time in the army. If they broke or cried out in any way, they would dishonor the rangers. They would dishonor Broad Bay. And they would dishonor their friend Robert without helping him. And then they would be executed for mutiny. He looked grimly at each sullen face. They knew they had to be there, to bear witness to the idiocy of this public killing. They might well desert the expedition afterwards, at the first chance they got. That would not surprise Johann. He might too.

They marched to the boggy field that had served as a drilling ground over the past weeks. The army was drawn up into three sides of a square, the fourth side open to the sea. The Broad Bay men were placed to the front of the formation's right wing. It was a prominent location, the sort usually occupied by grenadiers or Highlanders in brilliant and complex uniforms. Not by provincial rangers in drab.

Musicians, the same ones who played at General Wolfe's party the night before, stood behind the formation. They began the death march, a dirge Johann had heard too often while serving the Landgraf.

The first condemned man, from the Welsh regiment, walked before a sergeant, a corporal, and ten privates. The man stopped before a man-sized hole dug into the soft earth. The escort came to parade rest fifteen paces from him. Each of the other condemned men arrived with a similar escort, in a similar manner. McDonnell was the fourth of five.

With the prisoners in place, the musicians stopped. Thousands of uniformed, armed men stood at attention. The only sound was the breeze past their ears.

An officer walked across the open side of the formation, offering blindfolds to the condemned. McDonnell, standing erect, refused. Johann thought he had seen McDonnell's eyes sweep over the Broad Bay men, but he couldn't be sure. Johann didn't look at the other rangers. Each soldier retreated to his own thoughts. A few might feel self-righteous superiority over the condemned, and satisfaction that the army's code of conduct was to be enforced. More would feel simple gratitude to be neither one of the condemned nor in an execution party. For most, like Johann, the dominant feeling was horror. They had joined the army to kill the enemies of their king, of their nation, of their families. Yet they would start by killing their own.

Drums began a slow roll. The officer in charge called to attention the company that stood before the Welshman. More commands brought the company's guns level, aimed at the prisoner. Johann looked straight ahead, not at the execution. The cry, "Fire!" disappeared in the roar of ten muskets, a roar that triggered flinches through the army. Johann kept his eyes in front of him. He tried to control the tremble in his left hand. He waited. The acrid, sweet powder smoke blew across the Broad Bay men. Then, "Bang!" It was the pistol shot of the provost marshal to the prisoner's head, to be sure he was dead. Johann breathed. Four to go.

The officer in charge called the second company to attention. In the silence came the sound of hoofbeats. Johann forced himself to look to the harbor side of the formation. He saw the fallen Welshman, lying at an unnatural angle.

Wolfe rode a white stallion into the formation. He drew up before the remaining prisoners and held his head in an arrogant pose, his long legs reaching the bottom of his mount's deep chest. The general stood in his stirrups. "By the grace of our King George, the remaining prisoners are hereby pardoned and returned to the ranks."

Wolfe turned the horse, who pranced through the movement. "Colonel," he called in a high, ringing voice, "parade the army by the remains of this wretch." He indicated the Welshman. He turned the horse to look over the full formation, nodded to the army, and walked the horse back the way he had come.

Johann closed his eyes and breathed deeply. When he next saw McDonnell, he thought, he just might strangle the man with his bare hands.

CHAPTER TEN

†

"Look at these!" Sigrid ran toward a bed where low strawberry plants had spread. "Papa was right that they would grow here."

"Pick them all, even if they don't look ripe," Christiane said. "We don't want the rabbits getting them."

Sigrid, already kneeling with her bucket next to her, popped a bright red one into her mouth. The juice tasted sweet and lush. "Mmm," she said, "they're divine."

Christiane smiled as she reached the potato patch at Mayflower Hof. "Divine, are we? You're sounding a bit blasphemous."

"God made strawberries, didn't He? So they can be divine."

"Did He make these black flies divine also?" Christiane slapped at her neck, then pulled her shawl up over her neck. The day was cool and the sky full of clouds that ranged from silver to dark grey.

"The ways of the Lord are mysterious, I suppose. At least that's what Herr Nungesser says."

Christiane was relieved when she dug up the first potato. It was a good size. She should be able to fill at least two buckets.

Everyone in the stockade was hungry. Able to farm only four hours a week, they grew too little food. With so many off at Louisbourg, there were fewer to feed, but also fewer to hunt and trap and fish.

The Indians were growing bold. Only last week, Indian canoes had charged two Broad Bay fishermen, driving them off the river. If the guards had to protect the fishermen, too, that would reduce even further the settlers' ability to feed themselves.

When Armstrong's coaster arrived, it would take three more families to Boston. It hadn't come for weeks, which meant that the settlers hadn't shipped the firewood they needed to trade for the food they couldn't grow or hunt. Christiane suspected Armstrong was staying away because of the Indians. She had never trusted him.

Most settlers had felt better when Herr Leichter moved into the Prince of Wales stockade. Announcing that he would stay until Broad Bay's rangers returned, he took over the guards and supervised the stockades. Broad Bay needed someone to lead now, someone who could help stave off the frustrations and the isolation, but Christiane could see in Leichter's face an impatience, a desire to be somewhere else, after only two months in the settlement. He wasn't Johann. Not for her, to be sure, but also not for the others.

"Alec," she called out to the McDonnell boy, one of their guards. "Shouldn't you two spread out?" Johann insisted that the guards flank the settlers as they worked on their lands. The other guard was a boy, too, the Heilman boy, no longer chubby. They had been talking of trout fishing. "And watch the woods?" She waved at the forest behind their cabin, empty for nearly three years now and looking like it. The two boys stepped away from each other.

Christiane, halfway down the row, went back for her second bucket. She was ashamed now that she had lost her feelings for Johann until it was time for him to leave, to serve as a soldier, which he never wanted to do again. He took up his rifle without complaint. She was grateful to be with a man like that, one you could trust. The children trusted him too. Her eyes smarted to think of that. She would have to tell him that. It would please him. She tried to imagine him in front of her, his low voice covering her like a caress.

Freya's barks were rapid, angry. Christiane looked up. The dog jumped back and forth at the tree line, excitement making her voice climb.

"Sigrid!" Christiane called. "Sigrid!" The girl was at the far end of the berry patch, looking toward the frenzied dog. "Now! We go!"

The boy guards were alert, peering into the trees. "Missus," Alec called to her. "We should go." He fired a shot into the woods. Christiane didn't think he could see anything to shoot at. Right, she thought, the shot was the alarm. He had a cooler head than she did.

"Leave the berries!" Christiane called to the girl, who had stumbled and spilled her bucket. "Now!"

The four of them moved toward the path back to the stockade. "What about Freya?" Sigrid said, hesitating, looking back.

"Go!" Christiane ordered. "She's a dog."

Holding her skirts off the ground, the girl matched strides with the guards, her legs as long as theirs. When Freya's mad barking soared into an anguished cry of pain, they stopped short. "Go!" Christiane shouted. "Go!"

The path had never seemed so long. The slope after the Heilmans' farm gave Christiane a pain in her side. She couldn't keep up. Alec looked over his shoulder and waited, holding out a hand for her. "Missus, come on. We'll make it. Hurry now."

He waited for her to go by. Christiane's breathing was too loud. She wouldn't hear if anyone was behind them. When had she become so decrepit, an old lady to be protected by children? Maybe they were hurrying into an ambush? Johann always worried about ambushes. He said the Indians were clever, they fought only when they had the advantage. Was this the time when they would attack all of Broad Bay, as they had ten years before? She had to get to Walther and Hanna and Franklin.

Sigrid and the Heilman boy were a hundred paces ahead and pulling away. "Are they following?" Christiane gasped, looking over her shoulder.

"Can't tell, missus. Keep going, you're doing well."

He was so young. She put her head down and tried to go faster. As she rounded a curve in the path, she saw Sigrid fall into her mother's arms up ahead. Leichter stepped around them with two more guards carrying muskets.

Leichter trotted toward them. "That's everyone?" he called.

Christiane nodded, but her voice wouldn't come. "Yes, sir," Alec said. Leichter took Christiane by the arm as she doubled over.

"Did you see them?" Leichter asked.

Christiane was about to say no, but Alec said, "Two, in the woods. The dog alerted us. I think they got the dog."

"Freya!" Sigrid screamed, tears streaming down her face. Her mother hugged her hard and pulled her toward the settlement.

"Reload," Leichter said to Alec. He turned to Christiane. "Go on back. We need to be sure there's nothing more to watch for."

She held her arm across her middle as her breathing slowed. "You're not going back there?"

"Not all the way," Leichter said. "Far enough to be sure they didn't follow. Please, go."

"There's no other attack?"

"No. Not yet." He turned to Alec. "Get them to the stockade."

Christiane had to do her chores that afternoon with Walther and Hanna clinging to her. They had only a bit of salt fish for dinner, with some cabbage that Frau Heilman shared. Christiane thought bitterly of the potatoes and berries they had left behind. The children would have liked them.

In the evening, when Christiane walked out to empty the pot, she saw Leichter sitting before the fire in Ursula and Sigrid's room. They spoke in low voices. Sigrid was probably asleep, worn out by the scare. Christiane was surprised to hear Ursula call Leichter "Mathias." Christiane had never known his given name.

In the morning, Alec and a different guard came to take them back to Mayflower Hof. When Christiane explained that Walther and Hanna insisted on coming to look for Freya, Alec looked troubled. "Herr Leichter won't like that. Not such small ones. If there's trouble?"

Christiane said they could go by boat. They could take Johann's boat. The oars were in Johann's workroom. Alec went to get them.

When they reached the landing for Mayflower Hof, Sigrid ran up the slope, calling out, "They took the berries, and the potatoes."

"And the buckets?" Christiane asked, holding each child by the hand.

"Gone."

Christiane's anger made her walk more quickly. They stole food from the mouths of people who worked for it. Johann would say that the Indians were hungry too, but she didn't care about that. She hated the idea of them eating her potatoes.

"Wait," she called to Sigrid, who had already reached the cabin. "Wait for Alec before you go past there."

They moved together toward the tree line, searching for Freya. They walked from one end to the other, then back again. "Where is she, Mama?" Walther asked. "In the woods?"

"I don't know," Christiane said.

"We shouldn't go in there, missus," Alec said.

Christiane nodded and crouched next to Walther and Hanna. "Maybe she ran away." She couldn't say that the Indians, hungry as they were, probably took her. Or that, after being hurt, she may have crawled off to die in whatever sheltered place she could find.

"Why would she leave us?" the little boy said. "She protected us."

"Yes, she did protect us. She was a wonderful dog." Christiane fought to control her voice. "She may have been afraid. Or maybe she chased them away for us."

"Freya," Walther called out. "Freya, come home! Freya!"

When she looked up, she saw Alec turn his head, his face clouded with feeling, a boy pretending to be a man. The children hugged her as they cried. "Come now," she said, her voice now her own. "Freya wouldn't want you to cry for her. She was such a brave dog. She would expect us to be brave like her." The children nodded, each head against one of her shoulders.

"I hate them," Sigrid shouted to the sky. Then her shoulders slumped. She said quietly, "They take everything."

Christiane had planned to look for more potatoes, but she couldn't bear to stay there. None of them could.

Back in the boat, with Alec pulling the oars, Walther trailed a finger in the water even though he had been told never to do that. Christiane let him be.

"Mama," he said. "Papa is protecting us, too, isn't he?"

"Yes, Walther."

"Will he come back?"

"As soon as he can."

CHAPTER ELEVEN

Broad Bay's rangers thrilled to the spectacle of the fleet's departure from Halifax. Nearly two hundred ships stretched from one end of the horizon to the other, sails bellied out, bright pennants snapping in the wind. They included dozens of transports, more dozens of supply ships, and warships ranging from lightly-armed sloops to massive ships of the line. From the rail of their small transport, Johann thought that finally, finally the British were coming to the aid of Broad Bay. King George's fleet had many goals other than helping Broad Bay, but it would also do that.

A gale promptly scattered the fleet through the waters off Nova Scotia, though the Broad Bay men fared well enough. They knew bad weather and the water, so they weren't the ones hanging sweaty faces over putrid-smelling buckets. When calmer days arrived, they could see the beginnings of land as they headed for the fleet's rendezvous off Louisbourg.

Johann wasn't sure how the rangers would perform. Several, like Wilhelm Koch, had grey in their beards. They could wilt under the backbreaking labor involved in taking a fortress like Louisbourg.

A few, like the Wagner boy, were young and fit but still soft at heart. They all understood danger. Anyone who lived in Broad Bay knew the perils of the forest—those posed by humans, by wild animals, and by nature.

The rangers' anchors would be McDonnell, Meisner, Huffnagel, and Johann. That's how it had worked through their drilling at Halifax. It would have to keep working that way.

Johann watched for the men to show resentment, anger, any negative residue from McDonnell's near-execution. He hadn't seen it yet. The men decided that General Wolfe learned about the court-martial at the last moment, when he intervened in a triumph of British justice. Johann didn't tell them otherwise, though he thought the affair was a staged spectacle designed to terrorize the army into obedience. McDonnell had been lucky not to be the first one, the sacrificial victim.

"All right," Johann said, stepping into the circle the men formed on the ship's forecastle. "We've talked about the siege." Some of the men nodded. "Much of it won't be like the drilling we've just been through."

Koch, who felt most seared by McDonnell's near-execution, broke in. "So why do they drill us for a fight we won't have?"

"We may have fights like that, in the woods, or even out in the open. Maybe with the French, more likely with their Indians or the Canadians." Johann held his hand up to squelch further questions. "But attacking a fortress is different."

He talked about how Louisbourg had stout and irregular walls designed so defenders could rain wicked crossfires down on attackers. He had attacked fortresses in Germany. The only way to take one was for cannon to pound its walls to rubble. For the guns to do that, they had to get close. So soldiers had to dig trenches for them, zigzagging closer and closer to the fortress. He drew the pattern in the air with his hands. They had to throw up earthen defenses for each trench, then haul the artillery—often under enemy fire—to each new trench. Then they had to do it again, even closer. And again.

"But we're rangers, not ditch-diggers." This came from McDonnell. "We came here to fight and go home."

"We'll fight when the enemy sallies out to attack us, to disrupt our digging, to spike our guns. They'll ambush us when they can, sneak up at night. That'll be our fighting. But the way we win is to get the guns close and knock down the fort."

"How do they get the cannons off the ships?" Young Wagner asked this.

Several rangers looked around the deck, which had one gun at the front and one at the back. They shook their heads.

"Heavy bastards, those," McDonnell said.

Johann grinned. "These are the small ones. They'll take the big ones from the ships of the line."

"How?" Wagner asked again.

"There are engineers who know how to do that. You can watch and learn."

"How long will this take?" McDonnell asked.

Johann paused. This was the question on every ranger's mind. They wanted to get back to their families, exposed and vulnerable in Broad Bay. He believed in telling the truth, as much as he could, but he also believed in keeping their spirits up. "The fighting season is short up here," Johann said. "If we're not inside Louisbourg by September, I don't know that we'll get home this year." Shadows crossed their faces. What would their families eat through a hard winter without them? Would the St. Francis Indians sweep down on Broad Bay as they had years before? "So," Johann added, "we should dig fast, and fight hard."

* * * * * *

"Christ almighty, man," McDonnell called down to Josef Wagner, who dangled halfway out of the whaling boat that was to carry them to shore. A sailor holding the boat's tiller with one hand used his other to grab Wagner by the collar, allowing him to swing his legs over the side and roll into the boat. McDonnell, suspended from the rope ladder at the side of the ship, shouted, "Move, damn your German hide! I'd like to get in before the war's over."

"Goddamn. Can't see a fucking thing," Wagner croaked out as he scrambled forward. His recent education in army language had begun with cursing and stalled out there.

The heaving swells of Gabarus Bay brought the boat achingly close to the rangers' transport ship, then plunged it five feet below. Wagner's tumble was the result of poor timing.

McDonnell used a long leg to pull the boat closer to the transport, then leapt, landing on both feet. He pitched forward onto his hands and steadied himself. Johann followed, relying on McDonnell to catch him.

For eight days, the British fleet had loitered off the beaches of Isle Royale, miles from the Louisbourg fortress, leery of landing through heavy surf. Whenever the fog lifted enough to reveal the shore, the French fortifications seemed wider and deeper. The enemy kept digging trenches, throwing up protective embankments. They would be ready.

The Broad Bay men soon drowsed in the boat, their coats pulled tight in the damp air. It was early, barely past midnight. After so much waiting and so many false starts, they felt little of the pre-battle anxiety that steals into a soldier's heart. They carried two days' worth of bread and cheese. Each held his musket. Johann hoped they would sleep now. He allowed himself to think of Broad Bay. Not the stockade, but Mayflower Hof, with Walther and Hanna running and shouting. Franklin soon would run behind them, moving from his brother and sister to his mother and back again.

"From this godforsaken spot, a man's thoughts can travel all the way home, eh?"

McDonnell's voice was soft. He smiled in the shifting light of the boat's lantern. Johann smiled back. "Robert, you'll look after them all?"

"Like hell I will. I'll be telling the story of how the sergeant major made the French swim back to France. And you'll be bothering that skinny woman again."

Johann nodded. "I think we're going in this time." McDonnell looked the question at him. "The *Squirrel*, it's gone. So are some others." McDonnell craned his neck to look beyond Johann. They bobbed among a dozen longboats. Several ships had slipped away.

"So they've gone to shell the Frenchies."

"May they blow them to hell and back."

After another few minutes, the weak light of morning filtered into the sky. Cannon blasts jerked the rangers awake. The men grabbed for their muskets and shifted in their seats, straining to see the rocky shore. The two sailors who manned the boat's oars set to work.

The man on the tiller pointed to a rocky headland that peeked through morning mist. "We'll pull around that," he shouted to Johann. "Then straight on in. Have your men hang on. This could be dicey."

Johann crab-walked through the boat, passing the word, gripping each man by the arm or shoulder. This would be the worst, at the mercy of the sea and the French guns, able to do nothing but pray for luck. The cannon roars merged into a steady thunder, each blast swallowed by others. The wind picked up as the flotilla, dozens and dozens of boats, rounded the headland. Broad Bay's boat bounced in the surf, which flung them headlong into the bay and on toward the shore. They were near the front of the flotilla, the rockiness of the shore coming into focus.

McDonnell nudged Johann and pointed at the boat in front of them. It was the Highlanders. The sergeant who had fought with McDonnell was shouting fiercely, his beard pointed defiantly at the foreign shore. Johann was glad they wouldn't have to fight those men.

Suddenly the explosions were closer. Stabs of fire came from the land as the French opened up. The shelling from the British ships had done little good.

A cannonball splashed to their left. Another, farther over, took the head off a man, knocking his trunk back into his boat. Johann looked away. "Get down," he shouted, repeating himself in German. "Flat as you can." He tried to relax his jaw, to breathe steadily, then gave up trying. He felt the savagery of the moment. Those men were trying to kill him and his friends. They must be killed.

On an upswell, a shell plowed into the water beneath them. The boat plunged down, and a second shell whistled overhead. A man, off-balance, fell from the Highlanders' boat. No one looked for him. The boats drove on.

"Jesus," the man at the tiller shouted, "it's naught but stones ahead! Avast your rowing! Sweet Jesus, what are they thinking?" The beach was studded with rocks large and small. Johann could see nowhere to land.

The French cannon blasted as other boats slowed. The sound was like hailstones hitting the water. "Stay down," he shouted. The French had switched to grape shot, spraying the boats with scraps of fiery metal.

"Look over there," the helmsman called, slapping him on the shoulder. General Wolfe was standing in a boat two hundred yards away, waving a cane and pointing back out to sea.

"The lunatics are saying to go back."

Johann frantically scanned the shore. "There!" McDonnell shouted. "Over there!" He pointed at the Highlanders' boat and another one. They were veering right, toward the side of the headland. The shore there, below a sharp rise, seemed to have smaller rocks. Even better, it looked to be sheltered from the French lines.

Johann pointed to that place. "Follow them!" he yelled to the helmsman. "All the way in."

"Hang on," the sailor called. He swung the tiller and screamed at the men on the oars. "Pull, you worthless bastards! Pull for your lives!"

The boat rushed heedlessly at the shore, banging the men over waves that were no longer regular. One came from the right, the next from the left. The boat skidded on a crest. Johann took no notice of the cannon and rifle fire. No one could aim at them; they were moving too fast.

The sea tossed the boat forward, took a breath, then did it again. "Avast! Avast!" the helmsman called. "Ship oars."

The two boats ahead of them had crashed onto the stony shore, their soldiers clambering into calf-high water. Some used their muskets to gain their feet. Those wet weapons would be useless for hours to come. Johann gripped the gunwale with one hand and the seat with the other. He could smell the French powder smoke.

"Sweet Jesus," the helmsman shouted again as the sea heaved the boat a last time, smashing it into the Highlanders' craft. The bow stove in. The boat crumpled behind it. Rangers flew up like leaves in a hurricane. Some pitched headfirst into the water. Others became hopelessly tangled, shoved aside by splintering boards. A wave fell on the boat, drenching Johann and tilting him out the side. The cold water took his breath. His feet hit the bottom farther down than he expected. It was waist deep when the surf retreated. Shoulder height when it surged in.

"Move, you sons of Satan!" It was McDonnell's voice, rising above the clatter of musketry and booming cannon. "I'll kill anyone who's in this water five seconds from now!" He had Wilhelm Koch by the waist, holding him like a doll. Blood had drained from Koch's face. Likely a blow to the head.

Highlanders waded into the sea to pull drenched rangers onshore. Captain Grant pointed to the overhang of the rise. Johann herded the rangers to the spot, where others were sheltering. They had to climb over and through sharply pointed wooden abatis, but since French fire couldn't reach them, the men advanced.

More boats slammed onto the narrow beach. Wolfe stood in the bow of his boat and waved his cane for others to follow. He couldn't be a better target for enemy sharpshooters.

After a word with Captain Grant, Johann ordered his rangers to the right of the Highlanders and others. Officers and sergeants shouted for bayonets. The men fitted them on the end of their muskets. Muskets, cartridge boxes, powder—all were drenched. Only cold steel would work now. Since McDonnell's rifle wouldn't take a bayonet, he would have to use it as a club, then move on to the tomahawk. Not waiting for Johann's command, the rangers started up the slope.

Johann leapt up the hill, overtaking the others, using his free hand to grab anything that would propel him more quickly. Speed was key. The attackers had to keep the momentum. They had to rattle the enemy. The cannon fire was slackening. He looked back. The rangers were following, McDonnell roaring at them. More boats slammed ashore, spilling more soldiers into the sea to stagger onto land. Stinging powder smoke hung in the wet air. Wind gusts parted the smoke to allow glimpses of the defenders.

Johann didn't notice his soggy clothes or the swirling wind. He didn't hear the cannons that were pounding missiles of death in both directions. All he knew was fury. He had to get to the French lines and stop them.

He hurried the rangers to the right side of the British line that was forming on level ground. The French were trying to turn their cannon to meet the attack. Enemy soldiers ran to face the British. Time was slipping away. Finally a colonel strode before the attackers and raised his sword. Johann couldn't hear his order but understood the sword's downward slash.

"Rangers, advance," he shouted. They started at a double pace, muskets across their chests, bayonets reaching above their shoulders. The French prepared to fire a volley. The troops facing the Broad Bay men began to backpedal, trying to move at the same speed as the attackers. Emboldened, the rangers picked up their pace. Johann found himself shouting, a deep guttural roar. The other rangers picked up the shout as they reached a trot. A few French stumbled and fell, others turned and ran. The rest of the French line, now exposed on their flank, fell back as well. The British attack, sweeping up the fallen as prisoners, didn't pause until the edge of the woods.

Fire still burned inside Johann. He paced before his men, not out of breath, eager to pursue. They were getting away. The beach behind them was a jumble of boats, soldiers wading through the surf and climbing over the wooden abatis. Wolfe, shouting, red-faced, was forming up another contingent to attack the length of the French line, but they would be too late. The French, as many as two thousand, were streaming back into the woods, back to their fortress. If they had found their courage and turned at the edge of the woods, they would have had a heavy advantage, but now they were lost. Johann felt the fire inside begin to flicker and die.

"What are they waiting for?" McDonnell called.

Johann shook his head. The attack had won the day, but not the campaign. The siege would be a long one.

Johann looked over the rangers. Most were sopping wet, with the jangled look of men who recently feared for the lives. He didn't see Wilhelm Koch. He walked over to McDonnell, who was pointing at the fleeing enemy and laughing with two of the men. He drew his sergeant aside.

"Koch?" Johann asked.

McDonnell shook his head.

CHAPTER TWELVE

The sun warmed Christiane as she sat at the edge of the river, knitting a mitten and keeping an eye on Franklin. It had already been a long day. The baby, getting new teeth, was crying off and on. Not as bad as before, but he was hard to calm. They had walked to Mayflower Hof with two guards, but the hoe handle broke as she worked the potato plants, so she had to lean far over, which made her back ache. The children had quarreled, and there was only cabbage for dinner. The little ones didn't complain, but she could see they wanted more. She did too. She sighed. She must enjoy this bright summer evening, she told herself. It was early July, so the flies were mostly gone.

The baby had spent recent days hauling himself upright and staggering forward, then stopping and looking around with wonder. For this moment, he seemed happy to pick apart an old doll made from straw and cloth that his sister gave him. Hanna had judged it too old and tattered to retain. Christiane could hear the two older children behind her, screaming with a half-dozen others in a frenzied game of tag.

Walther, face flushed bright red, threw himself on the ground next to her. "No one can catch me," he announced.

Christiane smiled at him. He was still on the small side, but well put together. "Are you so fast?"

He scrunched up his face, thinking. "Not so fast, but I twist and turn a lot." He watched his mother's fingers move, quick and sure with the blue yarn. "Who are those for?"

"Papa."

"The last ones you made were for him."

"Your papa works hard. He goes through a great many mittens, all through the winter."

Walther picked up a rock and tossed it toward the river, but it fell short. "Can the next ones be for me?"

Christiane put her needles down and ran to the edge of the water, grabbing Franklin's arm and spinning him around on one foot before he reached the river. He looked up and laughed. She pointed him toward Walther. He took the suggestion and set off in that direction. Christiane followed and resettled herself.

"Can they?" Walther said. "Can the next ones be for me? I work hard too."

"Yes, the next ones will be for Walther."

Hanna ran to her mother and grabbed her neck, falling against her shoulder and crying. Christiane stroked the girl's hair with her free hand and asked what the problem was.

"It's my whistle, the one Herr Leichter made for me," Hanna said over her shoulder. "It's gone."

"Where have you looked for it?"

"I had a special hiding place, where Papa works. It's not there!" Hanna wailed.

"Let's go and look again," Christiane said, setting Hanna up on her own. The girl wiped her forearm over her eyes as her mother gathered up the knitting and picked up the baby.

They searched the room where the family lived and the one Johann used for carpentry, including Hanna's hiding hole under a piece of wood. The whistle was gone. "You didn't leave it outside, did you?" Christiane asked.

"No," Hanna insisted, "I put it in my hiding place. I always do. Herr Leichter said I should blow it if the Indians come. Now I won't be able to stop them, and they'll come and take us all."

"You couldn't stop them anyway," Walther said. He had tagged along during the search. "You're just a girl."

Christiane turned to him. "Do you know anything about this?"

"No," he said emphatically, folding his arms over his chest.

"My sweet," she said to Hanna, stroking her hair. "If there's an Indian attack, I know you can scream just as loud as any whistle." The girl wasn't mollified. Christiane announced it was time for tired children to get ready for bed.

Inside their room, she supervised the washing up and using of the pot, then had them say their prayers.

"Can I do it, Mama?" Walther asked. Christiane nodded.

Hanna started to cry. "I want to do it," she sniffled.

"You can choose the story," Christiane said.

The two older children knelt and put their hands together. Christiane lit a candle next to the bed. She pulled Franklin into her lap and rocked him.

"Thank you, Lord, for the blessings of this day," Walther began. "And please God, bless Papa and the other soldiers. And please God, care for the souls of Peter and Richard and Freya."

"Can I pick the story now, Mama?" Hanna asked. Christiane nodded. Hanna picked the story of the little tailor, her favorite. Walther flounced down on a far corner of the bed in protest.

"One day," Christiane began, "the little tailor fixed himself a meal of bread and jam, only to find his meal covered with hungry flies. He told the flies to leave. When they didn't, he attacked them with a cloth, killing seven at once. Proud of his triumph, he printed a sash for himself proclaiming, 'Seven with one blow!' and set off to tell the king."

"But he only killed flies," Hanna said.

"Wouldn't it be wonderful," Christiane said, "to kill so many of our flies like that?"

Christiane told how the king was impressed with the tailor's exploits and promised that if he could also kill two giants who were terrifying the people, he could marry the king's beautiful daughter.

"He's going to trick the king," Hanna said.

Christiane shushed her, then said, "So the little tailor found the giants asleep in a forest. He climbed a tree and dropped rocks on each of them until they woke up, then he hid so each blamed the other. After they went back to sleep, he did it again. And they blamed each other again. And then a third time. That time, the giants got so angry that they began to fight. They ripped trees up from the ground and smashed each other with them. Finally, they killed each other. So the tailor married the king's daughter and became king himself."

Hanna was almost asleep when the story was finished. "Papa tells it better," Walther complained. "He tells about all the fighting."

Christiane hummed until Hanna was asleep and Franklin was nearly so. She lay the baby down and went to Walther. His eyes were wide open, his hands gripping something. Christiane forced his fingers open. Hanna's whistle. During their search, through all of Hanna's tears, he had said nothing.

"Why you bad boy," she whispered to him harshly. "How could you do that to your sister? You know how much she cared about that whistle?"

He pushed his lips out in defiance and stared back at her. "I'm not sorry."

Christiane's hand flashed out and took his ear between finger and thumb. She pressed her thumbnail into the flesh, knowing how that hurt. Her mother had done it to her. Walther hunched his shoulder toward her hand, a useless act of self-defense. Pain screwed up his face, and tears ran from his eyes, but he made no sound.

Christiane let go. "Why?" she whispered. "Why do such a mean thing to your sister?"

Walther looked at her. "Papa told me," his voice caught with a small sob. "He said I should take care of you. It should've been my whistle." He sobbed again. "Papa didn't tell Hanna to take care of you."

Christiane held him until he stopped crying. "That was a mean trick, Walther. You must give the whistle back to your sister and ask her forgiveness, and also ask God to forgive you. And you must be sorry or God can't forgive you."

The little boy nodded. Then he hugged her fiercely and said he was really truly sorry. She helped him move over next to Hanna. She whispered to him that she would ask Herr Leichter to carve another whistle for him.

His eyes grew wide. "But Mama—"

"Yes?"

"Will you kiss Herr Leichter to get it?"

"Why would you ask that, my little lamb?"

"Aunt Ursula does, I saw her, and Sigrid's papa is away, like our papa."

Christiane placed a hand on his cheek. "They're just friends. And it's not the same." She sighed. "Uncle Fritz has been away for so long."

"He could be dead. That's what Dieter said."

"We don't know about Uncle Fritz," she said, "but we know about your papa." She tried to smile. "He's only been away for three months, and we know exactly where he is."

"He's fighting the French."

"Yes."

"And he's coming home when he's done."

"Yes. He's coming home when he's done."

The boy's eyelids started to droop. His lips drew together. "Mama?"

"Yes."

"I miss Freya."

"I do too, little lamb."

Christiane knitted for a while in the dark, her fingers, like always, knowing how long each row should be. Franklin cried out. She held her breath, but he settled again. The others slept. Franklin cried out again. Hanna sat up and looked around, but Christiane got her back to sleep.

She blew out the candle and lay down with them. Her thoughts raced up to Louisbourg, through the forests where Frenchmen and Indians lay in ambush. She thought of her hungry, unruly, frightened children. Wasn't she just as hungry and unruly and frightened?

She should pray, she thought. She rose, being careful not to brush Franklin. She knelt beside the bed and rubbed her face with her hands. Feelings swirled through her. She prayed every night for Johann to be spared, for the children to be spared, and for the souls of her lost children. But tonight she should pray for more. Tonight she would pray for God to let her love again.

CHAPTER THIRTEEN

Johann liked the spot McDonnell had picked, about five hundred paces past the small bridge over the shallow barachois. It was well past where most of the British ambushes had been staged and far enough from the fortress that Frenchmen on patrol would be thinking about their target—the guns northeast of the harbor—not about ambush. For weeks, British mortars and cannon had pounded Louisbourg, dropping deadly shells and cannonballs on the people huddled inside the walls. The guns still were too distant to smash the walls. They had to be closer. Men were digging new positions in front of the tidal flats, but still the guns on the heights thundered day and night, each blast shattering the air.

For this action, only fourteen Broad Bay men would fight. Three were down with the bloody flux, the soldier's companion, and two more had passed out that afternoon while digging gun positions near the Hill of Justice. Poor Wilhelm Koch, of course, was gone. Three British mortars boomed in quick succession to Johann's left. A French gun answered from the Dauphin redoubt. The blasts made it hard to listen for troops sallying out from the fort.

The Broad Bay men flanked the path from the bridge, half on either side. Johann's contingent was on the high side. If the French stayed on the path, Johann would strike after they had moved past. Then McDonnell's group would rise from the marsh side while the Royal Rifles swept in from the front.

The moon was still down, leaving the country dark. Fog shrouded the marsh fitfully, creeping onto the land, then slipping back to sea. Johann worried that the damp would soak into the rangers' powder. They might have to turn to the bayonet early.

He heard something. Men. Men trying to be quiet. The French had left the path and were working through the high ground, coming directly at him. They must have some Indians or Canadians with them. Johann gave the warning, the call of the cardinal. Each ranger should be burrowed down into a shallow pit he had dug for himself. Johann prayed that no enemy would stumble over a concealed ranger and trigger the engagement in a scattershot way. That would turn McDonnell's plan into shambles.

Figures loomed before him. Indians in buckskins led a column of French. The column was narrow enough that they shouldn't walk over any rangers, but they were many, at least a hundred. Those Royal Rifles better arrive fast or the rangers would be overwhelmed. Johann realized he was holding his breath. He exhaled.

The end of the column was almost even with him. Johann hoped for a cannon roar to mask the attack, confusing the French, but he couldn't wait very long for it. After the last Frenchman passed him, he counted to ten. He counted to ten again. No cannon. Giving the cardinal call, he rose to one knee and aimed at the sergeant trailing the column. He fired.

More musket shots followed. Johann saw muzzle flashes on his right. McDonnell's men must have seen the column and stolen up the hill to join Johann's group.

"Form up," he shouted as he reloaded, then repeated it in German. McDonnell's tall form topped the rise where the rangers were lining up, four feet apart, facing the French. "Fire," Johann shouted. The volley rang out. "Advance!"

They moved at a quick step, bayonets fixed, with McDonnell and Johann one step behind. A swale slowed them. A ranger tripped and fell. McDonnell, cursing, lifted the fallen man and shoved him forward.

They risked losing the shock of the attack. Voices came from the French column. They were forming their line to get a volley off. This moment would test every ranger. The enemy would fire at them. Each ranger could only hope they missed. "Rangers, spread," he called, adding space between the men. This wasn't a maneuver that the Landgraf's soldiers used, but Johann had introduced it for the rangers.

He ground his teeth. Why didn't they fire? Their officers were shouting. They might be waiting to maximize the volley's impact. Maybe they were falling into chaos, the ones in front not knowing what was happening behind, the ones behind in panic. The rangers advanced.

"Now!" he screamed. The men began to jog up a gentle incline. McDonnell moved to the front and picked up the cry. "Run, you bastards!" he shouted, his rifle over his head. Ragged shots came from the French lines, not a full volley. McDonnell staggered, switched his rifle to his other hand, and resumed the advance. Johann bellowed a war cry. No bullet had hit him.

Now in front, Johann singled out a tall grenadier in a light-colored jacket. He feinted high with his blade, then dropped it low and ducked under the man's thrust. Rising, he drove the blade under the grenadier's ribs. The impact drove the Frenchman back onto the ground. Johann turned the musket in his hands to tear up the man's insides, then put his foot on the man's chest to pull out.

McDonnell, next to him, warded off a blow from a clubbed musket. Johann thrust his bayonet into the side of that Frenchman, ripping the blade out his front. McDonnell had dropped his rifle and pulled out his tomahawk. He set on another Frenchman.

A musket volley exploded in front of them. The Royal Rifles. French voices shouted orders. They were forming on the path, sorting themselves into a double line.

"Down!" Johann shouted, hoping the other rangers could see the danger. He dropped to the ground, where he found McDonnell already prone. The powder flashes from the French volley showed that his friend was hurt. He crawled to him.

"Where?"

"My arm." He shouted. "Those bloody bastards shot me! Goddamn them to hell!"

By feel, Johann found the wound, above the elbow. McDonnell's sleeve was slick. He grunted in pain. Johann thought the arm was probably smashed. He tore a strip from his shirt and tied it off above the wound. He twisted his ramrod through the knot to tighten it.

"Jesus, you bloody German butcher," McDonnell muttered. "Don't need you trying to kill me too."

Johann called Josef Wagner over. He told the man to hold the ramrod tight, then headed toward the path. The French were retreating to the fortress. The Royal Rifles had reached as far as the rangers but stopped there. They weren't pursuing the way they should have. They could inflict the greatest damage in pursuit, but only the Rifles had the numbers to do it. The rangers were too few.

Johann called for his men to form before him. Counting McDonnell and Wagner, they were only thirteen. Someone was missing. Keller. Johann told the men to find him, then returned to McDonnell.

A crescent moon had risen to the horizon, offering dim illumination. McDonnell looked to be at the door of the next world. "Josef," he said to Wagner, "see if the Rifles have a stretcher." Johann took over the tourniquet. If McDonnell was lucky, the arm was all he would lose.

A horseman rode up. "A fine fight, Captain."

Johann looked up. It was Wolfe.

"Thank you, sir," Johann said, "I'm sorry, I can't release this wound."

"Yes, yes. There's a wagon coming with other wounded. I'll send it up here." The general nodded. "A fine fight."

* * * * * *

"Jesus, man, you look worse than me." McDonnell's words were brave, but his voice was weak. He'd been in the hospital tent for two fever-ridden weeks after a surgeon sawed off his right arm below the shoulder. He huddled under three blankets. Thirty men filled the tent to bursting. Artillery rumbled in the distance. Louisbourg's walls had begun to crack. For days now, the British guns had never been silent.

"Trenches still must be dug, and also," Johann touched his stomach and shrugged.

"Ah, Captain Quickstep has made a visit." McDonnell smiled and closed his eyes. He opened them again. "How long have you been here?"

Johann shrugged. "A wee bit."

"Don't even try, laddie. No one's ever going to think you're a Scot. You're too small."

"How does it go?"

"It goes. I guess I'm getting better. Thinking about how to be a one-armed carpenter. And the wrong damned arm, to boot."

"You'll do it. Make Alec and the others do the lifting."

"I've been thinking that way. Three inches to the side, and that ball would have barely singed my sleeve."

"Three inches the other way, and we'd have buried you."

McDonnell shrugged with his eyebrows and looked over at Keller, who was asleep in the next bed. In Broad Bay, he was a fisherman with four children. "Better off than that poor bugger. Took his leg clean off, they did." McDonnell wagged a finger at Johann. "Don't sit here too long or those sons of bitches with the saws'll cut something off."

"They didn't get *that*, too, did they?"

McDonnell smiled. "By God, Captain, that may be the first smutty remark I've ever heard from your proper lips." McDonnell shifted. Johann pushed a folded cloth behind the man's head, propping it up. "I've told Keller that we should go into business together. I'll lend him a leg if he'll lend me an arm." McDonnell had made the same joke during Johann's last three visits. He squinted out the tent opening. "What time of day is it? It's always grey in here. I can never tell."

"Afternoon. After two."

"Since when do ranger captains get afternoons off? Is this a Sunday?"

"General Wolfe can't think of any holes we need to dig right now, so we're at liberty."

A tremendous explosion sounded, making the ground shudder. Cheers came from all parts of the camp. The patients in the tent—those who could—began to stir. "Go on," McDonnell said. "Find out what it is."

Only a few steps from the tent, Johann saw the fortress and harbor. Orange flames were swallowing a French warship whole, turning it into a floating torch. After watching for a few moments, Johann hurried back inside.

"They've set afire one of the French ships of the line," he reported to McDonnell. "It's a sight to warm the soul!"

McDonnell started to roll onto his side, using his good arm to pull the blankets off.

"Here, here," Johann said, restraining him, shocked by how McDonnell's bulk had dwindled. "I don't think the doctors want you out in the damp."

"Bugger the doctors," McDonnell said. "I'm going to watch those bastards burn." He pushed his right shoulder forward to emphasize the absent arm. "I'll see them pay for this."

Johann put his friend's moccasins on and draped blankets over him. He crouched by McDonnell's side to lever him upright. McDonnell swayed when he stood, then steadied. He nodded. With his free hand, Johann grabbed the stool he had sat on. The two men slowly sidled between the patient cots and out onto the slope. Johann positioned McDonnell on the stool.

The spectacle in the harbor was hypnotic. Flames, fed by the pitch and tar in the ship's planking, soared hundreds of feet high. The British guns fell silent for the first time in days as the French sailors hurried to contain the inferno. Small boats circled the burning hulk to retrieve survivors, but the fierce heat kept them at a distance. A groan rose from the crowd on the slope when the blaze detonated the French ship's guns, sending ball and shot into the boats of the rescuers, capsizing several.

"Jesus," McDonnell said in a low voice. "It's awful, ain't it?"

The burning hulk drifted toward another giant ship. The flames leapt across the water, seeking new fuel. A violent explosion blew out the quarterdeck of the second ship as its sailors fled in lowered boats. The wind brought the sharp smell of woodsmoke and the sulphuric odor of black powder. No rain came to slow the flames, which ran up rigging, gleefully spreading across furled oilcloth sails.

Johann and McDonnell stayed out on the slope until late afternoon, though Johann made several visits to the latrine. When a third ship of the line ignited, McDonnell shook his head. "Bastards'll have to quit now," he said. "They can't have any more stomach for this."

Johann, seated on the ground, agreed. The fortress walls were falling down. The fires on the massive ships were destroying nearly two hundred French cannon. And the people in Louisbourg, blockaded for six weeks, had to be starving. "They'd better surrender," Johann said. "If they keep resisting, we'll give no quarter. They'll be massacred."

McDonnell made a face. "Why would we do that?"

"Rules of war. A town under siege that doesn't surrender—you give no quarter. Kill everything that moves."

One side of the Scot's mouth curled up in disbelief. "Bloody rules of war. Only English bastards could think up a rule like that." He shook his head. "I'm worn out."

Back inside, Johann held a bowl of soup while McDonnell, sitting on the side of his cot, spooned with his left hand. He ate with appetite, putting away a half-loaf of bread. He gestured with his crust. "That means we'll be going home," he said. "I'm going to see Maggie, find out what she thinks of a one-armed man. You can find out if that skinny woman hasn't done better for herself while we've been gone."

Explosions from the third ship punctuated his statement. Johann held out the soup for McDonnell to sop up with his bread. He felt a spring inside his stomach begin to unwind.

McDonnell fell asleep a few minutes after eating. Johann pulled the blankets up snug. He stopped with Keller for a moment. Sweat beaded on the man's forehead. His eyes were unfocused, but then he looked at Johann.

"Captain," Keller said.

"How goes it?" Johann took the man's hand. Keller didn't answer, lost again in his fever. Johann helped him drink some water, then left.

Johann lingered on the slope, watching the last French ship burn to the water line. He had thought so often of Broad Bay, the children and Christiane, Mayflower Hof, but he'd never allowed himself to think about going home, not until this moment. Maybe soon.

He and the other rangers, they had done their part. No one had asked them if they wanted a war with France, a war that threatened their homes, homes they had gambled everything for, homes they had to abandon for miserable stockades. He had come to America so he would no more be a slave to the whims of princes, yet here he stood at this cold, boggy outpost of two empires, having killed again, having risked his life again.

He was here, he told himself, to make his home safe. The French would lose Louisbourg, then Quebec. Then peace with the Indians would come.

He ached for home.

CHAPTER FOURTEEN

†

The harvest was thin again. Many potatoes had white mold spots. At least half were so blighted that Christiane threw them aside to dump in the forest. Ursula and Sigrid were building similar piles where they worked. Farms needed daily attention, not two-hour spasms every few days. Yet Christiane was grateful for the bright day, how the piercing blue sky and cool sun and fresh breezes acted as a solvent to dissolve her fears. The children chased each other near the river. Franklin poked the ground with a stick, mimicking the women's work, but then an animal turd attracted his attention. Christiane swooped over to dispose of it. She spat on his hand and wiped it, then brought him closer to her.

"Have you thought," she called to Ursula, "how we've crossed the ocean, built homes in the wilderness, yet we live as our mothers and grandmothers lived?"

Ursula looked up from her row of straggling plants and brushed a forearm across her brow. "My mother would take one look at our stockade and get on the next ship to Germany."

Christiane smiled. She straightened to check on Franklin and run her eyes over the other children. She turned back to her work. "I think about this. Here we live in a village, and we never leave it. We dig for potatoes. We have babies. We care for each other and for the sick and for those who die. Our men go to war. We pray and we hope." She shrugged.

"We have the lives of women," Ursula said. "But think what we've seen and done. They are wonders. We saw the great city of Amsterdam. We crossed the ocean. Did our mothers and grandmothers do that? We have seen and lived in a wild place, where the animals and Indians roam. And we have land. Our children will have land." She hacked her hoe into the ground. Both women were thinking of Fritz.

A boom echoed up the river, a much bigger boom than any musket.

"Armstrong," Ursula said. "He may have news."

Christiane kept digging, a cold chill seizing her.

"Christiane," Ursula said, standing, "it may be about Louisbourg." She called the children to get ready to leave, then told Sigrid to put away the tools. The guards arrived and lifted the buckets of potatoes. Christiane still knelt on the ground. "Christiane, we must go."

"Oh, Ursula," she said, dropping her head. "I'm so frightened. If only one letter had come."

Ursula took her arm. "We must go."

The guards rowed with energy, but the passengers were quiet with anxiety. At the landing, the settlers buzzed, their eyes on Armstrong's skiff as it left his coaster. He had come only twice that summer. He must have news.

From a hundred yards away, Armstrong waved his hat and shouted words they couldn't make out. When he had halved the distance from shore, he called again, "Louisbourg's fallen! Louisbourg's fallen!"

The settlers forgot their fatigue and hunger. They cheered, called thanks to God, held their arms skyward. Walther circled the crowd, screaming and blowing the new whistle Leichter had made for him, Hanna just behind with hers. Christiane blinked nervously and kissed Franklin. She held him tight and waited.

When the grinning Armstrong reached the dock, the cheers came again. Brandishing a letter, he walked quickly to Leichter, who broke the seal and scanned it. He stepped up on the dock and held his arms out for quiet.

"This is from General Waldo in Louisbourg," Leichter said in German, then waved to Nungesser to come forward. "The letter's in English, so I'll read it that way, and Herr Nungesser will translate."

He cleared his throat and began. The men and women, eager for each word, inched forward. Waldo began with a description of the military campaign. The landing on the shore, the bombardment, the fighting, the burning fleet, the final surrender. Christiane heard the words, understanding the English, then the German. But what of their men? What of Johann?

"The men from Broad Bay," Leichter read, "have fought with honor and bravery." When Nungesser translated the sentence, many heads bobbed. Tears tracked down cheeks. Christiane thought her knees might give way. "They landed with the first troops and were with the opening assault. They skirmished successfully against the enemy and were stout workmen for digging the works for our cannon." The tension tightened as Nungesser translated. What of their men?

"I am sad to report that the valiant Wilhelm Koch will not come home. We buried him on a hill here on Cape Breton Island with other soldiers who died for King George." All eyes turned to Frau Koch, a small woman with a steady disposition who had lived alone since the rangers had left for Louisbourg. Two women went to her.

"The other Broad Bay rangers," Leichter began again, "though they may have been wounded or sickened, will return." Christiane dropped to her knees. Blind with tears, she hugged Franklin. "We do not know when," Leichter read. "The fortress must be occupied and defended, and the regular troops will move on to attack Quebec. I hope they will be home before the winter, but we do not know if they will be."

"What's wrong, Mama?" Walther asked. She reached for him, then for Hanna.

"Nothing's wrong, lambie. Papa will come home. Just as he said he would."

The settlers lingered on the shore, digesting the news. A woman called out to Leichter. "Is this peace?" Another shouted,

"Can we move out of the stockades and back to our farms?" A man answered, "Yes, it's all over now. We've won. We can move back."

Leichter held up his hands. He switched back to German. "This is a wonderful victory," he said. "I expect that our trade will be better, since the French privateers have lost their home in Louisbourg." He looked at Armstrong, who nodded in agreement, though he understood no German. "But the war is not over. The king's troops are going to attack Quebec. There is no word of a peace between Britain and France." The people stood silently, taking in the deflating words. "No, we may not move out of the stockades. Nothing has changed the danger we face. The Indians—especially the Indians—haven't been defeated."

By dinnertime, the settlers regained their spirits. A great victory. The men coming home. In a community that had known so little good news for so long, this required a celebration. Leichter organized a bonfire. The women planned a supper of potato soup, fish, and sauerkraut. Heinrich Weber promised to bring out his barley beer, with small portions for the children.

Christiane, feeling lighthearted, cut potatoes for the soup with Sigrid. "Where's your mother?" she asked.

Sigrid pulled a lock of hair from her face with her smallest finger and tucked it behind her ear. She's old enough to wear a cap, Christiane thought. "Mama says she's not feeling well."

Christiane put down her knife and picked up Franklin. She found Ursula in her room, combing the hair of her younger girl, Herta. Christiane sat facing them. "You all have such beautiful hair," she said. Herta giggled, then squirmed as her mother started her braids.

"Won't you help with the soup?" Christiane asked.

"I don't think so," Ursula said.

"I should have thought of you, out there." Ursula kept braiding the little girl's hair. "But you don't want to miss this. There will be singing and maybe even dancing around the fire."

"Dancing, Mama?" the little girl said. "Like princesses do?"

"Yes, dear, though we have no ballroom for our dancing." She finished the braid and tied it off with a piece of red ribbon that had faded to pink.

"Can I dance?" Herta asked.

"Yes, you may dance all night."

After the girl had left, Christiane said, "And you may dance all night also."

Ursula shook her head. "You know how people talk."

"They will talk whether you dance or you don't."

"I can't have people calling me a whore when Sigrid is just coming into her age. What family will let their son marry her?"

Christiane giggled. "If you mean Maggie McDonnell, there's no one less likely to call you that, or to talk behind your back. She says you and Herr Leichter should marry." She grabbed her friend's hand when she saw the unhappiness in her face. "But tonight, just come be with us. We'll eat and sing and give thanks, and dance if we wish. Let Sigrid and Herta enjoy this party without worrying about you. We will all be sad if you don't." Ursula put her other hand on Christiane's. "Good," Christiane said. "Now come and bring some salt. We'll have to sneak it into the soup when Frau Krause isn't looking."

As Ursula gathered her shawl and looked for the salt, a cricket chirped in the room's far corner. "See," Christiane said. "At last, it's our time for good luck!"

* * * * * *

When Christiane woke up the next morning, she pulled the blanket up and shifted closer to Hanna for warmth. Outside, the stockade was quiet. Her neighbors seemed to think that their celebration included a late start to this day. She accepted the idea and slid back toward sleep. Franklin woke them all a few minutes later, needing to be cleaned. Christiane sent Walther for water. She gave Hanna the night bucket to empty.

She was alone with Franklin when the shot came. It made her jump. More shots followed. She wrapped the baby and ran to Ursula's room, where she pushed in the door. "Can you take him? The others are outside." She handed over Franklin without waiting for an answer.

Halfway across the courtyard she was shouting their names. "Walther! Hanna!" There were more shots still. It must be an attack. Half of the stockade gate hung open. Heinrich Berger, barely sixteen, was holding it, his musket at his feet. He waved for people to run inside. If the gate was open, the attack must be at another stockade.

She ran past the gate. Alec McDonnell, his face bright red, had Hanna in one arm, his rifle in the other hand. Walther was behind them, blowing his whistle and struggling to keep up. She ran to lift him, then turned back into the courtyard, his whistle deafening one ear. Heinrich Berger called out, "Anyone else out there?"

"Close it, close it," came a panicky voice from the watch platform above. "No one else in sight!"

Alec placed Hanna on the ground. "It's the Cumberland stockade," a voice, still on edge, called down from the watch platform. "It's a real attack."

"How many?" Alec asked.

"I can't see. They're not showing themselves."

Alec raced to the gap between the gates and peered out.

"Thirty?" came the voice again.

"More," Alec answered. "Listen to all the shots."

Christiane took the children to Ursula's room. She stopped by Johann's workroom for his rifle and cartridge box. Back in the courtyard, she heard no more shots. "Where's Herr Leichter?" she called up to the watch platform.

"Out there," came the voice, still tense.

When she stepped sideways, Christiane could see that the guard was Jurgen Wolff, a shoemaker with five children. He was probably the oldest guard in the stockade. Johann said he was no soldier.

She ran to Alec at the gate and handed over the rifle and cartridge box. "If you need them. How else can I help?"

"Gather any other cartridge boxes and pass them out," he said, not taking his eye from the gap in the gate. "Powder too. Tomahawks. Every weapon."

When she turned, she found Walther behind her holding a stick. "Come," she said, holding out a hand. They ran to each stockade room and demanded weapons, ignoring the anxious questions that came at them. Their search yielded two cartridge boxes and four tomahawks. She sent Walther to Alec with a tomahawk. She gave the cartridge boxes to the men on the platform, then took the other tomahawks to men who stood at the rifle loops that were cut into the stockade walls. She counted fourteen defenders.

"Fire out there," came Jurgen Wolff's voice. "Past Cumberland." Christiane's stomach tightened. That's where Mayflower Hof was. "Two fires now! No, three!"

Shots exploded from all sides around them. A child screamed, then stopped abruptly. "Shoot at their powder smoke!" Wolff shouted. His voice was under control now. "Shoot only at targets! Be thrifty with your powder."

The settlers began to fire carefully placed shots. Frau Wolff and another woman came into the courtyard from different rooms. Each carried a water bucket. "Yell if you need anything," Frau Wolff called, crouching down.

"Yes, over here too," the other shouted.

Christiane ran to Alec, who leaned back against the gate to reload his rifle. "Here," she said, taking it from him. "I know how." He reached for Johann's rifle and sighted down its long barrel.

She tore the cartridge with her teeth, then stood to place the ball in the muzzle and press it home with the ramrod. She knelt again, trying not to rush, flinching when Alec fired so close to her. She poured the powder into the pan and cocked the hammer, remembering to close the frizzen. The powder smell was strong. She exchanged rifles with Alec and started again.

Sporadic firing kept up. "They're staying in the woods," Wolff shouted. "Only shoot at a target."

Frau Wolff cried out. A guard on the stockade's north side had slumped against the stockade wall. He was bleeding. She ran to him and pulled him down on his back. Christiane followed. Blood pulsed from his head. Frau Wolff tore linen and pressed it against his wound, cradling him.

Christiane picked up the guard's musket. She checked the charge. She stood and rested the muzzle in the rifle loop, scanning the woods that began only fifteen feet from the palisade. One edge of the loop was splintered, probably by the ball that struck the guard. She shifted the muzzle from side to side. Her heart thudded. Control your breath, Johann always said. She remembered the gun's recoil, how it bruised her shoulder. Shots continued, some from the stockade, some from the attackers.

There. A flash of skin, next to a tree trunk. She pulled the trigger, and the barrel flew up. A man ran from the spot toward the river. Missed. She spun around to reload. She felt a hot anger. "What can I do?" Frau Wolff asked, blood splashed on her skirt and apron. The guard on the ground was grey, dead.

"The cartridges from his pouch."

Christiane fumbled the ramrod. She crouched to pick it up.

"Buckshot?" Frau Wolff said, holding it in the palm of her hand.

"Yes. Good." Johann said that buckshot didn't carry far but didn't require good aim. The woods were close. When the musket was loaded, she studied the forest again.

A musket flashed, not twenty feet away. A ball cracked into the palisade next to her head. She fired back. A voice yelped. She saw an Indian run deeper into the woods, favoring one side.

The gunfire was slowing. Christiane reloaded her musket and watched again through the loop. Five minutes passed. Then ten.

"Jurgen?" a man shouted from the back side of the stockade. "Where are they?"

"I think they're gone. There's two more farms burning. No, three. Maybe more. I can't be sure."

"Shall we stand down?"

"Stay where you are."

Christiane looked over at the dead guard. His blood had pooled in the dirt next to Frau Wolff. It was Alfred Shuler. In the spring, he made a doll for Hanna. When she turned to scan the forest, her vision blurred for a moment, then cleared. Her arms and shoulders ached from holding the heavy musket.

Wolff called into the courtyard. "Every other man stand down," he called. "We'll take turns. Fifteen minutes on, fifteen minutes off. I'll call the time. No one leaves the stockade."

Christiane helped Frau Wolff to her feet. They embraced quickly. "I'll get Frau Shuler," the other woman said. Christiane turned from the dead man. She took some water from Frau Wolff's bucket, elated to be alive. One hand shook. She hoped it was over. When she wiped her mouth with her apron, the fabric came away smeared with gunpowder.

They stayed at their stations for two hours, until Leichter came up the path with a guard. He stepped over an Indian corpse above the boat landing. "That was young McDonnell's doing," Wolff called down. "Good man in a fight."

Leichter gathered the settlers. The Indian band, with a few Frenchmen, were part of a large group from Canada that attacked Fort Georges the night before but were driven off. They caught a woman and her child outside the Cumberland stockade, killing and scalping them. They burned farms north along the river and killed some cows and sheep. They singled out the sawmills and gristmills, burning and smashing them. He said that Broad Bay would remain on alert through the night, but the attack was probably over. Parties were heading out to gather up the slaughtered livestock. There would be meat for dinner.

Leichter pulled Alec McDonnell aside as the meeting broke up. “That was your shot? That killed the savage?”

Alec nodded.

“The scalp is yours. The governor will pay a pretty penny for it.”

Alec looked around uncertainly. “I don’t know.” Maggie McDonnell entered the gate, carrying her youngest and leading the other four. They had run from their farm to the Governor Shirley stockade when the fighting started. She trotted the last few steps to Alec. He shied from the hand she reached out to smooth his fair hair.

“You decide,” Leichter said, and stepped away. “They’re taking two scalps down at the Cumberland.”

“Decide what?” Maggie asked. Alec explained. It could be a lot of money, he said.

She looked out the gate at the corpse, then back at her son. “If you’re old enough to kill him, you’re old enough to decide.”

Alec took a breath. “I don’t want it.”

His mother smiled and sighed. “God help us. Another poet in the family.”

Jurgen Wolff found Christiane on a bench in Ursula’s room. Franklin was climbing on her lap while Hanna washed the black powder from her mother’s chin. “You’re a brave girl, Frau Overstreet,” Wolff said. “I thank you. You don’t need to stand the watches.”

She nodded.

“I should see to Alfred,” Wolff said, then began to leave.

“No one else?” Ursula asked.

Wolff shook his head.

CHAPTER FIFTEEN

Every day until the river froze, Christiane hoped to see the ship, the Broad Bay rangers dropping into skiffs to come ashore. In November, when unforgiving skies were already cloaking the land with snow, Armstrong brought a letter from Johann. When Armstrong handed it over, she stared in wonder. He really was alive. And he was thinking of her. She thanked God, then curtsied to Armstrong before putting the letter in her pocket.

That night, she asked Matthias—as she now knew Leichter—to read it for her. Ursula and all the children gathered around. They lit two candles for the occasion.

In the letter, which covered one side of a sheet, Johann wrote mostly as captain of the rangers. The words were meant for everyone. The Broad Bay men, he wrote, had been more brave and more willing than any professional soldiers. General Wolfe had commended them. Now they defended the seized fortress. They had no idea when they would return to Broad Bay. Because the harbors would freeze soon, he was writing to say so.

But the last sentence was for Christiane and Walther and Hanna and Franklin. It is my fondest wish, Johann had written, to be home with my family. He signed, Johann Overstreet.

"Would you like to hear it again?" Matthias asked.

Christiane nodded. After the second time through, she took the letter from Matthias and spread it on the table before her. She stared at the signature at the bottom. She traced her finger along the last sentence. "You heard that?" she said to the children. "We are your papa's fondest wish."

Hanna and Walther, on either side of her, crowded in to look.

"I should tell the others his news," Matthias said. "They should know."

Christiane nodded. "But not the last part," she said.

* * * * * *

The ship was larger than most that stopped at Broad Bay, but the settlers didn't think it could carry the ranger company. It was only mid-April. Louisbourg's harbor probably wouldn't be open so early. Only Walther and a few other children watched as a brisk wind sped the ship up the bay.

The Indian raids had stopped, partly because of winter, partly because of the British advance inland from Louisbourg. Hunters from the settlement, always working in twos, were roaming more widely for deer or moose. The trading ships had sailed to Boston through the autumn, allowing Broad Bay to sell timber again and feed itself through the dark months.

It had been a cold winter, but they all were. This one had been a season of limbo, of suspended lives. A half-dozen children died from fevers. Frau Shuler's cough lasted for months then started to bring up blood. A wolf pack attacked a man while he walked his trap line, which showed what a hard winter it was. Wolves didn't usually attack people. The man fought them off but suffered terrible bites.

Ursula agreed to marry Matthias Leichter, but Nungesser refused to perform the ceremony without proof that Fritz was dead. Over winter fires, the settlers argued the question. Husbands and wives quarreled over it. Neighbors disagreed. Finally, a consensus emerged that the wedding should proceed, a consensus built on

Ursula's popularity and Leichter's status at the first man of Broad Bay. When Leichter announced he would take Ursula to Fort Georges to be married by Captain Shaw, Nungesser relented. He had conducted the ceremony only two weeks ago.

More than twenty farms, including Mayflower Hof, stood as charred, ruined reminders of the violent times. When Leichter tried to organize building and repair parties, few stepped forward, not even to work on the stockades. Timbers rotted at the bottom of the palisades. When the clay and dried grass fell from between the log walls of the stockade rooms, settlers stuffed cloth and sticks in the gaps. Rather than repair roofs, the people moved their beds away from the leaks and set out buckets to catch dripping water. They mulishly endured the frigid temperatures and blizzards.

So when the ship's cannon boomed, the families came running. Even though the bay was choppy, Alec McDonnell and three other boys launched a skiff to meet the ship. Alec scrambled up the ship's ropes. On the deck, he paused at the sight of his father's empty sleeve.

Robert spread his left arm wide and laughed in greeting. "Come on, lad," he said, "it means I'll do only twice the work of other men."

Robert and Johann and two others climbed into the boys' boat. The sailors lowered Keller in a sling, then handed down his crutch with the men's muskets and gear. So many other rangers piled into the ship's boat that it threatened to overturn. The boats raced to land, the men hooting and shouting challenges all the way in.

Johann stared at the wooded shoreline, the hills beyond, the clouds plunging across the sky. The breeze swept away the monotony and frustrations of the last months. The land was still here, as he remembered it. His land.

As they neared shore, he saw that the pier needed work. The stockade too. He would go to Mayflower Hof this very day. Christiane stood back from the crowd that had come down to the waterline. She was holding Franklin and waving. He had never felt so lucky.

The boys' boat arrived first. They rowed up on shore with a crunch. Walther ran into the water to meet them, tumbling into the boat, then Hanna followed. Johann laughed as he carried them ashore, complaining that they had grown so big. He went back to help two others carry Keller through the water, giving in to Keller's demand that he be set down at the first piece of dry land. He was still wedging the crutch into his armpit when his children piled into him, knocking him off his wooden leg and into the water with a shout.

Johann lifted his belongings from the boat. He handed his musket to Walther, the bag to Hanna, and walked up the slope. When Christiane put Franklin down, the boy ran to him, then stopped short. Johann crouched and opened his hands, smiling. The small boy, suddenly shy, turned sideways. Johann swept him up.

She was there, then, reaching around his neck and gripping him tightly. He held her close. "Oh, Christiane," he said.

PART III

1775

†

CHAPTER ONE

"Papa! Papa! I made a house!"

Johann looked down from his workbench to the three-year-old playing with scrap wood. Karl looked up at him expectantly.

With a low moan that seemed to accompany a lot of his movements lately, Johann knelt to examine the structure, which consisted of two blocks of uneven heights covered by a short board. "Yes, it looks very fine, very strong," he said. He absent-mindedly poked a finger into the open space between the blocks. "Such a large door. I like that. Many people can come in." He smiled at his son. "You will have many friends."

"It's not done." Karl said, crawling over to the basket of scrap wood to find other pieces. He had his mother's sturdy frame and dark coloring.

Johann blew on his hands, then twisted to hold them out to the fire, still necessary in early April. He inched closer to the fire. "Ah, Karl, no house ever is finished. It's good for you to know that so young." With a louder grunt, Johann turned back to the table leg he was trying to turn. "Perhaps," he continued, "you will make furniture some day with your big brother Franklin."

"I make houses," the boy answered, still shifting through the wood scraps, searching for one the right size.

"Houses, yes." Johann squinted to line up the leg on the lathe, which he'd made himself, attaching a wheel he could turn by hand to rotate the wood. His scrap basket held fewer botched table legs than it used to, but each one still was a struggle. He was working on a design for a lathe powered by a foot pedal, based on one he saw in Boston the year before. That would leave both his hands free to apply consistent pressure as the wood rotated. Muller the blacksmith got the dimensions wrong on the metal shafts, so he was making them again.

"Johann?" The door burst open, bringing a gust of cold air. "Catherine said you were back here!"

"Matthias." Johann wiped his hands on his apron to shake hands with Leichter, then closed the door against the cold. Leichter strode to the fire to warm his hands and spoke over his shoulder. "I see you have a new helper."

"I made a house," the boy said, pointing. He stood. "I go tell Mama." Johann helped him with his jacket, which had served four of his brothers and sisters before him.

After feeding the fire, Johann pulled a stool over to join Leichter, who was scratching under the wig he wore to cover his baldness. Johann had never tried a wig, though his own hair had whitened while retreating from his forehead at a steady pace. Catherine said he looked distinguished, which was as much as he could hope for these days.

They lit their pipes from a stick of kindling that Johann pulled from the fire. After ritual inquiries about family and comments about the weather, Johann waited and puffed. This was not a social call. Matthias Leichter didn't make social calls. Though he'd lost his official authority—Broad Bay was now an incorporated town named for General Waldo—Leichter remained a leading citizen. He was rich in land bought cheap from those who fled the settlement during the hard days.

"Ursula says we must have more cabinets," Leichter said, leaning back and extending his legs. "She wants them in the dining room. Large, with glass doors."

Johann stared into the fire, trying to remember the room. It was a wide one that could take a substantial cabinet. "And you? What do you think?"

Leichter smiled. "I think the mistress of the house has spoken, so thus it shall be. A couple of old dogs like us have learned that much." He plainly took pleasure in being able to provide such luxury in a house that was already the largest in Waldoborough. And in spreading his largesse to Johann.

Johann tried not to resent Leichter's self-satisfaction. The man had proved a doting husband for Ursula and took on her daughters without hesitation. Still, when the religious troubles fractured the settlement, the two men had disagreed. Leichter sided, loudly, with Nungesser and the established congregation. Johann, never churchly, sympathized with the Moravians. He admired their simplicity and willingness to wonder. He missed talking with their pastor, who had softened Johann's feelings about God, moving him from fear and bafflement to acceptance and hope. For two years, while the arguments boiled, Johann and Leichter spoke rarely and then only frostily. After most of the Moravians left for North Carolina, the friction faded but never disappeared.

"I should come by your home," Johann said, "and hear directly from the mistress. She can show me what she wants."

"Yes, by all means."

"It sounds a large project. It will come with high cost."

"It should be very fine. It will be in a featured place. That's why I insist that Johann Overstreet must build it." Johann smiled. He assumed it was Ursula, not Leichter, who insisted that the job go to him.

"I'll have to send to Boston for the glass."

"Of course." The two men smoked for a minute. "You've heard," Leichter said, "of the fighting there?"

"Something about it. More British soldiers coming, they say?"

"It's astounding," Leichter said. "Armstrong says they speak openly of rebellion. These rebels have stockpiled weapons, even cannons. Such fools they are, imagining they might stand against the king and his army. You've seen the king's army, the fleet. Who would send simple farmers against them?"

"Well," Johann smiled at the fire, "up at Louisbourg, simple farmers from Broad Bay fought very well."

"You were backed by the king's army and Royal Navy! Much easier to fight with them behind you than against them."

"Ah, Matthias, fighting is never easy."

Leichter sat forward. "Of course, the sergeant major knows about such things, but you agree that it's madness to oppose the king?"

"I agree that I accept your commission and will stop by to see the mistress of the house tomorrow morning, if that suits her. As for Boston and the king, I choose to remain here in Broad Bay and build furniture."

When Leichter was gone, Johann wondered how long it would take for Catherine to drop by. She had a nose for new orders. Sometimes after Sunday services, she would predict one based on the way a woman had looked at her, or passed an unexpected word. Often Catherine's predictions proved right.

"So?" she said as she opened the door. Not yet thirty, her generous figure filled the doorway, particularly with baby Klara on her hip. When Karl was born, Johann was surprised that Catherine kept most of the flesh she had gained in the pregnancy. Christiane never did. But perhaps with more flesh, Christiane would have survived the last birth, Liesl. Liesl, now eight, could unnerve him by looking up with her mother's solemn grey eyes, eyes that seemed to know much.

For three years, he and the children lived without a woman. He had attended the Moravian services then, where he saw Catherine, dimpled and cheerful. When she brought bread to the house, sometimes cakes, Johann knew what was afoot. Robert McDonnell told him not to marry. "You'll never be satisfied with another woman," he said, "nor should you be."

Robert had been wrong, but then Robert hadn't lived without a woman, not with so many children who needed mothering. Poor Hanna. As the eldest girl, she bore too much burden, forced to be mother to Franklin and the other girls. Johann remembered lying in bed in those years, beaten down with fatigue, staying awake to experience for a few moments the marvel of a quiet house.

Of course, Catherine was not Christiane. No one knew that more than he did. But she was a good woman who brought order, cared for his children, warmed his bed, and often smiled and sang as she did it. Where Johann thrived in quiet spaces, Catherine craved bustle and tumult. If those were missing, she produced them. She made Johann think of the psalm's advice to "make a joyful noise." He knew he had been fortunate a second time. The older children, Hanna and Walther, never warmed to this second wife, but Franklin had no such problem. Of course, Franklin had the knack with people.

"Come sit by the fire," he said without turning. "And close the door."

"I need to get back," she said as she sat, opening her cape and giving baby Klara her breast. She sighed. "It's always so nice and quiet here."

Johann smiled. She often said that as she vanquished the quiet. When he told her of Leichter's commission, her face lit up. "Oh, Johann, you must charge him every penny it's worth. Not like last time, no special price because of Ursula and her poor first husband."

"I think you're right, Katia. This time the special price for Herr Leichter will be because he's so prosperous and should not be allowed to rest in his prosperity. We must help his silver to get out and see the world."

"Johann, just imagine," she said, "all the fine people will see your work there and they'll want something just like it. You'll be buried with orders! You'll need to bring on apprentices."

Johann laughed. "First, I should build a very fine cabinet for the Leichter *Schloss*. Then apprentices." He gazed down at Klara, sucking greedily, then returned to his table leg.

"So where's Franklin?" Catherine asked. "Hasn't he returned with the firewood? He should have been back an hour ago or more. He should be helping his papa."

"It's coming to be spring, my dear. A young man may dawdle when he feels spring." He shrugged without turning. "Even an old man may."

"Ach," she said, lifting the baby to her shoulder and buttoning her cape, "so now you're going to learn how to dawdle? No one will recognize you." She stood. "You know you spoil that boy, that Franklin. He knows nothing of how hard things can be."

"That's good. I hope to spoil them all. That's why we came here, to Broad Bay—"

"When will you call it Waldoborough?"

"When General Waldo's family repays me for this land that I paid for twice because he cheated me."

Catherine smiled and kissed his cheek. “Wouldn’t that be a happy day!” She laughed. “Perhaps you should just take it out of their hides?”

“Such a pleasure that would be.”

She stroked his cheek. “The sergeant major at war again! Do you hear that, Klara?” she nuzzled the baby. “Your ferocious papa will impose justice upon the rich!” She twitched her skirt in a becoming fashion and stepped to the door.

“Mama! Mama!” Karl rattled the door from outside. When Catherine opened it, she caught him with one hand and guided him back toward the house in a single motion. “The girls,” Karl complained, “won’t let me taste the cake batter.”

“Of course they won’t,” Catherine said. “What have you done to deserve it?”

“Katia,” Johann called as he went to close the door, “town meeting tonight. I’ll be going with Robert.”

Catherine made a face back at him. “Yes, and you’ll come back complaining about all the talk, talk, talk, men just wanting to hear their own voices.” She sighed. “Fine. You and Robert should go and make everything right.”

CHAPTER TWO

The passage along the Medomak, past the riverside farms, was no longer a path. Over twenty years and more, the forest shrank slightly each time someone journeyed to trade or to visit neighbors or to attend Sunday services.

In the early days, only a few dozen people walked on the path in a week. That multiplied when peace released the settlers from the stockades. They spread out to till new land. They pushed deeper into the woods for lumber and game and pelts, which retreated before them. Footfall after footfall widened the way. Wet weather converted it to rutted mud, exposing stones and tree roots that grabbed at travelers until someone grew exasperated enough to hack them out. By the time the descendants of Puritans began to arrive in Broad Bay, it was already a bridle path.

Now that the land was safe and the Indians humbled, the new people coveted this land that only Germans had been hungry enough to settle. Horses broke off trailside twigs and branches; their heavy tread pounded the ground and the roots underneath and broadened the way further. The new people demanded more from the land.

They had a fever to improve it and the resources to do so. The Germans joined them in chopping down bushes and trees, grubbing out stones, producing a road wide enough for a team and wagon.

As Johann's mare picked her way, he held a lantern on the pommel of his saddle. His mind ran back in time, to the changes in Broad Bay. He remembered when there was no path at all, and when he buried a son and then a wife on the land he paid for twice. The Indians, so terrifying then, had yielded to a well-armed people who kept crowding in, seemingly without end. The Indians receded with the forest. Johann's oldest boy, Walther, now worked his own farm. Johann pulled up his collar against a chill.

"Johnny," Robert McDonnell called from his doorway. He turned back for a word to whoever was inside, then scrambled onto a tall black gelding. "I just about gave up on you."

"They never start on time," Johann said. "Not Loomis. The meeting's already two weeks overdue, anyway."

McDonnell's horse fell in step with Johann's mare. "They'll probably start on time to push through that tax Loomis wants, the one to pay the salary of Herr Nungesser."

A look of distaste came over Johann. "Such a swine he is. Surely we've not become so corrupt as to approve that tax."

"I don't know. Leichter's behind it. He's an influential man."

"But who can think we should collect tax to pay a man of God. Render unto Caesar that which is Caesar's! Nungesser, as a man of God—"

"A what?" McDonnell burst out.

"Fine, as a man who leads a religious congregation, Nungesser should not receive tax money. If his church wishes to pay him, that's fine."

"And if they don't, even better, eh?"

"Ach, he's rich enough from swindling the old people he pretends to help with his fake medicines."

Their talk turned to the gardens they would soon plant. McDonnell's son Alec was insisting on expanding the family's sawmill. "I swear," Robert said, "if I stand in his way, that young buck'll just run right over me, toss me out on my arse. Says we need to keep up with all the boatbuilders, also with the new houses going up. Talking about our own shipyard now." Robert's pride was clear from his tone. "These new people, they want good boards, not the logs and mud we used. And did you hear about Cushing? He's talking about putting in a mill above the falls. Say, John," he wheeled to look at Johann, "did Cushing ever settle that boundary dispute, the one with Penner?"

Johann shook his head. "The cheating started with General Waldo, and it's never stopped. Cushing's fence steals from Penner, Penner's steals from Soule, Soule's steals from Orff. There isn't an honest fence in Broad Bay."

"Which is why they appointed your upright self to straighten it all out."

"Because everyone steals, they give the job to a poor German with no power to make anyone behave like an honest man." Johann hawked and spat in disgust.

"Those other thieves, the ones who claim Waldo gave us all bad titles, they've filed their court suit in Boston."

"Robert, Waldo did give us bad titles."

"We took them in good faith and paid good money. I'll not pay twice." He looked across the space between the horses. "I'll never understand why you did. The old Johann would've pulled out his bayonet and chased Waldo straight into the river, along with this new bunch of thieves."

Johann shrugged. "I didn't care to spend my last years with lawyers. I've lost my appetite for war."

"Not me. I'll be goddamned if they'll see a shilling from me. I'll burn the house down and plow salt in the ground before that."

Johann smiled, "And so, shall we hear your report as deer reeve tonight?"

McDonnell laughed. "I have nothing to report and never will. If those asses in Boston want to protect the precious deer, they can get off their fat rear-ends and do it themselves."

"That's why you got the job."

"Exactly right. No one can ignore a stupid law better than I can. Besides," he snorted, "a little venison never hurt anyone."

At the new German meetinghouse, home to Nungesser's congregation, nearly sixty men had crowded into the unforgiving pews. A few leaned against the back wall and lounged in the side aisles. The multi-paned windows, lit by a dozen lanterns, reflected multiple versions of the scene, each square of glass set at a slightly different angle. The whitewashed boards of the meetinghouse gleamed.

Ten minutes late, Isaiah Loomis called the meeting to order. Johann didn't know Loomis to be a crook, but assumed he was because Cushing and Nash, the other two selectmen—and he knew this to a certainty—were men of low morals.

The meeting crawled through its agenda. The three selectmen showed neither emotion nor interest during the official reports, certainly not in Johann's account of the town's wayward fences. Most of the German farmers had learned enough English to follow the general direction of the meeting but not enough to understand everything.

The report of the fish warden triggered a sharp exchange. The first selectman condemned the millers' failure to build runways for fish to swim upriver to spawn. That, he insisted, was threatening people's ability to feed themselves. The millers dismissed his complaint. They had no duty, they said, to provide fish for the community.

To Johann's surprise, no one spoke on the proposed tax to pay Nungesser. After the first selectman read the resolution, silence fell. Men shifted in their seats. Two men in the back left to relieve themselves at the edge of the woods. Even Leichter said nothing. The first selectman called for the "yea" votes. Leichter's hand and three others went up. McDonnell kicked Johann's shoe and gave him a look. The first selectman said he saw no need to call for the "nays." He pronounced the proposal defeated. No tax money for the pastor.

Then Selectman Nash stood. He reminded the men of the fighting between the Massachusetts militia and the British. From a newspaper he read a resolution approved by the Massachusetts Provincial Congress. It called for 30,000 men to take up arms against the British troops occupying Boston. Nash moved that Waldoborough endorse the resolution and send a company to Boston to oppose British oppression.

Pandemonium broke out. At least five men, including McDonnell, stood and held their fists in the air, shouting huzzahs. A comparable number shook their heads and called out angrily. Individual arguments erupted. The first selectman stood on his chair and held his arms out in a mute call for order. After a period, the din retreated and Loomis could make himself heard. There should be full discussion, he said. He would hear one speaker in favor of the resolution, then one opposed, and so on until all had spoken who wished to. Johann stretched his legs and crossed his ankles. It was going to be a long night.

When Leichter led off for the opponents, Johann understood that Leichter had let Nungesser's tax die in order to employ his full influence against this resolution. Gesturing forcefully, Leichter urged his neighbors to rely upon the goodness of King George. Yes, he conceded, Parliament was treating Boston roughly, but even the most ardent must admit there was lawlessness among the citizens there, such as the dumping of tea in the harbor. The king, he insisted, had the power and the will to bring justice to all his subjects.

"It's a fearful thing," Leichter concluded, "to set our hands and hearts against our rightful king, against the order of society. That will return us to the world of the savages. We know what war is like. It not only kills and maims those who fight, but brings hunger and ruin to children, to wives, and to old people. It destroys trade and makes us all poor. At Louisbourg, our men saw the might of the British navy and the British army as they humbled France. What short work would they make of our poor efforts, with no warships, little in the way of arms, and with only our anger on our side? No, friends, our best course is not to rush into war, but to be wise, to protect our families, and to wait for the king's justice."

In high dudgeon, McDonnell shouted as he jumped from his seat. "Listen, by God," he demanded, "to one who has fought for this land of ours—*our* land, not King George's." He gestured to his empty right sleeve. The first selectman nodded to him. As McDonnell composed himself, Leichter called out, "You fought for your king."

McDonnell drew himself up to his full height. "I carried the king's rifle, that's true, but I and the sergeant major and our neighbors fought for this settlement and for our families, not for the king who left us naked before the attacks of savages. We mustn't be blinded by traditions," McDonnell turned to the others, "or by our wish for peace. Who among us doesn't wish for peace? I know what war brings. Look at me. But how much of your manhood, how much of your liberty, will you pay for peace? Will you wait for the British to slaughter us all?"

McDonnell paused. "Read the other news in Mr. Nash's newspaper. The king denies our right to appoint delegates to consider our situation. He cancels our government. The king wants us to lie down before him and trust in his goodness. As evidence of his trust, he sends troops to collect unjust taxes, to impose infamous restrictions on our trade. What *friend* sends warships and soldiers to reason with another friend? No, the king intends to break us, just as he has broken so many others. That's what we can trust about King George. Ask the world about the kindness and generosity of British kings, and you'll learn how much we should trust them."

"Spoken like a Jacobite," Leichter snarled from the front row, "still pining for Bonnie Prince Charlie."

McDonnell smiled broadly. "What I am, friend Leichter, is just another bloody American. I believe in American rights and American liberties, and I will rely upon myself and my neighbors to defend them, not on some pampered nancy on the far side of the world who sends his bullyboys to crush us."

A dozen men competed to answer McDonnell, then a dozen more to answer that speaker. No one even thought of leaving the building. The debate stretched on for an hour and then another. Some men shouted and shook their fists. At times, the hall was quiet, the mood contemplative. Selectman Cushing rounded the room to add fresh oil in the lanterns whose flames were guttering. When the final speakers were done repeating what earlier speakers had said, Loomis looked at Johann. "Does our captain in the last war wish to be heard?"

Johann paused for a moment, then stood. He gave a shallow bow to the selectmen and then another to his neighbors. "I am honored to address these grave matters, but not as your captain. I have grown old and will no more go to war." He paused, trying to order his thoughts.

"When I served in the Landgraf's army, I could never speak on such matters. It was not permitted. Tonight I have listened. You are my neighbors and my friends. I hear my friend Matthias, and I agree with much of what he says and with those who agree with him. My life is good here in Broad Bay. I have sons and daughters. I do not wish them to know war.

"Then Robert speaks and he makes sense, as do those who agree with him. The British have not treated us as they should. They don't treat us as equals, as men. So I realize that I haven't thought enough about these matters. I work all day. My mind is not settled. If we take a vote tonight, I will not vote. I am too uncertain. I would welcome the chance to think more, to talk to my neighbors, and to vote in a week's time."

Angry voices rose as he sat. Those supporting the resolution demanded a vote. The opponents embraced Johann's notion of a week's delay. The first selectman called for a vote on whether to reconvene in a week's time. It passed by two votes.

"You bloody fool," McDonnell sputtered as they stood. "You're playing into the hands of those rich bastards. Mark my word, it's the Waldos and the Leichters who will stand with this idiot of a king."

Johann shrugged. "You're probably right, Robert. But a soldier doesn't easily oppose his government."

"You bloody fool," McDonnell repeated when they were outside. Without another word, he mounted and rode off. Johann thought to call for him to wait for the lantern, but he held his tongue.

"Robert has a high temper," Selectman Nash said to Johann, "but he sees correctly what we must do." Nash held out his newspaper. "Would you like to read this tonight and return it tomorrow?"

Johann took it.

CHAPTER THREE

†

Sailing, as Franklin saw it, was the closest he would ever come to flying. Like the gull who shadowed him toward Pemaquid Point, the boat rode the wind. The gull made small adjustments to stay airborne. Franklin did the same with the tiller and spritsail, keeping his father's yawl splashing cleanly forward. The wind had been fresh since he left Walther's farm near Damariscotta. Though the water route from Waldoborough was farther than traveling overland, it was better for cargo like the chickens and sheep Franklin had taken to Walther's family. To satisfy his father, Franklin would have to use lye to get the smells out of the planking.

The *Christiane*, named while his mother still lived, was really Franklin's. He was only nine when his father, thinking to build boats for the coastal trade, started on it. Franklin hovered near the work until his father handed him a scraper and a plank to smooth. After months of labor, they produced a vessel that leaked grievously and sailed so slowly that passengers were tempted to swim. Franklin's father returned to making furniture and gave

Franklin the boat. Since then, Franklin had transformed it into a sleek, smooth-sailing vessel.

He ducked under the jib as he turned into Muscongus Bay. The sun struggled to shine. Low whitecaps raced toward shore, the swells now beating against the starboard side, rocking *Christiane*. Franklin loved this part of sailing, when he felt the wind and the water through the sail and the hull. The gusts were stronger in the bay. He might reach Mayflower Hof by mid-afternoon. He reached for the cheese and bread that Walther's wife sent.

He was almost to Louds Island, aiming to pass it on the landward side, when he saw the boat, not much larger than *Christiane*. The flag at its stern and the redjackets aboard meant it was a revenue cutter from Fort Georges, prowling for smugglers. In twenty minutes, the cutter was close enough for Franklin to drop his sail and wait.

"Ahoy," he called out. "You fellows must be after minnows today."

A sailor threw Franklin a line. They both tugged on it to bring the boats abreast. The officer on board, who appeared little older than Franklin, stepped onto *Christiane* and swatted Franklin with the back of his hand, catching him on the jaw. When Franklin turned and braced to retaliate, the officer bellowed, "You will show respect. Note, gentlemen"—he pointed at Franklin—"if this man raises his hand against an officer of the king."

Franklin stopped himself. "What do you want?" he shouted back, then swept an arm at the inside of *Christiane*. "You can see there's no smuggling here."

"What's your name and your business?" the officer asked.

"Franklin Overstreet. Sailing home from my brother's farm in Damariscotta. To Waldoborough."

"What was your business in Damariscotta, with your so-called brother?"

"If you find an Overstreet around here," Franklin said, "he's either my brother or my father. And my business was delivering chickens and sheep to his farm."

The officer wrinkled his nose in disdain. "That much appears to be true. You carried no tea?"

"Who can afford it, with the taxes?"

The officer glared at Franklin. "Your tongue could get you into trouble, young man. When one of His Majesty's ships makes toward you, do not in future continue on your merry way, but stop." He took a last look around *Christiane*. "Please tell your smuggler friends that their fat days are over and their prison days are coming." The officer pranced nimbly back to the cutter. "Good day," he called as his sailor pushed off. "God save the king."

* * * * * *

"Franklin, what happened?" Catherine, concern on her face, crossed the workshop floor. She held her hand out. "Does that hurt?" Johann looked up from his bench and squinted at his son's face.

Franklin pulled away, saying, "It's nothing. Really."

Johann smiled. "Catherine, run and get my spyglass so we can examine this more carefully."

She stepped closer to Franklin. "Is your mouth all right? Your teeth? What happened?"

"A cutter stopped me. Must be a new man, too new to know that no smuggler worth his salt would use a scow like *Christiane*."

"He hit you?" she asked.

"What did you do?" Johann asked.

"Papa," Franklin shook his head. "I'm not a child. I didn't do anything. He did it because he could."

Johann tightened his mouth. "They can be arrogant."

"But you're all right?" Catherine asked again.

Franklin smiled. "Of course." His eyes went back to his father, who had already returned to the table leg he was turning.

"Johann," Catherine said, "the talk is that you disrupted the town meeting last night."

Without looking up, Johann said, "How did I do that?"

"Must I squeeze every drop of information out of you? Must I hear from the neighbors what you do?"

Trying to concentrate on the lathe, Johann said, "You were asleep when I came in and when I got up. And you were visiting our neighbor at dinnertime." He cursed softly when the leg slipped. Luckily he hadn't been applying much pressure. "Katia, I have hopes yet of not mangling this job. May we please talk of the town meeting at supper?"

Exuding a dense air of grievance, Catherine left.

Taking his usual place at the bench, Franklin resumed his experiments with wood finishes. His father wouldn't pay for shellac imported from Britain, so they made do with mixes of beeswax and turpentine that produced a yellowish tint that Franklin thought ugly. He was certain that with a better finish, one with a rich glow that lasted for a longer time, they could please their customers and charge higher prices.

He mixed three batches, altering the proportions of wax and turpentine in each. He added linseed oil to a fourth. Then he applied the different concoctions to scrap wood and left the pieces outside to dry. He also tried holding each mixture over the fire and applying it warm. He numbered each piece of wood and wrote in the account book which mixture was on which numbered piece of wood. When he had stored the different mixtures, he opened the door to let in some air, picking up the newspaper that Johann had flung on the floor.

After ten minutes, Franklin looked up. His father was checking four table legs against each other.

"So?" Franklin said.

Johann nodded. "It's a miracle. They match. Tomorrow I attach the feet and we begin the chairs." He put the legs away. Wiping his hands on a rag, he shook his head, "I thought for many years that I would learn to work more quickly, but I've become only slower."

Franklin had heard this lament before. "How long did it take for you to get used to these fumes? They make me dizzy."

Johann smiled. "Every trade has its problems. Sailors drown."

"What was the problem at the town meeting? Will you fight a duel over Penner's fence line?"

"Exactly what you found just now in *Christiane*. What can we do with the British? What can they do with us? Or to us?"

"Please, Papa, tell me." Franklin leaned forward, his eyes bright.

Johann sighed and closed the door. He started to put his tools away, speaking over his shoulder. "Nash and Robert want war, to spit in the eye of the king and dare him to blow us into little pieces. You know how Robert is. He is magnificent but sometimes foolish. And Matthias Leichter and others want us to bow down to the British and kiss their lily-white feet."

"What did you do that caused trouble?"

"I said I agreed with both of them, so now everyone hates me and thinks I am the fool."

"Papa!"

"But I do agree with both of them!" He glanced at his son, then returned to tidying the workbench. "I want the British to go away. They have no idea what this American world is like and don't care to find out. They are greedy and impossible. They mostly want to bleed us dry. Robert is right about all of that. But I don't want to fight them. You know what I think of war. It is organized madness, men licensed to commit evil."

"How can you say that, Papa, after all your time as a soldier? Aren't there things worth fighting for?"

"Once, Franklin, only once did I fight for something worth fighting for, when we went to Louisbourg, and I still cannot be sure it was right, that God can mean for us to do such things."

"I'm sure."

Johann stopped. He leaned against the bench. "You must tell me then."

"I've been thinking about this. A lot. Walther and I talked it over. We can talk about the taxes and laws and the revenue cutters and stupid officers, but they're all small parts of the big problem. And it's the biggest problem. For those of us who know only life in America, it makes no sense to be owned by the British, these people on the far side of the world."

"Over this, you would fight and kill those men and have them try to kill you?"

"Yes, Papa. We have to. Otherwise, we are nothing."

"And Walther, he agrees?"

"He does, but he has Joanna and the babies and the farm. He can't leave them."

"You would go where a man would stand as far as you are from me and aim a gun at you and pull the trigger? Or lunge at you with a knife and try to rip your guts out? Because that is war. Or maybe you get sick in camp and die in a pool of your own shit. Yes, that's what you want? No one speaks the truth about war. No one. It's a butcher's trade. The lowest activity of animals. At least a butcher kills dumb animals for food. A soldier kills men with souls to satisfy some king's idea of his own glory.

"I crossed an ocean, Franklin. I've worked these years so my sons would never be soldiers, would never die choking on their own blood, surrounded by people who hate them. This place, Broad Bay, it's a good place. Compared to Kettenheim when I was your age, this is the land of milk and honey, even with those British around our necks."

"Papa," Franklin held his hands out, "you once fought for something worth fighting for. I know about Mama, how she fought too. Well, this is my time. Liberty is worth fighting for. I won't fight for a king, but I will for myself and for freedom." Trying to lighten the mood, Franklin added, "Perhaps I will be a good soldier like the sergeant major."

"You think I was a good soldier?" Johann wagged his finger then turned it on himself. "Me? There are no good soldiers. Only lucky ones and unlucky ones. When you stand on the field and face your enemy, and he fires a volley, and the man to the right of you falls and the man to the left of you falls, but you do not, what is that? Is that being a good soldier? Or is it being a soldier who stood in the right place, opposite a man who flinched when he fired and shot high or low?" He took a step toward his son. "Franklin, young men like me in Hesse had to be lucky to survive. I have been lucky. I know this. I won't have my sons rely on the same luck. It will run out. It has to. Don't you see? Look at Robert. See how war left him."

Franklin stopped the retort in his mind. He took a breath. "So, Papa, what happened at the town meeting?"

Johann pushed his fingers against his forehead. "When I said I needed to think more, some agreed. Enough agreed. We meet again in a week and will decide then. Many are angry with me. Robert is."

They stood in silence. "Papa, I don't need to think about it anymore. Marcus Straub and I, we'll be leaving tomorrow for Boston."

"No!" Johann's face turned red. His voice, gentle until now, became a shout. "I forbid it. You may not go. You don't know what you're doing!" He moved to block the door. When Franklin stepped toward him, Johann didn't move.

"Don't be like this, Papa," Franklin said, his voice level.

Johann shook his head. Franklin gripped his father by the elbows to push him aside. They grappled, grunting, faces contorted, neck cords standing out, not speaking. Franklin was larger, younger, and stronger. He wrenched his father from his feet and flung him to the side. Johann stumbled and fell.

"Papa!" he called.

"Go," Johann said, not looking up. "Just go."

* * * * * *

When Franklin burst into the house, the four young ones were standing next to Catherine, fear in their eyes. "We've been arguing," he said.

"So that's what it was," Catherine said. "We couldn't tell." She moved a child aside as she reached for a ladle. She filled a bowl with stew. "You must eat before you go." She placed the bowl on the table, wiping her hands on her apron. "You leave tonight? So you and your papa, you don't do this again."

"Yes. Yes. That's right."

"Yes, that's best."

Liesl ran to Franklin and grabbed him around the waist. He kept his arm around her as he sat before the stew. "I'm not hungry."

Catherine sat too. "You will be. You always are. Liesl and I will get your things together. Will you help me, Liesl, for Franklin?" She held her hand out to the little girl, who slowly relaxed her grasp on her brother and followed.

The stew did smell good. Franklin began to eat, mechanically at first, then with more purpose. He looked around the kitchen, which his father had built when Franklin was a boy. Mayflower Hof was the only home he remembered. His brother and sister talked about living in the stockade. They had liked having other children around to play with, but they'd been afraid too. Franklin didn't remember the stockade, but he knew this room like his own breath. The warmth from the fireplace. His mother watching porridge. Walther building the fire. His father cursing softly after lifting the hot coffee pot without a cloth.

"You're going to fight," Lena said. She had taken the chair next to him as he ate. She was thirteen now, shy but slender and graceful. Her movements were like their father's.

He nodded and offered her a piece of his bread. She shook her head. When he swallowed, it made a knot in his chest.

Catherine bustled in and took his empty bowl. Franklin accepted the knapsack from Liesl, who clung to him again. She hung on through his hugs with Lena and Karl, and his kiss for baby Klara. And then the farewell embrace with Catherine.

"Do you think I'm wrong?" he asked her. "Do you agree with him?"

Catherine's eyes were brimming. "I think no man loves his children more than your papa does." He crouched before Liesl and kissed her forehead. She wouldn't look up.

At the road, Franklin found his father standing with his good rifle in one hand and his bayonet in the other.

"You should stay," he said. "I'm not shouting now. You must be sure. This fight that's coming, it's not so clear."

"It's clear to me, Papa."

"Yes, I know. Things are more clear when you're young. I remember." He looked at the weapons in his hands. He held them out.

"Papa, you need the rifle for hunting."

Johann shrugged as Franklin took it. "I'll be fine with the old rifle. It will be a happy time for the deer." He handed over the bayonet. "I never talked to you about this—"

"Robert did."

"He did?" Johann shook his head. "If there was ever a man who didn't understand the bayonet, it's Robert McDonnell." He cocked a hip. "It only goes on a musket, so they'll have to give you the musket. You've seen, of course, they're not as accurate as the rifle, but in a battle, no one shoots straight. Rifles misfire. Powder gets wet. Cartridges are dropped. But the bayonet, the bayonet always works." He pointed at it. "Let them see it. Let them see you will use it. And don't poke with it. Drive it, with all your weight." He demonstrated.

Franklin nodded.

"Keep it sharp. It's a tool, like any other. It must be cared for."

Franklin nodded again.

Johann sighed. "Why not wait, just a few days? There might be a company formed here, from Waldoborough. If you wait until next week's meeting."

Franklin shook his head. "I can't. A coaster's stopping in the morning."

"Then stay here this night."

"No, I'll stay with Marcus. They're closer to the pier." He looked at his father directly. "I think it's best I go now."

Johann dug a pouch of coins from his pocket. Franklin stopped his hand.

Johann smiled. "It's not enough to say no to." He stepped sideways and stuffed it into Franklin's knapsack.

They clasped hands. Johann gripped his son's shoulder with his free hand and stared into his eyes. "You, Franklin, you come home to us."

CHAPTER FOUR

Franklin and Marcus rested against the starboard rail as the sloop swept inside the island that sheltered Lynn's harbor. To avoid Royal Navy patrols, the captain had run close to the shore, landing at Lynn rather than the larger port at Salem. Boston was, of course, out of the question. British warships filled that harbor. Franklin didn't ask why they had to evade the British. Perhaps the captain was smuggling. Maybe he planned to use his swift ship as a privateer against British merchantmen. The sloop had cannon fore and aft and the crewmembers had a desperate look. Since Franklin and Marcus shared the captain's wish to avoid the British, the reason for the captain's stealth didn't signify.

No customs officer greeted them, so the two men from Waldoborough paused only to ask for the road to Boston, which passed straight through town. Their trousers and felt hats labeled them as country folk. Their guns and their destination signaled their intent to join the Americans who, calling themselves patriots, were besieging the British.

Marcus and Franklin had been friends since their young years. A cooper's son, Marcus had strong muscles from wrestling iron rings around barrel staves. His fine looks and sunny moods had drawn the interest of Franklin's sister Lena, though Marcus seemed uninterested in her interest. Marcus favored fishing from the *Christiane* with Franklin at the helm. Franklin wasn't certain he would have left for the fight without Marcus as his companion.

The day was raw for early May. The muddy road, soaked by overnight rains, sucked at their boots. Horsemen and wagons splashed by while the two volunteers, afire with the urgency of their mission, trudged through the sloppy going.

As they neared the town, Marcus made a face. "Ugh. That's horrible. I've heard that Lynn stinks, but this is awful."

Franklin smirked in agreement. The stench intensified as they approached several tanneries. Raucous dogs warned them to stay away. A marsh stretched to their left, between a stream and the sea. The tanners' shops dominated the town. Stout wooden frames held the drying hides of cows and horses. Lime pits and tanning pools festered across the landscape, the air clotted with the perfume of soaking animal turds that would cure the hides. Piles of hair and flesh scraped from the hides added a different type of stench. When Marcus stopped to tie a kerchief over his nose and mouth, Franklin copied him, though the cloth provided little relief.

"You two goin' against the redcoats?" The question came from a figure leaning against a tree. Franklin broke stride to look at him.

"Indeed, sir, we are." The roughly dressed man had a crutch wedged under an armpit. One side of his face was puffy. Yellow-brown bruises ran from under one eye almost to the jawline.

"Figured as much. Couple of young men full of purpose heading to Boston with their Brown Besses. Well, I wish you luck, boys."

Marcus held out his hand and gave his name. Josiah Alderson of Lynn reciprocated. He offered them water from a bucket next to him. They took off their kerchiefs to drink from his dipper.

"Looks like you've been in a fight yourself," Franklin said, nodding at the crutch.

"That's the Lord's truth," Alderson said. He pulled a pipe from his trousers pocket and began to fidget with it. "That I have. And with those shit-eating lobsterbacks, I was. Say,"—he held up the pipe by the bowl—"you boys wouldn't have some tobacco, would you?"

They shook their heads.

"Ah, such honest lads. Haven't yet learned the dirty habits of this filthy world."

Franklin answered, "Tell us, Mr. Alderson—"

"I'm Josiah to fellow patriots such as you."

"Were you at Concord?"

"Not at the bridge, no," Alderson said, shoving the pipe into his pocket and leaning back. "But afterwards, in the scrape that went on afterwards. Then all the way back to Boston. Dear me, yes, I was by God in the thick of that."

Franklin and Marcus waited for him to continue. The man paused, building tension before launching into his tale.

"Well, I come hurrying up, a few of us from Lynn did, in the afternoon, when the redcoats were on the far side of the Menotomy, headed back to Cambridge as fast as their wicked legs could carry 'em. Well, we'd shoot at them from behind something like a tree or a building, like any damned fool would, then pull back into the woods or away from the road to reload out of their range. Then we'd run up ahead and find another good spot, crouch down and shoot again. There was quite a few of us doing that. I'll tell you," Alderson shook his head, "it felt like a damned turkey shoot. That's what it did."

"Looks like the turkeys started shooting back," Marcus said, pointing at the crutch.

"You ain't the first to say so," the man said with a sniff. "Wasn't their shooting was the problem. Around about Cambridge, the fighting became general, a regular scrap it was. The redcoats stopped and got in their formations and all, then the bastards charge us. This one officer type, he must have been at least a captain, I look over and he's riding down on me with his saber slashing. And me, I'd just fired at another officer, so all I have in my hand is a musket that isn't worth a damn. Well, like anyone would, I turn and commence to running. But I run straight into a damned hole, get my foot stuck in it, wrench the leg and knee something fierce, then fall right onto a rock, face first." He pointed at the bruises. "Yes, sir, I went out like a candle, right then and there." He shook his head with practiced wonder and dismay.

"Didn't come back to this world for some time after. The fight'd moved on by then, I could hear it a ways off, but I figure that officer and his saber must've decided I was already singing in the heavenly choir so they ride right on past me to slice up some other poor patriot."

"Are you going back to the fight?" Marcus asked.

Alderson squinted up at the tall young man. "Sure you don't have any tobacco?" He answered the confirming headshake with one of his own. "No, sir, I don't expect I will. The face is healing all right, but not this leg, though it's not so much to complain about compared to how it went for some of the boys. We lost some good men to those vicious sons of bitches. But for me, well, getting into a fight on the one leg just don't seem like a good idea." He shook his head. "No, sir, not a good idea. But if you boys are looking to get into a company with a good captain, you might look in on Captain Bellamy. That's Seth Bellamy, with the Essex County militia. He's a good one. Fought the French last time. Knows what he's about, he does."

The travelers accepted his directions to the workshop of Captain Bellamy, a cobbler on the south side of Lynn. The town's tanneries, logically enough, had attracted cobblers.

The sign next to the workshop door, set a few feet back from the road, said, "S. Bellamy, Shoes and Boots." The mephitic fumes were less pronounced here. The travelers left their guns against the shop's wall and entered, pulling off their hats. In the dark of the shop, Franklin could make out a woman delivering a pitcher and a cup to a worktable. Her cap couldn't quite contain her thick hair. She turned with surprise.

"Gentlemen?" A deep voice came from the left side of the room, where a workbench stood before a window.

"Captain Bellamy, sir?" Marcus said.

"He stands before you." The man straightened to Marcus' height. The slanting light emphasized the creases beside his mouth and across his brow.

"We've come from Waldoborough, on the Maine coast, and heard that your company might be needing men." The odors in the shop—the smell of fresh leather and the lingering tang of warm glaze—were a relief.

"This is my daughter, Jane," the older man said. As the visitors bowed, he added, "Thank you, Jane." She left by a back door. "Now, gentlemen," he said as he wiped his hands on a cloth, "what would commend you to the Essex County militia?"

Marcus looked over at Franklin, who cleared his throat. “Well, sir, we’re both patriots. We want to fight for liberty.”

“Well and good, sir, but what do you know of fighting?”

Franklin looked down at his hat, then back up. “Not much. My father was at Louisbourg, as a captain of rangers, though he doesn’t talk about it.”

“What’s his name?” When he heard the name, Bellamy shrugged. “Can’t say I knew him. Go on.”

“We can shoot,” Marcus broke in.

“Well, that’s fine,” Bellamy said, “but that’s not the hard part. The hard part’s being cold and sick and scared and what you do when your gun misfires.”

After a silence, Franklin said, “We’re going to fight the British, sir.”

With a small smile, Bellamy asked, “You have guns and powder and shot?”

“Guns, sir,” Marcus said, “but not so much powder and shot.”

“You’ll fit right in. Let’s see about your shooting.”

In a field next to the shop, Bellamy pinned a sheet of paper to a bale of hay, then led his visitors some fifty paces away. He told Marcus and Franklin to take a shot, reload, then take a second shot. He wanted to see how quickly they could shoot as well as how accurately.

Marcus hit the edge of the paper with his first shot but his second went high. “Always drop your aim a little,” Bellamy said. “It’s easy to shoot high.”

Franklin hit the edge of the paper with both shots, a disappointing performance with his rifle, particularly since reloading the rifle took twice as long. He would have to do better against the British.

“You’ll do,” Bellamy said. He looked at Franklin. “They named your town after General Waldo?”

“Yes, sir.”

“Hard to believe. He was equal parts thief and brave man. I wish I remembered your father at Louisbourg.”

“He said they mostly dug trenches.”

“Then he really was there.” He led the visitors back to the cobbler shop. “We won’t march out for a few days. We can put you up in our barn in return for some chores. My wife’s got a garden and could use some help before we go. You boys can sleep in the barn.”

CHAPTER FIVE

†

Franklin woke to the sound of a giggle. Then another one. Then came the drumming of liquid hitting the bottom of a wooden bucket. He brushed straw from his hair and pulled on his boots.

"See what comes forth!" Marcus called from the milking stool. "It's the champion sleeper of Lincoln County!" The giggle came again. Jane Bellamy was the source. The sun, bursting through the open barn door, gave depth to her dark hair and darker eyes.

"Good morning," Franklin managed.

"Breakfast'll be at eight," Jane said, adding an impish smile. "I believe my father's instructions will keep you busy until then."

"They'll keep us busy until breakfast tomorrow," Marcus said, eliciting another giggle as Jane left.

"Charming girl, ain't she?" Marcus said. Franklin grunted his agreement. He left to wash up at the pump.

The first chore was shoveling manure from the livestock pen into Bellamy's wagon for sale to a tannery. "The people here," Franklin said after spitting, "must have no sense of smell."

"All the same, bright things seem to grow here." Marcus aimed his chin at Jane, who was hoeing in the garden with two young boys as dark-featured as she was. "Just takes a bit of scrubbing."

When they were washing up again, Jane brought soap. "You won't get into the house without it. Mother insists."

Marcus accepted it with a grin. "Stay and show us how to use it."

"If you need instruction," the girl said over her shoulder, "I fear for the future of the cause."

"How does anyone here tell when they're clean?" Franklin muttered after she had left.

"Have you noticed," Marcus said, "how many people are walking by?"

"Sure. Who would linger here?"

"No, I mean where they're going. They're headed that way"—he pointed—"toward Boston. Toward the fighting."

"That's where we're going, and it can't be too soon for me."

A small boy opened the back door for them. Marcus took a step inside, then froze. Franklin nearly walked into him.

"Come in, come in," Captain Bellamy called from the table. "Biscuits are almost ready. Mrs. Bellamy made them in your honor."

Franklin nudged Marcus to get him moving again. A woman was reaching into an oven built into the side of the fireplace. Her long dark hair escaped from the back of her cap. Catherine had been after his father to build an oven like that. "That smells wonderful," Franklin said, his mouth watering. When the woman rotated to deliver the biscuits to the table, Franklin saw why Marcus had stopped. Though dressed like anyone, Mrs. Bellamy was Indian.

He smiled at her and gave his name, then shoved Marcus toward the table.

The breakfast featured dishes not served in Waldoborough, but Franklin and Marcus ate with enthusiasm, especially the baked beans and creamed codfish. The talk turned on the day's chores, which Captain Bellamy laid out precisely. "I'll be out in the forenoon," he concluded, "making preparations. We leave tomorrow, first thing."

Franklin said he'd noticed a hole in the barn wall with some lumber next to it. The Bellamy children smiled.

"Yes," the captain said. "Whilst saddling George the mule, Robert managed to annoy George sufficiently that the animal kicked those holes." The boy looked down at his plate. "We're lucky that George didn't kick any holes in his head. Any new ones, that is."

Franklin offered to patch the wall if there were tools. "By all means." The captain smiled. "Jane, will you show Mr. Overstreet the tools?"

"And shall I do the fence, too, sir—over on the east side?" Franklin said.

"It would be rude for a host to take advantage of his guest so."

Franklin insisted, explaining he liked to work with wood. "It'd be small return for the holes that we're eating in your larder."

"You're not going to get to that fence before you go, are you?" Mrs. Bellamy directed the question to her husband.

"Indeed, not," he said, turning to Franklin. "Shall we have young James serve as your helper?" He wagged a finger at the younger boy. "Watch and listen. You might learn a few things."

After breakfast, Marcus placed the mule George into harness while the older Bellamy boy recited the animal's likes and dislikes. Captain Bellamy, in a faded green uniform coat with buff breeches, waved as he set off down the road. All three paused to watch. "That's from the last war," Robert said. "And the one before that. The one where they found my mother."

"Found her, they did?" Franklin said.

"Yes, her whole village had either been killed or run away. The Barlows"—he pointed at the next farm to the west—"have a scalp from then, but I'm not allowed to look at it."

"You wouldn't want to, would you?" Franklin asked.

The boy pursed his lips and shook his head as he climbed up to drive the wagon filled with manure. "You two can walk alongside," he said. "George can't pull both the load and you."

It was nearly noon before they had delivered the load and washed down the wagon. When Jane came toward them, wiping her hands on her apron, Marcus said he would start digging out the second garden plot that the captain wanted. As he passed the girl, Marcus nodded and touched the brim of his hat, but didn't speak. She walked on without expression.

Franklin turned to the wall patches, which came hard at first. He missed his own tools. The lumber was a mishmash of lengths and widths, scraps and leftovers from other jobs. Franklin had James sort them by type of wood, width, and thickness, while

Franklin filed off and squared the damage the mule had wrought. Preparation, he preached to the boy, was the key. How many times had Franklin heard that from his father?

When the call came for dinner, Franklin was near the end of the second patch. He sent James in to eat, with the message that he was making progress and wanted to finish up. He didn't mention that the neighborhood's pestilential odors were suppressing his appetite. Franklin was looking over the last gap in the wall when he realized that Jane was behind him. She held a plate with a cloth over it, a mug in her other hand.

"Oh," he said, "I didn't mean to make you do that."

"Father didn't want you interrupted, but mother insists. This is the compromise. You must eat—mother's codfish cakes shouldn't be missed—but I've saved you coming inside and having to be polite."

Franklin smiled, "Right." He gestured to a stump. "Why don't you sit there and I'll practice being polite with you."

When he returned from washing up, Franklin sat on the ground with the plate, leaning against the barn. The sun lit one side of her face. He first drank off half the beer. His appetite rallied at the sight and smell of brown bread and more codfish.

"Your mother's a marvel," he said around a mouthful of bread.

"For an Indian, you mean."

"No. I say what I mean."

"And what of your friend? Who barely said a word through dinner?"

Franklin shrugged. "He's not like that. Not really."

"He's exactly like that."

He swallowed the bread. He started coughing, then drank some more beer. She waited. When he was settled, he said, "Your brother said your mother was found as a child. Where?"

"Out east, towards where you're from. She's Penobscot. Her people were. She doesn't remember much. She was only four."

"There's still some Penobscots up our way, not far from us. We get along with them. I guess we didn't when our people first got here. Our people came from Germany." Her dark eyes looked levelly at him. A man could lose himself in those eyes. That must be what happened to Captain Bellamy with Jane's mother. He tried the bread again. "Is it hard? Being part Indian? I mean, around here?"

"Sometimes my brothers get into fights. Most folks around here are used to us. A few stay away. Like your friend. My father, he's pretty well respected."

"He seems a fine man. Your mother too."

"She seems a fine man?" Jane was smiling.

Franklin smiled back. "I guess you're making me nervous."

"You're always nervous around Indians? Worried that I've got my scalping knife under this apron?" She reached underneath it.

"No, around girls who seem nice."

Jane nodded at the patches on the barn wall. "You're a carpenter?"

"My father makes furniture. He favors making fine pieces, though there's not so much demand for them in Waldoborough. He's taught himself the trade, did that here in America."

"And he's taught you."

"Yes, we made a boat together, when I was a boy. He taught me everything, then we kept learning together." He told her about the *Christiane* and sailing. "There's nothing like it. The air's so fresh and clean out there."

She wrinkled her nose. "Not like here."

He smiled. "No, not like here."

"You and your father should make more boats."

"He won't. He says he doesn't have any feel for them, not like I do. He says we have the two boats we need, so why make more?"

"Then you should make boats by yourself. You have the feel for them."

He nodded. "I plan to." He almost started to tell her about his plans, which were for more than boats, for ships, coasters, even big ships. Waldoborough was a good place for it. The lumber could float down from forests upriver. Pitch could come from local pines. Hemp for ropes grew nearby.

"I should get back for my spinning." She stood, then paused. "Why are you going to fight?"

"Why, for liberty. So we can rule ourselves."

"Does it matter so much to you?"

"You know, my parents, the people who settled Waldoborough, they say they came from Germany for land. That's what my father says. He's got the land, so why fight? He says he doesn't understand why I'm going. When he was young, he fought for

King George, the one before this one. But when he talks about it, why he came, I don't think it was for the land. That's just the way he says it. I think he came to get out from under the thumb of the Landgraf—that was the ruler where they lived. He hated that. But here we are, under the thumb of the king and Parliament."

"My mother keeps asking why."

"What does the captain say?"

"Much like what you say. Without the German part."

"Do you understand?"

She shook her head. "Not entirely. I think fighting's more important to men."

Franklin stood and held the plate out. She was tall. They looked eye-to-eye. "Jane," he said, then his mouth felt dried out. He locked up.

"Yes?"

"Well, I'd like to come back here after the fighting."

"You'll be a member of the Essex County militia, fully entitled to breathe the restoring air of Lynn at your leisure."

"No. I mean, to see you. Come here to see you. If your folks didn't mind."

"I wouldn't mind. And I'm sure they wouldn't." She took a step back, then looked at him again. "It would be fine."

After supper, when Franklin and Marcus were settling down by lantern light, Marcus said, "You looked to be having quite a chat with that girl."

"Jane?"

"No. I mean Helga!"

"She's interesting."

"Because she's part savage?"

"Why do you say that? She's Captain Bellamy's daughter. She speaks better than we do. And why did you go off like that? They had to notice."

Marcus sat down on a hay bale. "I'm not sure. I was surprised, that first time, when we first went inside. I hadn't figured on that."

"So?"

"I don't know. It felt wrong."

"We see Penobscots in Waldoborough. That's what Mrs. Bellamy is. Or was."

"See?" Marcus looked at him. "You don't even know how to describe her. It's confusing. It doesn't seem natural. Not right."

"The captain doesn't seem confused."

"I suppose not. Do you like her? Jane?"

"I guess I do."

"Because she's part Penobscot?"

"I don't know. Because I like her."

After a few seconds, Marcus said, "You ready?"

"Yes."

Marcus blew out the lantern. After a minute, he said, "Are you going to try to see her again?"

"If I can. The British may have something to say about that."

"I've been thinking about that. About the fighting."

"Yes. I think we're lucky to be with Captain Bellamy. He's done it before." Franklin rolled on his side. "My father says it's all luck."

"What is?"

"The fighting. Whether you live or die."

"He ought to know." Marcus added, "Is that supposed to make us feel better?"

"He wasn't trying to."

CHAPTER SIX

Shortly after dawn, Captain Bellamy's company mustered on the town commons. Most of the forty-two men carried muskets. Each wore the clothes he thought best for the expedition. Most chose trousers and work shirt, waistcoat, and jacket, with a blanket for cool nights. Hats ranged from broad-brimmed felt ones like Franklin's to beaver caps to the straw hats of farmers. Only the captain had a tricorn, and only he wore a uniform. Ancient swords dangled from a few belts.

Ages ranged from younger than Franklin to older than the captain -- a few were considerably older. The company had three pairs of brothers and a couple of fathers and sons. The men shifted from foot to foot, impatient for the march to start. Families waited at the edges of the company. Wives and mothers and fathers smiled gamely while young children chased each other. Josiah Alderson was there, leaning on his crutch and calling out good wishes. Franklin and Marcus stood to the side while the Bellamys struggled to master their feelings. If there were Tories in Lynn, they stayed indoors.

Two wagons pulled up. One held bullets and two kegs of powder; the other held canvas and lumber for temporary shelters. In view of the sparse equipment, Franklin judged that no one was going to give him a musket to fight with, which meant he might never have a chance to use his father's bayonet.

When the march began, the two volunteers from Waldoborough fell in at the end. Franklin was glad to have someone to wave farewell to. The morning gave him no chance to speak with Jane, but he waved specially to her. He thought she waved specially to him. Maybe.

The company's progress varied between a walk and a trot. The men were eager to get to the action but rarely stayed in formation. Captain Bellamy, having drilled them for months, knew enough to insist on only a rough order. The narrowness of the road forced them to advance no more than three abreast, moving aside for mounted and horse-drawn traffic in either direction. At noontime, when they crossed over the Charles River, Franklin pointed out British warships in the harbor. Those were ships of the line, he said, bigger than anything he'd seen on his one trip to Boston with his father. Each carried sixty-four guns.

As they neared Cambridge, Captain Bellamy insisted on better order. He led them briskly past crowds of lounging men who chatted and shouted to each other, walking here and there on a thousand different errands. The atmosphere felt closer to market day than to a military camp.

"Where we headed, Captain?" a man in the front called.

"Harvard College grounds. Just up on the left."

"Hear that boys?" the same voice called out. "We're going to get educated before we fight!"

But the college grounds were filled. The company walked to an open field a mile beyond. Captain Bellamy ordered the men to stay put. Taking one man, he left to find the wagons, which had fallen behind. He said he'd also look for someone who was in charge of the camp.

Marcus flopped onto the ground, only to spring back up, twisting to looking at the seat of his trousers. The others laughed at the manure stain. Franklin grabbed a handful of grass and handed it to his friend to clean himself up. "Guess it's pastureland," he said.

"More like it came from our fellow soldiers," an older man said. He pointed to the side of the field. A man crouched to perform an act usually conducted in private.

"Good Christ," another said, "like beasts of the field they are."

"We won't be beating the British if that's the kind of camp we have," the first man said. "No discipline. Can't win a fight without discipline. Did you see those characters we marched by? Some of them already stewed to the gills. The rotgut peddlers are having a big time."

"Didn't you see the fine bottles they were swigging?" said the other. "I bet they've been off plundering Tory houses for better stuff than these fellows have ever drunk before."

The two men, who proved to be the brothers Ben and Christopher Talbot, sat with Franklin and Marcus. Each of them pulled out some bread to share. Franklin didn't know where the rest of their meals were going to come from.

Ben, the older brother, had been on campaign with Captain Bellamy twenty years before, against the French. "That's where the captain got that gorgeous uniform," he said with a smile.

"Where's yours?" Franklin asked.

"You're looking at it. That Seth Bellamy, even the British could see he was a natural soldier. They recruited him for one of their American regiments. Went all the way to Quebec with Wolfe, he did. He'd fought in the war with the Indians before that one, when I was a boy."

"Is that when he found Mrs. Bellamy?"

The brothers looked at each other. "So, you heard the story?" Ben asked Franklin.

"Just that he found her." A gunshot startled them, then another. Jumping to their feet, they looked back toward town.

"Nathan," Christopher Talbot called to a laughing man near the road. "Who's shooting who?"

"Some of the boys opened up on a regiment from the goose army, a fierce-looking group they are. We drove 'em off, but no meat for dinner tonight!"

It was mid-afternoon before Captain Bellamy arrived with the wagons. Looking grim, he called the company together.

"All right, boys," he said, "this camp ain't exactly organized yet. We have a chance to show the rest of them how a camp should be set up and how soldiers should carry themselves. I've spoken to General Ward, who's commanding. We picked up provisions for the evening. Apparently the local folk are sharing very generously."

"You mean the Tories?" a man asked with a laugh.

The captain didn't smile. "We're here to fight the British, not our own countrymen. There's a provision system set up and that's how we'll feed ourselves. Now, Jonathan and I are going to lay out where the tents should go up. Leave at least five feet between them and keep them orderly. You'll have to share the tools.

"Now, Mr. Talbot—" he turned to address Ben — "back next to those willows looks a good spot for the latrines. Could you direct our stout young friends from down east in the proper preparation of such a facility? And"—he turned back to the full group—"if you see any fool taking a shit on this field, you have my approval to open fire. Run 'em off with their pants around their ankles. We're going to be dirty enough without other men's shit under our feet."

The men began to break up, but the captain raised his hand and shouted, "One other thing. Drill begins directly after breakfast, at nine. We're soldiers here, not picnickers."

"You need to tell the rest of those boys over there," a man called out.

"We'll show them," Bellamy answered. "Now let's get our work done."

Ben turned to Franklin and Marcus. "I'll just get you boys a couple of shovels. You've got the most important job here." He slapped Franklin on the shoulder. "It's been a wet spring. The ground'll be soft."

* * * * * *

The gleaming furniture around Franklin appeared to be cherry wood, a kind his father valued above others.

"What've you got there, lad?"

Franklin's pulse, already elevated since he entered the house by the back door, shot up. He hadn't heard the man. Franklin wasn't certain it was a Tory house, though no one but a Tory would leave his home unattended with thousands of foraging soldiers around. Foraging had become a principal pastime of the American army. Most of the food had long since vanished from the homes of Tories who sought British protection in Boston. Some soldiers had been eating better than they ever had at home, acquiring a taste for clams and hams, imported coffee and tea. The first round of foraging targeted liquor cabinets and wine cellars.

On one of the early days, the Essex County company marched past a scene worthy of Roman times, two casks broken open and soldiers squatting to catch the wine in their mouths. Captain Bellamy stopped that directly, but he couldn't be everywhere. What would he think if he heard that Franklin was acting like the least disciplined recruit from Connecticut?

When he turned to the voice, Franklin resolved to brazen it out, "What's it to you? Are you the owner here?"

The man, whose clothes were as filthy as Franklin's, grinned. One hand held a sack and the other a short sword. "*Rightful* owner I am, sir," he said. "That's it. I'm the rightful owner. By my mother's side. Terrible injustice they did, stripping all this away from dear old mum while they go off and live like dukes and earls."

Franklin picked up his rifle. "You'll want to be speaking to General Ward about that," Franklin said, "or maybe Dr. Warren."

The man pushed his sword through his waistband and lifted a candelabra from a side table. "They're busy men. I'd hate to bother them with family troubles. Especially when those can be easily fixed." The man spun and offered his wolfish grin. "That is, if you're not feeling too greedy yourself."

Franklin resented being in league with this scoundrel, but he was in no position to make moral judgments. He had two pilfered bottles of brandy in his own sack. "I wish you joy of your family home," he said with a small bow. He held up the sack so the man could see he wasn't taking much. The bottles clinked.

"Hope you left some for me, young fellow. Soldiering's thirsty work."

Franklin rapped on the cabinet he stood next to. "You have a thirsty family."

"Aye, it's been our downfall." The man let out a belly laugh as Franklin left by the back door.

After a half-dozen strokes, the water spurted from the backyard pump. Franklin put his head under the cold stream and ran his hands through his hair to dislodge the worst of the dirt. He pumped again and used the next spurt on his hands and face. He stepped easily into the road. There was little chance he would be challenged now. Filthy soldiers carrying sacks of looted goods were a familiar sight. The only man he feared meeting was Captain Bellamy. He had a good reason for taking the brandy, but the captain could be particular.

Franklin lengthened his stride, ignoring achy muscles. For six days in a row, they had dug entrenchments. They dug them in Roxbury, and in Chelsea, and everywhere in between. The men grumbled about it, complaining that they were digging entrenchments that lazier militias would occupy without any effort of their own.

Captain Bellamy paid no attention. "Many a battle's been won with the shovel, not the musket," he liked to say. "That's how we took Louisbourg. We dug and we dug until the French knew they couldn't win." That wasn't how Robert McDonnell told about that glorious triumph, but Franklin's father always warned that Robert tended to improve on the truth.

Franklin thought that Bellamy was keeping the men busy so they wouldn't fall into the bad habits that afflicted other volunteers, bored by the wearisome standoff with the British. Just a few days before, the Americans had cheered an escapade led by General Putnam, a feisty old number from Connecticut who lured a dimwitted British sea captain to wait too long in shallow water as the tide ebbed. When the ship became grounded, the British had to abandon it. Putnam's men ripped out its cannon and rigging, then set her on fire until she exploded, a fireball in the night. Captain Bellamy said he'd watched warships explode at Louisbourg, but never expected to see such a sight again. That part agreed with Robert McDonnell's accounts.

The Essex County men had no role in Putnam's adventure. They concentrated on digging. Franklin wondered what the people in Waldoborough knew about this great confrontation, and whether the town had approved a call to oppose the king and Parliament. Most days Franklin was impatient for the armies to get on with the fighting. Some days, though, he wondered whether he should be happy with this bloodless stalemate.

The problem was that men were starting to get sick. Marcus definitely was. He began with a fever and aches. Neither he nor Franklin thought much of it. They were tired from the digging, from sleeping out in the cold air. And there was the stink of sweat and unwashed clothes, of dirt, of latrines and of men who were too ill or too drunk or too lazy to make it to the latrine in time. The stink was a degradation.

When it rained, water ran into the shelter Marcus and Franklin had built, then pooled under them. One storm blew off their canvas covering, forcing them to scavenge wood and bricks to build a stronger base for the shelter. Then Marcus started to puke. Spots came out on his face and hands. After one look, the captain said it was the pox, they had to get him into a hospital before he infected the whole company. Franklin worried that he might have picked up the disease, too, but so far he felt all right.

Marcus's sores were becoming vile and angry-looking. There was no hospital system, so he was quarantined in a Cambridge house where a royal official had lived. Some local women managed it. They kept Marcus as clean and comfortable as they could. After seeing Marcus, a physician said there was nothing to do but let the disease run its course. With the captain's approval, Franklin spent most nights there, with Marcus.

He halted in surprise as he stepped into the parlor of the Cambridge house, which held five sick soldiers plus an unexpected figure. "Well, look who's here," Bellamy said from Marcus's bedside. "It's that other man from Waldoborough. By the looks of him, he's brought you something."

The sack in Franklin's hand felt like it held an anvil. "I, well, I," he stammered, "Mrs. Pendleton, one of the ladies here, she thought some brandy might comfort Marcus, might help with the fever. Might help him sleep."

"She sounds a wise woman," Bellamy said, reaching for the sack. "How'd you come by this? Two bottles!"

"I traded for them."

Bellamy pulled out a bottle and appraised it. "Shrewd trading indeed. Why don't we give it a try? Private Straub could certainly use a boost."

Franklin looked to Marcus. Some sores had crusted while others still wept. What skin was visible beneath the sores was whiter than any sheet. Marcus clutched the blanket to his chin. His eyes were bad.

The captain spilled the contents of Marcus's cup out a nearby window and poured in a healthy slug of brandy. Franklin fetched a chair from across the room. "Now just sip it," Bellamy said, his hand cupping the back of Marcus's head. Marcus swallowed and coughed. Then took a swallow without coughing. He nodded and let his head fall back.

"I was just telling Private Straub," Bellamy said, keeping his voice bright, "about our brilliant progress digging entrenchments."

"The men are saying," Franklin answered in the same tone, "that we'll tunnel to Boston and surprise the redcoats by coming out of the ground, blinking and shading our eyes like moles." Marcus, his eyes a little better, smiled. He seemed to have no energy to talk.

"Don't joke about that," the captain said. "It's been tried for centuries, though not quite such long tunnels."

"Does it ever work?" Franklin nodded at Marcus, suggesting some more brandy might be in order.

"Ah," the captain grunted as he helped the sick man drink again. "Not often, but let's hope no one proposes it to our commanders. They might try it."

"Captain," Franklin said in a lower voice, "I hope you don't mind the question, but who exactly's in charge? There's talk that General Putnam's attack on that ship wasn't even authorized. That there's no general in charge."

Looking down at the cup, Bellamy said, "It's not easy to create an army out of farmers and carpenters and cobblers. Us, in other words. The British Army's been around for centuries. They know what they're about. Everything's written down and orderly."

Franklin nodded.

"But war's a difficult business, even if you've been about it for centuries. Even the British get beat. More times than they like to admit."

"But who's in charge?"

The captain poured more brandy into the cup and fed it to Marcus, who nodded again. "I wish I knew. There's General Ward, who's supposed to be. He's a well-spoken gentleman. A patriot. He's been trying to get us organized and fed and armed, and that's no small matter. I'm not sure he's had time, or taken the time, to think about fighting. Then there's General Putnam, who thinks about nothing but fighting, lets the devil worry about supplies and organization. He comes across as the tavernkeeper he is, and the old ranger he was, but he looks to be a fair man in a scrap.

"One thing you may be sure," Bellamy said as he moved his gaze between the younger men. "The British aren't going to sit in Boston all summer. We're going to fight. I don't think it'll be long now. We'll be short of powder and ball, and not very disciplined, but we'll fight."

Marcus's eyes were closed. Captain Bellamy rose from his chair. "The brandy," he said to Franklin in a low voice, "was an excellent idea. You do whatever Mrs. Pendleton says."

"Yes, sir."

"And we'll see you at morning muster?"

"Yes, sir."

"We'll be having several hours of drill."

"After all the digging, that sounds very good."

A sad look passed over the captain's face. He put his hand on Franklin's arm. "I'll pray for your friend."

CHAPTER SEVEN

The order came for the Essex County men to muster on Cambridge Common at 6 p.m. They were to bring blankets and guns. The men knew. Something was about to happen. Maybe now, one of the men joked, they'd dig trenches in the dark.

When the company reached the common, the day's heat was spent. A breeze whispered through the leaves of the arching elms. Captain Bellamy led the men to the near side of the open area, where Colonel Brickett stood before the rest of Frye's regiment. Franklin marched with the Talbot brothers, his companions since Marcus died. They had come to the burial, along with Captain Bellamy. Then, without saying anything, they took Franklin on. Christopher still spoke little, Ben a bit more.

Two other regiments stood two-deep in their stinking clothes and broad-brimmed hats. Most men wore a coat or long waistcoat, stained brown with walnut or sumac bark. Their guns were mostly muskets.

Colonel Prescott paced before them, his tan coat flying out each time he pivoted. When he took off his hat, his bald head reflected the slanting sun.

A man in black broadcloth, a minister, emerged from Hastings House, the army's headquarters. As he climbed a platform, Prescott gestured for the men to come forward. Franklin took off his hat and bowed his head with the others. The minister was red-faced with passion, but Franklin couldn't make out his words.

Prescott, now with a cloak over one arm, ordered the men into marching formation, a drill Captain Bellamy had emphasized lately. The Essex company was near the end of the line. Ben put his head next to Franklin's and Christopher's. "If they're praying over us," he said, "look sharp."

Christopher gave a slight smile and pointed behind them. Two wagons stuffed with shovels and picks were pulling up at the end of the column. "Oh, Lord," Ben said. "We *are* to dig by moonlight."

They took the eastern road to Charlestown, which lay close across the water from Boston and its British ships and British soldiers. No one spoke as they marched, skirting swampy ground and crossing two bridges across the same meandering creek. As the sky darkened, Franklin could see the pale bobbing glow of two hooded lanterns, carried just behind Colonel Prescott. Beyond, the city's lights sparkled through the road dust raised by the march.

The column came upon some American soldiers idling silently on a side road. They swung in behind Bellamy's company. Franklin couldn't tell how many marched now, but it was hundreds. They passed a pond and another empty stretch, then turned onto a narrow isthmus and halted. Before them rose a hill. Franklin would learn it was called Bunker Hill.

For thirty minutes, no orders came. The soldiers kept quiet, shifting on their feet. Some knapsacks and rolled blankets slid to the ground. Bellamy's company stood at parade rest, just as the captain had been drilling them. Christopher cocked an eyebrow. Ben shrugged. "Idiots," he muttered, "have no idea what they're doing."

When the column started again, it passed between Bunker Hill and Charlestown village, then ascended a second, gentler slope. At the crest, with a half-moon hanging large in the sky, they waited as the wagons pulled to the middle of the column. The night air felt warm and soft. Boston looked near enough to reach out and touch. It was a commanding position. From there, the Americans could threaten every location in the city, including the anchored British warships. The British, Franklin realized, would never let them stay here, not if they could help it.

Orders came down the line. Start digging.

With ropes, an officer had laid out a perimeter about forty yards square. Overnight, they were to raise a fort there. Captain Bellamy called it a redoubt. He told them to be as quiet as possible. The men traded guns for tools. They knew to build earthen walls as vertical as possible on the inside, so they could take aim by resting their muskets on the top. On the outside, the walls needed more slope so the base was stable and the walls were thick enough to stop a cannonball.

Franklin and the Talbots were on the village side of the redoubt, at a point where the wall thrust forward several yards. That would allow defenders to angle their fire at attackers. Franklin started swinging a pick, feeling it bite into dry soil. The brothers shoveled behind him. First they dug down the inside wall, working along Prescott's line. Then they climbed over to dig on the outside, creating a ditch that attackers would have to cross. After an hour, they rested amid muffled sounds of thudding picks, shovels sliding into loose earth, and shovels thumping loose earth into shape. The city lay in silver moonlight, with a few evening flames still flickering. Christopher fetched a jug of water from his knapsack and passed it around. Their neighbors on either side asked for a taste, so it was quickly gone. Christopher took the pick from Franklin.

By the beginning of the third hour, the redoubt wall stood about four feet high. Franklin felt fatigue taking over. If he paused, his eyelids drooped. His back and his legs ached. Though the night had cooled, sweat ran down both sides of his face, stinging when it carried crusted dirt into an eye.

"Good work, lads." He looked around. Colonel Prescott, still wearing his long coat, stood behind them. He spoke in a low voice. "Build them out nice and thick. Our lives'll depend on it."

"Colonel," a man to Franklin's left called in a hoarse whisper. "Is there any water or rum? It's thirsty work."

"Not yet, lads. We're saving it."

"Christ," Ben muttered. "That means there isn't any."

Twenty minutes later, Prescott was back. He poked his head over the wall to speak to the men on the outside. "That's good," he said softly. "Now I need some of you over on the Mystic River side. We need a breastwork there in case the British come from that direction. Just a bit more." Captain Bellamy came behind the colonel, carrying the shovel he'd been using. "All right, boys. We know how to do this."

Christopher's eyebrow went up again. Ben spoke indistinctly. After stopping for a breath, Franklin scrambled over the redoubt wall and followed the others to the site for the new breastwork.

After an hour of digging on the Mystic River side, the sky behind Boston began to lighten. The men were leaning on their shovels more often. They licked parched lips and swallowed with dry throats. Muscles cried out for rest and sleep. No one knew what the morning would bring.

Before he heard the hollow boom of a cannon, Franklin saw the first puff of smoke and flash from the sloop off the eastern point. A cannonball whistled overhead and landed hard. Several men dropped to their knees and covered their heads. Franklin's stomach turned over.

"Seems like our secret's out," Ben said in his normal voice, using his foot to drive the shovel. "At least we can talk now." He threw his shovel load on the breastwork.

"You figure we'll be having company?" Franklin said.

"Amen, son," Ben said. "If we had any damned artillery, we could rain bloody murder down on them." He shook his head. "They'll come after us for sure."

Franklin nodded, then swung the pick again. Another cannon boomed. Then a different sound, like a gourd being squashed. The soldiers on the breastwork looked to the redoubt. A body lay on the ground, its top part mashed to jelly. Franklin looked away. "Dig, son," Ben said. "May the Lord bless that poor man's soul."

Soon five ships were firing up at the redoubt and the breastwork. Across the harbor, British artillery on a facing hill opened up. Balls constantly arced overhead now. The Americans could see them against the high, white sky, bending down to smash whatever lay at flight's end. Their impact was sickening. Fear revived Franklin's weary body. He swung the pick with a vengeance. Maybe he could burrow deep into the earth, away from this insanity.

The men's grumbling was gaining volume now. The officers were fools who knew nothing of war. The soldiers were fools to follow them. They'd been led to their deaths, sent up on this godforsaken hill with more hope than water. It was suicide. If the cannonballs didn't get them, they were sure to die of thirst or exhaustion. Captain Bellamy, working a few yards from Franklin, didn't chastise the complainers. He kept digging. When Franklin looked to his left, he saw a gap among the men. A dozen were walking uphill, away from the redoubt, some singly, some in twos or threes.

"Captain." It was Prescott again. Bellamy stepped back to confer with the commander, who was animated. The captain picked his coat off the ground and pulled it on, then began walking the line of the breastwork, speaking in low tones to the men, encouraging them.

Prescott stalked off. When he neared the point where the breastwork met the redoubt, he made a long-legged leap onto the lower wall, then sprang up on the redoubt wall. Waving his hat with one arm, he flashed a broad smile. "Boys," he shouted, "we'll let those bastards aim at me first, so you can get your work done."

He strutted down the rim, calling out to soldiers he knew, swatting others on the shoulder with his hat. At the corner closest to the British ships, he turned his back on Boston and faced them all. "Those sons of bitches've got the same chance of hitting me," he called, "as I have of dining with King George this afternoon!" Some of the men smiled and shook their heads. As if to make Prescott's point, two cannonballs passed harmlessly overhead and a third fell short. Prescott spread his coat to put his fists on his hips. "Which is lucky for me, because Mrs. Prescott would insist on a whole new rig for such a dinner, and I can't afford it!" The grins spread. A few men called out to the commander.

Resuming his walltop saunter, Prescott threw jokes to the men, praised the work, told them they'd soon be grateful for every spadeful of earth they packed down.

"Now that's a man," Ben Talbot said. "I'll follow that one."

Prescott's stroll on the redoubt stanched the trickle of men heading to safety, but only for a while. For two more hours, the British barrage kept up, doing little real damage beyond smashing two water casks, a bitter loss to thirsty men who hadn't eaten in fifteen hours or slept for thirty. The guns fell silent in the late morning, leaving the ascending sun as the Americans' chief tormentor. Exposed on a hill without trees, the men suffered. Thirst and fatigue mounted. Captain Bellamy pronounced the breastwork completed and led the company back into the redoubt. They dropped their tools, fetched their rifles and muskets, and collapsed.

When the British cannon resumed, spirits plunged anew. Why no reinforcements? Thousands of Americans loitered in camp in Cambridge a few miles away. Why didn't they send food and water? Had the men on the hill been forgotten? Were they to be sacrificed?

The exodus began innocently. General Putnam strode into the redoubt and exclaimed that no battle could be fought with all those shovels and picks lying around. He called for volunteers to carry them up Bunker Hill. Dozens leapt at the opportunity to leave, many carrying a single shovel. "Say good-bye to those fellows," Ben said. More left, many not even pretending to carry any tools. Franklin felt anger, fear, and envy.

Captain Bellamy crouched before him. "There's a call for a squad of sharpshooters to drop down to the village." He stood and pointed southwest from the redoubt. Franklin rose to look. "The villagers have left, it's empty. You can find a good spot to shoot at the redcoats when they land." His finger swept around to a beach next to the buildings, directly across from Boston. "With that rifle of yours, you could do us proud."

Franklin nodded. He followed Bellamy to the high end of the redoubt, where a dozen soldiers clustered around Prescott. All held rifles. "We need you boys to disrupt them, make them think twice about their choice of profession. Aim at the officers. Without officers, their men'll lose heart."

"How do we pick them out, the officers?" a man asked.

"They'll have the brightest uniforms," Bellamy broke in. "Pure scarlet. Soldiers can't afford a new uniform every year, but officers can. Look for the brightest colors."

"And," Prescott said, "aim for their belts, where they cross each other, right here." He put a hand to his solar plexus. "If you're new to this"—he looked straight at Franklin—"shoot lower than you think you should. We all shoot high." He looked at each man in turn. "Don't stay too long. When they start after you, pull back into the trees behind the village, there's a farm there. Or even slip up here and lend a hand."

The best part of the assignment came early, when they reached the village. One of the sharpshooters discovered a well. Franklin drank deeply, letting the cool liquid filter down his throat, washing out the dust of the digging. He felt reborn.

It took nearly an hour to find a spot he liked. Some shooters settled inside houses, their rifles poking out the windows. Franklin didn't feel right stomping into someone's home, bringing war with him. Also, he didn't want to get trapped inside a building. He found a thick oak at the village's eastern edge, the pride of a grove surrounded by heavy undergrowth. He set up there, plotting how after each shot he could move to another sheltered spot, confounding return fire. He cleared passages between those shooting stations, so he wouldn't stumble.

He settled down to wait, grateful to be in the shade, to be kneeling. When his head hit the tree trunk, he realized that he had fallen asleep. He was startled by two blasts that came from up the slope, at the redoubt. Had American cannons arrived? That would help. They were drowned out by answering fire from the British cannon.

He studied the sloops in the channel as they fired up the hill. The largest had ten guns facing the Americans, puffs of white smoke billowing with each blast. Two smaller sloops had seven gun ports on each side. Without return fire from the Americans, they rode at anchor, firing at steady intervals. He wondered how fast the ships could sail with such heavy guns. Franklin felt a guilty relief that they were shooting up the hill, not at him in the village.

Movement on the channel's far shore drew Franklin's eye. Lines of redcoats were entering boats. They didn't hurry. When loaded, the boats launched across the channel. The water was calm, lending the procession a majestic quality. He counted two columns of fourteen boats each. Franklin drew himself up to firing position, but the boats veered north and came ashore far beyond his range. The redcoats walked up a small rise and lingered there while the boats went back for another load. The process took much of an hour.

At midafternoon, a detachment of redcoats broke from the main body and marched toward the village, then swerved right, massing for an attack on the redoubt from this side. Franklin settled on one knee, the rifle barrel on the ground. They were in range, but he waited for another shooter to fire first. He noted three of the enemy whose uniforms sparkled in the afternoon sun. Officers. Targets.

He wiped sweaty palms on his shirt, then rubbed dirt into them. He had never shot a man, or at a man. This was no time to dwell on that. He thought of Marcus, who made the sacrifice without getting into the fight. He thought of his father and the battles he survived. He thought of Jane. He had a job to do for all of them, and for his friends in the redoubt. His heart was beating hard.

A shot came from his right. Franklin had a target in his sight, a tall man with a uniform that fairly glowed. He squeezed the trigger. The rifle jolted. His target fell backward. Franklin spun round, his back to the tree trunk, and reloaded, reminding himself to slow down. Others fired. He had no cartridges, so he had to pour the powder down the muzzle, load the ball, then level the rifle to pour powder into the pan. There was no return fire. He decided to shoot again from this spot.

When he turned to take aim, the sight was shocking. None of the British troops had moved. They weren't kneeling or lying down or making any effort to protect themselves. They weren't firing back, probably because their muskets couldn't reach this far. He couldn't decide whether to admire their bravery or scorn their stupidity. He fired again and cursed. He had to keep his mind on shooting. Nothing else. He hurried his next shot and the gun misfired, only a click sounding after he pulled the trigger. Taking a breath, he cleaned the muzzle, emptied the pan, and concentrated, then moved to another shooting station.

Franklin was at his third station when he heard the whistle of a cannonball, then a crunch as it hit a building to his right. So that was it. The British would blast the sharpshooters with artillery. He aimed in a standing position, impressed that targets in the brightest coats still presented themselves. Didn't they notice the danger? He shot. He thought it hit home. He decided to move back to his first station. More cannonballs shrieked into the village. One whumped into the ground. Others smashed wood and glass.

When he set up for his next shot, Franklin sniffed. He turned around. Black smoke spiraled up from two houses. The village was burning. More British shells flew in. Two sharpshooters were running toward the farm, back toward Bunker Hill. He fired a last shot and didn't stay to watch. The smoke was billowing now, blowing toward Franklin and the British troops.

He jogged through the grove, then out into open ground. The sharpshooters had gathered near a stone barn. "Can't burn this," one of them said, but Franklin wasn't so sure. The roof, any hay inside, all would burn easily. He decided to keep going. He looped around so he could climb the hill. His breathing grew labored. This hill was steeper than the hill where the redoubt stood.

At the summit, he stopped to catch his wind. Hundreds of Americans milled aimlessly there. Some looked anxious. Others looked bored. The slope down to the redoubt was dotted with traffic, soldiers fleeing the redoubt and others—fewer—approaching it. British troops on the Mystic River side had formed into a line, two-deep. They were moving against the breastwork and another structure that looked like a fence. In the front, wearing tall hats that made them seem a race of goliaths, marched the British grenadiers. Franklin's heart pounded. The battle was starting. A man near him called out, "Who's for the redoubt? Who stands with our men?"

Franklin joined the group that formed behind the man, walking next to a black soldier carrying an ancient-looking musket. He wondered how an African ended up descending this hill to fight the British, but then focused on the British advance. The line of red on the river side had started to move forward.

CHAPTER EIGHT

"It's young Overstreet," Ben Talbot cried out as Franklin threw himself against a rampart. The older man gave him a sidelong look. "You're showing more loyalty than judgment." Christopher clapped Franklin on the back, but said nothing. Both brothers, coatless now, leaned against the embankment. "We were hoping you'd have drove the bastards off by now," Ben added.

To their right, the village was aflame, thick smoke cloaking the British muster. Nothing could survive that conflagration. On the other side of the redoubt, the British still advanced along the river. Stumbling over pasture fences, the attackers stopped to batter them to pieces. Their lack of haste was unnerving, like the ice coming down the Medomak in spring.

As the redcoats kept coming, the British cannon fell silent. The stillness left a ringing echo. Tension built inside the redoubt.

Franklin looked around after he loaded his rifle. "We could use a few more men."

"See Dr. Warren there," Ben said. Christopher nodded his head to the right. Amid the dirt-crusted soldiers stood a handsome fellow in a black suit, holding a musket and chatting with a neighbor. "Boss of the whole colony he is, and came here to stand with us."

Franklin grunted.

"Also," Ben said, "we're not to shoot until we see the whites of their eyes."

"Hope the redcoats don't squint," Franklin said.

Ben smiled. "Good man."

Franklin felt lightheaded under the blazing sun. Lifting his hat, he wiped his forehead with a sleeve. He still hadn't eaten or slept, but he'd had water. He closed his eyes and thought a short prayer. The men climbing the slope were offering the same prayer. How would God choose?

Well beyond rifle range, the redcoats had formed a long line before the village, one that curled around the redoubt's eastern and northern sides. Overlapping both ends of the American walls, the line looked like a vise that would slowly close, crushing the fort and everything within it. Drums began a steady, slow beat. At the pace of a Sunday stroll, the redcoats started.

Some Americans were leaving the redoubt wall on the river side, across from Franklin and the Talbots. Colonel Prescott rushed to them. "Fellows, you've built these stout walls," he said in a steady voice, managing a smile. "We can do this now. We must do this. This is why we're here." The men paused. They looked uncertainly at each other. Prescott spread his arms to herd them back. They resumed their positions.

Franklin peeped over the wall at the British advancing from the village. They had stopped, evidently to wait for three small cannons to be muscled past fences. The drums kept pounding. Then the line of red coats, white belts, and white britches started again. They looked a proper army, not like the men in the redoubt, who resembled impoverished gravediggers. Nor did the British look thirsty or hungry or unslept.

The redcoats stopped to send a volley up the hill. Musket balls thumped into the redoubt wall. Others whistled overhead. No American cried out.

Some Americans fired back, but Prescott stopped them. "The whites of their eyes," Ben muttered, taking his own peep over the wall. The British line began again. Franklin took aim. They marched closer. And closer. So close that he barely needed to aim. He could simply point the rifle in the right direction. When the British were thirty yards away, still at their Sunday pace, Prescott shouted.

Franklin's shot was swallowed in the roar. Flames sprang from muzzles up and down the wall. The British front line fell, swept to the ground as though a giant scythe had swung across them. Or the hand of God. The American musket fire kept up. By the time Franklin had reloaded, the British were moving back down the slope. Few fired back. Some British officers shouted, smacking soldiers with the flats of their swords to drive them forward, but the red wave was ebbing. As they backed away, they left behind a scattering of broken and bleeding soldiers. Franklin heard cheers from soldiers around him. They had stopped them.

But the redcoats weren't through. They stopped out of musket range and reassembled. Franklin thought his rifle could reach them. He aimed at a man trying to organize a new line. He kept the muzzle on the man as he strode up and down the line, waiting for him to stop. The man paused to shout at a soldier. Franklin squeezed the trigger. He saw the man jerk, drop his sword, and fall to his knees.

By the time Franklin had reloaded, the drums were beating again. The British line was moving. They're not cowards, Franklin thought. He tried to ignore the groans and cries from the enemy wounded who lay before the redoubt.

The next scene was an eerie reprise of the first attack. The Americans held their fire. And held their fire. The British kept coming. And kept coming. Franklin remembered his father's words. On either side, the soldier's comrades are shot down, but the soldier continues on. It was madness.

Prescott shouted. The American line erupted. More redcoats fell. The men behind them tried to get past crumpled bodies. Some tripped. Others wavered. More shots came from the redoubt. The redcoats fell back down the slope.

Prescott screamed to stop shooting. This time there was no cheering. Prescott walked behind the men. Powder was low, he said. Make every shot count. Retreating to the middle of the redoubt, he started tearing open artillery cartridges for cannon that had never arrived. Men trotted over to receive loose powder from him.

"I'm out," Ben said to his brother.

"Yup," Christopher agreed. Franklin poured his remaining powder into his hand.

"Four shots?" he said. The brothers nodded. "One of you take enough for the second shot, since you're faster."

"Chris," Ben said. "He's the fastest."

When they looked back over the wall, the British had regrouped. Bodies writhed on the ground. Others lay still, in impossible postures. Franklin couldn't make out faces, but he could hear voices crying out to God, to comrades. One called for mother. Many groaned. The voices reverberated in Franklin's head. He saw a redcoat slither downhill, using one arm to pull himself, holding the other against his body. It felt inhuman to stand there with his gun, ready to make more bloody wrecks like that one, to watch other men die.

The British cannon resumed, announcing that the battle would go on. The British soldiers dropped their knapsacks so they could advance more quickly. Franklin thought of the bayonet in his knapsack, which he had left at the redoubt's sally port almost eighteen hours before. He rested his rifle against the wall and ran for the knapsack. With the bayonet in his belt, he resumed his position.

Again the drums beat. Again the red wave came. Again the Americans waited. And again a wall of flame leapt out, the blast from two hundred guns ripping the air. Its force staggered the red wave. This time, the British stopped to fire back. Most of their balls hit no one. The American firing fell off, the lack of ammunition beginning to tell. The red wave gained fresh heart. Foot-long bayonets flashed at the end of their muskets. The wave started again, this time with a roar of angry voices. Some redcoats wore bandages. One had an arm in a sling. His good arm cradled his musket.

The advance faltered when it reached the wall. A few intrepid souls scaled the embankment only to be clubbed to their knees, their skulls or bones smashed. Other redcoats gathered at the base of the wall, where the Americans couldn't get at them. The standoff lasted for seconds, then a minute. Something had to give.

Behind him, Franklin heard the roar of close artillery and the screams of wounded men. The British had their cannon in play on the other side of the redoubt. More redcoats sprang up in front of Franklin. A man to his left jumped over the American defenders then pivoted and plunged a bayonet into the throat of a short man in shirtsleeves. Blood spurted into the redcoat's face. Franklin swung his rifle at the attacker, aiming to smash his skull. The man ducked while the swing pulled Franklin down on his knees.

Redcoats were leaping from the walls. There were no lines of battle, only a melee, men in sweaty uniforms grappling with filthy men in work clothes. The Americans, reduced to using their rifles like clubs, had to get in close to avoid British bayonets. Shouts and screams mingled with grunts and gargled agony.

Franklin couldn't see the Talbots. Next to him, an American wrestled with a redcoat. Franklin smashed his rifle barrel into the British soldier's knees, bringing him down. The American picked up a rock and threw it. He missed. Franklin jumped on the redcoat's back and tried to throttle him with his hands, but the man threw him off. They both lay on the ground panting. Franklin reached for the bayonet and sprang at his enemy, the bayonet in his hand ready to thrust. When he pushed it forward, the redcoat gasped yet still reached to push Franklin off. Their eyes locked. Franklin leaned his weight on the bayonet, but it began to twist from his hand. It wouldn't go in. It had snagged a belt or a strap. Both men strained for an advantage.

Franklin bore down with all his strength, his forearm at the man's throat, yet the blade wouldn't budge. The redcoat's eyes bulged. He thrashed from side to side to throw Franklin off, one arm pushing up to protect his throat, the other pounding on Franklin's arm and shoulder, the power of the blows sapped because he was on his back. If Franklin drew back to thrust the blade again, seeking a softer target, he would give the man an opening to twist away. He could smell the man's breath, feel his fingers dig into his arm and hand.

Franklin stole a glance around him. There were too many redcoats. The redoubt was lost, whether he killed this man or not. What was he doing? He needed to go.

He stared into the redcoat's eyes. Keeping his arm at the man's throat, he let up on the bayonet. The redcoat nodded. Franklin released his pressure and rose to his knees. The Englishman's eyes filled with tears. He didn't move as Franklin scrambled to his feet, grabbed his rifle, and headed to the sally port. He jammed the bayonet into his belt.

Other Americans pushed toward the same goal. Redcoats atop the redoubt walls fired into the struggling mass. Franklin ran up against a pile of Americans. He held the rifle across his body and pushed, driving ahead with his legs, step by step. When he burst through the sally port, he stumbled, then gathered himself. More redcoats stood to the side, firing at defenseless men fleeing up the hill. Franklin needed to be lucky now. He started to run.

After only a few strides, he slammed face first into the ground. A searing pain scorched his scalp. He lost track of the day.

"Ben," Christopher shouted, "the boy!"

The brothers had never separated during the brawl. With a glance, they'd silently agreed to withdraw. They fell in behind Franklin but couldn't keep up with his younger legs.

"Christ," Ben said, leaning over, "all that blood."

"Come on." Christopher jammed the fallen man's rifle under his arm with his musket. Each brother grabbed an arm and began to drag. One side of Franklin's whitened face was smeared red. After a hundred yards of slow progress, another soldier called over. "I'll carry your guns. You take the man."

They lifted Franklin, draping one of his arms over each brother's shoulders. At the hilltop, they laid him on the ground. Ben tore a strip from his shirt and wrapped it round Franklin's head. The boy breathed yet. The British, stalled by a brace of Americans who fired from behind a stone wall, abandoned their pursuit and turned to their own dead and wounded who ringed the redoubt.

On the far side of the hill, Christopher found a barrow filled with shovels and picks. He dumped the tools. They loaded Franklin, his arms and legs spilling out every side, and laid his rifle across. Each brother lifted a handle with one hand, his musket with the other.

"Keep an eye out for something to drink," Ben said. "I'm parched."

CHAPTER NINE

The scene around Franklin was unaccountably domestic. Captain Bellamy, spectacles perched halfway down his nose and legs crossed, was reading a broadsheet. Franklin clenched his eyelids against the sunlight that poured through a window over the captain's shoulder. The sheet pulled up to his chin smelled of soap. His shirt was clean. Where was the frenzy of those final moments in the redoubt, the desperate struggle with the redcoats, the flight up the slope?

"Good evening," the captain said, lowering his broadsheet.

Franklin struggled for words. His voice wouldn't come. His throat felt raw, coated with hair and scabs. Bellamy lifted a metal cup to Franklin's lips, supporting his head. The water went down hard, making Franklin sputter and cough. Pain burst in his head. He groaned. The water felt good on his lips, in his mouth. They tried again. He swallowed some that time. They kept at it until the cup was empty.

"How do you feel?" Bellamy asked.

"Like someone's pounding my brain with a hammer." He closed his eyes and felt the pain relent. "What hit me?"

"Musket ball, ran right along your scalp." Bellamy ran a finger along the side of his own head, from back to front. "It took a pretty good gouge out. They had to cut off your hair to dress the wound. If it doesn't grow back, you'll have a very distinctive scar." Franklin lifted a hand to the left side of his head. "Don't touch it. It bleeds easy." Franklin let his hand fall.

"When is it? Now, I mean."

Bellamy looked at the broadsheet he had dropped to the floor. "After dinner, Monday, June 21."

Franklin tried to calculate. It seemed like it must be two days, but he couldn't stop his eyelids from descending. Bellamy sat back and pulled his watch from his waistcoat pocket. He had to leave soon.

"More water." After another cupful, Franklin asked, "This house, is it where Marcus was?"

"Down the street." Bellamy looked around the wood-paneled room. "It's a fine place. I imagine the Jenkins family is missing it."

"We lost." Franklin had his eyes closed.

"We did." Bellamy sat back and crossed his legs. "The British are digging in up on Bunker Hill like they're planning to stay a while. But they won't."

"It's all right with me if they do."

Bellamy shrugged. "It's one hill on a big continent. Our spirit is good. They can't win this war. We won't let them. It's our home, not theirs."

"They won."

"Conquerors always lose in the end. Look at Rome."

Franklin sighed. He lacked the energy and the knowledge to talk about history and conquest. "How did I get here?"

"Ah. The Talbots dragged you all the way from Charlestown in a wheelbarrow, then they sat here like a couple of mother birds waiting for an egg to hatch. When I got here an hour ago, they were both asleep, still in their same clothes. I sent them to get some proper rest. I hope they're stretched out on cots."

"I owe them a debt."

"You do, but they were proud to do it. You're the closest thing to family they've got around here. Queer ducks they are, but steadfast." Bellamy leaned forward. "How about some food? You must be famished."

Franklin shook his head, then regretted it. The movement set off a nausea that threw him off balance while lying flat on his back. He closed his eyes and waited.

Bellamy smiled. "I don't know about you, but when we were up on that hill, I could have eaten a horse, hooves and all." Lying on the makeshift bed—really planks with a mattress laid across—Franklin looked very young. Being awake had softened the waxy sallowness he wore when Bellamy arrived. Maybe it was the water.

"Did we lose men? Up there? The company?"

Bellamy cleared his throat. "There's Jonas in a house down the road." He turned to point across the room. "Took a ball to the shoulder. Went clean through. The doctor's not sure about him. He's got fever." The captain scratched the back of his head. "Sergeant Upton. He was killed at the wall, near me. And Collier and Miller too. Some others have been hurt, but not so bad. It wasn't as bad as I feared, but it was bad." Bellamy pursed his lips. "You fought well, son. You didn't have to come back up from the village. The men know that."

Franklin let his eyes stray from the captain's face. He was looking at nothing when he spoke. "At the end, at the wall, when it was like a brawl…" His voice trailed off.

"Yes."

"I could have stayed and probably killed one of them. I had him down. I had the bayonet blade in my hand. I could have done it." Franklin fell silent again.

"It was a hard fight."

"I left. I saved my own skin instead of staying to fight."

"The day was lost. It was time to leave."

"That wasn't it. Or not all of it." He looked back at Bellamy. "I didn't want to kill him."

Bellamy nodded. "Are you sure you don't want some food? It's been three days." Franklin grunted no, then allowed himself to drift away.

When he opened his eyes next, a lantern lit the room. Ben and Christopher dozed in chairs next to him. Christopher woke first and prodded his brother. When Franklin declined food, the brothers acted as though he hadn't spoken. Ben had fixed some porridge. He hurried off to warm it.

Christopher wedged a blanket behind Franklin's head, then put a shirt to the same use. The pain wasn't as bad now, but the dizziness came back. After a silent time, Christopher offered the water cup. Franklin sipped it steadily, feeling its cool through his whole body. He recognized a passing interest in food.

Ben fed the porridge to him slowly, letting him rest between spoonfuls. Franklin had never properly appreciated the sweet flavor of porridge before. It flooded him, full of life itself. The warm food after the cool water was almost heavenly. He let his head drop back. "Enough," he said.

Ben sat back. The spoon jutted from the bowl at an angle. "More in the morning."

"I owe you, you both, my life," Franklin said. "I know that. I'll find a way to repay you." Ben smiled. Christopher looked down at his hands.

After a silence, Christopher cleared his throat and looked up. "Make something of yourself."

* * * * * *

The lady nurses of the Jenkins house changed his bandage and tried to keep him quiet, but Franklin only grew more restless. Recovery was taking longer than he thought it should. One of the nurses, an older woman with a fluty voice named Flora Lewis, read to him in the afternoons. For several days, she also read to him from whatever in the Jenkins library struck her fancy. Franklin asked Mrs. Lewis to read something about history, perhaps about empires. He wanted to know more about what the captain said, that conquerors always lose in the end. She started reading about the Roman Empire, from the time of Jesus.

At other times, Franklin was content to lie still and think. Perhaps it wasn't quite thinking, more like imagining. He imagined going back to camp with the Essex County boys. He imagined digging, marching, sitting around campfires, facing cannons, shooting, and brawling. He imagined becoming an officer, wearing a uniform, the thrill of victory. He imagined rooms with sick and wounded soldiers. Men like the one in the bed opposite him, who thrashed with fever for several days, shouting in a vexing gibble-gabble until he gave out. Now there was a man from Connecticut who tried to stop a rolling cannonball with his foot. He lost the foot.

Franklin thought about Jane Bellamy too. That thinking was closer to dreaming. He had spent only two days around her. And part of a third. Why did she make such a strong impression? She reminded him of his mother, though there was no physical resemblance. It was her way. He dreamt of a life on the banks of the Medomak, dark-haired children, his father making child-sized furniture. And where was he, Franklin, in this dream? He couldn't see.

Most days, the Talbots stomped in after dinner, caked with dirt. They were digging more than ever. American commanders had learned one lesson from the battle—always keep thick walls between them and the British. So for a while, the company dug trenches in Roxbury. Then up in Medford. Wherever the lines of the siege extended, they worked to put something solid between them and British bullets.

By early July, Franklin could rise from the makeshift bed and walk a little. His strength came back day by day. From the head wound down to his toes, he didn't recognize his body. His legs were unsteady, like a newborn pup's. He learned to avoid the mirror in the central hall. He didn't care to see the emaciated stranger who stared back.

He could feel a scab forming over most of the wound, but he preferred to keep it bandaged. It opened once when he walked in the garden, sending blood down the side of his head in a dramatic cascade. The lady nurses didn't flinch. They had seen worse.

He read for himself now. He stayed with the book about Rome. On bright days, he pushed a chair into the sunshine and read until he drowsed. He wondered how much history the captain knew. The Romans were losing in the story, the conquered peoples rising against them, but it seemed like it was taking lifetimes. He hoped it wouldn't take so long to drive the British from America.

One day Franklin asked for paper and ink and a quill. Flora Lewis set them out in what had been the dining room, making space amid heaps of bandages, blankets, and sheets. For a long time, he wrote nothing, lost in the memory of working in the shop with his father. Those hours had slipped silently by, Franklin watching how his father coaxed the wood into the shape and size he wanted, unwilling to have it be off by the slightest margin. If a chair made by Johann Overstreet wobbled, the floor was uneven. The chair was not.

Franklin thought of his sisters, Lena and Liesl, and how they never really knew their mother. He wanted to be home. He missed sailing the *Christiane* into Muscongus Bay. He missed all of it.

The blank paper stared back at him. He had to begin, at least to tell them he was alive. He realized he would also tell them he was coming home. He didn't know when. As soon as he could. Before winter.

It was mid-July, a rainy day, before Captain Bellamy came back. He looked drenched as he sat, shaking off his tricorn. Franklin was propped on his bed. He had dropped off while reading about Rome.

"More digging, Dorchester today," the captain said. "I've spent so many years leaning over leather and tools that it's a shock to be outdoors all the time."

"I should be there to help," Franklin said.

"You're still not able. From the look of you, a strong gust of wind would blow you down."

"I'm getting stronger." Franklin shrugged. "The headaches come less often. It makes you appreciate how good it is to be healthy."

The captain picked at his hat, pulling off grass and dirt. His face was serious. "We need to replace Sergeant Upton, you know." Franklin nodded. "I've talked to the men about it. That's how we do it in the militia. I make the appointment, but I need to know what the men think."

"I've been reading about the Romans. I don't think that's what they did."

Bellamy smiled. "Have you? Is that Gibbon?"

Franklin held out the book for Bellamy to inspect. "Wonderful stories in this," the captain said. "About all the forms of human folly." After a moment, he said, "Well, back to New England. Some said you should be the new sergeant."

Franklin frowned. "I'm too young. There are men my father's age in the company."

"How old are you?"

"Twenty my last birthday."

"Alexander had won most of the known world by your age."

"I'm not Alexander."

"Nor I. You needn't worry about it. I've appointed Christopher Talbot."

"Not Ben?"

"I figure that if I appoint one of them, the other comes along."

Franklin thought for a moment. "You know, my father was a sergeant, back in Hesse, where he came from in Germany. The Romans had a lot of trouble with the Germans. I like to think those were our ancestors giving them a bad time."

"I thought you said he was at Louisbourg."

"He was. He was a ranger captain there."

"He'd be proud of how you fought."

"No. He didn't want me to come."

"I see." Bellamy scratched the side of his face. "So he's loyal to the crown. That must be hard for both of you."

Franklin shook his head. "No, it's not that. He says he came to America to get away from kings and nobles, so his sons would never be soldiers." He paused. "We argued."

The captain sat forward. "It's a righteous cause, Franklin. It's our liberty at stake. Your father may have come here to get away from the kings, but here we are with King George breathing down our necks. We have to fight."

"That's what I said, though not so well as you say it."

"Has anything changed your mind about that?"

Franklin shrugged. "Maybe. Maybe I've changed. I've fought. I've shot men, probably killed them, and then I couldn't keep doing it. No one needs a soldier like that, one who can't do what needs to be done."

"The men you serve with, they've taken your measure. They don't agree with you."

"They don't know, Captain. This man I was fighting with, the one I told you about. I was trying to use the bayonet on him, but it wouldn't break through his belt. I had all my weight on it. I think back on it now, and it's so clear to me. I see his face. I feel his breath. I'm pushing down and pushing down. He can't move, but I can't kill him. And now I know it was my fault. I hadn't kept the blade sharp. I never sharpened it, not once. It's old, hasn't been used in twenty years. My father told me to keep it sharp." He looked up at Bellamy. "You see, he told me. But still, I'm not sorry. I didn't want to kill him. What kind of soldier does that make me?"

Bellamy held his gaze. "I don't know, son. Battle's the hardest thing you and I will do."

"I keep thinking maybe there's another way I can help our cause. That I should find another way."

The captain looked uncomfortable again. "I have something for you." Franklin looked at the man's serious face. "I wrote to my family and mentioned you were wounded." He pulled a folded paper from the inside band of his hat. "It's from Jane. I didn't suggest she write to you." He handed it over. "You see the seal. I didn't open it."

Nor did Franklin. He thanked the captain and set it aside. "Well," Bellamy said, shifting in his chair. "Have you heard about our new general?"

"One above General Ward?"

"Yes, sent by Congress. The whole continent is watching us. The new man almost rode me down just now. He's a big fellow, from Virginia, rides a white horse and takes his slave with him everywhere, almost like his shadow. His name's Washington."

"Does he know what he's about?"

"They say no one can understand him, the way he speaks, so I'm not sure. Evidently he fought the French—not up here, down in Virginia—so he must know something." Bellamy raised his hat to his head. "I'll be off," he said.

Franklin made himself wait at least a minute. His pulse was racing when he broke the seal on the paper and unfolded it. He cast his eye quickly over it. The note was only a few lines. Then he started again and read each word carefully. It contained nothing that Captain Bellamy couldn't have read. Jane sent her wishes for his speedy recovery. She was sorry to hear of Marcus's death. She related the progress of the Bellamy garden. The berries had been sweet, but the corn needed rain. She signed it "your friend."

Franklin read the letter several more times that evening, then placed it in his knapsack. Jane's words were ordinary ones. Her sentiments were unexceptional for a young woman. But she wrote.

CHAPTER TEN

Only three miles past the Charles River, Franklin's spirits became lighter, much lighter than the dreary day. Flat, grey clouds clotted the sky without offering much hope of rain. A sharp September breeze promised colder days to come, though only a few leaves showed autumn colors. Wagons filled with harvest goods clambered south toward the army that Franklin had left behind.

The farewells that morning had been grinding, especially with the Talbots. Ben was kind. He insisted that Franklin was making the right choice. "You've pulled your weight," he said, "and no one can say you didn't. Others have left and new ones come in. Leave the fighting to washed-up old bachelors like Chris and me."

It was true that others went home after the battle, but Ben's words tied Franklin's tongue in knots. Franklin had depended on the brothers. They saved him. But he was leaving them to fight his war.

For once, Christopher filled the silence. "Anyway, soldiering turns out to be a lot like farming. You dig holes and build walls."

They had laughed. Franklin tried to tell them what they meant to him, but Ben cut him off. "You don't have to say anything, son. We've been the best of friends."

Leaving Captain Bellamy was no easier. In his dingy, frayed uniform, he looked up from the tree stump where he sat reading, a leg crossed over the other knee.

"Sir," Franklin said, saluting as smartly as he ever had.

"If you're saluting, this is serious." Bellamy pulled a folded sheet from the back of his book and handed it over. "This is a formal notice of discharge from the Essex County militia, if anyone should give you difficulty. Apparently some towns are getting particular about their soldiers turning up back home."

"Thank you, sir. It's been an honor to serve in your company." Franklin waited a beat. "Sir, I also should say that I hope to stop in Lynn on my way home, and to see your daughter."

"Ah." Bellamy closed his book and took off his spectacles. "Is she expecting you?"

"I did send her a letter, yes, sir. I want you to know, sir. My intentions are serious."

"She's not like other girls, you know."

"I know."

"Did you warn her about . . .?" He pointed to his head. The hair around Franklin's wound was still patchy, with parts of the scar exposed.

"I'll keep my hat on, sir."

Bellamy stood. "Perhaps you would carry a letter, and some small things for my family. Can you wait?"

"Of course, sir."

Returning minutes later, the captain handed over a leather pouch. Franklin stuffed it in his knapsack, then shouldered the load and his rifle. He began to salute again, but Bellamy held out his hand.

Franklin started to tell him how much he admired his leadership, but Bellamy shook his head. "Godspeed," he said.

A rough voice broke into Franklin's reverie. "Watch where you're going, will you?"

Franklin stepped away. "Sorry," he said, "my mind was elsewhere."

The man, whose lank black hair reached to his shoulders, smiled and nodded. “With that rifle on your shoulder, looks like you’re headed the wrong way. The fighting’s back there.” The man jerked his thumb behind them.

“I’ve been there since May,” Franklin said. “Discharged.”

The man shook his head. “Only lasted a few weeks myself. Didn’t get on with being told what to do. Nor for the digging. Moles is what they need, not men.”

“Well, it wasn’t all digging.”

The man grabbed Franklin’s arm with a dirty hand. They stopped. “You were there, at Bunker Hill?” Franklin nodded. “What was it like?”

After a moment, Franklin said, “Bad.”

“Huh.” The two men began to walk again. “Another fellow said that sort of thing.”

They fell into step together, though Franklin labored to match the man’s stride. His wind wasn’t back yet. He was sorry when the man, Ned Rogers of Saugus, left the road. A gull followed him for a short way, but soon veered off in search of better company.

Lynn didn’t smell so bad after the army camps. He walked first to the town pier. A northbound coaster was leaving in two days, provided the British didn’t turn up. The captain was willing to stop at Waldoborough. Franklin arranged to be on it.

Jane was in front of the Bellamy house when he came along the road. The sight made him smile. Even better was her bright look when she saw him.

* * * * * *

Next day, after morning chores, Jane and Mrs. Bellamy packed a lunch for them. Franklin sat against the kitchen wall, luxuriating in the food smells, the room’s regularity, how ordinary it was.

Her brothers tagged along when Jane and Franklin started, staying near as the couple turned off to climb Osprey Hill. Jane told them for the fourth time there would be no food for them at the top of the hill. They finally believed her. Grumbling, they turned back.

Jane had to slow her pace to match Franklin’s on the hillside path. The crown was bald, affording views on all sides under a clearing sky, but Franklin looked only at the bay. The altitude made the waves look small as they churned shoreward in thin white lines. Dozens of birds crossed the sky without apparent effort.

"Where are the osprey?" he asked.

Jane smiled. "I've never seen any up here. One of our local mysteries."

When Franklin sat on a rock, Jane asked to inspect his scar. He took off his hat. "It must have been awful," she said.

"It was worse for those who had to look at it, like your father and the Talbots. I can't see it, which is fine with me."

"You could use a mirror."

He shook his head. "I guess I'm afraid my brains really are leaking out, or already have."

Jane started pulling food from the bag—a large cheese, a loaf of bread with butter in a pot, apples, pears, and a jug of beer.

"Quite the feast," he said, then pointed behind her to Lynn. "The town's so settled. People have lived here so long. I saw a gravestone at the churchyard that was from fifty years ago. It gives the place a different feel. Waldoborough's still rough. The people who settled it still live there."

"My mother's people," she said, "have been here a lot longer than fifty years."

He broke off a piece of bread. "All right. That was stupid of me. I don't know much about the Penobscots."

"I don't either," she said. "Nor does my mother. All her family, her people. They're all gone."

"They were killed?"

"Or got sick, or ran away to the north. Which probably was a good idea."

"That must be hard for her."

"I think it left a hole." She leaned back to look at him. "Why did you leave my father's company?"

He shook his head. "I don't think I'm much of a soldier."

"Father said some wanted you to be sergeant. Then your letter came saying you would stop here on your way home." She looked over. "What happened?"

"I'm still thinking on it." She waited. "See, there's this friend of my father's back home, a great big man, lost an arm fighting the French. Wonderful storyteller. He fought alongside my father. And he rides my father—he rides everyone, but my father too. He calls my father a natural killer. And I could tell my father hates being called that, so I didn't like it either. But now I've been in battle, I maybe know what he means." He stopped and reached for the words. He'd been working on them.

"My father's a hard man. Not mean, not like that. That's not what I'm saying, or even what his friend is saying. But hard. If he thinks something's necessary, there's nothing he won't do."

"You admire him."

"Yes, I do. When I was young, he always made me feel safe, even in Waldoborough." It was easier not to look at her. "I'm not so hard. I know that now. Even if something's necessary, I'm afraid I may not do it."

"You mean killing?"

He nodded. "Killing, yes. Making men bleed, smashing their bones, making them suffer like I've suffered with this wound. Making orphans and widows. What I can't get straight is that I know the redcoats are here to do all of that to us, so that means it really is necessary. I know that. And I did it. During that fight, I shot men. I probably killed them. But now that I've done it, I doubt myself. In a fight, doubt's a poison. It could get you killed, get your friends killed." He shook his head. "I don't know if I can do it again. But that's not the whole thing. I don't want to do it again."

He looked over at her. Her eyes seemed dark. "Do you understand?"

She was quiet longer than he wanted. "Do you still believe in the cause?" He nodded. "And you left my father and your friends to fight for it for you?"

Franklin colored. He stood and took a step away. He spoke to the bay again. "When I was mending, lying still most of a day, I worked out this plan. That I would go home and build boats for the fight against the British. I would use my skills for our cause. But the way you say it…" He shook his head. "It sounds empty. An excuse."

"What did the other men say?"

"They told me to go." He sat down.

"That should matter more than what I think."

"It doesn't."

She was quiet for a minute more, then took his hand. "I don't have to make your decision, to fight or not, but I worry for my father." She pulled her lips tight. "I know you didn't have to come to the fight. You fought—father says you fought well—and you were hurt. Of course that should be enough."

He heard it. It was in the "should be." That meant it wasn't, not for her, but he wasn't just going to give up, not yet. He'd rather fail than not try. He took her hand, then kissed it. "You're easy to talk to, Jane. I told your father I had serious intentions."

"Franklin," she said. "How could you say that? You barely know me."

"I don't know how I know it, but I do. I knew it when we met, when you were flirting with Marcus."

"Oh, poor Marcus."

"Yes, poor Marcus, but back then all I could think was why wasn't I handsome and charming like him."

"I was wrong about which boy I should be talking with."

Franklin took her other hand. "Jane, if you can imagine putting up with me, with this scar and with my short career as a soldier, we could have a good life together. There's so much I want to do, to do with you. I want to build boats, lots of boats, even ships, big ships that sail the ocean. Maybe we could go off on one of them and see the whole world."

"Oh, Franklin. Really, Franklin." She let go of his hands and stepped away.

He followed. "You can't be entirely surprised, not after I said I was coming."

Her eyes flashed. "Of course I can be surprised. Don't tell me what I can be or can't be."

He held his hands out. "All right, all right. Here we are. I've said what I said. What do you say?"

"Can't you build boats here in Lynn?"

Franklin looked puzzled. "No one builds boats here."

"They do in Salem, and in Boston."

"The British are in Boston."

"They won't be there forever."

"Jane," he took her hands again. "Waldoborough's my home. I wish you could see it. The coast there. It's wilder than here. It's powerful. The ocean and the bay. The forest. And the air—it's clean and fresh, not full of tannery smells. It's beautiful, and there's so much for us there. My sisters would love you, and my father and his wife."

"How many half-breeds live in Waldoborough?"

His mouth fell open. No words came for a moment. "I, I don't know. I can't think of any, not right off. I never thought about it. But that doesn't mean anything. You'll be my wife."

She shook her head. "I can't leave my family. My brothers and I, we know what we all live with. We live with it together. We rely on each other, more than most families do. I couldn't leave them."

"Jane, what can I say to change your mind?"

"Nothing."

"Won't you come look at Waldoborough, at Broad Bay? Come meet my family. Won't you give us a chance?"

She shook her head and started gathering the remains of their meal.

CHAPTER ELEVEN

A light snow fell as Franklin crouched at his end of the long oak strake. He'd shaped it to serve as the sloop's portside garboard. Ethan Tucker grunted as they lifted and began sidestepping toward the frame that Franklin had based on the ships at Alec McDonnell's shipyard. With the Royal Navy still patrolling the coast, traders had to become smugglers. They needed fast ships like this 35-footer. Franklin meant to build the fastest ones.

"Christ," Ethan muttered as they sidestepped gingerly, facing each other.

"Gently, gently," Franklin said, his muscles quivering. He nodded. With a final heave, they brought the strake up to shoulder level, across and down, nestling it next to the keel. Both men gasped when the frame took the strake's weight. They nudged the strake back and forth until it lay flush up to the keel. Franklin walked the length of the frame, running his hand along the junction. The fit was snug.

"What about rigging up that hoist you were talking about?" Ethan asked, shrugging his shoulders.

"Why would I do that when I've got a mighty shipwright like you?" Franklin blew on his cupped hands, then flexed the fingers. Alec said that Waldoborough shipbuilders grew accustomed to the cold, but never came to like it.

Ethan snorted. He was half a head shorter than Franklin, who was no giant himself. He waved at the pine mast that lay under ice-crusted canvas. "You'll need a hoist by the time we get to that monster." Good mast timber was getting hard to find, so Franklin had bought this one from a yard that was failing. He dreamt of seeing it lean under a full weight of sail and wind, powering a sleek hull through the water.

They turned to one of the other strakes. It was mounted on sawhorses, waiting to be adzed to the right dimensions, molded, then tapered at each end. Franklin's yard, on a scrap of land that Alec rented to him, was on the west side of the bay end of Waldoborough. He had storage space and room to build two boats, so long as they weren't too large. He lived right there in the one-room cottage that his father and brother Walther helped him build, with a shed on the landward side for his tan mule, Oatmeal. Because he had no dock, deliveries came to the McDonnell yard. In return, Alec kept some of his equipment on Franklin's lot.

The hesitant March daylight was slipping away. Franklin knew firsthand that shipbuilding done in weak light sometimes had to be redone. "I guess that's it," he said, arching and twisting his back. He wiped down the adz and the unfinished strake, covered everything with canvas, then anchored the canvas with rocks.

"Payday tomorrow?" Ethan asked. Hunched against the wind, he jammed his hands in the pockets of his greatcoat. The snowflakes dodged crazily in the shifting breeze. "Did Gilchrist come up with what he owes?"

"You'll get your wages. Don't worry."

"I don't know about that fellow. You may need another buyer."

"If I do, there'll be one. There may even be a bidding war," Franklin smiled. "She's going to be a beauty."

Ethan said good night as Franklin stored the hand tools in the mule shed. He was about to take Oatmeal out when he heard his name. He turned to find Alec beckoning him.

"The rent's not due for another week," Franklin said as he neared his tall, fair-haired landlord.

"And a damned shame that is," Alec said with a smile. "Early payments are always welcome, of course." He nodded at the frame under canvas. "You need a hoist. Why don't we set one up there tomorrow?" He started walking toward his shipyard office, gesturing for Franklin to follow.

"That's a generous offer," Franklin said, "but Ethan and I are doing fine."

"A brilliant designer like yourself shouldn't be muscling strakes around. You could use some more hands too."

"True enough, but I'll be needing to find a pot of gold for all that."

"Ah," Alec grinned as he opened the office door. "Then you've come to the right place."

The office, smoky from a poorly vented wood fire, was lit by two lanterns. Franklin was surprised when Alec's father, Robert, greeted him with a one-armed embrace. "My God, lad," Robert said in his booming voice, "it's a curse! You look more the spit of your old man every time I see you. I trust you're not acquiring his vile disposition."

Franklin couldn't help but grin. "I'm sure my father returns your good wishes."

Robert offered barley beer in a tankard, which Franklin accepted. "Death to our foes," the older man toasted.

When they were seated, Franklin asked Robert, "You've got something on your mind?"

"Aye, that we do. But this is Alec's program. I'm just here to hold the purse."

Alec sat forward. "We've got good word that the British'll be leaving Boston. They're already boarding their ships."

Franklin smiled broadly and leaned back. "I'll be damned."

"You boys at Bunker Hill did better than you knew. They're running away, taking their Tory friends with them."

"We did our share of running that day," Franklin said. He shook his head. "I'll be damned."

"So, this has got us to hurrying up a thing we were on about already." Alec said the rebellion would stretch on now. The British, stung by this defeat, would fight even more fiercely, that much was sure. With the British out of Boston, New England ship captains wouldn't need to be smuggling their goods in fast boats, but another line of business would boom now.

"Privateering," he said with emphasis, the color coming into his face. "Grabbing British cargoes and selling them for ourselves, dividing up the booty. There's money to be made there. That's where the smart boys will go." The state government, he said, was issuing privateering papers. With the British out of Boston but still needing to sail through New England waters, privateering would surge.

"That makes sense," Franklin said, "though it's never seemed much different from piracy."

"Franklin, such words from a man who fought at Bunker Hill? We're fighting to win our independence. They've got a navy that spans the blasted globe. We've got nothing like that, so we have to be clever, use the weapons we've got at hand, one of which is privateering."

"Which just happens to include getting rich by taking other people's cargo."

"You and I don't make the rules for wars. If we're helping the cause, where's the crime in helping ourselves? We're going to do both."

"You're going into privateering?"

Alec nodded.

"And you want my ship for it?"

"We do," Alec sat back. "It's a good size. A small crew can handle it. It can hide in coves along the coast, but it's big enough to take on a lot of the supply boats."

Franklin waited.

"And it has to be fast. There's going to be British warships to outrun."

"It'll be fast. Don't worry about that." Franklin scratched a cheek with one knuckle. "But I've got a buyer, a man named Gilchrist from Bath."

"We bought him out." Alec held out a paper. Franklin took it.

After looking it over, he said, "This doesn't say what you paid."

"That shouldn't matter to you. He confirms that we're the owners."

The McDonnells, Franklin figured, must have got wind of Gilchrist's troubles, which were no secret, then swooped in with a cash offer that he jumped at. "Why don't you build privateers here? Why buy mine?"

"We've got other contracts to fill. And we like your design."

"And you don't take any risk if the British show up. My yard's the one they'll burn."

"Aye, there it is," Robert burst out, "that miserable German suspicious streak. Straight from your old dad. Listen, son, we're not trying to take advantage, not of you. We'll take out the letters of marque from Massachusetts—in our names, the McDonnells, big as life. We'll buy the bond to be posted with the state. We'll share out the equipment you need and get you more workers so you can get this one on the water, quick as six jiffies. We'll take the same risks you do. Maybe more."

Franklin took a few moments. Getting equipment and more hands for building, that part sounded good. But he knew he'd be losing control over the project. "What do I get? Other yards will want this ship too. Old man Wilson, or Storer, or any of 'em."

"By speeding up the project," Alec said, "you get your money sooner and can move on to build more. And we'll give you five percent of whatever the ship clears."

"Do you have a captain?"

"Some villain from Salem, James Corcoran by name. He's reputed to be crafty and vicious both. When the ship's ready, we sail to Boston for the papers, then pick up Corcoran in Salem. If Corcoran's luck holds, this won't be the first ship we put out there. We'll be wanting more. If his luck's bad, you've still done fine for yourself." When Franklin was quiet, Alec added, "There's other ships we could get, but we like yours and we like you. We'd prefer to keep this in the family."

Franklin figured a sharp businessman sitting where he was sitting—a man like Alec, for example—would haggle over his share of the booty, but Franklin wasn't of a mind to. What they offered would move the sloop's completion ahead by months. He could build another ship while still having an interest in the sloop's profits. It would, as Alec said, all be in the family. And there was that connection to Salem, which was near to Lynn, which put the whole business in an even better light.

He stood and held out his hand.

* * * * * *

Franklin rode Oatmeal across the Medomak where the ice was thickest. His mind kept cycling back to his trip through Salem the year before, and his days at the Bellamy household. Jane would be surprised to find him on her doorstep again, already building ships for the cause like he said he would. Perhaps he could name the sloop the *Jane*. He smiled. He was getting ahead of himself.

A hundred yards from Mayflower Hof, the smell of sausage reminded him that he was hungry. His father was enjoying some success now. The elegant cabinet he made for Leichter had spread his name among the gentry who craved fine pieces but cringed at Boston prices. So the Sunday before had brought a butchering party at Mayflower Hof, with a fiddler and dancing in the front room and food in the kitchen. The men had lined the hog pen, wielding axes and knives. They took pride in every splash of pig's blood on their clothes, but mostly they drank beer, smoked, and told stories. Johann, who liked to share his good fortune, had insisted that Franklin come back for the blood sausage towards the end of the week.

"Franklin!" "Franklin!" "He's here!" Shouting and laughing, his little sisters and brother Karl burst from the house. The placid Oatmeal ignored the children and also the three dogs barking at his knees. After dismounting, Franklin scooped Karl up for the short walk into the barn, with dogs and Liesl in hot pursuit. Lena said she'd look after the mule, so Franklin veered off to the kitchen door with Karl on his shoulders, his arm around Liesl.

"There's big news, little Liesl," he said.

"Tell me first! Tell me first!"

"Everyone at once."

Catherine was at the fireplace oven, peering at something that smelled miraculous. "Close that door! It's freezing!" she shouted. Thick slices of blood sausage sputtered in a large skillet. A second skillet sizzled with sliced apples and potatoes. Franklin kicked the door shut while setting Karl down.

Catherine gave Franklin a bear-hug greeting.

"I have an announcement for everyone," he said. "In the front room."

"If you want your dinner," Catherine answered, "you'll wait a few minutes for me, and for your father to come in." She shooed them out of the kitchen, handing baby Klara to him.

Promptly, Franklin was on the floor portraying a wild bear while Karl, Liesl, and even Klara climbed over and under him, shrieking with tickles and pokes and growls and roars.

Johann and Hanna came in through the kitchen, both carrying wood. Franklin called his greeting from the floor.

"A fine thing," Johann said. "With all of these young, strong arms and legs, they send an old man out in the snow for wood."

"Hanna!" Catherine's voice came from the kitchen. "I need you! And where is that Lena when I need her?" Hanna leaned down to kiss Franklin and hurried to the kitchen. Johann knelt to rebuild the fire.

"Papa," Franklin said, crossing the room on his knees. "Let me do that."

Johann leaned back. "An excellent idea." He produced his pipe and began to scrape it out, then packed the bowl and lit it. When the tobacco smoldered, he moved to the rocker he had made for Christiane years before. It was everyone's favorite chair, but Johann had first claim on it. "So," he said, "when will we see you playing with some babies of your own?"

Wiping his hands against each other, Franklin shrugged. "You and Walther don't need my help with that, Papa."

"We have a whole continent to fill."

"Soon enough. I have news, Papa."

"Yes?"

"For everyone."

Johann rolled his eyes. "Then we wait for Frau Overstreet."

"Mama," Karl called out. "Franklin says you should come."

Following thumps and clashing noises, Catherine and Hanna entered with Lena behind them. "So," Catherine said, "what is it that can't wait for dinner?"

"Nothing much," Franklin said as he sat up on the floor, then stood. "Except I've just learned from the McDonnells that the British are abandoning Boston. We've won!"

When the cheering and hugs subsided, Johann enlisted Lena to help him tap a fresh keg of beer. Liesl asked Franklin, "Does that mean the war is over?"

He shook his head. "No, but it means we're winning. And we can celebrate with this grand meal that Catherine and Hanna have made."

"How," Catherine asked, "do the McDonnells know this before everyone else?"

"That's their business, knowing things first," Johann said as he entered with two schooners of beer. He handed them to Catherine and Franklin. "Don't underestimate those two. They'll make money from this."

After a noisy meal that bordered on the riotous, Franklin and his father sat together in the front room. Catherine was putting Karl to bed while the girls cleaned the kitchen.

"Tomorrow," Johann said, relighting his pipe, "we can tell this news to Walther and Joanna when they come by."

"You'll have to do that, Papa. I'll be at the yard."

Johann puffed for a moment, the narrowed his eyes. "Alec and Robert, I'm thinking they shared this news for a business reason?"

"Turns out they've bought the rights to my sloop and they want it finished faster. So tomorrow we're moving a hoist over from their yard and we'll hire more men."

Johann grunted. "That reminds me," Johann said, switching to English so the others wouldn't understand, "I have new orders for two large tables, good work. I have some cherry wood for them. Can I get you for a few days, maybe three? You'd be working inside, near the fire."

"Sorry, Papa. We need to get this ship on the water." Franklin was glad to have a solid reason for saying no. Johann often insisted that only Franklin's touch would satisfy his clients, but Franklin hated neglecting the work in his shipyard.

Johann chose not to press the matter. "Don't let the McDonnells rush you. What matters isn't that you finish it two days faster, but that it is excellent, that everyone sees that when it sails by and says, 'Who built that beautiful ship?'"

"Like an Overstreet cabinet, eh, Papa?"

"It's the same, yes. What we have is our work." He pulled his pipe from his mouth. "So, what are the McDonnells really up to?"

"Where is your trust in your fellow man?"

"I've known Robert and Alec longer than I've known you. They're up to something."

"They're going into privateering."

"Not with you as captain?"

"No, no. I'm just the shipbuilder. They have a captain from Salem."

"Will this bring danger?"

"The letters of marque will be in their names, and they're arranging the bond."

Johann puffed for a moment. "Keep your eyes open, Franklin. Privateering is risky. Maybe even for the shipbuilder."

"Don't worry. They say it can be a rich business."

"Oh, yes, it can be that, but more for men like Robert and Alec, not for men like you and me."

"We're so different?"

"Yes. Yes, we are."

The girls arrived at the same time as Catherine. "Did I hear something about the ship you're building?" Catherine asked.

"You see what I tell you," Johann said with a smile. "This woman has a nose for business."

"Yes, there's a new purchaser, and they want it more quickly so they're paying for more shipwrights and a hoist."

"You'll build it faster then," Catherine said.

"Yes, much faster."

"Do you know what you'll name the boat?" Liesl asked.

"Ach, my sweet Liesl flower, how do we raise such romantics in this house?" Johann said. "Franklin is in business. The boat will have whatever name the buyer wants."

Franklin didn't contradict his father, who was probably right.

When Franklin went to mount Oatmeal, Hanna carried the lantern for him. Though she was only three years older, they both acted as though the difference was a decade, a gap created from their motherless years. Like Liesl, she had their mother's slender poise, the cool grey-blue eyes, the attention to everything around her. At least that's how Franklin remembered their mother. After so long, his memories had dwindled to a few feelings—her touch when she helped him, the calm she brought into a room. He could still feel her voice in his ear, vibrating through her warm breastbone as he snuggled close. Her voice had been deep for a small woman.

"Liesl is learning English," Hanna said.

"Isn't she the clever one! Does she understand when Papa and I speak?"

"Some of it. She tells me."

He smiled at her. "Our mother would approve."

"I know Mama could understand, but I don't remember her ever speaking it. I think she liked it that way. She knew what people said when they thought she didn't."

Franklin patted Oatmeal and turned to Hanna. "You've been doing that for years."

Hanna smiled and shrugged. She switched to English. "But I have no one to speak it with. Catherine and many of the women don't know it."

"You can speak it with me, and with Liesl." Franklin cocked his head. "Wait. I'm being stupid. Someone's courting you now, in English. That's it?"

She blushed slightly. "Not courting, I don't think, but how he acts, I think, well, maybe he will, maybe soon."

"Does he have a name?"

"He is old. He has children."

"Does he have a name?"

"Andrew Sherwood."

"The sailmaker? He's not so old. He has two boys?"

She nodded again. "They are small yet."

"He was at Papa's party. Do you like him?"

"I think so. We have not had much time with each other." She looked up at him. "What do you know of him?"

"Not a lot. In the yards, they think he's reliable. Honest." Franklin shook his head. "I've been a bad brother, not noticing this right under my nose. Shall I speak to Mr. Sherwood about his intentions?"

She smiled and held up a warning finger. "Not a word to Papa. We must see how Herr Sherwood goes."

"He would be a fool not to come see you, and to see Papa. I don't think he's a fool."

He reached for the reins, but she held them back. "And you? Did I hear that you go to Salem with this ship? Do you go to that girl there?" Hanna was the only one he had told about Jane. She could keep a secret. "You will go see her, right?"

He drew his mouth into a tight line. "I can't be sure. I might."

"You think of her still? Yes?" He nodded. "So you go. Write to her, a letter like before. So she knows."

"I've tried. I don't know what to say."

"You say you're coming. That way she knows. That's enough." He reached again for the reins. This time, she handed them over. "You should, you know."

He shook his head. "Maybe, but I feel like my chances are better if I don't." They walked the mule into the yard.

"Will you go back to the war?" Hanna said.

"Why would I do that, with the British leaving Boston?"

"But you and Papa say they keep fighting."

"Yes."

"So I worry that you'll go back. I think you want to." She reached to the side of his head, where the bullet had passed through his scalp. "You did enough. Don't make us afraid again."

He kissed her on the forehead and climbed onto the mule.

CHAPTER TWELVE

"The wind's strong," Ethan said. "Look at those high clouds. I don't like straining the mast so soon."

Franklin shook his head. "Alec wants to leave today. He's meeting with the governor's man to get the papers. If we have problems, we'll fix them on the way or when we get there." They had loaded planks, tools, and caulking, both to deal with emergencies on the way, and also because more work would go into the ship in Salem, beginning with installing four swivel guns.

Ethan pointed to two men dawdling on the pier. "We're sailing with just four of us?"

"Plus Alec. The crew comes aboard in Salem, where Captain Corcoran recruits. Privateering takes special skills, Ethan, like with a cutlass." When he pantomimed a sword thrust, Ethan flinched. "That's no job for peace-loving shipbuilders." He pointed up the shore. "There's Alec. Let's get going. The longer we delay, the more your wind freshens."

The sloop had been on the water for less than a week. Every morning Franklin searched for leaks or moisture on the seams, hammering in new caulking wherever he found the slightest flaw. Each defect mortified him. He had taken such pains, generously applying pitch and oakum to each joint and seam, sealing them as tight as possible. But temperature changes, time, and water conspired to create new gaps. On the starboard side, he had already reinforced the planking in two places. Wood degenerates in water, but it shouldn't happen in only a few days. He worried that the McDonnells had sold him some bad wood.

Still, Alec had shelled out for new sails and new rigging. Their principal conflict had come from Alec's relentless pressure to build faster. Even that, Franklin recognized, wasn't all bad. He knew that demands for perfection could be unrealistic. Every wooden ship leaked somewhere.

Franklin had been disappointed by the sloop's naming. The McDonnells called it the *Margaret,* for Robert's wife, Alec's mother. The matter was settled before Franklin could propose *Jane,* so he never did. In truth, he hadn't been sure how to explain that he wished to name the boat for a girl he had known for only a few days and hadn't seen in nearly a year. He aimed to change those facts when they fitted out *Margaret* in Salem, which was so close to Lynn. He still hadn't written to Jane, though. He figured either she would be willing to see him or she wouldn't. If she wouldn't, he didn't need to find out ahead of time.

With Alec on board, Franklin eased *Margaret* from the pier. She took to the water eagerly, sails filling as the wind sang through her rigging. Franklin had shifted the ballast after each cruise, trying to get the ship to lean into the wind the way she was designed to. In Salem, after they installed the guns, he'd shift it again. Halfway to Bremen, Franklin gave the tiller to Ethan and began to inspect the ship. Alec joined him with a wide smile.

"You're like a mother hen," he said, "always clucking and fretting."

"You'll be glad of it when she's in rough waters or trying to outrun a British man of war."

Alec slapped the rail he was leaning against. "I've seen enough ships to know what I think of *Margaret*. She's a good one."

Franklin nodded, then dropped down the steps into the crew's narrow quarters. The crew wouldn't want to spend a lot of nights in this cramped space, but they would be out of the weather. He lit a lantern to examine the planking under his feet and along the ship's sides. He didn't like the look of a spot on the starboard side. Why was it always that side? In Salem, he probably should tear out some of the planking so he could reexamine the timbers. He might be able to reinforce them, then reseal the joints. He went back on deck to collect the kettle of pitch he had set to warm over a fire. He wanted to work over a couple of places. It might not make much difference, but Franklin needed to do something useful.

* * * * * *

Margaret was barely tied up in Salem before Alec set off through the warm September day. Franklin, still fussing over the ship's performance, had to hurry to arrive with him at The Sailor & Mermaid, the tavern preferred by Captain Corcoran.

Their business in Boston had met the customary snarls but was completed. Alec now held valid letters of marque for *Margaret*, and the ship was showing some of the speed they wanted. But when she was about to leave for Salem, deflating war news had crashed in from New York. British and Hessian troops had routed the Continental Army, draining away the euphoria of the victory in Boston. Alec was worried. If the independence movement crumbled, the British would move swiftly against privateers and the men who financed them. And might the news from New York sap Captain Corcoran's enthusiasm for the venture? How eager would sailors be to sign up on a patriot privateer if the British were winning? *Margaret* might be reduced to hauling lumber to Boston and rum back to Maine.

The tavern sign featured a brawny sailor eyeing a mermaid who looked as lascivious as possible for a creature with a tail of green scales. Asked about Captain Corcoran, the landlord pointed to the tap room. Alec clenched his teeth. His captain shouldn't be in the tap room before noon.

Inside, a solitary figure was reading a broadside at a table next to the lone window. "Captain Corcoran? James Corcoran?" Alec called out.

The man let the sheet drop in front of him. His face was in shadow. "And who is it wants to know?" When Alec introduced himself, the figure rose in his chair, though not very far. The wily mariner who was to skipper the *Margaret* through war-torn seas was little more than five feet high, slender as a whippet. His hair was shaved nearly down to the scalp to allow for his wig, which lay on the table under the broadside. Franklin couldn't peg his age. He might be thirty. He might be fifty. "There's coffee if you care, gentlemen." Corcoran's speech was precise despite teeth nearly black with decay.

"Thank you, Captain," Alec said. He moved to a side table where a tin pot stood next to several mugs. Franklin declined the offer while enjoying the experience of looming over Corcoran.

Once reseated, Corcoran expressed disgust at the news from New York.

"How do you think it might affect our chances, Captain?" Alec asked.

Corcoran waved his hand dismissively. "It'll take longer to beat the lobsterbacks, which should be good for business. Gives us more time to snare what we're after." He had turned in his chair so his eyes reflected the sunlight, giving him a predatory look that suited his reputation.

"Do you have enough of a crew?"

"Upwards of a dozen."

"Is that enough?"

Corcoran looked impatient. He plainly disliked being questioned. "Mr. McDonnell," Corcoran said, speaking with emphasis for the slow-witted, "the more men, the more shares to parcel out. Neither of us wants unnecessary shares. Numbers alone don't tell the story in a sea fight. Have you ever stopped to think why there's so many small dogs in the world?"

"What?"

"You heard me. Why are there so many small dogs in the world when there are so many big dogs too?"

Alec, suppressing his irritation, shrugged and looked away from the black stumps of the captain's teeth.

"The little ones figured out that most big dogs don't like to fight. So the small dogs act like the thing they want most in the world is a fight, that they don't care how big the other dog is, and most big dogs just back off." He leaned forward. "Well, we're the little dogs, and we always act like there's nothing we'd like better than a good tussle, don't much care who with. You'd be surprised how many of 'em'll come along quiet-like if that's what they think about you. They start thinking, well, they've got insurance, no need to get all banged up over some cotton or timber."

"How'd you figure out this particular secret of life?" Disbelief was written all over Alec's face.

"Let's call it the lesson of a lifetime as the smallest man in the room."

Alec smiled at that.

"So," Corcoran said, turning to Franklin. "I take it you're the builder. How much longer do I have to wait to see this ship?"

The men from Waldoborough swallowed their coffee and led the way to the wharf.

The captain said nothing while he walked alongside *Margaret*. On board, his inspection began below, by lantern light. When he ran his hand over the repairs on the starboard side, Franklin began to explain. Corcoran raised a hand to shush him. Up on deck, he took the feel of the tiller, yanked on the rigging, and gave the sails a close look.

"All right," he said to Franklin, "Mr.…"

"Overstreet."

"Yes, let's start a list. If you must look more at the starboard planking, be my guest, but it's no worse than I've seen in a dozen ships and none of 'em sank. I'm going to need stations for eight guns—three on each side and one fore and one aft."

"Wait," Alec broke in. "Your letter specified four swivel guns. That's what we've arranged for."

"Yes, that's right. The other four gun placements will be wooden dummies. Coleman in town can fix us up with those. Look just like the real thing, they do."

Franklin nodded. "So you get the intimidation value without slowing the ship down with heavy guns."

"Or with ball and powder for them. We're not looking for an artillery duel, blasting away at fifty yards' distance. Either the bastards'll strike their colors when we challenge them, or we board 'em and take 'em in close fighting. If neither happens, we're off to the next one, and for that I need speed, not more guns."

"Swivel guns fore and aft," Franklin said, "and amidships?"

"You're catching on, Mr. Over…"

"Overstreet, sir."

"Right. Let's get to work. Then we can take her out in the bay. I want to see what we've got."

Over the next four days, Corcoran kept Franklin and Ethan busy, with Alec lending a hand when he could. They stripped out the starboard planks and rebuilt both the outer sheathing and inner supports, then installed fresh planking. They built the eight gun stations, four for the dummies (with dummy cannonballs) and four for the swivels. Corcoran redistributed the sails off the main mast, increasing the canvas that powered the ship. He insisted on a new configuration of the powder magazine, one that would afford greater protection from hostile shells and blunders by crewmen.

On the evening of the fourth day, the three Waldoborough men collapsed at a table at the Smiling Cod Tavern. After asking for ale and oyster stew, they stared into space. Corcoran had banished them from the Sailor & Mermaid for the night since he was signing up the crew. "They'll answer to me for everything," Corcoran had explained. "I don't want them thinking they can get around me to the owner or shipwright. I'll answer for their quality."

When their ales arrived, Franklin, Alec, and Ethan offered halfhearted salutes, then drank the reviving liquid.

"He's a tartar, he is," Alec said. "These damned changes have cost a pretty penny."

Franklin nodded. "He knows his business. If we build another one, I'll do it better." After a long draft of ale, he asked, "So you don't pay the sailors at all? They just gamble on their share of the goods?"

"It's a gamble, sure, but a sailor knows it's the only way he'll ever get ahead. A sailor's wages go to drink and women as soon as they're earned. But a successful privateering cruise with a good captain—one like Corcoran—well, a sailor might just end up with enough to buy a stake in a tavern or a cordwainer shop."

Over their dinners, Franklin broached the subject that had been on his mind since they reached Salem.

"We won't be leaving for two more days," he said, "while Corcoran works the crew on the ship."

"They'll be working the guns too," Alec agreed, shaking his head. "Shooting off perfectly good powder that I have to pay for."

"If you were the captain, you'd want your gunners to have some practice." Alec snorted. Franklin pressed on. "I'd like to go down to Lynn, look up some people there. The captain I served under, Seth Bellamy."

"See here, Franklin. I'll need you around. You know Corcoran's going to want a dozen changes after he sails with the crew. Why not just ride down and have a meal with your old captain? You don't need two days for that."

"Actually, I do."

The two men locked eyes, then Alec shook his head. "I can't spare you. Go for dinner tomorrow."

Franklin looked away, then back. "Ethan can deal with the captain's needs. I need both days. It's not just Captain Bellamy. I got to know the family too."

Alec sat back and wiped his mouth with the back of his wrist. A glint came into his eye. "Family as in girl children?"

"Family."

"If you haven't noticed, my friend, there's plenty of female companionship around the wharf, if that's what you're missing."

"That's not what I'm talking about."

"Damn me, Franklin, I never saw you as one to conduct some long-distance romance." He lowered his voice and leaned forward. "Look, we've got the ship here, and we'll be heading back east. Tell you what. We can go to Lynn, grab the girl, then whisk her up to Waldoborough to reign as the Duchess of Broad Bay. You know, like the Romans with those Sabine women."

Franklin smiled. "Let me try my way first."

"All right. Still and all, you might think about having me come along to help you. Women like me."

"I'll leave in the morning," Franklin said, "and be back the following night."

Alec sighed. "It's lucky your father saved the old man's life up at Louisbourg. Otherwise, I would never indulge this lovesick escapade of yours."

"You're a grand fellow."

"Just be sure you bring her back. I'm not spending two days at Captain Corcoran's beck and call and then have you turn up with a broken heart."

"Neither of us wants that."

"Plus, I'll expect you to name the first son for me."

CHAPTER THIRTEEN

Franklin hired a wagon for the short journey to Lynn. Having arrived at the Bellamy house on foot twice before, he intended the wagon to demonstrate his improved fortunes. A steady morning rain, however, dashed any hope of arriving in style. An oilcloth kept his clothes from a complete drenching, but there was no helping his hat, the wet wagon seat, or the depressing experience of cold and damp.

When he turned into the Bellamy yard, his heart barely stayed in his chest. Hurrying into the cobbler shop, he peeled off his hat to shake it out and rake his fingers through rain-matted hair.

"Well," came Captain Bellamy's voice, "it grew back."

Franklin eagerly clasped the man's hand. After getting permission to leave the horse in the barn, Franklin hurried through the task, wondering about the changes in his old captain. Though Bellamy's voice was unchanged, his frame had shrunk. He bent over slightly. He had less vitality.

Back in the shop, Bellamy shrugged in response to Franklin's inquiries about his health. In the winter before, still with the company in Boston, fevers seized him, several in succession. Too weak to travel on his own, Mrs. Bellamy and Jane had fetched him home.

"Like you," he said with a trace of rue, "I missed when the British finally abandoned Boston, that moment of triumph, but we did our part. I'm working now, a bit more each day."

Franklin asked after the other Essex County men. They never fought the British again, and never stopped digging. They helped install the big guns that the army dragged on sleds all the way from Fort Ticonderoga, the guns that persuaded the British to give Boston up. The Talbots, Bellamy said while his hands stitched the sole of a black shoe, served to the end, but now were back at their farm.

"I thought I might catch them at breakfast tomorrow," Franklin said, "if you could tell me the way."

"Of course—"

The shop's rear door pushed open roughly and a woman bustled in. "Seth, that door still sticks." Mrs. Bellamy lay back the damp hood of her cape. "Oh, Mr. Overstreet," she said, then smiled. "How good to see you looking well, and on such a mean day." Franklin offered his greeting as she set a pot down on the captain's workbench. "Here's coffee," she said, "but I brought only Mr. Bellamy's cup."

Franklin had no need of coffee, he assured her, but she waved his refusal aside. "Why, you're soaked to the skin. You need a warm cup. I'll send Robert out with one for you. Have you asked Mr. Overstreet to dinner?" she asked the captain.

"I haven't had a chance yet, but," he turned to Franklin, "we insist you join us."

"Yes," Mrs. Bellamy said, "Jane isn't here right now, but she'll be home from the Coopers' in time." She turned to her husband. "Have you told him?"

"I haven't had the chance of that either. We've been catching up on war news."

"Well, hadn't you better?"

"Yes, of course."

As she left, Franklin's insides clenched. He braced for the information he had dreaded for months.

"Well," Bellamy said as he put the shoe aside, a thick thread still dangling. "I suppose you're suspecting this. Jane has a suitor."

Franklin said nothing. The silence stretched out between them. "Can you," Franklin said, "say more?"

"He's a tanner here in town, Daniel Brewster. He and his brothers have a good business. Though they've married, he has not."

"Is the matter settled? Between Jane and him?"

"Jane, as you perhaps recall, has her own mind on matters."

"Yes, sir."

"All matters."

"Yes, sir."

"If I was to speak to you more as an army comrade, and not as Jane's father, I might say that matters are less settled in her mind than in Mr. Brewster's."

Franklin felt hope flicker. "Tell me, Captain. Did he fight? This other fellow."

Bellamy looked surprised. "Why, no, he didn't."

Young Robert slammed into the shop with the second coffee and launched into a stream of questions about why Franklin was in Lynn, which allowed Franklin to start describing *Margaret*.

* * * * * *

Jane looked as poised and winsome as Franklin remembered, though more a woman and less a girl. She was friendly but not entirely warm. Franklin could detect no special light in her expression when she first saw him. She was now, he told himself, a woman with a suitor. And he had been away for many months.

Over dinner, Franklin regaled the family with stories about *Margaret,* and especially crusty Captain Corcoran, only slightly exaggerating the sea dog's high-handed ways.

"So," Jane asked with a serious look, "how would you compare Captain Corcoran to Captain Bellamy?"

"I would never compare them," Franklin answered immediately. "I was blessed to serve in the Essex County company under such a fine man."

"And," Bellamy inserted, "to serve with Ben and Christopher Talbot."

"Yes, sir, them too."

The younger boy, James, jumped into the brief silence. "Will you fight on the ship too?"

Franklin smiled and shook his head. “I want to *build* ships now, not sail them. Maybe even build more fighting ships.”

“Did you see,” Jane said to him across the table, “that the Indian tribes of Maine have joined the Patriot side?”

“I heard that. We can use all the help we can get.”

“So, are you people in Maine now sorry to have killed so many of them?”

“Jane,” Mrs. Bellamy said after an awkward silence, “what’s got into you? Mr. Overstreet is our guest.”

“No, wait, ma’am,” Franklin said, “maybe I should speak on this.” He spoke to Mrs. Bellamy, not Jane. “It’s a sorrow that so many were killed, on both sides. Both happened in Waldoborough. It was frontier. For three years, we lived inside a wooden stockade with other settlers, afraid of being attacked. We were attacked once. I was little, I don’t remember it. My father and mother, they both fought. My father’s best friend was taken and hasn’t been seen since. It was war. But with the Indians our allies now, that feels like progress. Maybe someday we’ll be friends with the British again.”

“I hope so,” Mrs. Bellamy said. She looked around the quiet table. “It seems the rain has stopped. Seth, why don’t you men see if there’s anything outside that needs attention.”

“Perhaps,” the captain said to Franklin, “you’d enjoy seeing how your repairs to the barn have held up. Robert just repainted. And there’s the garden plot you and Marcus helped open up.” Jane made no eye contact with Franklin as she gathered dishes from the table.

Halfway across the yard, Franklin said, “I hope, sir, I’ve not given offense.”

“If you have, the fault isn’t yours. Jane will speak her mind. You should have no other expectation.”

“Yes, sir.”

“You have sisters?”

“Four, sir. One older and three younger.”

“So you are familiar with the sex.”

Franklin praised the barn’s paint and condition. They walked the rows of the garden, though everything but a few squash had been harvested. When Bellamy saw Jane coming across the yard, he said he needed to attend to matters in the shop. He called for the boys to follow him.

Franklin smiled as Jane approached. She had a shawl over her everyday frock and still wore her apron. She was as tall and straight and lovely as he remembered. She didn't smile back.

"My mother says I've been rude."

"I didn't think so."

"I meant to be."

"Why?"

"Why!" She looked away quickly then back. "You go away for a year, just disappear. Never send a letter or a message. And then you come sashaying in here with your fancy wagon and your tales of privateering and you expect me to be thrilled about it."

"Jane, you said no. You sent me away."

"Are you so easily discouraged?"

He smiled. "I'm here now."

"Franklin—"

"Aren't I?" He took her arm and led her back toward the barn. "I know I didn't write. I didn't know what to say, the way things were. I didn't want to argue with you in a letter, but I couldn't write and just ignore what you said. So I didn't write at all. But I was thinking about you, and what you said, the whole time."

"You should've written."

"That's what my sister Hanna said."

Jane looked over. "You told her about me?"

"And now I had to tell Alec McDonnell, my partner and owner of *Margaret*, which means that as soon as we get back, all of Waldoborough will know of my suit."

"Is that what this is? Your suit? After a year of silence?"

He took a moment. "Some of the things you said then, they were right. About my leaving your father and the Talbots to fight the war for me."

"Oh, Franklin, that was a stupid thing I said." She reached over to the hand he held on her elbow.

"No, no, it was what I was feeling. I needed someone to say it."

"But what did I know? When my father came home, and I saw how sick the war made him, and you with your poor head, of course. You all had fought while I sat here in my safe home—I know I had no right to say that. I don't always think before I speak. Mother's forever telling me that."

Franklin stopped and took both her hands. "And another thing you said. This one you weren't right about. You mustn't think I have the least care that your mother is Indian. It's you that I care for, just as you are, every part that makes you dear. That has only grown stronger through our separation and won't change. It will never matter to me, nor to anyone who's my friend."

The moment, looking into her dark eyes, felt electric. He pressed on. "Your father said there is a man here, named Brewster, who also feels in this way. About you."

She looked down and nodded, then looked at him directly. Her eyes were troubled. "He's a good man."

"If you say I should, I'll go back to Waldoborough." He tried to pour into her the emotions that welled inside him, holding her hands more firmly and holding her warm, dark eyes in his gaze.

One corner of her mouth lifted in a trace of a smile. "And what would you tell your partner, the one with the big mouth?"

"I'd think of something."

"Perhaps that I died?"

He grinned. "That might work."

They began to walk again, hand in hand, no longer aware of exactly where they were. Franklin took a deep breath. "There was one more thing you said."

"Yes. I know."

"About moving to Waldoborough with me."

"Yes."

"Jane, I have no answer for that. It's where I must be."

After a silence, she said, "I see."

He stopped. "Do you have tasks this afternoon?"

"My mother has released me, on condition that I conduct myself so as not to embarrass her further and determine once and for all whether I have a future with this unpolished frontier type from the far reaches of Maine."

"Excellent. We should get started. I thought we might ride over to Salem wharf and I could show you the ship."

She brightened. "I must meet Captain Corcoran, the angry midget who presides over the ocean." She laughed merrily. "He sounds irresistible."

"And perhaps supper at an inn before we return?"

"I'll fetch a lantern for the ride home."

* * * * * *

At the Sailor & Mermaid, over bowls of overcooked stew, Franklin could only shake his head as Jane pronounced Captain Corcoran a perfect gentleman.

"You will admit," she insisted, "that he was nothing but courteous and winning today?"

"To you, yes. Did you hear how he snarled at Alec?"

"What do you mean?"

"Nothing. Nothing at all. You plainly have the power to charm snakes from their lairs and soften the hardest of hearts."

"All very flattering, sir, but I think you take a harsh view of that sweet little man. He even offered to take all of us on that cruise tomorrow. My brothers will be thrilled."

"I'm not sure you appreciate how remarkable that is. He complains at having Alec and me on those cruises. Insists we're in the way. I can't wait to see what he makes of your brothers."

"He'll probably terrorize them into good behavior, and bless him for it. Besides, don't you realize that the way he was with me, and the cruise tomorrow, are his way of trying to advance your suit?"

"Well," he smiled, "is it working?"

She took a breath. "There is that last thing."

"Waldoborough." She nodded. "Can I tell you more about it? About my family?"

"Please."

He tried not to paint too rosy a picture. He admitted it was small and far from Boston. She said she'd been to Boston twice and that was quite enough.

He described his cottage at the shipyard. She pronounced it cozy, but allowed that it might stand some improving. He agreed that improvements could be made. Whatever she wanted, he said, then caught himself. Within reason, he added. She smiled.

He talked about his family, Walther and Hanna and the younger ones. They could be no more unruly or burdensome, she answered, than her own brothers.

Waldoborough held many German families, he added, like the Overstreets. "German," he warned, "is spoken. Often."

"Not to me, surely."

"Oh, yes. Many women have no English."

"I doubt that. I imagine they know more English than you think."

Franklin smiled. He told her how Hanna had been listening to English without letting on that she understood it.

"See?" Jane said, then cocked her head. "Hanna's the one you told about me?"

"Yes."

"She'll be our friend."

"Yes. She'll love you." He sat up straighter. "Your family, I know, is the hard question. We would come here every year, for long enough for you to know their lives."

"Franklin, how long is that? And if they get sick and they need me for the things a daughter should do? You see how my father looks now. What will I do? I won't even know that they need me."

"News can find you in Waldoborough, and then you may return here."

"That could be weeks or months. In the winter, when ships cannot get through the ice."

He waited a moment. "I have no answer for that."

They were mostly silent during the ride back to Lynn. Jane rested her head against his shoulder. When they arrived, he saw that her eyes were shining. A tear formed at the corner of one eye. His heart leapt. "So, you will?"

She nodded and whispered, "I think I'll be sad sometimes. I won't be able to help that. But I'll be more sad if I'm not with you."

CHAPTER FOURTEEN

†

When Franklin stepped off the mule at Mayflower Hof, Liesl came running. She grabbed Oatmeal's reins.

"Have you seen," she asked excitedly, "the chest of drawers that Papa made for you and your new wife?"

"Her name is Jane. You'll meet her in just a bit more than a week now, after the wedding."

"Have you seen it, the chest?"

"I have. I think it was supposed to be the Stoningtons' until very recently."

"Papa says it's yours and Jane's now. Papa says it's too good to go out of the family."

He and Liesl led the mule into the shed. "You're right, Liesl. It is beautiful. And Papa's right to keep it in the family."

"What will he make for me when I get married?"

"Something very special, I'm sure. Perhaps he will help me build you a boat."

"Would you?" Her face was bright.

"Of course, I would," he said. "Perhaps a small one."

Franklin had been back from Lynn for eight weeks, mostly frantic ones. The improvements to his cottage had proved time-consuming, and Alec was pressing to start on the next ship. This one would be named for Jane.

"Where is everyone?" Franklin asked when they found only Hanna in the kitchen.

"Church supper tonight," Hanna said. "You were told."

"I've been told so many things. I can't remember them all." He fell into a chair and rested his head on folded arms. Liesl sat next to him. "And why," he asked his little sister, "aren't you at the church supper?"

"Hanna and I had to work on her dress and bonnet for the wedding. You're leaving the day after tomorrow, you know."

"Ah, I do remember that."

"Liesl," Hanna said, "why don't you get the bonnet with your needlework, to show Franklin."

When she was gone, Hanna sat next to him. "Is something wrong? Has something happened?"

He sat up. "Mostly I'm just tired." He looked around the kitchen. "But also, we have bad news."

"Yes?"

"There's been a storm, up in Nova Scotia. They say *Margaret* broke up on some rocks."

"How do they know?"

"There was another ship that just missed the rocks. They couldn't get close enough to save anyone."

"And the sailors? Did they get to shore?"

He shook his head. "We don't know. We're not even positive it was *Margaret*. But Alec's worried. He could find no insurance when we were in Boston, because of the war, so if it was *Margaret*, the loss is his."

"Does that affect you?"

He shrugged. "Alec hasn't paid me all the cost of *Margaret*. I took some of the payment in a share of the profits."

"Oh, dear." Something in his expression caused her to add, "What else?"

"Well, we won't go ahead with the new ship until we know for sure what happened. If it really is gone, I'll need to find another buyer for the next one. Alec won't have the money. And some folks might decide *Margaret*'s fate was because it wasn't built right."

"I'm sorry, Franklin. It's a bad time for such troubles."

"Worse for the poor men on board." He gave her a thin smile. "I can always build other men's ships if I have to. Let's leave it for now. I have a wedding to celebrate."

"Look, Franklin," Liesl said as she came in. She turned so he could admire the pale blue bonnet that sagged slightly on her too-small head.

"Ach, Liesl flower, it is perfect! Your sister will be the center of all attention at the wedding."

"That," Hanna said as she stood, "will be your bride. Catherine left some bread and cheese and ale. Let's have it."

Franklin explained that he'd come to borrow his father's scorper to engrave the headboard of the new bed which he and Walther had finished just that day. "You know," he said, "how Papa refused to help us. He said he would be ashamed to have sons who couldn't build something as simple as a bed."

"I wish I was going to the wedding," Liesl blurted out.

"Papa can't pay the fare for everyone," Hanna said. "Just for him and me. And Catherine needs you to help prepare for the party when Franklin and Jane return. Everyone will come for that."

"Why does Hanna get to go?" Liesl asked Franklin.

"Because she's my oldest sister," he said, "and because she's taken such good care of you and me that she's entitled to some fun."

"Imagine that!" Hanna said with a smile.

After supper, the girls showed off Hanna's dress. Tomorrow, she was planning to bake bread for the Bellamy family.

It was nearly eight when the others returned from the church. For the third time, Johann showed Franklin the craftsmanship of the chest of drawers. When the young ones were going off to bed, Franklin started back to his own home.

Oatmeal worked carefully along the uneven road. He seemed not to trust the shifting light of the lantern that bobbed on the pommel of the saddle. After nearly half a mile, Franklin cursed to himself. He'd forgotten the scorper. He was forgetting everything. With a groan he turned around the uncomplaining Oatmeal.

A single light burned in the front room, but Franklin didn't need to disturb anyone. He went back to his father's darkened workshop. Dismounting, he heard voices speaking German in the shop, which was odd. It was a cold November night for sitting in the dark. As he neared the door, the voices fell silent. Across the yard, trees blocked most of the moonlight. Franklin could see nothing through the shop window.

With a knot in his stomach, he knocked, then opened the door. “Papa?”

“Franklin, yes. What is it?”

“I wanted to borrow your scorper.” In the light of his lantern, he could make out a form huddled on the far side of the shop. Something was wrong. “Papa?”

“Yes.”

“What’s going on? Who is this?”

Johann sighed. “There’s nothing going on. Close the door.”

CHAPTER FIFTEEN

†

Franklin sidled in the weak light to the workbench on the left, the one he had always used. He could make out the huddled figure better from there. The man's hair hung in stringy clumps. He seemed large, but that might be from the shadows thrown by the lantern. His father had no fear of this stranger, Franklin told himself, so he shouldn't either.

"Franklin," Johann said in a low voice, speaking German, "our guest is Horst Scheuer." The man nodded but didn't leave his spot in the corner. Franklin nodded back. "Herr Scheuer is from Hesse, near my old home."

"He's been fighting for the British?" Franklin said. He turned to the man. "You've been fighting for the British, haven't you?" Not waiting for an answer. "He's from the fighting in New York. They've been brutal."

"Yes," Johann said. "That's right. Horst has had a bad time. He was separated from his regiment, ended up alone. Once on his own, he's decided he doesn't like to fight this war."

"He's a deserter?"

"He's a man who wishes to fight no more."

"And you believe him? You've always said, Papa, that soldiers of the high troops, who serve the Landgraf, they never leave their duty. They have the highest discipline. So he means to fight again." Franklin took a step forward and leaned down to speak to the man. "Isn't that right, you're looking to fight again, no?"

Johann didn't move, but his voice turned harder. "Franklin, I explained that Herr Scheuer is our guest."

"He's our enemy, Papa." Franklin spoke in a hoarse whisper, his voice probably louder than he intended. "If this man had been at Bunker Hill, he would have tried to kill me. He might have killed me. He is not a guest. He's a prisoner of war."

Johann picked up his pipe. Lacking any way to light it, he chewed the stem. "Franklin, this man is no better or worse a man than your father. He joined the Landgraf's army because his family is poor. He fights for King George because the Landgraf rents out his people like animals. Herr Scheuer does not wish to fight any more. Surely, you understand that, how a man can feel like that." Johann sucked on his dead pipe. "All of us here understand that." He let the silence fall among them. "To return Herr Scheuer to the war," Johann said, "would be like turning myself in as a criminal."

"Papa, we have neighbors, Waldoborough men, who still fight. They were with the army in New York. Your Herr Scheuer may have shot them, or run them through with his bayonet. We have news today that *Margaret* is lost at sea, the sailors likely drowned. They were fighting against this man and his army."

"Come, Franklin, don't be a child. That ship was a business proposition for the McDonnells. I'm sorry for the sailors, but the sea is harsh, and this man had nothing to do with it."

Scheuer sat mute, his shoulders hunched and his head drooping to his chest.

"Would you set us against our neighbors?" Franklin said. "Against our country? We're Americans, not Germans. We're not in Hesse. I was born here." He nodded. "I'm an American, and this man is my enemy. I don't care how he got here, or what bad things happened to him or his family. He came here as my enemy to fight against my country, and he still is my enemy. I must deliver him to the sheriff."

Johann pulled the pipe from his mouth and ran his index finger around the edge of its bowl. "Franklin, can there be no moment when our enemy ceases to be our enemy? Look at this man. Herr Scheuer says he will fight no more. I believe him. Don't you want war to leave our hearts?"

"I'm sorry, Papa. I also want the British to leave America, but instead they spread the war to new places. This man may be cold and weary and beaten now, but when he gets to Halifax and has a few weeks of warm fires and good food, the British will have him ready again to carry a musket and kill our friends. Isn't that right, Herr Scheuer? You know nothing except war, isn't that right? You are a soldier, nothing else?"

The unshaven man looked up. He was younger than Franklin had thought. His filth and air of misery made him seem older. "I don't care for your rebellion," the man said in a hoarse voice. "The world has no need of rebellion. Rebellions get people killed but change nothing. I don't like rebellions or rebels. But I also don't care for King George or for the English. I have a little one at home. I have a wife who should not be poor. My parents grow older and need their son. I want only to get home to my family."

"Listen to him," Franklin said to his father. "Why is he here? He has come a long way from New York."

"He says he hopes to escape to Halifax and board a ship back home," Johann said.

"Really? Who's being the child here, Papa? The only way for him to get home is in a British ship. Do you think they won't know that a German man his age, trying to sail to Europe, is one of their soldiers? They'll put him back in uniform and send him to slaughter Americans."

"That's not true," the man said. "I would refuse to fight. I will fight no more. I only want to get home."

Franklin shook his head. "I wish I could believe you, Herr Scheuer, but I don't."

Father and son stared at each other. "All right, son. It's late. There's no need to get Sheriff Palmer out of his warm bed in the middle of the night. Come in the morning and we will decide, the three of us, what is to be done."

"I'm not going to change my mind, Papa."

"Well, then maybe I'll have to."

Franklin opened the door to leave. "Wait," Johann called. He reached behind his bench and pulled the scorper off a wall peg. "Keep it as long as you need it."

CHAPTER SIXTEEN

†

Johann could find no sleep that night. Franklin made sense. Their guest was a man trained only for war. He had little chance of evading British authorities and sneaking back to Germany. Yet Johann ached to help this man return to peace. If Johann could bring this one man to peace, that might atone for some of the violence of his life, violence that had echoed through Franklin's life. It wouldn't be a full atonement. It couldn't be. Yet it would show what his heart felt. That seemed important.

What if, as Franklin said, Herr Scheuer ended up back in an enemy uniform? He would still know that Americans are people of honor and generosity, people who loved peace. Wasn't that also important?

He rolled off the bed and pulled on clothes while Catherine slept. In the kitchen, he placed a chair next to the fire. He had banked it for the night, but it still threw off a little warmth.

He felt the quiet of the house, these rooms that usually overflowed with talk and shouts and laughter and argument, with coming and going and cooking and washing and spinning and sewing. He knew he was still a prideful man. He had never conquered that sin and was old enough to know he never would. He was proud of this home, of his children, of the two fine women he'd taken care of as best he could, of the life he made here in Broad Bay. Walther had started his family, and now Franklin would. It was not a bad life for a man from Kettenheim with no parents and no land.

He had lost much. Peter and Richard, gone before he could know them. And Fritz. And Christiane, which was the hardest. His eyes clouded. He had a new fear now, that Hanna, so much like her mother, should not marry this man, this sailmaker with two sons already. He told himself that she was strong like an Overstreet and would always prevail, but still he worried.

He had liked having Horst around for the past two days, speaking proper German with a man who could tell of the old land, of the old army, neither of which seemed to have changed. Johann thought he understood Horst, how much he wished to get home, how weary he was of this American war, this family quarrel among English. It wasn't Horst's fight. Then again, a soldier of the Landgraf never fought for himself or his country, only for his *dienst*. Horst shouldn't fight Americans, but at least he knew it. Johann knew the black feeling of killing men for reasons that mean nothing to you. For no reason. He wanted to help Horst escape that.

Johann couldn't disagree with most of what Franklin had said. They were Americans now. Overstreets, not Oberstrasses. He came here for his chance, so he fought at Louisbourg for Broad Bay and King George. Yet Franklin had fought for their home against the new King George. Their duty was to America, to Broad Bay, to Mayflower Hof and their friends. This was their home.

He sucked on the cold pipe, then stood and placed it on the mantel. There had to be a way to help this man and still to be true. He pulled on his boots and let himself out. Rolf, the black dog who loved the water, met him and licked his hand. "Good boy," Johann said, scratching behind his ear.

When Johann pushed the shop door open, he could see Horst's eyes glistening out of a nest of blankets. "Sleep eludes you also," Johann said.

"I am trying to decide whether to run away into these cold woods or stay and go back with your son."

"There's no dishonor in being captured. That's just bad luck." Johann leaned an elbow against his bench.

"I know."

"There's another way. You could settle here, in Waldoborough. My son couldn't object to that. You could start out working for me, here in this shop. I need help. My son, he builds boats now so he cannot help me. I would pay you a fair wage."

"I'm not a carpenter."

"Neither was I. You're a young man. You would learn. When the war ends, you can send for your family. You can find land here. Think of that, Horst. Land of your own."

They were quiet. The guest stood, keeping a blanket around his shoulders. "I know you wish to help me. I've been thinking of that too. Staying here would be desertion, but so is what I want to do, to go back to Hesse and be with my family. That's what my officers would say."

"So stay. No one will bother with one more German in Waldoborough. This war, it can't last forever. It always seems it will with wars, but they all end. By then you will have money and can send for your family."

"So I should leave my family for more years? They will be lonely and have little money. And I will be lonely also. This is only the second year of this war, whenever it may end." He turned to the window. The moon, higher in the sky now, cast shadows across the bare yard. "You have built a fine home here. I envy you."

"You can do it, too, Horst. I was like you."

"No, you chose to come here. I wish to go home."

"You'll die in the forest. It's very cold. The British or the Indians may shoot you—they won't understand who you are. There are bears and wildcats."

"Then I'll die trying to get home. Being faithful."

Johann sighed. "I know you must be from my home because you won't listen to reason. All right. I will help you, but only if you make a pledge."

Scheuer raised the question with widening eyes.

"You must give your word as a soldier, that you will not fight, ever again, against Americans."

"I don't wish to fight anyone."

"I know that. But things happen. Times may change. I need your word. I must have your pledge as a soldier that you won't fight against Americans."

Scheuer nodded. "You have my word on it."

Johann held his hand out and the other man took it.

"What about your son? He will be angry that I have left."

"You gave me your word as a soldier. He will understand it." He cocked his head. "Eventually, I hope, he will understand it." He nodded as he picked up a pencil he had recently bought. It was made in London, a self-indulgence for an old furniture-maker. "All right, we must get you on your way. I will gather some things. It will take little time. Roll up those blankets. You'll need them."

"I have no money to pay for these things."

"Yes, I know."

Johann lit a candle in the kitchen, then fetched a piece of paper. Using the new pencil, he drew a rough map. He gathered bread and cheese and salt pork. Flint for fires. Some coins. Mittens. Catherine stirred when Johann took the socks from the chest in their room, but she didn't wake. Scheuer had a knife. Johann had seen it. He thought about giving the man a pistol but decided against it. It was little use against animals and too useful against men. He stuffed all but the mittens in a canvas sack with a drawstring.

He found Scheuer pacing in the shop, two blankets rolled tight around his neck. He handed the man the sack and the mittens, then gestured for him to follow. When they were a hundred yards from the house, Johann stopped in a shaft of moonlight. He showed Scheuer the map and explained in a low voice the best route north. Johann would take him as far as the path through North Waldoborough, one the smugglers used. If Scheuer traveled with some of the smugglers, he would be safer from the Indians. His best chance for getting out of America would be to sign onto one of the British ships as a crewman.

"Yes," Scheuer said. "That's a good idea."

"Do you know anything about ships?"

Scheuer smiled. It was the first time Johann had seen him smile. "I will be sure to know that very soon."

Johann told him the bears should be sleeping, but wildcats might be out hunting. He should move slowly away from either. No quick movements. Fording rivers was the most dangerous time. If part of the river was frozen and part open, he should stay off the ice and just walk through the water. It would be cold but there would be less chance of falling and having worse things happen.

He shouldn't travel while snow was falling. It was too easy to get lost. Scheuer would find no Germans beyond Waldoborough.

Then Johann had no more advice. They walked without words. Scheuer turned his head from side to side, searching out hidden dangers. When an owl hooted, he jumped. Johann hadn't been in the woods like this for a long time. It was in these woods, managing his traps, where he first began to understand this new land. Yet the woods he had known were shrinking. The Indians were fewer. The beavers were gone, and the trappers had moved west. He thought of the Indian he ran down and killed in these woods. Johann didn't believe in ghosts, but that man's face, the feel of his skin as Johann squeezed the life from him, had never left. The feeling of shame and regret came back, but that also was the night when Hanna arrived. God wouldn't have blessed his life with Hanna if the killing was so wrong.

Johann stopped at a frozen stream. Scheuer, he said, should walk up this stream bed until he reached a huge oak. That marked the trail to the east. It would be clear.

"You have been generous," Scheuer said, taking his mitten off and holding out his hand. "I will remember you, Herr Overstreet. That is the only way I can repay you."

"Good luck, Horst. You repay me by honoring your pledge."

"Yes. I will."

The Hessian adjusted his load and looked around. He ducked his head and started up the stream. Johann stood and watched. After the man had gone fifty yards, he stopped. He took a few more strides, then halted again. He peered into the woods in all directions. After a full minute, the Hessian let the canvas sack drop to the ground. His shoulders slumped. He crouched where he stood and put his hands over his eyes. Johann looked away. Then he followed the man's path.

The Hessian looked up at him. "Come," Johann said, "in the morning, you'll meet my family. Sooner than you know, it will be your home."

"But your son. He will take me to the sheriff."

"We will talk to him."

The Hessian nodded. "I must write to my family."

"Of course. Right away."

They walked back through the quiet of the cold woods. The

clean smell of pine needles filled Johann. He smiled up at the brightness of the moon. In the black half of the heavens, clouds played hide-and-seek with stars in a sky pierced with the spires of great firs.

Johann's mind turned to Franklin's wedding. That would be a joyous day, except for missing Christiane. He wondered again what this young woman was like who had so bewitched his son.

AUTHOR'S NOTE

The story of the German settlement of Broad Bay in the 1750s is told in a few sources, most extensively in a remarkable two-volume local history by Jasper Jacob Stahl, *History of Old Broad Bay and Waldoboro* (1953). Stahl, a descendant of the settlers (as am I), provides not only names and dates and events, but also a rich picture of the world of mid-coast Maine in the eighteenth century. It was a tremendous resource for me. Other sources on local history included Samuel Miller, *History of the Town of Waldoboro, Maine* (1910), the collection of the Waldoborough Historical Society, and one of the historical society's trustees, Bill Blodgett, who showed me his town and answered questions that were doubtless annoying. For information about the Penobscot tribe, I looked at Bruce Bourque, *Twelve Thousand Years: American Indians in Maine* (2004). Some of the characters in the story are inspired by Broad Bay's early citizens, though most are wholly invented. Even those inspired by real historical figures (such as General Waldo and General Wolfe) are imagined by me, not strictly based on historical accounts.

To understand the siege of Louisbourg in 1758, I relied on Hugh Boscawen, *The Capture of Louisbourg 1758* (2013), and also looked at a biography of General James Wolfe, Stephen Brumwell, *Paths of Glory: The Life and Death of General James Wolfe* (2008). The Bunker Hill fighting is recounted in Nathaniel Philbrick, *Bunker Hill: A City, A Siege, A Revolution* (2014); Paul Lockhart, *The Whites of Their Eyes: Bunker Hill, the First American Army, and the Emergence of George Washington* (2011); Richard M. Ketchum, *Decisive Day: The Battle for Bunker Hill* (2014); and James L. Nelson, *With Fire and Sword: The Battle of Bunker Hill and the Beginning of the American Revolution* (2011). As always, I'm indebted for the assistance of the Library of Congress and its outstanding professionals.

I'm grateful to those who read early versions of this story and improved it with their comments: Gerard Hogan, Prof. Daniel Krebs of the University of Louisville (who kept me from blatant errors about German culture, tradition, and military concerns), and my wife, Nancy, who continues to light my days.

PREVIEW OF
BOOK TWO

The
BURNING
LAND

CHAPTER ONE
DECEMBER 1862

†

The word spread fast. Corporal Henry Overstreet passed it on to his platoon as soon as he heard: Two men in Company C froze to death in their tents the night before. The bodies were blue.

The platoon gathered around campfires in the thin morning light, kicking at four inches of early December snow. They shook their heads. They warmed their hands over the flames or cradled them around tin cups of coffee with more heat than flavor.

"Glory be to God," said Joe Maxwell. "That's a hell of a thing. What in God's name happened?" The flaming red of his face reflected both the cold and his temper.

Henry kept his voice level, fitting for a corporal. "They didn't seal their tent flaps."

"And they died for it? Men from Maine shouldn't freeze to death in Virginia."

Henry met Joe's gaze. The other man dropped his eyes and muttered, "Glory be to God."

Henry couldn't show how nervous the news made him. He resolved to check the men's tent flaps at night, to make sure they stuffed their rubber blankets into every crevice and gap. He couldn't mention this to Katie in his next letter. He didn't know how he could make sense of it. His fingers were too cold to write, anyway.

Captain Clark came down the row of tents, stopping to talk at each knot of men around each fire. A few men saluted but he paid little heed to the formalities. As he spoke, heads nodded slowly. Then he moved on.

"Corporal Overstreet," Clark said.

"Captain, sir."

Clark scanned the faces around the fire. Joe Maxwell loomed over the others, his sandy hair poking out from all sides of his kepi cap, the brim drawn low over his eyes even though there was little morning light to shield against. "We march at ten. This is it. The whole army. Twenty extra rounds for each man."

"Fredericksburg, sir?" Henry asked. The extra cartridges definitely meant a fight. For days they'd heard rumors about an attack on the rebels dug in there. Of course, they'd also heard rumors about attacks on Richmond, or rebel assaults against Washington. But Fredericksburg was the tale they heard most.

"Nobody's saying. The newspapers say that's where General Lee has his army, so that seems like a good guess, but it's a guess." He nodded and spun on his heel, his officer's cape billowing behind him.

"Well," Maxwell said, his eyes following Clark as he moved back up the row of tents. "The secesh can't complain about us surprising them, can they?" The others grunted their agreement. They assumed their generals weren't as smart, or as tough, or as daring as the rebel generals. That's how it had been so far.

"Eat hearty," Henry said with a small smile. "Easier to carry it in your stomach than in your pack."

The march took three days. On the third, bugles roused them at three in the morning but the march didn't start for another two hours, triggering a cascade of grumbles. The regiment stayed together on this march, all the way to the Rappahannock River across from Fredericksburg. The rebels were across, up on the crest of a slope that rose from the town streets. They had a commanding view of the settlement, the river, and the Union Army on the far side. The regiment joined the rest of the Fifth Corps in a muddy field, hard by the house where General Burnside had his headquarters. They stood there for most of the frigid day while the engineers tried to assemble a pontoon bridge across the river and messengers on horseback rushed to Burnside and then rushed away.

Company E stood at ordered arms near the front right of the formation, close to Colonel Ames and Colonel Chamberlain and their aides. For once, Henry could overhear at least something of what was going on. George Young, his sergeant, kept stopping by for news.

"What do you hear?" George asked in the late morning.

"Every time we get the planking on the boats near the other side, that's when the rebel sharpshooters – they're hiding in the houses over there – they start picking off the engineers and the whole business falls to pieces."

"Bad day to be an engineer," George said.

At mid-day, with little rise in the temperature and no orders to advance, Colonel Chamberlain approached Henry.

"Corporal," he said. The officer loomed nearly a head above him, his drooping mustache ends expressing a sadness that his eyes confirmed.

"Colonel, sir." Henry snapped off the best salute he could manage.

Chamberlain nodded absently. "Have the men eat what they have. We've no idea how long we'll be here."

"Yes, sir. And, sir?" Chamberlain had started to move away but looked back. "May they stand at ease?"

Chamberlain looked around the ranks of blue-clad men who filled the cold soggy field. "I'm afraid not, Corporal. General Burnside wishes us to be ready to march on short notice." Henry thought he could hear a soldier's skepticism in Chamberlain's voice. "Tell them they may ground arms."

"Thank you, sir."

At that moment cannons bellowed. "Ours," Chamberlain said, his eyes flicking over to where cannon smoke was rising. "May they do some good."

The bombardment went on for hours, cannonballs pulverizing the empty buildings of Fredericksburg, but the Union Army's attack never launched over the river. Captain Clark ordered the regiment back a mile into night camp. The bridge was built, he said, but the assault would be in the morning.

Henry's nerves were strung up. Everyone was cold and getting colder but there was nothing for it but to swallow some hardtack and sleep as they could. Henry checked from man to man, reminding each to seal his tent against the night. Joe Maxwell and Teddy Meisner sat on their rubber blankets before a fire that smoldered with damp wood.

"Might as well sleep, fellows," Henry said. Both nodded but kept their eyes on the low flames. Voices murmured close by. They were tense, all of them. They were afraid. Henry was, too. Tomorrow their war would change from one of misery and discomfort to one of fighting and killing. Henry said good night. They grunted in answer.

Flagg was asleep when Henry slipped into their tent. As he lay down, Henry couldn't rest. His mind kept turning to the battle to come, the fighting. Through the long day, he had thought mostly about each task before him that minute and then the next one and then the next one until now, when it was time to wait for sleep that would not come. Now his stomach tightened with the idea of gunfire, cannons, raging men tearing and clawing at each other. He wished he was somewhere else. The idea slipped from his mind as he drifted off.

* * * * * *

In the morning, the regiment descended through heavy river fog to the bridge. The rebels still held the high ground across an open plain on the other side of the town. It looked like the generals were going to fling the Union soldiers through the city, then across the plain and up against the Confederate lines. While the regiment waited, Joe Maxwell looked over at Henry with a tight grin. "Sure hope old Burnside has some trick up his sleeve," he said, "'cause otherwise this looks to be pure murder."

The attack didn't start until midday. A Union division that had crossed the bridge during the night started out across the open field.

As the blue-clad soldiers neared the rebel lines, fiery streaks erupted from the higher ground. The angry roll of explosions took a second to reach Henry on the safe side of the river. Smoke bloomed from the rebel cannons. The cannonade gouged gaps in the blue lines, finally causing them to melt into the ground. Some patches of blue fell back down the slope, seeking shelter where they could find it. Pure murder it was. Henry felt weak. His skin prickled. How could they march up that hill to die? Would he have to do that?

Another blue line advanced, then sputtered out on the green slope, adding more slashes of blue to the ground. Then another. And another. Nothing, Henry thought, was up Burnside's sleeve today. Or between his ears. The men in Company E watched with horrified awe. They breathed oaths and took off their caps to scratch their heads. Johnny Baxter's eyes were wet.

It was near the end of the short December day that orders came for the Twentieth to cross the bridge. Shells screamed overhead and cannonballs splashed the water around them. Henry felt the air press down when a shell passed close by. Anxious men and horses ducked and weaved on the bridge, making the boats under the planks wobble and sway, threatening to spill them all into the river.

When the regiment reached the town's battered buildings, the men shed their packs.

"Hey, look," a man in Company G shouted. He held up a bank note. The men realized there were hundreds of them in the breeze. Henry picked one up. It carried the name of a Virginia bank. The printing was splotchy, some of the words smeared. He showed it to Maxwell, who shrugged. "Worth even less than ours," he said. Henry stuffed it into his tunic.

A hungry-looking black dog ran to the men, who were crouched behind what must have been the bank building. The dog nuzzled Johnny Baxter urgently. The young soldier placed his rifle on the ground and hugged the dog, whispering to it. Colonel Ames' shout sliced through the din. Other voices picked up his cry. The soldiers began to move. Baxter shoved the dog toward the pontoon bridge and pointed, shooing him away. The animal, his tail straight down between his legs, stared back. He was shivering.

The regiment, exposed to the Confederate cannons, filtered carefully through the ruined streets. Henry heard a thud and cry behind him. Meisner swiveled to look. "Keep going," Henry shouted, shoving him forward. Fighting to keep his legs moving, not to turn and sprint for the bridge, he couldn't understand why they were being sent up the same slope where so many had already died. Didn't anyone else know that this was suicide?

They broke into the open land just as the sun fell behind the Confederate lines. Grateful for the spreading dark, they advanced a short way before reaching a low ridge, still a hundred yards from the enemy. Even the officers saw that they could advance no further. A few men fired their rifles up the slope but Henry didn't. He couldn't see anything to aim at. Word came to settle in for the night.

Without blankets, without overcoats, Henry's platoon burrowed into the ground to get out of the wind that whistled down the slope. Moans came from the wounded men who lay around them. Some begged for water. Some for their mothers. Some for death. A few for God. Two stretcher-bearers crept past the platoon and knelt next to a fallen soldier.

"Wish they'd take the loud ones," Joe murmured to Henry. They were hard up against each other, sharing their warmth against the chill that was seeping into their bones. "Jesus. We're all gonna freeze. Save the rebs a lot of trouble."

"I know. The South shouldn't be so damned cold."

When the stretcher carriers came back, leaning down as much as they could, Henry whispered to them, "Hey. Any of those men dead right there?"

"On the right" came the reply.

Henry crept out in that direction. He found two corpses, one sprawled over the other. He stripped the tunic off the top man. By touch, he found the frigid blood and exploded intestines of the bottom man. He moved on, sliding to his right. Another corpse yielded a blanket and another tunic. A fourth corpse wore an overcoat. Though covered with gore, the coat was too thick to pass up.

Henry crawled back to Joe and shared his haul. When they had covered themselves, they looked out to see Colonel Chamberlain dragging one of the corpses Henry had just plundered. The officer shoved the body to the rim of the shallow swale he occupied with two other men. Then he turned back and started dragging another over.

"Jesus," Maxwell said, his voice filled with awe and revulsion.

Henry started up over the rim again. Joe's hand grabbed him. "My turn," he said, then pushed forward.

They positioned four bodies between the enemy and the dip where they huddled. Other forms moved in the dark, working at the same grim task. Henry covered his face and head with a dead man's tunic and pushed hard against Joe in spoon position, partly for warmth and partly to affirm that each was still alive. "Sing out if you're going to roll over," Henry said, squirming to pull the extra blanket underneath them. The wet soaked through it as they sank into mud. The weakening voices of the wounded still came through the dark, the cold finishing what the enemy had begun.

"Reckon we'll die here?" Joe said.

"How the hell do I know?" Henry gritted his teeth. He looked longingly over his shoulder, down the slope. Why not crawl back down in the darkness? He squeezed his eyes shut, tried to close his mind off.

When the morning sun sneaked over the trees on the east side of the river, Henry couldn't tell if he'd been awake or asleep. He rubbed his hands together and twisted his neck. Shots began to sputter from the Confederate lines. Henry reached for his rifle but stayed down. A bullet thumped into one of their corpses. Henry bent his head against Joe's back to stifle the scream that surged into his chest. They had had no choice, he told himself. Colonel Chamberlain started it. He showed them how to stack the bodies.

After a few minutes, Joe said, "Gotta piss."

"Downhill."

Joe twisted around and fumbled with his pants. He leaned back against Henry and began to moan. Henry turned his head and saw the yellow arc.

"Tarnation, Joe. That'll run right back on us."

The only response was more moaning. The odor arrived in a few seconds. Henry closed his eyes and told himself it wasn't the worst thing about the day. He had to piss too.

An hour later, the urine stink was overpowered when a confederate ball struck one of their corpses in the abdomen. A pop and *ssssss* signaled the escape of gas, which soon enveloped them.

Hour after hour, the regiment lay there. If a blue-coated soldier raised his head, the rebels shot a hole in it. After a while, the Maine boys started to fire their rifles blindly up the slope, twisting awkwardly to load, then poking the barrels between sheltering corpses. It was an act of defiance, not a military maneuver.

By noon, their water gone, their food gone, Joe and Henry no longer paid any heed when enemy bullets thudded into the dead flesh that protected them. It seemed to Henry he could get used to anything. He stopped thinking about getting off that slope. They couldn't move, or stand. Had the generals forgotten they were out here?

The sun was sinking when the enemy mounted an attack to the right, dozens coming out of their lines to flank the shallow depressions where most of the Twentieth still lay. If the Union boys raised up to meet the attack, the rebels still in their lines would pick them off, quick as a wink. Some fast-thinking soldiers stacked more corpses at the right edge of the swale so a whole platoon had shelter for firing back at the attackers, who quickly withdrew.

Dark brought orders to leave. The men knelt to begin scraping out graves for the dead who had protected them through that long night and day. Henry used his bayonet. Joe favored a wide, flat rock. The wet ground yielded readily. The sound of digging ran down the slope. The graves were shallow, just enough to cover each body with dirt. For head boards, most used the butts of the dead men's guns. Not knowing the names of the dead, they carved into the wood the number of their New York regiment.

"Duck," Joe whispered harshly as they finished the fourth burial. Henry flattened against the new grave. A pinkish light washed over him. There was no explosion, no firing. He rolled up onto one shoulder. Light streaked and flashed across the sky, sometimes in wide sheets. "I'll be damned," Henry said. He had seen the northern lights before but didn't know they showed so far south.

"What's it mean?" Joe asked. Henry could hear emotion in his voice, but didn't answer. He rolled back and stared upward. The colors made the sky look as bloodthirsty as the men on that slope, but what could one have to do with the other? What did anything mean?

When the lights had finished, the men used the dark to slide down the slope. At the base, they rose to walk. They passed smashed wagons with wheels jutting at odd angles, decapitated draft animals and more dead soldiers. Henry wore the blood-stained overcoat he had borrowed. Joe clutched another man's blanket around him.

They breathed easier when they reached the ruins of the town. At the beginnings of the pontoon bridge, Henry felt the coiled spring in his stomach begin to loosen. Rain started. Dirt had been spread over the bridge planking to muffle their steps.

The regiment did all right. They weren't cowards. They knew that now. They stayed together. They lost only a few killed, a few more wounded. But the army had lost again. Their minds were filled with the horrors of that slope.

They stopped for the night with neither rations nor shelter. Rain fell. Henry and Joe found tree stumps to sit on. Neither cared to lie down in that rain. They wore out the night on those stumps, sometimes asleep, mostly not. Henry tried to think of Katie but couldn't bring up anything about her. Not her face. Not her words. He had her letters in a pouch that hung around his neck but he couldn't take them out in the rain. He had only her name, which he thought over and over in the dark.

From the time they left the slope until the next morning, neither he nor Joe spoke a word.

About the Author

After many years as a trial and appellate lawyer, David O. Stewart became a bestselling writer of history and historical fiction. His first novel, *The Lincoln Deception*, about the John Wilkes Booth conspiracy, was called the best historical novel of 2013 by Bloomberg View.Sequels include *The Paris Deception*, set at the Paris Peace Conference in 1919, and *The Babe Ruth Deception*, which follows Babe's first two years with the Yankees.

Stewart's histories explore the writing of the Constitution, the gifts of James Madison, the western expedition and treason trial Aaron Burr, and the impeachment of President Andrew Johnson. In February 2021, Dutton published Stewart's *George Washington: The Political Rise of America's Founding Father*.